Barbara Kloss

Printed in the United States of America.

ISBN-13: 978-1466372702
ISBN-10: 1466372702

For my best friend, Ben, who ignited the spark.
I love you.

Contents

A Segment from Gaia's *Orbis Terrarum*

*The above is merely a sketch from the *Orbis Terrarum*, and lacks all magical properties present in the original, making this image suitable (and safe) for anyone on Earth.

Chapter 1

The Unexpected

A bolt of blue light exploded from the bruised clouds above, and Cadence froze.

No, she didn't stop. She didn't slow or jerk to a halt. She just...froze, with her front legs clawing at the air and her mane splayed in chaos like it was styled that way. And what was worse, I was frozen, too.

My body hovered inches from the saddle and my dark hair floated in a cloud around my face. I tried wiggling my fingers off the horn but they wouldn't move. Nothing would move. I couldn't even blink.

It was like my mind existed in another dimension, like someone hit the pause button on my life and time came to an abrupt halt. And I was watching it as an outsider.

But what was that light?

I searched the golden fields and there, way off in the distance, was a shadow—a man, veiled in a black cloak. I couldn't see his face, but I could feel him watching me. My blood ran cold. Strangers didn't frequent these parts, and when they did, they wore Wranglers and cowboy boots. Not cloaks.

Something burned in my hands and I glanced down. The horn was...glowing. The crystal, the one buried in the tip, radiated a blue light. It pulsed with life and singed my hands, but I couldn't pull them free. They were stuck, clamped around the horn.

I looked back toward the shadow and wanted to scream.

I hadn't seen him move, but now he was only a few hundred yards away, and I could see his face. He didn't have any hair and the bones in his face were sharp and emaciated. His skin was so pale it looked blue and where his eyes should've been were two black, empty pits.

But I felt him staring at me.

Slowly, he raised his arms to the sky. The air around me pulsed and in one sweep, he brought his arms down. The

1

grass flattened before him as if pushed down by an invisible force. I couldn't run, I couldn't move, I couldn't even scream.

The force barreled through the fields like a wave, flattening everything in sight. It would only be a matter of seconds before it hit me. The horn of the saddle singed my palms but still, I couldn't let go. It burned and burned, sending fire up my arms.

Twenty yards...ten yards...

I braced for impact.

Sharp pressure engulfed me and the light in my palms blazed white. Air exploded in my ears with a cry of fury, and everything went silent. When I looked back, the man was gone.

The clouds vanished, the sun shone brightly, and Cadence ran on as though she'd never stopped. Birds chirped overhead and the breeze whipped the hair in my face. I looked down but the glow in the horn was gone. There was no sign of what'd happened.

Had I imagined it?

I think you need to get more sleep.

I brought Cadence to a halt. I lifted my hand to wipe the sweat from my brow, and paused. There, seared along my index finger was the faint outline of the crystal.

I never knew my mom. The day I came into the world, she went out of it. At least, that's what Dad always said. Asking him about it never did any good. Even after all these years his forehead would do that crinkly thing, his lips would fold into themselves and his eyes would glaze over. And then he wouldn't say another word to me, for about a day.

Dad was private about, well, a lot of things. I assumed that was why he moved us to the middle of nowhere, otherwise known as Fresno, California. Living in the middle of nowhere meant having more conversations with cows than people. And staining your skin forever with the stench of manure and hay. And not needing an alarm clock because your neighbors had roosters so loud you could swear they woke up all of China. But I learned to deal with it because I thought it would end. Right now, actually. I thought I'd get my freedom right when I graduated high school.

2

Actually, let me rephrase that: I just *finished* high school. Graduating implies that huge ceremony with caps and gowns and some person on a stage handing you a rolled up diploma. Graduating implies celebrating with all of your friends and being excited about where you were going to go next. And, let's be honest, none of that happens when you live on a farm and you've been home-schooled all your life. All I did was take an exam. No cap and gown. No friends. No ceremony. I guess if I'd really wanted to have a celebration, I could've invited the neighbors. All five of them. And their stupid roosters. Some party.

What would we celebrate anyway? My future? I have no future plans, thanks to Dad. I can't figure out why he cares. He's gone most of the time on international business anyway. You'd think a successful businessman would want to see his only daughter excel on her own. Apparently not. I probably would've driven myself to San Francisco by now and flown out of here, but he won't even let me get my driver's license. I don't know where I'd even go, but I'd go somewhere. Preferably somewhere without cows.

Before you jump to conclusions, let me clarify that my dad's not a tyrant or anything. He just happens to suffer from a severe case of overprotection. Everyone thinks their parents are overprotective, I know, but mine installed video *and* thermal surveillance in our house, around the perimeter, and a few miles down the road. You be the judge.

So, you can imagine how well he reacted when I told him my plans to study abroad. Actually, I couldn't say anything about my future without that same look crossing his face like it does when I ask him about mom. But I had to. Thinking about being stuck here any longer gave me this drowning sense of despair, as if the world was charging forward, leaving me behind. In a pile of manure. Was it possible to devolve?

And what was my reward for finishing high school? Dessert. By itself, dessert wasn't so bad. But this was dessert at the home of my worst enemy.

My stomach flopped. I couldn't believe I'd agreed to go. When Dad had come home early from Rome, I knew he had something up his sleeve. I thought it had to do with my future, and that maybe he was finally ready to talk about it. But no. He had decided to torture me instead.

"I'll be in the car!" Dad yelled from the hall.

Why was I so nervous? I hadn't seen Mr. and Mrs. Anderson in years. Three, to be exact. It wasn't like *he* was going to be there. He'd made it pretty clear three years ago that he hated me, and had proved it by never speaking to me again. Come to think of it, not speaking to me would have been the nicer thing to do. He just disappeared. Somehow apathy hurt a lot more than hatred.

It was no use. All of my clothes were stained with Eau de Farm. I put on my only white blouse and dug through my creaky wooden drawers until I found a pair of jeans that didn't look like they'd been attacked by a barbed wire fence. I hid the tears along the bottom of my pant leg with a clean pair of riding boots, pulled my long, dark hair back into a braid, and paused to look in the mirror.

I looked as nervous as I felt.

There's nothing to worry about. It's just Mr. and Mrs. Anderson. They're like another set of parents.

Yeah, but they were *his* parents.

"Daria Jones!"

"Coming!" I leapt over my pile of books, bolted down the hall and out the door.

Dad already had the engine of our Subaru thrumming as I climbed in.

"Did you tell Mr. Arashiro—?"

"Already taken care of." Dad backed the car out of the driveway.

Mr. Arashiro was my ju-jitsu instructor. He'd been coming to our house every week since I could walk. Part of my dad's over-protectiveness. While Dad was out of town on business, he consoled himself knowing I'd be able to defend myself. And, I could. Against a cow. Maybe.

We left our lawn of brown grass behind and started for the Andersons'. Other people lived out here because there was land to be had, but not us. Why we lived on the only plot of land you could mow in a single day, I didn't know.

It wasn't long before the mountains loomed overhead and we entered Yosemite Valley. The Andersons lived in the Valley, as very few did. Their family had purchased property there before it turned itself into a National Park, affording them a luxurious home in one of the most beautiful locations on the planet. The sun always seemed to shine on them. Giving them such a residence was rubbing it in.

I'd spent many summers there while my dad was away. Sonya Anderson had been the mom I never had, ever since I could remember. I liked her husband, Cicero, well enough. He was Dad's best friend, and overprotective just like him. I didn't mind that, because he was at least reasonable about it. He wasn't the one installing thermal sensors. But the other reason I had loved going there—the main reason—was to visit their son, Alex.

Even thinking his name sent pains through my stomach.

"There's no need to be nervous." Dad broke the silence.

Startled, I jumped. "I'm not."

Dad raised a brow. "Yes, you are. You've been twirling your braid since we left. You always play with your hair when you're nervous."

Sure enough, I was clutching my braid like I was afraid it would fly out the window. I promptly let it go and dropped my hand in my lap.

He grinned. "You look beautiful. Thanks for coming with me."

"Wait, so I actually had a choice?"

His smile fell as he focused back on the road. "Princess, we won't be there long. Sonya wanted to see you, and I couldn't say no to her this time...especially since she's been more of a mother to you than I've been a father." There was pain in his eyes, a kind of silent regret. I'd never seen him like that before.

"Dad, just because you're gone a lot doesn't mean you're not a good father. Besides." I grinned, trying to nudge the life back into him. "That's how we get along so well—you're never home long enough to argue with."

He smiled, but it didn't touch his eyes.

Something was bothering him. I mean, Dad could get into these withdrawn moods, but he'd been particularly quiet lately. As I watched him, I realized his bronze hair was a mess, and the skin around his pale eyes sagged with fatigue. I hadn't noticed it earlier, being so preoccupied with my own nervousness. Dad was never good at hiding things from me

5

because his countenance would give him away. Which was good, because if there was one thing I hated, it was being lied to.

I grabbed my iPod out of the glovebox and filled our silence with Coldplay. It was the only modern band Dad and I could agree on, because their lyrics weren't "inappropriate" and their music didn't "offend his ears." He preferred classical.

We rounded that last wooded bend, and there, emerging between thick walls of giant pines, stood the Anderson home.

It didn't matter how many times I'd seen it. Their gothic Victorian mansion still inspired awe: dark wood paneling framed stonework equipped with gables, a stone turret, and a roofline that matched the rim of the surrounding mountains. It was the kind of home I'd read about in fairytales, and visiting it always made me feel as if I was part of one.

I didn't know how the Andersons had such a beautiful home, considering Cicero and my dad worked together. In fact, I was pretty sure Dad was Cicero's boss. Dad always said it had to do with protecting investments, whatever that meant.

My dad pulled the car around, halting before the broad stone steps that led to the rustic oak door. When I was younger, that door had represented complete and utter happiness. Looking at it now, I suddenly couldn't believe I'd allowed Dad to bring me here.

With a deep breath, I climbed out of the car. The air was crisp and the scents of earth and pine seeped into my soul, bringing with them the string of memories I had tried so hard to shred.

You can do this. You won't be here long. And it's not like he is going to be here.

Our shoes crunched on their gravel driveway. Part of me wanted to run back to the car, but I knew it was too late. I'd already let him drag me this far. We stood before the door and I stared at the gargoyle head holding an iron ring knocker in its teeth. It hung lower than I remembered, but no matter where I stood, those empty eyes followed me. I never did like those eyes. Dad glanced at me before clasping the ring, letting it clank against the wood.

6

Was I imagining it, or did he seem guilty about something?

Just as he released the ring, the door swung inward, replaced by a woman I knew well.

Sonya Anderson stood tall, her elegance unmatched as always. Her lustrous dark hair was pulled back loosely, dark eyes smiling as though seeing me made everything right in her world. And before I could say a word, her slender arms wrapped around me. It was an embrace only she could give— one that seemed to hug you on the inside, too.

When she pulled away, her fingertips lingered at my cheek. "My darling, I've missed you." She searched my eyes. "Thank you. For coming."

Sonya was the kind of person who didn't really need to speak because her eyes communicated everything. Right now they were overflowing with love. "Sure. Thanks for having me."

"You know you never need an invitation." She led us into the foyer, closing the door.

I stepped onto the familiar crimson rug as my nose filled with the scents of spices and wood smoke. An iron chandelier hung above, its rows filled with squat, ivory candles. I'd counted them once. Alex would throw random numbers at me to throw me off track, but one day when he was preoccupied, I finally succeeded. There were exactly twenty-three.

Sonya appraised my disheveled dad with a frown. "I figured as much."

Dad grinned. "Nice to see you, too."

Sonya had always worried about Dad's health. When you internalize everything like my dad does, "everything" turns your outward appearance into a haphazard mess.

Sonya sighed. "Well, it's a good thing Daria knows how to take care of herself. There are some clean towels in the bathroom upstairs. Just in case."

"Alaric!" It sounded like the entire house had spoken.

Cicero's tall, strong build appeared beside his wife and he smacked my dad hard on the back. "You look terrible. I mean, even for you."

Dad chuckled. "Well, one of us needed brains, so I sacrificed good looks. You're welcome."

Cicero shook his head. "I really only stepped out to see little Daria." His bright eyes found me, his grin spreading. "Not so little anymore, are you?" He wrapped a thick arm around my shoulders. "The world's newest graduate! Good to see you."

I smiled. "You, too."

Nothing ever seemed to faze Cicero, and that quality influenced everyone around him, me included.

Cicero studied me a moment, then smirked at my father. "She still doesn't look a thing like you."

Dad arched a brow. "You don't think so?"

"Not in the slightest," Cicero said. "She'd never be that beautiful if she did."

My dad chuckled.

"Actually—" Cicero glanced at Sonya. "There's something I need to discuss with Alaric in private." I thought I saw Dad stiffen. "Do you mind?" Cicero fastened his startling green eyes—Alex's eyes—on me.

It wasn't like them to be so secretive, at least not in front of me. "Oh, that's fine," I said.

Dad held Cicero's gaze a long moment, then shot me a quick glance. "Be right back." The men disappeared down the hall.

When I looked back at Sonya, I caught traces of worry on her face, but the moment she caught me watching her, that worry transformed into a smile.

"It's been so long."

"About three years, I think."

Who was I kidding? She knew exactly when I stopped coming, and why.

"It has. You've turned into a beautiful young woman, and I've missed all of it."

The regret in her voice, the love in her eyes—it made me feel guilty. Sonya hadn't done anything wrong, but in my anger toward Alex, I'd cut myself off from her, too. And I could've used her advice on so many things over the past few years. I'd always been able to confide in her in ways that were impossible with Dad. She understood emotions. "I'm sorry." I sighed, and I meant it. "I've missed it here. I've missed *you*. But, you know, with Dad's schedule it's...hard to get away."

Those dark eyes saw and understood everything I didn't say. "I know."

"Mrs. Anderson," spoke a soft voice that lifted my spirit.

Clara, their maid, appeared before us, just as slight and as happy and gentle as I remembered. Her face brightened at the sight of me. "If it isn't Miss Daria."

I beamed at her. It didn't matter how old I was, Clara always made me feel like a little kid again. She was the kind of woman that would let you stay up way past your bedtime, and then she'd slip candy under your bedroom door when you were supposed to be sleeping. I wasn't sure if Sonya knew that, but Alex and I certainly never tried to find out.

"Clara, what it is?" Sonya asked.

Clara's gaze flitted to me before landing on Sonya. "The gentlemen would like to speak with you."

A look passed between them, and then Sonya turned to me. "I hate leaving you so abruptly after finally getting you all to myself, but will you excuse me a moment?"

What was going on with everyone? "Uh, sure."

"I'll be right back." She patted my cheek and disappeared down the hall. Clara lingered, eyes bright and twinkling as she took me in. But instead of saying another word, her expression grew distant and she left.

Now I was alone, feeling completely out of place. I wandered into the sitting room, where a fire blazed in the fireplace. An ivory chaise lounge sat beside it, accented by a mahogany side table standing on flared legs, and sitting on top of the table was the glass bowl. It was half filled with water, and floating on the surface was that lurid orange flower. The flower always reminded me of a flame—a flame even water couldn't extinguish. Sonya always had a fresh one in the bowl, but I'd never been able to figure out where they came from.

I stared through the window at the yard beyond. Alex and I had lived in that yard. It had been the home of wrestling matches, stick fights, and snow forts. There, we'd sprawled out on the grass in exhaustion while gazing up at the clouds and dreaming of our futures.

A future he had and I didn't.

My heart sank. I couldn't stop the unwanted memories from replaying in my mind.

A transparent shape floated above the yard. It took me a second to realize that it was a reflection in the glass. There was something behind me. Someone. I turned my head toward its source and my breath caught in my chest. It was Alex.

Chapter 2

Lost Secrets

Alex stood in the entryway, much taller than I remembered. His fitted, dark jeans revealed a lean, muscular build, and the sleeves of his white button-up shirt were rolled to his elbows, exposing strong forearms. Not the scrawny boy I'd known all my life. He wore his hair longer, too. Dark strands now framed his face, sharpening the angles, and the green in his eyes was much greener. And more penetrating.

Three years had turned him into a man. I should've expected it, but all I could do was stare, and the walls started closing in around me.

His face was unreadable and, even though his sharp gaze never left mine, I felt like he was taking me in from head to toe. It made me even more uncomfortable than I already was.

"Daria." He spoke my name softly, lingering on each syllable.

I was so shocked by the depth and richness in this new man-voice that I couldn't speak. My words were trapped somewhere between surprise and indignation.

He took a step forward. "*You* at a loss for words? This is unusual."

I suddenly realized I'd been standing there, staring at him. Heat flooded my face and I forced myself to speak. "Maybe I've changed."

A knowing grin twitched at his lips as he raised a dark brow.

Really, Daria? You prepared to rip him to shreds if you ever saw him again and the first thing you say is "maybe I've changed"? You haven't even left Fresno!

He continued studying me, as if he was waiting for me to say something—anything. The longer we stood there staring at each other with this thick wall of silence between us, the more flustered I felt. It didn't help that I was having trouble

11

breathing, and my hand ached from clenching the arm of the sofa. I had to get out of there.

"Good." Sonya beamed at the pair of us. "You found each other."

My dad and Cicero were right on her heels. I caught my dad's gaze, and then he seemed a little too interested in finding a seat for himself. I should've known. That was why he'd been acting guilty. He'd known Alex would be here, and he continued avoiding my murderous glare as he fidgeted with the buttons on his shirt.

Clara entered with a tray of tiramisu and I couldn't have been happier for the distraction. She passed around plates filled with layers of cream, chocolates, and cookies compressed into a strong tower, topped with raspberries and mint leaves. It was too beautiful to eat. Almost.

Just as I lifted my spoon to carve into my tiramisu, Sonya spoke.

"What are you going to do with yourself now?"

At first I didn't realize she was addressing me, but when no one else answered, I glanced up. Everyone was watching me.

"What do you mean?" I asked.

Sonya smiled. "I mean now that you 're all done with your studies. You just took your graduation examination a few weeks ago, didn't you?"

Dad watched me, his face flushed. He was probably worried about my answer, and with Alex—the successful, impressive world traveler—I was worried about my answer, too. I didn't want Alex knowing how uneventful my life had been, or about how much I really hadn't changed.

"Yes, I did," I said to Sonya, glancing down at my plate. "I'm interested in Medieval European History. I'd like to start at a junior college in the fall, and then maybe study abroad."

Sonya's smile fell, and so did Cicero's gaze. Alex frowned, and the red in my dad's face started spreading down his neck. Since I'd just effectively killed the conversation, I went back to my dessert.

"Are you still riding?" Sonya asked. The smile returned to her face, but there was unease in her eyes.

"Yes," I replied. "Every day."

"I was hoping you kept up with it."

This obvious avoidance of discussing college irritated me. "It's a nice *hobby*."

Sonya's gaze flitted to my dad, and Dad cleared his throat. "She's fast too. I can't even keep up with her."

"Get used to it." Cicero grinned. "We certainly aren't getting any younger."

They all chuckled, and thus began an exclusive discussion about the inevitable woes of the aging process.

My hope sank. The topic of my future was not on Dad's mind tonight. He still wasn't ready to talk about college, or jobs, or anything about my future, and the Andersons would respect that. But if my future wasn't weighing him down, what was?

An obnoxious chirping interrupted the chatter. It 'd come from Dad's phone. He pulled his cell from his pocket, glanced at the screen, and he went completely still.

"It's Stefan." He frowned and his wary eyes found mine. "Princess, mind if I talk to Cicero and Sonya in private?"

All these private conversations this evening. "Oh...sure. Go right head." I started getting up from my seat.

"No, dear." Sonya stood. "You stay here. Alex?" A knowing look passed between them.

"I'll stay with Daria." He leaned back in the chaise lounge. "Fill me in later."

I wondered why Alex would need to be filled in. He'd never been included in their business transactions before. Sonya and Cicero followed my dad from the room, leaving me with my favorite person, Alex.

I turned my entire body toward the crackling fire, trying very hard to dispel Alex's presence from view. This wasn't at all going how I'd planned. I was to come here with Dad and spend a nice, leisurely evening eating dessert with Cicero and Sonya. There wasn't even the hint of Alex being in that picture. In fact, he was supposed to be in another country.

I braved a glance up. He was studying me, but his expression was unreadable. Alex had always been as transparent as a window, at least with me, and this mask of emotion was making me lose my nerve. I dropped my gaze back to my plate, but then I became too aware of the fork in my hands. It seemed awkward in my fingers, and I fumbled as I sliced into the tiramisu. I raised the bite to my mouth, but the bite slid right off the prongs and back onto my plate, and I ended up with a bite of fork. Frustrated, I dropped the fork on my plate with a clang and set my dessert on the table.

"Have your tastes...*changed*?" There was that man-voice again, and this time it was tinged with amusement.

I pinched my lips together. "I'm full."

He leaned forward, elbows resting on his knees. His eyes searched mine, but for what, I didn't know.

My face felt hot and the creases in my joints began sweating.

Dang it, Daria, stop acting so ridiculous. You know what he's doing. Probing. Sticking out his feelers. Trying to find a weakness to manipulate you again.

He glanced at my plate. "You were never too full for that."

I didn't like being reminded of how well he knew me, and fury pulsed through my veins. "And you were never one for small talk, so where does that leave us?"

He studied me a moment more before leaning back in his chair, his features more guarded than before. He continued to sit, silent with his thoughts as if was waiting to see my next move.

So I moved.

I got to my feet and left the room. I couldn't let him see me so weak and unnerved by him. Why was he here anyway?

He lives here, genius. What are you doing here?

I loathed my conscience sometimes.

Once I reached the heavy oak doors to the library, I paused, sighing in relief. I pushed them open with a creak, tiptoed inside and closed them behind me.

I loved this room. Enormous dark, wooden bookshelves covered the walls, all crammed with books—there was even a ladder to reach those on the topmost shelves. Many of them were history books, because Cicero was both a lover and collector of any manuscript written about a time other than the present. His influence was the primary spark of my own infatuation.

Two tall, narrow windows with window seats stood along one wall, separated by a large canvas of Yosemite's Bridal Veil Falls. I'd never seen the real falls in person, because no one had ever bothered taking me there, but this portrait was so vivid and lifelike I never felt the need to go, as if this frame were a magical window to a beautiful world.

Being in this room put my nerves at ease. In here, I could escape my own head and spend time in someone else's, and right now, I desperately needed someone else's head to get my mind off of *him*.

I made my way to the sliding ladder, my fingers trailing the smooth wood. This ladder wasn't the original. I'd broken that one after jumping up the rungs, despite Alex's warning. I'd climbed up pretty high, too, so the fall hurt. After being assaulted with "I told you so's", Alex had built this one, and I had helped him stain it.

The memory taunted me as I climbed to the top, where we'd chiseled our names in the wood. Alex's name was legible; he'd always been so good with tools. But mine looked more like "Dam" than "Daria."

Maybe coming in here wasn't such a good idea.

I scanned the books on the top shelf for *The Count of Monte Cristo*, and found it wedged in its usual spot, between a dragon-shaped bookend and *Treasure Island*. This part of the library was what I'd always referred to as the "adventure section." Dad didn't let me out much, but even he couldn't control the trouble I got myself into on paper.

Grabbing the copy, I climbed back down the ladder and curled into the corner of the window seat. I didn't remember having so much space when I was younger, probably because Alex would always cram into it with me then.

I shoved away the memory, flipped on the reading lamp, and began to read.

My plan was to lose myself in Edmond Dantes' betrayal, but my thoughts kept flitting back to Alex. He looked so different, sounded so different, and I'd acted...

I flipped through the book, forcing myself to think about anything but Alex, when a slip of paper fell to the floor. I bent over to pick it up, and when I opened the single fold, my stomach turned. It was a note, in Alex's handwriting.

Daria--
There is so much I want to say to you. I know you sense my distance, and I wish I could explain it. Until then, I need you to do something--something that may help you

15

understand. Go to the desk. Underneath the top panel, push upward. You'll find a key. Take the key to the portrait of Bridal Veil Falls. Along the bottom of the frame you'll find a keyhole. Try it. Make sure no one sees you.

I'm sorry.

--Alex

I read the note again. When had he written this? It must've been sometime before he left, because the ink had faded and the paper had yellowed slightly.

Overwhelmed by curiosity, I walked to the desk and set my book down. I read the note again, following his directions, and soon enough, sitting in the dark space between panels, was a rusted, bronze skeleton key. It was the kind of key no one used any more—the kind the size of your hand and unlocked some secret treasure. I rushed to the painting and found a large keyhole. All these years, and I had never noticed it.

I slid the key into the keyhole, and turned. With a satisfying click, the painting swung forward on a hinge, leaving behind a large, gaping black hole in the thick stone wall.

"What in the world..."

A cool draft touched my face. I was staring at the top of a narrow, circular staircase that wound down, disappearing into darkness. I grabbed a flashlight from the desk and hurried back to the painting.

My boots scraped on stone as I made my way down, step by careful step, ending at a wooden door with a single bronze knob. The knob turned easily and the door creaked inward an inch. Whatever lay beyond was hidden in darkness. I hesitated, heart pounding in my ears.

Calm down. Alex wouldn't try to kill you, not even back then.

Inhaling a deep breath of stale and musty air, I gripped my flashlight, pushed the door in and stepped inside.

All along the walls were shelves of books and lots of eerie shadows. Too many for my comfort. I moved forward, eyes alert. It looked like this room was used, and often. There was no dust or cobwebs. A few antiquated portraits hung along the walls, each canvas depicting someone of power from

16

centuries long ago. They looked like they belonged in a museum. An engraved golden plate was fastened to the bottom of each, all members of some Regius family. I didn't remember ever learning about them.

I trailed the light along the book spines. *Gaia's Potentate Directives, Guide of Militant Stratagems, Magic and its Proper Uses, Prophetic Verses.* I paused in front of one in particular: *The Creatures of Shadow.*

Curious, I pulled it from the shelf and lifted the stiff leather cover. The binding creaked as it opened, and the pages were stiff as I turned them. I held my flashlight over a page filled with "B". Balcan, Banshee, Barghest...

A horrid drawing stared back at me, some hellion of a hairless dog, with fangs exposed and blood-red eyes. Beneath it was a description.

Barghest: Created by the Dark Sorcerers during the Great Deception to destroy all that is of light. Banished to the great depths of Mortis for their insatiable thirst for light's destruction.

I shut the book and returned it to the shelf. Scary drawings didn't do much for me, and never in the dark.

A strange sensation swept over me, as if something was tugging at my consciousness, and I turned around. My eyes settled on a large globe sitting atop a wooden stand in the corner. And the globe was...turning.

My heart beat faster as my eyes darted around the room, searching for signs of life, but I couldn't see any. As far as I could tell, I was down here alone.

Then how was the globe spinning?

I took a few cautious steps forward, my mind drawn to the strange object. The surface of the miniature Earth depicted topography, but as I studied it, I realized it wasn't Earth at all. There was a single giant landmass and a few smaller lands separated by strange seas. A thick smear of white settled over a piece of the largest landmass. I stretched out my pointer finger to touch it and gasped. It felt cold and damp, like mist.

But that was impossible. Globes didn't depict the weather.

Footsteps echoed from somewhere above. Someone was coming.

17

I sprinted for the door. Just as I went to close it, I looked back at the globe. A small spark flickered where the smudge had been. That spark had looked like lightning.

I slammed the door and bolted up the stairs, two at a time.

The footsteps in the hallway had almost reached the door to the library. I swung the portrait shut, locked it, and hurried to return the key. I just managed to shove it inside when the library door opened.

Chapter 3

Enough is Enough

Alex stepped inside, closing the door behind him. His eyes moved to the canvas, and then settled on me, pinning me in place. "Not enough light?"

The flashlight. I forgot to put it away. How was I going to explain this one? "It was dark by the window."

His eyes narrowed as he stared at the window seat with the LED shining brightly. "I...see."

You've got to do better than that.

I had no idea what to say. I'd just discovered something he wanted me to find years ago. I should've bombarded him with questions about it, but I couldn't get past my anger. Anger at him for leaving, anger at him for lying, anger that, after all these years, I was still angry.

"Time for me to leave?" I asked.

His gaze moved back to mine. "No."

A cold cloud of awkwardness settled in the room, and his presence filled the empty spaces, making it a tight fit for me. Why wouldn't he leave me alone? I had come here to spare him the misery of my company, and to spare myself the pain of his. I also wished he'd leave so I could investigate that room some more.

"Do you need to use the room, or something?" I asked.

He opened his mouth to speak, but thought the better of whatever he was about to say and closed his lips. A flourish of emotions passed over his face, but the mask triumphed once again. His gaze flickered to the desk, and then he walked further into the room.

There was a sort of grace to his step, one that made him seem light and agile despite his muscle. He continued past me, pausing at the desk to thumb the cover of the book I'd been trying to read.

19

A grin curled his lips as he glanced back at me. "Aren't you tired of this one yet?"

Something inside of me snapped. "What I'm tired of is *you*. Quit acting like everything's fine when it's not. You're nothing but a liar. And if I'd actually known you were going to be here, I never would've come." The heat inside me burned with fury I couldn't contain. "I hate you."

My words slapped the grin from his face, and I wanted to take them all back immediately.

He didn't move, his gaze hardened and locked on mine. I tried ignoring the sharp fingertips of guilt that were already poking at my heart. Everything I'd said was true, but for some reason the idea of speaking the truth sounded infinitely better in my mind than when it had actually been coming out of my mouth.

And you could've left out the part about hating him. You know that's not true.

But I'd wanted him to hurt. I wanted to hurt him how he'd hurt me. Guilt dug into my chest, deeper and deeper.

Alex's gaze bore into mine with a fire I couldn't comprehend.

The sound of footsteps echoed down the hall.

Alex didn't look at me as he stalked to the door. He hesitated, his back to me, his fingertips lingering on the doorknob. At last, he turned it and left, the door closing shut behind him.

I stared at the door. The room suddenly felt too empty, too cold, and a mass hardened in my stomach. What had I just done?

Cicero and Sonya entered the library, followed by my dad. Their eyes darted around the room, probably expecting Alex to be with me, but thanks to my unfiltered words, I doubted he'd ever come near me again.

But that was what I wanted.

Is it?

"Ready to go?" Dad asked.

"Uh...yeah. Sure." I heard my own words as though someone else had spoken them. I flipped off the lamp near the window seat and returned the flashlight, ignoring the curious looks on their faces.

Cicero and Sonya escorted us to the front door, where we all hugged and said our goodbyes. Sonya insisted I visit her more often, and with honest intentions I said I'd try. We both knew "try" was all I'd do, but she had to say it, so I'd know how much she cared.

As Dad and I walked out into the drizzled night, I glanced back, searching the windows, but all of them remained dark and deserted. There was no sign of him.

Our drive home was quiet and contemplative. Dad seemed preoccupied with thoughts of his own, his jaw tight and eyes focused on the road ahead. I didn't mind because I had enough to think about, like that room. The spinning globe and foreign manuscripts and portraits. What did they all mean and why were they hidden there? I thought of the spinning globe, its clouds and the streak that'd looked like lightning. Had my eyes been playing tricks on me? The more and more I thought about it, the more certain I was I'd been seeing things. Globes didn't just turn on their own, and they certainly didn't depict the weather. It had to be some new technology. But what about the pull I'd felt? It was as if the globe had been beckoning to me—wanting me to find it. It really was too bad I hadn't been able to investigate the room more.

Was the globe what Alex had wanted me to find? And what, exactly, had he been sorry about? That he'd never shown me that room before? I could've asked him about it when he'd caught me with the flashlight, if only I hadn't been so flustered and angry.

Regret washed over me. I didn't know why, because I had done precisely what I'd planned all these years: I had told him exactly how I felt. That should've been my closure—my vindication. But I felt even more unsatisfied than before I'd assaulted him.

You should've given him a chance to explain.

He'd had plenty of chances.

Maybe if you'd kept your mouth shut, he would've explained everything.

Dear conscience, shut up.

But what if that was his intention, seeking me out in the library? Maybe he wanted to explain the hidden room, or maybe I could've confronted him about that day once and for all.

I was fifteen and he was seventeen. It had been a slow progression, but I'd sensed it. I'd known him like I knew myself—better in some ways. We had shared everything, talked about everything, and depended entirely on the other as an accomplice in the small world we'd lived in. There had never been any barriers between us, not until he started creating them.

At first I thought it had been a figment of my imagination. Then one day, reality punched me in the gut. Dad had been off to the Andersons and I had the grand idea to go and surprise Alex. When we'd arrived, I crept up the hardwood staircase, careful to skip the seventh, creaky step, and continued all the way to Alex's room. It'd been tough catching Alex off guard, but I'd mastered it after years of practice. Not telling him I would be coming would definitely help.

His door had been cracked open just a few inches and he'd been talking to someone. I peered through the crack and realized he was on the phone. It should've been simple—easy, even. Just as I'd adjusted my stance to lunge, I froze. He'd said my name.

"Yes, my mother said she's on her way, but I'm not supposed to know," he said to the person on the other end. "No, she still has no idea...it's hard for me...I've been pretending since we were kids...my parents are making me." *Pretending? About what?* I'd been afraid to keep listening but I couldn't pry myself away. "I'm trying to figure out a way to tell her before I leave...I go insane when I'm around her..."

The floor creaked beneath my foot as I'd shifted, and Alex spun around in his chair. I could still see his face: surprise, guilt, fear, worry. He'd hung up the phone and rushed to me, his true feelings already hidden behind tenderness, but it was too late.

"What's wrong?" he'd asked, searching my face.

He'd been prodding, trying to see if I'd heard what he said. I told him I didn't feel well, and he believed me. After a hasty goodbye, Dad took me home.

I didn't cry often. With a dad gone most of the time, and no real mother figure, I never learned how to deal with emotion. I walled it off, burying pain deep inside, but that night the pain was so immense that even the Great Wall wouldn't have been able to contain it. My tears came, and came. The entire night.

Once my tears dried up, I built an impenetrable barrier around my memories of him, tucking them away far from reach. I never saw him again. I never heard from him either. To me, that only confirmed the fact that he'd never cared about me or our friendship. He'd just pretended all those years because his parents had made him. But he had pretended so well, and I had been a fool.

That was the first time in my life I ever truly felt alone. Sure, I'd been left alone most of the time, but this was different. Alex's abrupt absence left me empty and hollow, the shell of a human. If someone had punched me, I doubt I would've felt it, and I had wanted someone to punch me, to take the focus off the invading emptiness inside. Anything but what I had felt then.

Dad would sometimes talk about Alex, even though I never asked. Alex had gone to study abroad, far, far away from here, while showing great success in ventures unknown to me. His parents—and my dad—were so proud.

After that incident, I stopped going to the Andersons. It brought back the happiest moments of my life, which were now tainted with pain and bitterness.

"What's going on over there?" My dad broke the silence.

I realized we were almost home, winding past the empty fields that had encased me all my life. "Nothing."

"Oh, really?"

I was twirling my hair again. I dropped my hand. "Did you know Alex was going to be there?"

Dad licked his lips as he flexed his grip on the steering wheel. "Last minute."

"That wasn't the question."

"If I told you Alex was going to be there, would you have gone?"

I opened my mouth to argue and then glared out the window. "No."

"Then do you blame me for not telling you?"

"Of course I blame you! There was no reason for me to go." Dad opened his mouth to speak but I cut him off. "And don't say it was because of Sonya. I barely got to talk to her anyway."

He took a deep breath and exhaled slowly. "I wanted...or hoped, that you might talk to Alex. Move on from whatever it is you're still upset about. He's not the same person, you know. Neither are you. You could at least give him a chance."

Without a doubt, when it came to issues between Alex and me, my dad took Alex's side. That was where my conscience learned it. "I did talk to him."

Dad looked over at me, doubtful. "Maybe we need to have a little discussion on the definition of 'talk,' because you hardly said a word all evening."

"We talked in the library," I said. "When you were busy with Cicero and Sonya."

"Must have been quite the conversation since he didn't meet us at the door when we left."

I shut my mouth and stared out the window again. I loved Dad, but he inferred way too much about things, and I wasn't in the mood to talk about what happened. I still didn't know what happened. "Look," I started. "I'm sorry. It was...hard for me, seeing him again. It's been so long, and—"

"Princess..."

I knew that tone. It meant he was about to lecture me, so I braced myself.

"I'm not saying you shouldn't hurt from the past," he continued. "Pain isn't unhealthy, but if you keep it too close it'll father bitterness, and bitterness will eat at your soul like poison." He paused. "Your mother always told me that, and she knew from experience."

The moment he said the word "mother," I forgot about the lecturing and looked back at my dad. I expected to see pain there, but the deep creases in his forehead vanished and his lips held traces of a smile. I studied him, waiting for him to revert to his usual state of despondency when it came to my mother, but it didn't come. Instead, he kept talking about her.

"You look just like her." He glanced at me. "I don't need to remind you that she was a beautiful woman, but it was her loving and honest heart that made her the loveliest woman I'd ever known. To this day, I've never met her equal."

24

That hurt a little. I prided myself in honesty, but loving? My track record wasn't looking so great, this evening included.

His next words tumbled out so quietly I almost didn't hear them. "I was a changed man after I met her."

Considering his unusually nostalgic mood, maybe he'd tell me this time. "How did you meet her?"

My dad shifted in his seat. "Traveling. But that was a long time ago."

His smile disappeared, his forehead re-crinkled, and he focused back on the road ahead.

Or...maybe not.

My dad ended every discussion about anything important to me during, well, my entire life, and now I was starting to reach my threshold for dealing with it.

The clouds huddled over the mountains, as if they were ready to attack. We turned down our long country road in silence, while my irritation amplified. We couldn't talk about my mom; we couldn't talk about my future. He, and my conscience, always took Alex's side, as if I was the root of every problem.

Frustration simmered beneath my skin. He wouldn't tell me anything. He wouldn't let me go anywhere. He was gone all the time. And because he was so overprotective, I had been forced to live in the middle of nowhere my entire life without prospects of an exciting future—any future. Worst of all, I was forced to admit all that to Alex—the guy who'd just spent the past three years studying abroad with friends so interesting he had no need of me. What a successful life I'd led. And what a bright future.

All of the anger and resentment I'd kept submerged burned so hot it melted the little filter I had.

"We need to talk," I blurted as we pulled into our driveway.

"You suddenly remember what it means?"

"Dad, I'm serious. I'm eighteen! I just finished high school—alone. I don't have college plans. I don't have any plans because *you* refuse to talk about it."

My dad pulled the Subaru into our driveway, and the low thrum of the engine came to a halt.

"Fair enough." He sighed. "I know I haven't said much to you on the subject."

"Much? You haven't said anything."

He continued saying nothing, his strong hands gripping the steering wheel, and then he looked at me. I knew that look. I wasn't going to win, not this time. Not ever. "Dad, *please.*"

"I'm sorry, but I can't give you my reasons yet."

"But—"

"We'll talk about this in a few years..."

"This is ridiculous!" I couldn't take it anymore. "A few years? You think I'm going to just...sit in this house until *you're* ready? Until you install thermal sensors throughout the world? You can't protect me forever. I'm leaving, whether you like it or not. This summer."

He studied me with suspicion in his eyes. "Does this sudden outburst have anything to do with Alexander by chance?"

I threw open the car door and jumped out of my seat.

"Daria."

I couldn't believe it. He was smiling.

"Where are you going?"

"To see Cadence," I called over my shoulder. "Don't worry, you can keep an eye on me through your video cameras."

I had to get away. I felt Dad's eyes on my back as I leapt over the fence and into our neighbor's yard. And then there was nothing but a sea of brown grasses before me.

What was wrong with me? It wasn't like my monotonous life was a new thing. I'd been dealing with it since I could say the word "cow." It just took someone like Alex—doing all the things I'd always dreamed of doing—to expose my life for what it was, to illuminate my own misery, to remind me that I was a boring, mundane farm girl. Worse than that, I technically didn't even live on a farm.

Seeing me, Cadence whinnied. It seemed my taking Cadence for a ride was the only freedom either of us had. Her hooves pounded the ground, clumps of earth kicking up behind us as we ran. Air whistled past my ears as my braid whipped my back, my eyes watering from the chilled air. I'd always found peace through riding, but it wasn't taking the pain away tonight.

I pushed Cadence harder.

We ran to the farthest corner of my neighbor's property, the only side without a fence. It didn't have a fence because it ended with a steep cliff. We stopped at the rim, and Cadence panted as I sat, breathing in the cool, damp air.

Reaching in my pocket, I pulled out Alex's letter.

"I need you to do something—something that may help you understand."

Understand what? And how was that room supposed to explain anything? All it did was form more questions, reminding me of something else he'd known all these years and never shared. But why would he? He hadn't been honest with his feelings. Being reminded of his lies when I'd trusted him more than I'd trusted myself hurt all over again.

I crumbled the paper in my hand and threw it at the canyon. The wind grabbed hold with invisible fingers, lifting and carrying the wad farther and farther. Back and forth it floated through the air, away from me, taunting me, like Alex.

I sighed. Dad was right, again. My current circumstances hadn't changed. I knew this moment would come, that I'd have to take my future into my own hands, and I wasn't really that upset Dad wouldn't help. I wasn't thrilled about it either, but that wasn't my issue. Right now, my issue was with Alex. For years I'd denied his memory rights to my thoughts, and now they attacked with a vengeance, stabbing and tearing at my insides. All this time they'd been idle, waiting for that opportune moment. Problems conspire with each other behind your back and when they unite against you, you don't stand a chance.

A gust of wind ripped through the fields, and Cadence whinnied, her mane blowing all over the place. The clouds above had grown dark. I'd been so focused—so angry—that I hadn't noticed them sneak upon me, and from the looks of things, I'd be lucky to return home only damp.

Cadence and I ran hard back to her stable as thunder cracked overhead, rumbling like a bass drum through the sky. As I ran across the neighbor's yard, large droplets smacked my forehead, falling faster and faster as I ran. I reached the fence, leapt over, and stopped dead in my tracks. Something was wrong.

The car was there, in the same spot. But our house was dark.

Rainwater spilled into my eyes as I sprinted across our small yard, my boots splashing through small puddles, soaking my pants. Our front door was cracked open, but the space beyond was hidden in shadow. My heart hammered against my ribs.

I shoved the door in, my breathing ragged as I scoured the shadows. "Dad?"

Scorch marks stretched like black veins across the walls and down the hallway, and crumbles of charred plaster littered the tiled floor. What had happened? I took shaky steps forward as my pulse skyrocketed.

And then someone grabbed me from behind.

Chapter 4

The Andersons

"Daria it's me. Calm down!"

Cicero released my arms and I stopped trying to attack him. His eyes were hard and determined as he looked me over, his features tight with strain. I'd never seen him so serious. "What are you doing here? And where's my dad?"

Sonya bolted around the corner, her hands on my cheeks the moment I was within reach. "Thank the spirits you're safe."

Thank the spirits? And if she was so worried about my safety then, "What about my dad?"

"Your father is…"

The back door opened and slammed shut. Heavy footsteps hurried toward us and Alex appeared in the hallway, drenched. "She's not…" His voice trailed as his eyes found me. There was so much concern in his face, but then it melted away into something hard and inscrutable, and he turned back around and disappeared down the hall.

"What's going on?" I asked.

"Daria." Cicero's voice was careful. "Something happened and Alaric asked us to come and get you."

My heart lurched. "What do you mean…something happened?" My eyes jumped from Cicero to Sonya.

"Don't worry about your father," Cicero said, his hands spread, placating. "For now, you'll have to trust us until we can explain at our home."

"Don't worry about him? There are scorch marks along the walls in my house, and you don't want me to worry about him? I'm not going anywhere until you tell me what's going on."

Alex appeared again, this time carrying a burlap bag. He didn't even glance at me as he tossed it to his father and opened the front door.

"Someone *please* tell me what happened!"

Alex halted, and all three of them stood there, staring at me. They were in my house. Why did I feel like the intruder?

"Daria." Sonya pleaded with outstretched hands. "Please, calm down. Your father's fine. I promise you. He was worried about your safety, and asked us to take you back with us tonight. You'll see him first thing in the morning."

Were they serious? My dad would leave me notes just to say he walked to the mailbox. "My dad would never just...leave. Not without telling me first."

"Of course he wouldn't." Cicero took a step toward me. "That's why he had us come and get you. We'll explain everything back at our home."

"Right here seems like a perfectly good spot."

"It's not safe here." Cicero leaned close, his eyes holding a ferocity I'd never seen before. "And you wouldn't believe us."

Without giving me the chance to argue, he turned and followed his son through the front door.

This was so out of character for Dad. In fact, I couldn't remember the Andersons ever coming to *our* house. I didn't think they knew where we lived.

"Come on." Sonya grabbed my arm.

I didn't budge, staring at the charred, black lines streaking the walls. They were narrow and laser-focused, making the walls look like they had a web of black veins.

"Sonya, *please*," I said. "I need something to go on. Can't you understand how this looks? We should be calling the police!"

Her gaze flickered to the door, in the direction of the men, and then she grabbed my face in her hands and stared straight into my eyes. "Listen. You are being hunted."

My eyes widened. "Hunted...?"

She glanced again at the door. "We don't know who, and we're not sure why, but your father's gone to find out."

That didn't help my anxiety at all. "*Alone*? What can he possibly do—"

"Shh." She cut me off. She didn't want the men knowing she'd said any of that. "I wish I could tell you more, but I can't. Not yet. You have to trust me when I say your father is perfectly able to handle himself. We can explain a little more at our home, but we need to get you out of here. It's too dangerous now."

I studied her face. She was telling the truth, I could feel it. I hated leaving like this, with so many questions left unanswered, but I trusted the Andersons as much as I trusted my own dad, and being that they were my only lead, I decided to go with them.

Casting one last glance about the house, I followed Sonya out the door and we ran through the rain toward the Subaru. "We're taking *our* car? But what about..."

My words were cut short as Sonya all but shoved me in the back seat. Alex already had the engine running. His eyes narrowed, surveying our surroundings. and he seemed a little tense, almost predatory. I didn't see the Andersons' Mercedes anywhere.

"Where's your car?" I asked. "Wait a minute. How did you even get here?"

I caught Alex's sharp gaze in the rearview mirror.

Sonya grabbed my hand and sat beside me. "We'll tell you what we can when we get back to our home. The rest...your father will have to explain in the morning." She squeezed my hand, reminding me of her words earlier.

Cicero sat in the passenger seat, slammed the car door, and we were soon backing out of our driveway—fast. In fact, I didn't know our Subaru could go this fast, and I had no idea where Alex learned to drive like this. The road seemed to move for him.

The drive back to the Anderson home was the longest hour of my life. Once we arrived, my anxiety increased tenfold. I didn't realize I'd held out hope my dad would be waiting for me until I felt the sting of disappointment when he wasn't. Where could he have gone? What was he doing? Was he really able to handle himself as Sonya had said? And why had he sent the Andersons for me? I'd bear with Sonya for now, but if I didn't get some answers soon, I'd search for him myself.

The Andersons escorted me straight to their library without any explanation. Cicero walked over to the desk and retrieved the key.

My anxiety grew unbearable. "Don't tell me my dad's hiding down there." I pointed at the painting.

31

Sonya and Cicero both glanced at me, startled, and then their gazes landed on their son.

"Alexander?" Cicero accused.

Alex's eyes narrowed at his father. "I never told her." Alex almost sounded bitter.

"Now's not the time," Sonya said, taking the key from her husband. She grabbed the flashlight, walked over to the portrait, and opened it. "Daria?" She peered back at me.

If I hadn't grown up with the Andersons, I might have used the opportunity to run and call the police. I was wasting time being here, having fled the scene of the crime. But I trusted this family—at least two-thirds of them. I knew they loved my dad and me, and if they wanted me to follow them to a hidden room beneath their home, I should at least give them the benefit of the doubt. To me, that translated to approximately ten minutes.

Taking a deep breath, I followed Sonya.

Cicero and Alex followed on my heels, their whispers harsh in the empty stairwell. I couldn't tell what they were saying, but I thought it had something to do with Alex defending his honor while simultaneously ruining mine. Sonya pushed open the door and went around the room lighting candles. Ribbons of smoke snaked through the air as the library flickered with a warm glow. The candlelight hid the shadows that'd seemed frightening hours ago, and the globe stood in its corner, still spinning around its axis.

I had the sudden urge to walk over to it, but hesitated. I needed answers first. Cicero rummaged through a small wooden box sitting on a shelf, withdrew a folded piece of paper and walked back to me.

Eight minutes.

"Read it." He held the paper to me.

I eyed him then took it. The paper was thick, stiff, and the crease was perfect, folded once and never opened. The writing was in my dad's hand.

My lovely daughter,

I'm entrusting this letter to the Del Contes, whom you have known your entire life as the Andersons. Even as I write this, I hope it never finds your hands, because that would mean your safety has been compromised. You know I'm not one to take chances with your safety—probably to a fault. But if you do find yourself reading this, I must ask you to do something for me. Listen to the Del Contes. Trust them with your life, as I've trusted them with mine. They will be my voice in my absence. I hope that whatever situation has caused our separation is momentary, and that I will see you again soon within Gaia's realm. There is so much I need to explain that I should've done many, many years ago.

Please forgive me,

I love you,

Dad

I read the letter again. What on Earth was he talking about?

"You...are the Del Contes?" I asked.

Cicero and Sonya exchanged a nervous glance. "Yes," she said.

They studied me, waiting to see how I'd react.

"You drove me all the way from my home and brought me down here just to tell me you have a different last name?"

Cicero's eye twitched. "Did you read the entire letter?"

"Twice!" I was so mad the paper trembled in my hands. I couldn't believe I followed them here for this.

"And...?" Cicero prodded.

I glanced back at the letter, my rage intensifying. Five minutes. "Fine, where is this G...how do you say it?"

"Guy-uh," Cicero said. "Gaia is another world."

My eyes snapped from the paper to Cicero, then to Sonya then Alex. Nothing in their expressions even hinted at humor. These people I'd known all my life, this family I'd trusted—I may have been experiencing slight hysteria at my dad's sudden disappearance, but it didn't mean I'd believe any explanation thrown at me.

"Just how stupid do you think I am? Is this story really easier than just telling me who's after me and why?"

Cicero leveled a look of disapproval on his wife for telling me this bit of information, and his wife returned that look with something full of helpless exasperation. "There's no harm in telling her that much, Cicero," she said.

"Alaric made us swear to keep quiet. Telling her only puts her in more danger!"

"Yes. Danger." My breath came quick and shallow with panic. "Would either of you like to tell me why you're not at all worried about my dad, considering he's *alone*, chasing after whoever's pursuing me?"

Cicero and Sonya stared at one another, each of their faces hard. They didn't disagree much, but this whole situation seemed to strike a dissonant chord. Sonya folded her arms over her chest, her eyes demanding Cicero answer me.

Cicero sighed and looked back at me. "Your father is...not the international businessman you think he is."

I waited, sweating and shaking, and for some reason, I feared what Cicero was going to say next.

"Alaric is an ambassador from Gaia—the world he's from. The world we're all from. Including you."

My breath lodged in my throat. Cicero's words repeated over and over in my head. My heart raced as the edges of my vision darkened, and I gripped the nearest bookshelf to steady myself. My dad goes missing under very strange circumstances, and then people I'm supposed to trust abduct me. Although, considering I agreed to come with them, I couldn't call it abduction. But, in my defense, they hadn't said anything about another world. If they had, I never would've followed them. Then again, they'd known that, which was why they hadn't bothered telling me any of this before. What next, magic?

"I don't believe you." My world slowly tilted. "And I don't see how any of this explains anything about why someone's after me or why my dad's suddenly gone missing."

Cicero looked to Sonya, and Sonya said, "Daria, we really aren't certain why someone's after you. Your father has speculations, but he'll have to tell you himself, when we all meet him in Gaia tomorrow."

Spots floated and swirled in my eyes, and the ground tilted faster and faster. I sat down in a cold sweat, focusing on keeping my consciousness close.

A square, dark object appeared before me.

Cicero was holding a large, leather-bound book. The binding was worn and dried, and the stitching in the leather frayed at the edges. "This is probably the best way to show you, in a way that *you* might understand."

34

Shaking, I took the oversized manuscript from him and set it in my lap. Right across the front, in faded bronze embossed lettering, were the words:

THE ORBIS TERRARUM
and other obscurities of Gaia's anatomy

This wasn't a manuscript. It was an atlas.

He was going to explain a hypothetical world with a map? Cicero waved for me to continue. I refolded my dad's letter and shoved it in my pocket, then lifted the large cover and stared at the large page beneath it. Ostentatious handwriting was scrawled at the bottom.

Seekers beware.
What was there, was there before, and will not be, evermore.

I glanced up at Cicero.

"Turn the page."

Scrolled across the top of the next page was the word *Regent*. Right below, filling the rest of the page, was a giant black square. "What am I looking at exactly?" My voice trembled despite my feeble attempt at strength.

"Where we're going tomorrow. Where the Aegis Quarters is located."

"The...what?"

Sonya laid a hand on my shoulder. "Where we're meeting your father."

"But I don't see anything."

"That's because it's night."

"What does that have to do with...?" I ran my finger over the page and my breath hitched. My finger sank *into* the page. Right where my finger pressed into the darkness, I felt a wet chill. I jerked my hand back. "What is this?"

"*The Orbis Terrarum,*" Sonya said. "It's a sacred Gaian manuscript. One other exists, but it is kept in a vault. This is an atlas of the present."

I trailed my fingers over the page again. They sank in like before, disappearing into the blackness as if the manuscript was a living, viable object. My mind tried refuting it, but my eyes won the battle.

The Andersons—Del Contes—or whoever they were, all hovered around watching me, their apprehension palpable. I flipped through more pages, some of them black, others muted in color. One was so bright it was as if I'd unleashed the sun in the room.

A page entitled *Sea of Despair* made me stop. It was dark like the others, but I thought I heard distant whispers, almost like the crashing of waves. Blinding white lines forked across the page, followed by the boom of thunder.

I slammed the book shut.

Sonya leaned close to me, her eyes warm and trying so hard to comfort me. "Cicero wanted you to see this so that you would believe."

"Believe what?"

I couldn't be sure, but it seemed as if the candles dimmed a bit.

"Gaia is a world full of magic."

I knew it. They weren't done dropping bombs on my sanity. My mouth opened to argue, but the words wouldn't come.

Magic wasn't real. I knew that.

Are you sure? You know you've never seen anything like this before.

So what? Technology's incredible these days.

This isn't technology. It's a book.

That was it. It was bad enough having everyone I knew turn against me. My own conscience doing it was unacceptable.

I went back to the book in my hands, searching for mechanics, hardware, wires—anything that could unveil the truth behind this phenomenon—but all I could find was paper, leather, and old adhesive. An unsettling truth began to wiggle its way into my very soul.

This book was supernatural.

I couldn't deny its uniqueness, or its power. Cicero had known that. They all had known that. They expected me to need some sort of hard proof, and a magical book would be the most convincing tool for someone like me. It was also why they'd been so insistent I come with them here before explaining anything. I could deny their words, but I couldn't deny my sight.

"This atlas shows the present," Cicero continued. "It isn't so much a map as a way to see places throughout Gaia at any given time, and it is all possible through magic."

I stared dumbly at the atlas. It was all too much.

"You've been down here before?" Sonya asked.

Even though it'd only been a few hours, it seemed like so long ago. "Yes, I...found it when Dad and I were here earlier."

Alex looked a little startled. He also received an apologetic look from Cicero.

Sonya glanced around the room, her hand still on my shoulder. "These shelves are filled with books from Gaia: concordances, histories, biographies, magic." She glanced at me before crossing the room to the globe.

She lifted it by the supports and brought it before me. Clouds floated in their manufactured atmosphere, lingering over landmasses and hiding them from view. Here, in the ambient candlelight, it looked magical. I remembered the little flash, thinking at the time it reminded me of lightning. Maybe, just maybe, that was because it *had been* lightning.

"This—" Sonya's eyes were fixed on the globe "—is a miniature representation of Gaia."

The object held me entranced.

"Do you notice anything unusual?" she asked.

The little sphere continued rotating on its axis. "The entire globe is unusual," I said.

She smiled.

"How is it rotating on its own like that?" I asked. "And is it really showing current weather systems?"

She nodded. "Yes, and like everything from Gaia, it's fueled by the magic inherent to that world."

That little white smudge continued moving from water to land, as the world turned.

"It's where we are all from—including you."

I looked back at Sonya. Her gaze was tender, confident, and I could almost feel the truth in her words, even though my mind still fought against it. But something deep within me accepted it against my will. Some part of me already knew it existed—my backstabbing conscience—and it had waited all my life for this moment, unbeknownst to me.

"Magic runs through your veins," Sonya whispered. "It is as much a part of you as your own blood, just as it is a part of your father. You feel it. You know—deep down inside—that it's true. You've always wanted more from your life, you've always felt a pull for more, and that's because this world is not your true home."

Sonya always understood me better than most, but after she said that, I was certain she'd crawled in my head and poked around when I wasn't looking. My whole life I'd yearned for more, begged for more. But not for this.

I felt Alex's eyes on my back even though I couldn't see him. He'd remained in the shadows ever since we'd come down here.

"The atlas." She nodded to the book in my hands. "It focuses on different territories within our world with greater emphasis on the portals."

I swallowed. "Portals?"

Cicero grinned. "Yes. Those bloody things are the only way between worlds, and they keep us employed."

"You're serious."

"Well, about the first part."

He waited for my response but I was too overwhelmed to say a word. All this information supersaturated my brain.

Cicero continued. "At one point, well before anyone remembers, Gaia coexisted with Earth. They were one and the same." He paused a moment, his eyes fixed on the spinning globe. "As mankind continued turning to their own ways, they turned their backs on Gaia. They wasted her gifts and powers—disregarded them under the false notion that they didn't need her. What they failed to realize was that the only reason they had any power at all was because Gaia had given it to them. So, Gaia left. She took her spirit to a place where it would be safe, in balance with all other powers, and Gaia became her own world.

"Gaia's strongest remaining vestiges of influence are where the portals formed, linking parts of Gaia to Earth. Like everything in this world, they've been forgotten over time. Now, only the citizens of Gaia know of their existence, and they're guarded." Here, he winked at me. "Gaia's magic is too dangerous in the hands of the people of Earth now. That knowledge might destroy both worlds."

38

My eyes were trapped on the sphere. "These portals. Where are they?"

"There are seven in total, all of them in unique places around Earth."

Dad. He'd always traveled to the exact same locations, in the exact same rotation.

"Let me guess. London is a portal?"

Sonya nodded. "Stonehenge."

Which meant Rome, Cairo, Moscow, Auckland, and Lima were all portals to another world. London was closest, but there was no way Dad would've had the time to get there, meet us in the morning, and expect us to meet him. As I turned the locations over in my head, I realized they only added to six.

I looked at Cicero. "Where is the nearest one?"

"Bridal Veil Falls."

Seven.

I thought of the portrait in the library upstairs. How ironic. "But how...with that many tourists?" I asked.

"You'll see in the morning, when we take you to your father." Cicero climbed to his feet.

Morning seemed so far away, but what could I do? They were the ones who had seen my dad, or so they'd said. I would be patient for now, as they'd asked, but there was one more thing I needed to know.

"How did you get to my house?"

Sonya knelt at my side. "This," she whispered. In her hands was an object: a round, bronze amulet hanging by a circuitous bronze chain. Engraved on the surface were foreign symbols I'd never seen before. They reminded me of runes.

"It is a magical device," Sonya continued. "Your father insisted we keep one in case of emergency. It stores power. Since Earth is no longer a magical world, it takes a great deal more effort to perform magic here, especially magic like this. This amulet has accumulated power over the years, and even then it was only enough power for the three of us to wrap it around ourselves and use it just this once."

"For what?"

Her warm eyes stared straight into mine. "For transporting ourselves straight to you."

Chapter 5

The Portal

Tap-tap-tap.

The sound pounded against my skull. I fought against the haze and opened my heavy lids. Moonlight slipped through a crease in the thick draperies. Wait, those weren't my draperies. I didn't even own draperies. Where was I?

Tap-tap-tap.

The memory dropped on me like an anvil. I was in the guest room at the Andersons, except they weren't really the Andersons. Well, they were, but they were from another world, they'd used magic to get to my house, and their last name was actually Del Conte.

My temples wrenched in pain.

The door creaked open, the light from the hallway stabbed through the shadows, and I winced.

"Morning, dear." It was Sonya.

I tried answering her but a yawn came out instead.

"Time to go." She flicked on the lamp beside my bed.

Craning my neck, I looked at the hands of the little, round clock standing on the bedside table. Three-thirty in the morning. I plopped back down on my pillow and stared at the ceiling. I was about to follow them through a portal into a magical world to meet my dad.

It was highly probable my sanity got fed up and deserted me.

Sonya sat on the edge of my bed. "To your father, remember?"

How could I forget?

"Clara made fresh maple scones for you," she said.

Well, there was one thing about my morning that wasn't disastrous. "That was nice of her." I slowly propped myself up on my elbows.

At my reply, Sonya seemed to breathe a little easier. "She wanted to help you ease into your ...unusual morning."

I took a deep breath. "Clara knows then?"

Sonya nodded, studying me with eyes full of remorse. "I know you're upset." She touched my hand. "And we understand if you're angry with us. I wish I could tell you more, but we've sworn an oath to your father to not only protect *you* but to protect certain information. And he'll share that information with you once he feels it's safe."

Her regret was sincere, but I couldn't rid myself of resentment. How could they do it? See me all these years, knowing things this fantastic existed, and never—not even once—allude to it. And it sounded like they'd sworn an oath that would force them to continue keeping things from me.

"We'd like to leave within the hour," she said. "Feel free to go back to sleep till then. I just wanted to give you the opportunity to gather yourself. I laid out some towels for you in the bathroom." She kissed my forehead and stepped out of the room.

I rubbed my eyes and looked around the Andersons'—Del Contes' guestroom. I'd slept in this room too many times to count, but things were so different then, and simple. The stained mahogany armoire filled with blankets that Alex and I made forts with, the old school-desk in the corner that screeched in pain every time I wiggled in its wooden chair.

Hanging on the wall above was a painting of an enormous, gothic castle surrounded by mountains, but not even they could outshine the magnificence of the stone structure. It loomed over the world it sat upon, daring anyone to disrupt the tranquility of the valley below.

I used to wonder if that castle really existed somewhere in our world, if people really lived there. As a kid, I imagined stories of goblins and trolls and a knight that fought dragons to rescue the fair maiden trapped inside the tallest tower. I didn't really care much for fair maidens. If I lived in that castle, I'd be the knight. I'd slay that dragon, send the maiden back home, and be crowned the ruler. Alex had laughed at me when I told him that, but stopped when I punched him in the stomach so hard it knocked the wind from him. I would've been a just ruler, too.

To dream of a magical world is one thing. To be told one exists is quite another.

Shaking off the memories, I crawled out of bed and took my shower. Hot water ran over me while the steam brought back my senses. Was I really about to abandon everything I'd ever known? But abandon what, exactly? My life in borrowed fields? Cadence? Hours spent in solitude while yearning for adventure? Here was my chance, and besides, what did I have to lose? They were still my only real lead, and I couldn't deny everything they'd shown me last night.

The shower ended, I toweled myself off, dressed, and made my way downstairs with wet hair.

I wonder if Alex is awake.

Angry that my mind would think such a thing, I focused on the strong scent of maple coming from the kitchen. I ignored the fact that my eyes kept scouring the rooms for him.

Clara was busy frosting her last batch of scones when I entered. She glanced up and smiled. "Morning, miss. Sleep well?"

I couldn't be angry at that smile. "No, but I woke up well, thanks to you. They smell fabulous."

I felt like a kid again, running downstairs early on a Saturday morning, Clara waiting for me with her scones and milk. Alex would be waiting for me, too, so we could plan our adventures for the day.

Light footsteps moved behind me as I grabbed one of the scones.

"Good morning, Alexander." Clara smiled past me.

I didn't turn around. In fact, my jaw froze mid-bite.

"Smells incredible in here, as always," said that man-voice.

I focused on finishing my bite, trying to enjoy the taste of cinnamon and maple glaze. From the sounds of things, Alex was rummaging through the pantry.

"It does my heart good to see you two together again," Clara said.

I choked on my scone just as something slammed to the floor behind me. Struggling to swallow my misrouted bite, I met Alex's gaze right before he bent over and picked up the water bottle now rolling across the kitchen floor. He left without another word.

Clara watched after him, glanced at me, and then turned her curious eyes back to her cooking.

After I finished my breakfast, I meandered down the hall. Everyone was gathered at the front door.

"Are you ready?" Sonya asked.

No, not in the slightest. I nodded.

Her smile was full of relief. "Great. Let me fetch Clara. Meet us out back?" She said to her husband. Cicero nodded.

Alex was out the front door before Sonya even started back down the hall. Cicero glanced at me, scratching the back of his neck. It seemed as if he was trying to think of something comforting to say but I wasn't sure. Cicero wasn't the most delicate with words. In that way he was a lot like my dad.

He eventually just opened the door. "Ready?"

The land beyond was blanketed in darkness. We walked into the chilled morning air and waited on the front porch. My dad's silver Subaru appeared around the corner with Clara in the driver's seat, smiling. Alex hopped out of the car and held the door open, motioning for me to climb in back. I caught his gaze as I crawled in, but he abruptly looked away, sat beside me and shut the door. He took up more space than when we were younger, and I didn't remember his frame being so solid and immovable. It was impossible to keep my shoulders from touching his, even though he was conveniently leaning away from me.

Cicero buckled himself in the passenger seat. When Clara shoved down the pedal, I thought the car was going to throw me out the back window. For such a passive creature, her aggression while driving was shocking.

We reached the end of their long driveway in record time and headed straight for Yosemite Valley. As many times as I'd visited the Andersons, not once had I gone to the Valley.

The sky lightened and we drove through a short tunnel. When we emerged, my gaze fell captive to the valley. Water glittered over granite cliffs, carving its way through rock, plunging into beds of green. It looked like a big crack in the Earth, the valley a hidden paradise protected by thick walls of stone and snow-capped mountains.

The road wound through a forest of colossal pines. Huge boulders dotted the land, having fallen from the cliffs above. We passed column after thick column of brown bark. Every so often, Sonya would turn and look back at me, her smile both sad and encouraging.

I still couldn't believe I'd allowed myself to accept this. Dad goes missing, someone's after me for reasons I can't fathom, and I believe he's gone to another world to find them. Not only that, I was trying to go there myself. But then there was my traitorous conscience. It was confident this Gaia existed, and was appalled that I wasn't.

Clara pulled the Subaru into an almost empty parking lot, designated for the Bridal Veil Falls trail, and the pull within me intensified. All of us, except for Clara, climbed out of the Subaru. Alex walked around back, lifted the hatchback, and retrieved a stack of blankets. Maybe this other world was colder than Earth.

If it existed.

It does exist.

I pushed my door shut, silently cursing my conscience.

The roar of rushing water filled the valley. From here Bridal Veil Falls looked like it fell from the heavens. It careened over a cliff, widening as it fell, veiling the ground below with a swirling white mist.

"Everyone ready?" Although Cicero's question was addressed to everyone, everyone was looking at me.

So I nodded.

Cicero began trudging down a paved trail with Alex right behind him. This was it. My sanity was about to abandon me forever. I glanced one last time at Clara, who was smiling.

"Don't worry, miss. It's beautiful on the other side. Once you see it, you will understand."

Before I could respond, she rolled up her window and backed out of the parking spot. No Subaru had ever gone from reverse to drive so fast. It was only a few seconds before the car was gone. Maybe Clara was the one who taught Alex how to drive.

"Let's go," Sonya said.

Sonya and I jogged ahead, the thrum of the falls growing louder and louder the closer we got. After a few bends I saw the khakis and whites of Cicero's and Alex's clothing.

44

The closer we came to the falls, the more I needed to get there. It was as if there was an invisible force yanking at my soul, beckoning me forward. At first I thought I imagined it, but it grew stronger with each step. If Dad had been hiding another world from me—for whatever reason—he was smart not to bring me here. All of them were. In this place, I felt there was something more, something greater.

The trail disappeared into a mountain of mist that rose and swirled from the base of the crashing water, and the thunderous roar reverberated around me, blotting out all other sound. Cicero motioned for us to follow him off the path.

The pull continued and I wanted Cicero to hurry. I wasn't even sure where we were going, but I had the urge to move. Cicero led us parallel with the granite wall, our clothing getting soaked with each step. He halted right beside a smooth spot in the granite then scanned the area around us.

He placed his hand on the rock surface, his eyelids closed and his lips moved. I couldn't hear what he was saying, but when he dropped his hand, a faint shimmer caught my eye, right on the rock's surface. The etchings of a word began to appear on the granite, glittering with a faint glow:

Porta

Then the letters moved, spreading apart until they formed an arch just above Cicero's head. He cast one last glance back at me before stepping forward and vanishing into the solid granite wall.

My jaw dropped with a gasp. "How...?"

Sonya grabbed my hand, pulling me toward the wall with the letters shimmering above.

"Hurry before it closes." She let go of my hand, took a step forward, and disappeared in the wall.

I was frozen in shock, unable to believe my eyes. I had just witnessed two people walk through a solid, granite wall. That had to be a major violation of at least a dozen laws of physics.

Alex stepped forward, pausing beside me. He didn't speak or glance at me, he just stood there staring after his parents.

45

I thought he was waiting for me, letting me go first to make sure I didn't change my mind and run off, but then he walked on and was swallowed by the rock.

The golden lettering began to spark and fade. If I didn't hurry, I'd be stuck here alone taking an unwanted shower. What was the worst that could happen? I'd run into a rock wall. As long as no one saw me, I could live with that.

Closing my eyes, I took a deep breath and stepped away from my world and into the unknown.

Chapter 6

Gaia

I winced, preparing to smack hard into the wall. Instead, my foot landed on solid ground. The air was so damp it tasted wet and my clothes were heavy with dew. I opened my eyelids slowly. Everything was dark except for a golden haze in front of me, and before I could wonder where I was, my attention was drawn to the voices coming from the glow.

"Where's Daria?" It was Cicero, but his voice sounded muffled and distorted, as if he was talking underwater.

I took another few steps toward Cicero's voice. When he spoke again, his words were clearer. "You were supposed to wait for her!"

The darkness vanished and I ran into something, hard. My arms flailed as I tried to keep myself from falling, and something gripped my shoulders, holding me upright.

"I've got you."

I glanced up into Alex's face. Amusement sparked in his eyes but it quickly faded back to cold nothing. He released my shoulders and stepped aside, exchanging a quick glance with his father. Cicero's face was bright red, but when he looked at me his frown disappeared.

We stood in a large, round stone room with an arched ceiling. The walls glistened and glittered from torchlight that splattered upon moist rock, and the air was stale and heavy with mildew and smoke. Torches hung on the wall, separated by large stone doors spaced at intervals around the room. They all looked exactly the same, no handles or markings, just sheets of smooth rock embedded in the circular wall. But that wasn't the only thing I found strange.

There was life to this room—a life force I felt—and I could hear distant voices. They were coming from the doors, pleading in whispers, begging me to pass through. A shudder

47

ran through me. "What is this place?" My voice echoed in the empty chamber.

Cicero studied the various doors, his forehead creased in concentration. "It's called the Room of Doors. It's a boundary of sorts, and it's necessary to keep people from coming in and going out."

My fingers trailed the surface of the cool, stone door we'd walked through, trying to find some unique marking—anything that would set it apart from the others—just in case I needed to go back. Intuition told me I didn't want to be caught choosing the wrong door.

"It doesn't matter." Cicero watched me as if he'd heard my thoughts. "What lies beyond them shifts regularly. If you pass through the wrong door, you may never find a way out, and because of that, only those like myself attempt to cross."

I never should've followed them in here, but it was too late to regret that now.

"One of these doors leads to this...Gaia?" I asked.

Cicero nodded as he took a blanket from Alex. I soon realized it wasn't a blanket at all. It was a cloak. The wool hung to Cicero's feet, broadening his already-broad shoulders. It reminded me of the man I'd seen in the fields. That was only yesterday, the same day Dad disappeared. Was he the one who was after me? If he was, I didn't like the idea of Dad going after him alone. Not at all.

I was about to mention that encounter to Del Contes, when Alex stood before me, holding a pile of wool.

"I don't need one, thanks."

The flickering torchlight sharpened the angles in his face. "Put it on."

I ripped the wool from his hands with more gusto than I'd intended. He raised a brow but said nothing else.

"We need to hide our clothing." Sonya was already cloaked. "The style is...different on the other side."

I hadn't given much thought to the style attribute of another world.

My cloak was enormous. I bunched up as much fabric as I could at my neck, forced the silver clasp to hold it together while feeling completely awkward doing it, but I was still swimming in wool. Alex had already put his on. The wool clung to his shoulders, rustling ever so slightly as he moved.

The cloak looked elegant on him—natural, even. It seemed as much a part of him as the dark hair on his head. Not at all what I imagined I looked like.

Cicero stood before a door about thirty degrees to my right. It looked just like the others and was shaped just like the others, but unlike all the others, this one was quiet.

I felt Alex's eyes on me as Cicero laid his hand on the door. A few slow seconds passed and the stone rumbled as it slid into the wall. And then Cicero stepped into the pure blackness beyond.

With a deep breath I followed, Sonya and Alex right on my heels. The door slid shut behind us. The glow from the torch-lit chamber narrowed and dimmed into a fine line, and was gone.

The darkness that followed was so thick I couldn't see my own hand. Here, the air was damp and a cool breeze brushed against my clammy skin, making me shiver. A constant drip—drip—drip echoed from somewhere in the distance. I was about to say something when a light burst to life. It came from a single torch hanging on the wall to our right. The flame burned bright, casting a soft glow down the stone tunnel to where it was swallowed by darkness. Cicero proceeded forward, and we all followed.

Just as we reached the end of the torch's golden halo, another burst to life up ahead and the flame behind us snuffed out. On and on we walked, torch after torch dimming and glowing as we moved from one to the other. They were lighting on their own and I didn't think it had anything to do with motion sensors.

What was this place?

There was a strange reverence to the silence, one that sank deep into my soul, overwhelming me with intrigue. The walls felt *alive*. Life was everywhere, reaching out, wrapping over me and through me. What the source was, I had no idea, but I couldn't shake the need to move forward. It was becoming unbearable.

My eyes flitted about, watching the shadows dance along the rock. It was as if the walls were watching us, whispering to each other as we passed. And that's when I ran in to something.

"Sorry!" I was thankful for the darkness. Hopefully, Alex wouldn't see the blood filling my face.

He peered sideways at me and kept walking.

Well. He could've at least said *something*.

The cave turned. Up ahead, beyond the glow of the nearest torch, the blanket of darkness lifted with a soft, white light.

Daylight.

We were almost at the end of the tunnel. My need to move forward bordered on irresistible, and it was all I could do to keep from running. With each small step, the invisible string pulled harder, gripping my consciousness until I couldn't hold myself back any longer.

My legs moved faster and faster. I walked ahead, brushing past Alex, Sonya, and Cicero. My speed walk turned into a dead run. The light amplified as I ran, pitching headlong toward the opening. I felt the Del Contes' eyes on my back, but I was compelled by an insane desire to keep moving. Leaving darkness behind, I ran from the mouth of the cave and was bathed in blinding sunlight.

My spirit was ablaze, my skin tingling as a myriad of emotions engulfed me, drowning out my awareness of self. My surroundings felt alive, and I felt connected to all of it. Overwhelmed and dizzy, I sat, closing my eyes. So many feelings pressed against me and I swam against their strong current trying to stay afloat. The world encased me with its life force, holding me in strong, invisible hands, as if my body had returned from a long sojourn, and the world was my spirit, rushing to unite with its flesh. A few long moments passed, the chaos in my mind abated, and I became aware of my own feelings again.

Waves of concern poured over me. Even though my eyes were still closed, somehow I knew the concern was Sonya's. I could *feel* her approaching. My hand was in hers just as I felt Cicero move beside me. Then I sensed Alex.

I opened my eyes and found his at once. They were burdened and heavy, but the joy flowing from him was so pure and potent it intoxicated me. For a few moments, I struggled to push their emotions away so I could find my *own* again. Once under control, I peered at Sonya, who looked a little worried.

"Are you all right?" Her eyes searched mine.

"I think so." I stood, releasing her hand.

My senses were acute and powerful, more so than I thought possible, and they had connected to this strange place without my permission. The Del Contes said this world magical, but this? They hadn't said anything about this. Reaching a new sort of equilibrium, I finally looked at the land before me.

We stood on the rim of a deep, lush valley with a glittering blue river dividing it in half. Magnificent mountain peaks stood all around, their caps like white arrowheads piercing the sky. The valley itself was veiled in a blanket of giant trees, while exotic wildflowers dotted the rare open spaces, accenting the deep green with splashes of lurid colors. Everything here was vibrant, as if I was looking at a world in high definition. The air tasted crisper and cleaner, and the light breeze was scented with flowers' perfume. The thrum of rushing water echoed throughout the verdant vale, and everywhere I looked I felt life—in the air, in the trees, in the rocks—everywhere.

This place made me *feel* to the core of my being, and it held a knowledge and wisdom of its own. It was then I realized my need to press on had left, because I had arrived. There was no turning back now, not even if I wanted to. No more brown fields, no more fences. No more loneliness.

Just...life. Pure, powerful life.

"Beautiful, isn't it?" Sonya whispered beside me. I'd almost forgotten they were there.

"Yes," I said, but I didn't think the word "beautiful" was enough. I wasn't sure there was a word that could capture the magnificence of this place.

"Are you all right to keep going?" Cicero asked.

I nodded. "This place...it's unbelievable."

"This is only a piece of it." His eyes narrowed ahead. "Better get moving before someone sees us."

He walked down a narrow, rocky ledge that hugged the granite wall behind us. Sonya touched my arm and beamed, and continued after her husband, but Alex remained. He stood fixed, staring beyond with that same weighted gaze while the light breeze ruffled his cloak and dark hair. He looked majestic standing there, as if he were a prince guarding over his realm, burdened by the safety of its citizens. Deep down inside, a part of me ached. That part wanted to throw my arms around him and tell him how much I missed him and how happy I was to be with him again. I was furious at that part of myself.

His gaze met mine then, those deep green eyes seeming to hear everything I didn't say and everything I didn't want to feel. I glanced away and hurried after Sonya and Cicero into the veil of dense foliage.

It was much cooler beneath the shade of the trees. Shadows slithered along the ground as light pierced through the canopy above. I glanced up, tilting my head to the green cathedral walling us in, and the effect was dizzying. Boughs creaked and moaned as they strained with all their might, reaching out to cradle me in their arms, their leaves rustling in the breeze. When I looked back down, I realized I was alone. I didn't see Sonya or Cicero anywhere.

Just as I opened my mouth to call out to them, a hand grabbed my cloak and yanked me off the trail. The hand belonged to Sonya, and we were now hiding behind a large boulder with Cicero. Alex appeared right behind me.

"What's going—"

"What is it?" Alex cut me off.

"Guards. I think someone saw us come through." Cicero's brow furrowed as he peered into the forest. All I could see was green.

"We're hiding from—"

"Are you sure?" Alex interrupted me again, peering around with his father. Sonya held her finger to her lips, motioning for me to remain silent. As if talking got me any answers.

I heard a muffled patter in the distance, and my ears perked. I knew that sound. I knew it like my own voice. It was the rhythmic pounding of horse hooves, and it was getting louder.

Cicero mumbled something and Alex shoved me on the ground, forcing me to lie flat between Sonya and him. The pounding roared in my head, drowning out my racing heartbeat. Whoever was coming rode hard, and it sounded like there was more than one of them. Whatever they were after, I was about to find out.

52

The pounding ceased. They were here.

After a few seconds of unbearable silence, I had to look. I lifted my face inches off the ground and peered over Alex. Silver glinted through the trees on the ledge where we'd stood moments ago. I counted four riders, and they looked like some sort of guard. They wore breastplates of silver, dotted with greens and blacks, their baldrics holding swords. The hair on their heads and faces was long and unshaven, and their expressions were filled with so much hatred my breath stuck in my chest.

A fifth rider appeared in my line of sight, but he was different from the rest. His face was hidden beneath a drawn hood and the rest of his powerful frame was veiled in rich, black wool that blended with his velvety black stallion. A long silver blade hung at his waist, glinting in the sunlight. He looked out of place in this world filled with color and life, as if the night had delivered Death himself.

My head was shoved back down and my eyes locked with Alex's, his face rigid with warning, his eyes flashed with violence.

One of the riders jerked his horse around and started in our direction, and the others followed him. My heart thudded in my ears. The rider stopped in front of the boulder we were hiding behind, his horse raking at the ground.

I held my breath.

"So he was wrong," the soldier barked in a gruff voice.

"Keep searching," answered a deeper, velvety voice. The black rider. "Considering the current circumstances, you shouldn't be so hasty to forfeit your assignment."

His voice unnerved me, touching my newfound awareness with a stiff chill.

"We're wasting our time," said a third. "There's no one here."

"My Lord is never wrong," growled the black rider.

Everything went silent and I was smothered in the anxiety of my companions. I didn't move. I didn't breath. I didn't even dare to blink.

The silence menaced. A stiff breeze barreled through the forest and the trees bended and creaked loudly in response.

"Search the grounds, and stick to the main road," barked the voice. "I shall notify my Lord at once."

Leather reigns snapped, horses whinnied, and the riders vanished down the trail. All but the black rider.

He lingered there, just on the other side of our boulder. There was a darkness to him—a malevolence that made my soul recoil. Ice-cold fingers grazed me then, as if some invisible hand were searching and sifting through my mind. Sweat beaded on my forehead as I shut my eyes tight, fighting against the invasion. Another gust of wind ripped through the forest, the chill ceased, and the rider spun and rode off after his companions.

The moment the guards were out of sight, the Del Contes leapt to their feet, their concern and anxiety overpowering. Running from guards didn't seem like something any honest person would do. Which made me wonder, what if my dad's role in this other world was bad? I hadn't thought of that. What would I do then? But I'd seen those guards and how dark and frightening they'd been, and that voice had left me shaken. It didn't matter whether or not Dad was good or bad. I needed to see him, if anything to know that he was safe from men like them. And to know that he was alive.

"They weren't...after me, were they?" I whispered.

Sonya shook her head—whether in dismissal or denial, I didn't know—and she tugged on me to move. The shadows in the forest were much deeper than before. I glanced up. Thick clouds loomed overhead, just visible through cracks in the green barrier. These clouds were darker and more menacing than anything I'd ever seen—not the sort of thing you want from a storm.

We strayed from the path this time, winding around huge trees and thick underbrush. The wind gained strength, ripping through the forest, nipping at my damp skin. I kept seeing movement in the corner of my eye, but every time I looked, all I could find was a rock or pile of shrubs.

Then I bumped into something.

Not again.

"Sorry." My cheeks burned hot, and, unfortunately for me, Alex noticed this time.

He lowered his mouth to my ear. "You know, if you wanted me closer, you could've just asked. It'd be a lot less painful for both of us."

My eyes narrowed. "Like you know anything about pain."

54

His lips formed a tight line and he stepped aside. When I walked on, I felt his eyes boring into my back.

You got your wish. You wanted him to say something last time.

That's it, conscience. If you don't keep quiet I'll tie you to a tree and leave you there.

The breeze continued beating at my hair and cloak. I wrapped my arms around myself, trying to contain my body heat, hoping that wherever we were headed wasn't much farther.

My teeth were chattering by the time a solid gray structure came into view. The roof was made of thatched coverings and the walls were composed of neatly laid stone. Ribbons of smoke rose and curled from the chimney and my spirits lifted at the prospect of a warm fire. Soft light flickered behind one of the beveled glass windows and shadows moved beyond. Someone was inside. Was it Dad? Was he safe?

The front door creaked open, and my heart sank. It wasn't my dad. It was a young man about my age, maybe younger. His light-brown hair was a disheveled mess and his hazel eyes held an intelligence that contrasted his youthful features. His loose-fitting tunic was slightly large for his skinny frame, and the extra fabric of his tan pants was tucked into tall leather boots. If this was the style, no wonder the Del Contes wanted us to wear cloaks. This guy was dressed for the nineteenth century.

The young man halted right before us, and even before he opened his mouth to speak, I knew the news wasn't good. His apprehension was strong.

"Thad." Cicero gave a curt nod of acknowledgment to the young man called Thad.

Thad nodded in return. "Sir." His voice was scratchy.

"Where's Alaric?"

Thad's gaze flashed to me. "Gone, sir."

Cicero stepped forward. "What do you mean...gone?"

"He left this morning. He said he couldn't stay." Thad hesitated, glancing briefly at me. "Someone helped the Pykans through the portal."

The Del Contes' anxiety stabbed through me, but knowing my dad had come and gone turned my heart to lead. "But you promised me he'd be here," I said.

"Quick, inside." Sonya looped her arm through mine and pulled me after her.

Thad stole a few glimpses of me as he led us to the cottage. Thunder cracked above, rumbling throughout the valley as large droplets began falling, and my sense of despair expounded. From the very moment I'd been told about this world, the one hope I'd clung to had been seeing my dad. Without him, I wasn't sure how much longer I could hold it together.

We reached the porch's protection just as the clouds unleashed their fury. Rain fell in a curtain behind us, blurring the landscape as we walked through the doorway.

Dad wasn't here.

Everyone scattered while I stood in the foyer, paralyzed by anxiety. What should I do now? I'd followed the Del Contes here only because they'd promised we'd meet my dad for answers. That obviously wasn't happening, and now I was stuck in a strange world with no one I could really trust. My dad was somewhere in this world, but I had no possible way of finding him—not one clue as to where he could've gone. But even if I knew where he was, how in this world would I get there?

Quick patter echoed from somewhere. There was a blur of movement and then a large mass of grey fur lunged at me. Its paws landed on my chest, shoving me against the wall while lavishing my neck and chin with dog drool.

"Egan!" Thad's voice reverberated down the hall.

Egan dropped his paws. His tail whipped behind him as he paced at my feet with his tongue lolling out of his mouth. The grey streaked his silky fur like the shadows in drifting snow and his eyes were like two shards of blue ice. He looked like winter on four legs, assuming winter also had a long and slobbery pink tongue.

"Sorry about that." Thad chuckled as he strolled into the room. "Egan gets excited with company. Especially pretty girls."

My cheeks warmed as I reached down and scratched Egan's soft neck. He nuzzled his wet nose into my palm. "What kind of dog is he?"

Egan licked my fingers, careful not to leave any piece of skin dry.

"Akita. And an ornery one at that." Thad stuck out his hand before me. "I'm Thad."

There was a childlike vigor to him I liked. Maybe I could trust him to help me.

"Daria." I shook his hand with the one not dripping with dog drool.

"Your cloak?"

"I'm all right. It's keeping me warm."

A drop of water fell from my cloak and onto the floor as another one slid down my back. I shivered.

"Right." Thad grinned. "Hand it over. I'll get you something dry."

He held his hand open in expectation. I peeled off my wet cloak and handed it to him. He took it away, and I looked around the room for the first time.

The walls were made of stone and dark wooden beams, the view beyond the windows smeared from rainwater. A fire crackled and blazed in the corner, the warmth slowly seeping into my skin. Candles sat in sconces upon the walls, their light diffused in golden halos, chasing away all shadows. This place was comforting, and even though I wasn't sure what was happening, I felt safe here, as if these walls would protect me at all costs from the unknown world beyond them.

Thad grabbed a wool blanket off the couch and threw it at me. I managed to catch it before it fell to the floor.

"Make yourself at home, *Daria*." There was something knowing to his smile that matched the intelligence in his eyes.

He started walking out of the room but halted mid-stride. Egan crouched at the door, growling with a spine of hair standing on end. Thad's brow furrowed as he strained to look out the smeared window. I couldn't see a thing, but his eyes narrowed in concentration, and then I felt a surge of his anxiety.

"Oh, hellfire," Thad said beneath his breath. "Del Can't!"

Before I had a moment to wonder who Del Can't was, Alex rushed into the room. Alex's gaze fastened on the window, then me. He rushed to a corner in the room, lifted the edge of a rug and loosened a floorboard beneath it. "Get my parents," he said over his shoulder. Thad didn't need to be told twice, and Egan stayed crouched at the door, snarling.

Alex lifted a square panel of wood attached by a hinge. Beneath it was a dark hole. He looked up at me, his features taut.

"What's out there?" I asked.

He motioned for me to come close. "We have to hide you."

"Hide me?" I asked. "Why? Is it those men again?"

Alex shook his head as Cicero and Sonya appeared. "They're here?" Cicero asked.

"Almost," Alex said.

Sonya glanced at me. "I'll hide with her."

"You all have to hide," Alex said. "If they discover you and Father are here, we'll have a much greater problem on our hands."

Something about his voice stole away my urge to argue.

Sonya and Cicero exchanged a glance, and I watched Cicero lower himself into the black hole. He landed below with a soft *thud.*

"Hurry!" Thad stood at the window.

Sonya dropped in after her husband, and I crouched at the ledge to follow them when Alex grabbed my arm.

There was an intensity in his eyes that held me still. His rigid mask was gone, all defenses stripped away, and what lay beneath was full of tenderness. But he quickly looked away and lowered me into the space below until my feet touched the floor. The hatch closed right as a loud banging sounded on the door.

Chapter 7

Decisions, Decisions, Decisions

The front door creaked opened. The storm outside wailed as Thad restrained a snarling Egan. The visitors walked inside, the wooden planks in the floor creaking against the heavy *callunk—callunk* of their footsteps. The front door shut behind them, muting the storm outside.

"Good morning, gentlemen, may I help you?"

I was shocked by Alex's perfect control. His voice was calm and authoritative. Not at all as if he had three fugitives hiding in his basement.

"I hope you can," one of the men replied, his voice throttling like an old car engine. He meandered farther into the room. There was a metallic clang when he walked, and his boots scraped across the floorboards as if they were carving into them. "We think someone's passed through the boundary. From the other side."

He halted right above us. I could see his shadow through the narrow cracks in the floorboards. Sweat beaded on my forehead as I held my breath. I didn't know who these men were, but they weren't friends. Even from here, their anger and hostility seeped inside of me, leaving a bitter taste in my mouth.

"Are you sure?" Alex asked. "I haven't been notified."

Even I believed Alex.

"No doubt you haven't. We believe their passage was aided by someone of power."

"Then King Darius is aware?"

A king?

"No." A board creaked as the man shifted his weight. "We'd like to take care of the problem without worrying His Majesty and causing a public disturbance. You know how the people can be when it comes to the boundary."

Alex was slow in his response. "I see. So then, if I may, what is your purpose here?"

"To find out if you've seen anyone out of the ordinary."

"Other than Thaddeus here, no."

I heard sharp movement, someone grunted, and then Thad cried out, "Spirits! He's joking. I live here."

"Yes." There was a smile in Alex's voice. "Unfortunately, Thaddeus is correct."

I had to hand it to Alex. He was a talented liar.

There was a soft thump and one of the men chuckled. The sound grated against my ears.

"Perhaps you've seen Aegis Cicero?"

Sonya squeezed my sweaty palm. Alex had been right to hide all of us. Those men already knew Cicero crossed the boundary, and Alex didn't miss it.

"I haven't seen my father in a few weeks, and I can assure you if there was anything to worry about, he would have handled it already."

I felt the men's surprise along with their dawning comprehension. "You're...Alexander Del Conte?"

"Yes."

"Spirits take me." This voice belonged to the other man. It sounded squeaky and muddied as if his nasal passages were being pinched.

"My apologies," said the other. "I wasn't implying that—"

"Will that be all, gentlemen?" Alex's voice was polite, but it had an edge that didn't invite further conversation.

"Yes," said the man with the grumbling voice. "And if you don't mind, we'd like to keep this from His Majesty for now."

Alex didn't respond.

Their footsteps stomped and clunked across the floor and the front door opened. The sound of howling wind filled the air and the clunking halted.

"Glad we weren't forced to cross blades, boy. Good day to you."

The door closed and the room returned to silence.

Footsteps crossed the room and light flooded in from above. Alex held open the hatch. "All's clear." His arms reached in to help us up.

"Who were they?" I asked Alex as he pulled me through.

60

"Hold on." He helped his mom and dad out of the opening.

Egan returned to my side as if our momentary interruption never happened, and he resumed licking my hand, as if that also never happened.

"Were those the same men we saw near the portal?" I asked.

"I think so," Alex replied.

"Were they wearing Valdon's armor?" Cicero asked.

Armor. Of course. That was what had been making all that noise when they walked.

"They were," Alex said. "It was old, but it still bore the sigil."

"Valdon?" I asked.

Alex looked at me with tired eyes. "Valdon is the name of this region."

"Any idea who sent them?" Sonya asked.

"No, but it obviously wasn't King Darius."

There it was again. "Gaia has a king?" I asked. I hated being on the inside of a conversation I understood nothing of.

Sonya, Cicero, Alex, and Thad all turned to look at me. Even Egan perked his smoky ears.

"King Darius Regius is the ruler of Gaia," Sonya said.

Gaia had a king—an authentic, living monarch. I felt excited and horrified at the same time. I knew about kings from my history books. "Is he a...good king?"

"Yes," Cicero said as Alex made a faint grunting noise.

This earned him a glare from his dad, so he took the opportunity to leave the room, and Thad followed after him. I was glad because I'd rather ask my questions without Alex listening. "Does this king monitor the portals?"

Sonya glanced at Cicero. It was like I'd asked them to open Pandora's box. All I wanted was more information, anything to help me make sense of this place.

Sonya was the one who answered. "King Darius has a contingent of high lords who serve directly beneath him, and their territories are near the portals."

"You live near a portal," I said. "So are you one of these...high lords?"

"No, the high lords of Gaia are some of the most powerful in our world, second only to the king himself," Cicero said.

"My title is more of a duty than a rank. I'm called an Aegis, which means I'm an appointed protector. My lovely wife—" Cicero grinned at Sonya "—has inherited the role by marriage, and I fear it may be the only reason she married me."

"Don't listen to him." Sonya smirked. "He has an unfortunate habit of remembering things in a way that will make a good story." She then moved about the room closing the curtains.

But Cicero wasn't finished talking, and his lips weren't done smiling. "I tell it like I see it. The day I went from squire to being appointed an Aegis, Sonya finally decided to take my hand."

"No." Sonya glared over her shoulder, her hand still clutching the curtain she was closing. "I didn't marry you sooner because you were a squire with an irritating need to follow every knight on duty. I needed stability."

Cicero laughed at that. "Eighteen years in Yosemite valley stable enough?"

The Del Contes had been protecting investments. Quite literally. "All these years, you lived there protecting..."

"You and Alaric," Cicero answered for me.

I'd been about to say "portal," because that seemed the obvious token to protect. But protect Dad and me? I was no one and Dad was just a businessman—ambassador—whatever.

"Why, exactly, were you protecting Dad and me?" I asked.

A look passed between them, and Sonya said. "I'm sorry, Daria, but your father is the only one who can tell you that."

And we were here again. "But if those men were searching for someone who traveled through the portal, then my dad's in trouble!"

Thunder crashed overhead as rain threw itself against the windows with renewed fury.

"Your father isn't in any trouble. Besides—" Cicero gazed at the window as if he could see through the curtains "—we can't do anything tonight."

How could they know my dad wasn't in trouble? I'd worry about him alone in this storm, even without armed men searching for trespassers. My patience snapped, my blood boiled, and I reached the end of my short rope. "The *only* reason I came with you was because you told me my dad was going to be here, and he's not. If there are dangerous people out there looking for him, I have to find him, and I'm going to do it with or without your help."

I wasn't sure how, but I would. By the looks on their faces, they knew it, too.

Sonya placed her hand on her husband's arm. "The letter?"

Remembering something, Cicero reached into his pocket, extracting a small, folded piece of paper. The same sort of folded paper the Del Contes had given me in their hidden room.

I frowned. "Another letter."

Cicero held it before me.

Anxious, I unfolded the heavy sheet. Just like before, it was in my dad's writing, but this time it was much more rushed.

Cicero—

My apologies for not waiting. I'm sure Thaddeus told you the Pykans crossed the boundary undetected. I fear something greater is behind this. I'm off to see Lord Commodus. If anyone knows of a resurgence in Pykan activity, it will be him. I'd ask that you come, but it is more important you watch over Daria.

Bring her to Amadis and I'll meet you there. A week's time should be sufficient for me to extract what details I can and meet up with all of you. The magic of the Arborenne should protect and hide you. Not a soul, whether it is good or evil, can know she's here yet. Not until I get to the bottom of this.

Stefan is to act in my absence. He's sending necessary supplies to you via Rex Cross morning after next. Trust few. Remember your oath, because more than Daria's life may be at stake.

I thank you with all I am,
Your friend,
Alaric

There was a postscript at the end of the letter, addressed to me.

Daria,

63

Forgive me for not explaining this life to you sooner. My regret is greater than you can possibly imagine. I promise I'll explain everything to you soon—once it's safe. Listen to the Del Contes. They will care for you as their own, as they always have. Know that the only reason they're sworn to secrecy is for your own protection. I love you, princess. I'm so sorry. –Dad

After a second reading my panic waned and my anger ignited. Most of the letter didn't make sense, but there were three points I understood clearly. One, my dad was alive. Two, there were still secrets only he could tell that he'd forbidden the Del Contes to share with me "for my own protection." And three, in the meantime he expected me to trust and follow the Del Contes without arguing about it.

How could he do this to me? How could he throw me in this situation without any explanation, continue being secretive, and expect me to just go along with it. It was almost like being wedged between a rock and a hard place, but this was worse. I'd been given a third barrier: solid ground, brought to me by my dad. I wasn't going anywhere unless I learned how to fly, but at the rate I was losing control, the sky would probably fall on my head and lock me in completely.

What to do, what to do...

I couldn't back home. Now that I knew this world existed, that was out of the question. So, I had two alternatives. I could march out of here alone, with no sense of direction and no one to trust—except, perhaps, Thad. Or, I could follow the Del Contes, who had lied to me my entire life and still wouldn't share my dad's secrets. But at least they knew the way through this world.

I hated admitting it to myself but the Del Contes would get me to Dad the fastest.

As much as I didn't like it, my best option was to follow the Del Contes. I'd learn everything I could from them along the way, just in case I was left choosing that other alternative.

After folding the letter back on its creases, I glanced into the faces of a worried Cicero and Sonya. "These Pykans. Who are they?"

64

Cicero studied me a moment looking a little relieved. He'd probably expected my other alternative.

"Why don't we all have a seat?" he asked.

I picked a seat on the floor beside the fire. Egan bounded back into the room, carrying a large bone in his mouth. It was a strange looking bone, black and about as big as my entire arm. He dropped it at my feet, took a couple steps back, and stared at it.

"Egan, not now," Cicero said as he and Sonya sat down on the small leather sofa.

Egan whimpered and slumped to the ground. He rested his head on his paws while his sappy eyes stared at the bone with longing. I felt bad, but I was too eager to learn about this place to play with him.

Cicero took a deep breath. "Long ago, the Pykans were a powerful people from the lands of Visigoth."

"Visigoth? As in Alaric of the Visigoths?"

"No, here, Visigoth is a large island, far off the coast of Orindor—Lord Commodus' territory."

"Lord Commodus...as in the person Dad's gone to see?"

Cicero nodded. "The Pykans were strong people— beautiful people—with many magical talents given them by Gaia herself. They became puffed up and proud, forgetting who gave them their power. As their pride swelled, they turned vicious and violent, lusting for more power. A great wizard—"

"Wizard?"

Cicero bristled, but continued. "Yes. A great wizard—"

"Wizards exist here? Really?" I couldn't believe it.

Cicero smacked his hands on his kneecaps. "Confound it, Daria. How am I supposed to answer your questions when you keep interrupting?"

"Maybe if you'd all told me about this world when you should have, I wouldn't have so many questions."

Cicero sighed and leaned back on the couch. "All right. Would you like my explanation now, or would you prefer to wait a few weeks for your father's?"

I folded my legs, rested my elbows on my kneecaps and glared at the fire. "I'll listen."

"A *wizard*," he paused, "cursed their lands to waste and they were banished to them. They still keep some of their powers, since they are fueled by evil and even a wizard can't touch all that is dark. The Regius dynasty and the high lords have done an adequate job keeping the Pykan fury contained to nothing more than their ruined island of Visigoth."

This supposed history sounded like a fairytale to me. However, under the current circumstances, my line between fact and fiction had blurred. I was establishing my foundation of knowledge all over again, much like a child would. But it was easier as a child because I hadn't already established any rules of the world yet.

"These Pykans were at our home," I said.

Cicero hesitated, but then seemed to realize there was no longer any point hiding this truth from me. "Yes. Alaric contacted us when you got home. He said you were safe, but two Pykans had been there, waiting for you."

"I thought you didn't know was after me."

"We don't know who sent them," Sonya said.

"We also don't how they got through the portal without any of us knowing," Cicero added. "You see, as an Aegis, that is part of our job. Not just protecting you, but monitoring the portal from the other side. It is protected by great magic, and since the Pykans were able to get past that detection, that can only mean someone powerful sent them for you."

In a land of magic and wizards and Pykans and kings, someone wanted me. "What would anyone want with me?"

They exchanged a glance.

"At this point, we aren't sure," Sonya spoke slow and careful. "But your father is trying to figure it out. Lord Commodus's territory is closest to any port the Pykans may have used to get on the mainland. If anyone knows of their presence, it would be him."

I thought about that for a minute. "So let me get this straight. Dad is traveling alone, where more of these Pykans could be hiding, to talk to Lord Commodus, who might know more about the situation?"

"Yes." Cicero and Sonya answered together.

"And what was he planning on doing if he found any of them? Fight? My dad won't even kill a spider!" I was distantly aware that I was now standing.

My other alternative was sounding better and better.

"Don't worry. If anyone can handle himself, it's Alaric." Thad had reentered the room with a smile and tray of steaming mugs.

I glared at Thad. "You don't know my dad."

"Sounds like you don't either." Thad smirked, and it made me even angrier. I was so tired of all these dual identities.

"Thaddeus's right." Cicero grabbed an orange, ceramic mug from the tray. "Alaric is perfectly able to handle himself."

"Pyxis has probably taken him halfway across Valdon by now," Thad commented.

"Pyxis?" I asked.

"Alaric's horse," Sonya answered.

"My dad has a horse? He hates riding."

"Earthen horses, maybe," Thad said. "They're nothing like ours. *Your* father is one of the best riders in the land, and Pyxis is the fastest stallion of his kind."

Secrets, secrets, and more secrets. What else didn't I know about *my* dad, the one person in the world I thought I did know?

"Here." Thad held out a glazed, green ceramic mug.

I shook my head. "No thanks."

He pushed the mug toward me. "Take it. It'll help."

I glanced into his buoyant face. "What is it?"

"Tonic. Made from callaberries. Trust me, you need it."

My hands trembled as I took it from him.

"Thaddeus, you've outdone yourself." Cicero wiped frothy white film from his lips.

Thad grinned as he handed one to Sonya. "Nonsense, sir. I just happen to know you like extra froth."

I took a whiff. It smelled sweet, and there were hints of spice. I held the cup to my lips and sipped, the thick liquid coating my mouth. It was the best thing I'd ever tasted, like drinking a freshly baked sugar cookie. The warmth spread down my chest and through my limbs, all the way down to my fingers and toes, giving me back my feeling. My next sip was a gulp.

"Careful," warned Thad. "It's hot. You'll burn off your tongue."

"Daria doesn't feel the way most of us do." Alex took a seat near me. He met my gaze, and then sat back down on the floor beside Egan.

My anger began to dissolve but I didn't know if it was from exhaustion or the tonic. I wouldn't put it past them to give me a mild sedative. But at least my dad was safe. My rider-extraordinaire dad.

"My dad is *not* an international businessman."

Cicero chuckled lightly as Sonya answered. "No, darling. He's technically an ambassador. From this world."

Ambassador and businessman didn't seem like they were so different. Unless, of course, you threw in the concept of other worlds. Then Dad's line of work took on an entirely new meaning. All these years, he'd been monitoring the entrance to Gaia, or the entrance to Earth, depending on how you looked at it. No wonder he never wanted to talk to me about college. It was a minute detail in the grand scheme of things, whatever that grand scheme was.

"If," I continued, "my dad is an ambassador from this world, then why did we live so far from the entrance?"

"Your real home is where we live," Cicero said. "The guesthouse is where we should be living. Alaric asked us to live at the main house so he could move you somewhere safer and less obvious, but still relatively close. He was concerned something like this—" he waved his hand toward the window "—might happen."

Their beautiful house had actually been mine. Maybe that was why I'd always felt at home there.

I didn't think I'd ever recover from all of this, but for now I would wait. I would wait and follow them to my dad. After that...I didn't know, but it wouldn't involve them. My body was weary and my emotions were drained of fuel. What I needed was to lie down, close my eyes, and lose myself to slumber's purging.

"Daria," Cicero continued, "your father is much more powerful than you think. We aren't exaggerating when we say Alaric knows what he's doing. He was always one to seek justice on his own." He smiled as if remembering something.

Cicero was right about one thing. If my dad saw a problem, he always took it on himself to fix it. I'd always admired that trait about him, but right now I found it incredibly irritating and highly inconvenient.

Sonya walked over to me and laid a hand on my shoulder. "Lake Amadis is protected by ancient powers. We'll be safe there. We'll journey through the Arborenne, a forest filled with of all kinds of magic that will shield our path. Your father knows this, which is why he chose that location. I promise we will get you to him safely, and then he can explain everything and hopefully give us some answers as well."

Waiting was going to be the hardest part. Waiting for things that were beyond my control. I hated when things were beyond my control.

"Why didn't any of you tell me about this sooner?"

The silence in the room was thick, and I could see Sonya's mind working, trying to figure out the best answer.

"I would be breaking my oath to your father if I told you. But I will say this: he knew your character, your strength and independence. He knew that if he told you about this world, he'd never be able to keep you from it. He needed to ensure your safety before bringing you here. It was hard for him...after losing your mother. He trusted no one after that day. Something inside him snapped. He couldn't bear it if he lost you, so he tucked you safely away with others he kept employed to monitor you while you were there."

Cadence. "Our neighbors?" I asked.

Sonya nodded. "And his strategy worked, until now."

"But why is this world so dangerous for me?"

"That," Sonya said, "your father must explain. Once it's safe."

I always thought paranoia had driven Dad to extreme measures, but it wasn't paranoia at all. It was evil from another world, and in his aim to protect me from that evil, he was forced to protect me from the truth.

My gaze flitted to Alex. "How long have you known?"

His eyes didn't leave mine. "I've always known."

My heart sank. All those years we spent together, and he'd always known. I felt like such a fool.

My dad keeping this world from me, I could understand. He was my dad, and he was obsessive with my protection. Cicero and Sonya, I might be able to excuse some day, for the same reasons. But Alex? I couldn't excuse him. We were peers. We were equals. We had been the closest, and his lies hurt the most.

"Daria," Cicero said, sensing the direction of my thoughts. "Alex was forbidden to tell you—by your own father. He's been living here—at the Aegis Quarters—for the past three years."

"Studying abroad." I muttered to myself, but I knew Alex heard me.

He had been a thirty-minute drive and a one-hour walk from his home in Yosemite. And he never once bothered contacting me.

There had to be a limit on the questions that could form in a person's head. The more I learned, the more questions I had, and I knew it was only the beginning. Maybe I should be writing it all down in case I needed it when on my own. But then one small question wormed in the back of my mind.

"Who's...Stefan?"

"Your father's assistant," Sonya answered. "You'll meet him eventually."

"I know it's a lot to comprehend," Cicero said, "and I'm sorry things have happened this way. It was never our intention to keep this from you at the expense of your love and trust. You are handling everything remarkably well, and I—we—are grateful you've come with us this far. The rest you'll learn from Alaric. In exhaustive detail, I'm afraid. Until then—" he stood "—we have a journey to prepare for. Alex? The shed?"

Alex stood, grabbed his cloak, and the two men disappeared. And I hoped against all hope that I'd made the right decision.

Chapter 8

Preparations

As much as I wanted solitude, I wasn't going to get it. The Del Contes left to make travel preparations, but Egan continued pouting at my feet. His desperate eyes stared at that little black bone, longing for someone with an arm— namely me—to throw it, and Thad was still lying across the lounge with his legs dangling over an armrest.

I had the distinct impression he was watching me, even though I fixed my attention on Egan the faithful, rightful guardian of this home, protector of his owner, master of fetch. When I raised my hand to pet him, he crouched lower, tail whipping in the air, eyes fixed on that bone.

"No," I whispered. "I'm not going to throw it. You'll break something."

Egan whimpered and curled around so that I was facing his rear. Typical.

"You're nicer to the dog," Thad said.

I glanced up. There was a definite smirk on his face.

"And?" I asked.

Thad shrugged. "Maybe you need another drink."

"Maybe you should mind your own business."

He stopped swinging his legs and grinned. "Considering you're in *my* house, it is my business."

"This is your house?" I looked at him, doubtful.

"Well..." He folded his arms behind his head and leaned back. "It's Alexander's, but I live here. He needs me for protection."

"Alex doesn't need anyone," I mumbled.

Thad studied my face with that smirk. "Sore spot, eh?"

I glared at him but he just chuckled. There was a recklessness to those youthful features of his, and I wondered if Thad and Alex actually got along. Alex might have been my fellow conspirator at one time, but he'd never

71

been reckless. That's also why my dad had always trusted him so much.

"How did you two meet?" I asked.

Thad dropped his legs to the floor and sat, taking a swig from his mug. "The Academia."

"The what?"

He choked on his tonic, his hazel eyes opening so wide I thought they were going to fall out of his head. "You're joking, right?"

"I found out about this world just yesterday, remember?"

He didn't miss the bitterness in my voice. "Right." He rested his chin in his palm and studied my face. "It must be difficult."

"You have no idea," I snorted.

"Makes you wonder what else the secret service isn't telling you." He nodded toward the direction the Del Contes had gone.

Uncomfortable, I looked away. It was hard sticking to my plan when I thought about all their secrets, and his words weren't helping. Egan sulked over a few feet, and plopped to the ground again with his rear still to me.

"So what is it?" I asked. "This...Academia."

Thad came out of his trance and ginned. "I don't think the secret service will care if I tell you about that." He craned his neck to check down the hall then leaned forward. "It's a school. But it's the Gaian version."

"Gaian version?"

That mischievous grin spread wider. "It's more like a training ground."

"For?"

"Fighting."

I stared at Thad, impatient for him to continue.

"All Aegises-in-training—like me and Alex—study with Masters in the art of fighting and magic. We train to fight against evils of this world—including abominations like those Pykans."

That sounded incredible, and insane. I wondered how my ju-jitsu training would hold up in a place like that.

"Which reminds me. I wanted to warn you," Thad continued. "Watch out for the Black Bard on your journey."

"Black Bard?"

72

Thad's voice dropped low as he leaned closer to me. "He's a powerful sorcerer that lives deep in the mountains. He was banished long ago for doing terrible things—things that would make your blood curdle. No one has ever seen him because no one has lived to tell. Rumor is he travels as a shadow. Keep watch so that he doesn't sneak up on you." His gaze was penetrating, his features serious. And then one corner of his mouth turned up. "I'd hate to lose my newest acquaintance."

"Considering you're the self-proclaimed master protector, I'm surprised you're not coming with us."

He chuckled, leaning back in the lounge again. "If it was a journey to worry about, I'd be going."

I rolled my eyes. "This Academia. Is that where you met Alex?"

"Fine. Ignore my warning at your own risk." He smiled. "But to answer your question, yes. The Academia isn't far from here. That's why Alex let me live with him."

"Does your family live far away?"

Thad glanced down and examined his hands. "They move a lot."

The rest of the day was filled with raindrops and dark clouds. The Del Contes made various preparations for our journey, while I sat in the sitting room with a chessboard and Thad. I'd tried to help prepare. I thought it would be a good idea to see what the Del Contes thought necessary for travel in this world, but after multiple instances of being shooed away from Sonya, I gave up and accepted my fate of losing incessantly to Thad.

I admit, he was a master chess player, but despite my losses, the game kept my mind preoccupied, and Thad's exuberance kept the mood light. Egan remained our faithful audience, his tail beating at the air every time I moved a piece. He probably thought I was going to throw it.

"Check mate!" Thad leaned back in his chair with that smirk.

As many times as he'd won today, I thought he'd be used to it by now. Apparently not.

"I don't see why you act so surprised," I said. "You've only chastised every move I've made since we started."

Thad smiled at me, and then went back to setting up the pieces. Again. "You learn a lot about a person by their strategy."

"What about when that person has none?"

Thad grinned. "Having no strategy is still a reflection of character."

"Oh? So what does that tell you about mine?"

Thad held a pawn over its square. "You're impetuous and you don't understand the consequences of your actions. And you don't have the patience to learn, which prevents you from making good decisions."

I scowled. "That's ridiculous. You're judging me on a game I don't even like."

Thad flashed me a knowing smile as he returned to his task of arranging the pieces. "That reveals something else, actually."

"What, that I don't like chess?"

His eyes held something sinister in them. "The fact that you've spent all afternoon playing a game you don't like with someone you don't know tells me you are trying to keep yourself distracted from something else you don't know how to deal with. Or should I say...someone?"

My jaw dropped as I glared at him. He preened.

"You little—"

"We should probably get to bed." Cicero stepped into the room. "It's getting late and we've got extensive traveling ahead."

With all the curtains closed and no sign of a clock anywhere, I hadn't noticed the day pass. Sure enough, the Del Contes had filled large packs with food and supplies for our journey, and the bags were tilted, resting against the wall beside the front door.

Alex walked into the room, his face blank as he eyed Thad and me.

"Hey, Del Can't." Thad grinned. "Didn't you ever teach your old friend here how to play chess?"

Alex walked over, glanced down at the pieces, and then his gaze lifted to mine. "You hate chess."

74

I wanted to punch the satisfied smirk off Thad's face. "Actually, I had fun."

Alex wasn't buying it.

Thad looked at Alex and placed a hand on his shoulder. "I know, I know, it's not every day a woman chooses me over you. But don't be too jealous, Del Can't. I'm pretty sure the only reason she hung around me is because she's too nervous to be around you."

Horrified, I gaped at Thad. On second thought, maybe I would punch him. "That's not—"

"Alexander." Sonya poked her head in. "Show Daria to her room, please. And Thaddeus, thank you for allowing us to intrude under such late notice."

"Always a pleasure, Mrs. Del Conte." Thad smiled, all innocence.

"See you in the morning." Sonya smiled, and she and Cicero disappeared, leaving me all alone with the pair of conspirators. I was too humiliated to look at Alex and much too infuriated to look at Thad, so I crouched on the floor and petted Egan.

"I think she's angry with us." Thad pretended to whisper.

"I'm not angry." I scratched the soft fur between Egan's ears. "You're just making ridiculous accusations."

"Hmm, I don't know about—"

"Thaddeus," Alex interrupted with a tone so firm I glanced up.

His gaze was fixed on Thad. Something passed between them and the humor in Thad's features transformed into something more like respect.

Thad looked back at me, but only the shadow of a grin remained. "Del Can't to the rescue. Well, thanks for keeping me entertained all afternoon, Rook. Even though you're a terrible chess player."

Thad started walking away. "Egan, come."

Egan dropped his head and followed Thad out of the room. When I glanced back, Alex was eyeing me without expression. "Rook?"

"Yeah, well." I looked away, still embarrassed from Thad's comment earlier. "According to your *friend*, it's the one piece I misunderstood and misused all afternoon."

I felt a wave of Alex's amusement. "Thad compared you to your chess strategy."

"Oh, so he's done it to you, too?"

"Once." He stared at Thad's empty chair and the edge of his mouth turned upward. "He never asked me to play again after that."

"I can see why. You're such a good liar I bet you were a formidable opponent."

I wasn't sure why I'd said it. Sure, I was thinking it but I hadn't exactly planned for it to come out. Which seemed to happen every time I was with Alex.

Alex's smile disappeared and when he looked back at me, his eyes looked more brown than green. "I'll take you to your room."

He led me down a darkened hallway and up a narrow flight of stairs. The floorboards creaked beneath each step and shadows danced on the walls as light from the sconces flickered. Even though I could only see Alex's silhouette I knew he was upset. One hand was latched on his front jean pocket and the other raked through his hair—something he always did when he was very, very agitated.

Alex stopped before a door at the end of the hall. He pushed it in and held it open, gesturing for me to go inside. I glanced at him as I walked by but he didn't meet my gaze.

An enormous bed occupied half of the room. Next to it was a small wooden table with a glowing lantern, the window behind it hidden behind brown curtains. The other wall housed a small dresser and a pair of sturdy wooden bookshelves stuffed with books. The room was simple, uncluttered and tidy, and I was suddenly suspicious.

I glanced back at the door. Alex hadn't moved. He leaned against the doorframe with his arms folded over his chest, watching me.

"Is this your room?"

His jaw clenched and unclenched. "Yes."

A small feeling of guilt began creeping inside of me. "That's really nice of you, but I'm fine sleeping on the couch."

"You can't. That's where I'm sleeping."

We stared at one another in silence, the muffled rain splattering against the window. I couldn't sleep here, in his bed. And considering how little he thought of me—and how I

76

kept speaking to him—I was certain he hated the arrangement as much as I did. This was ridiculous. "Really, Alex, I'm just fine—"

"Do you need anything else?" He cut me off in a tone that was both weary and firm.

"No," I said. "Thank you."

He held my gaze. Something sad and pained flashed in his eyes, and then he closed the door behind him.

Leaving me alone.

It was strange being in Alex's room. I felt like an intruder, but somehow worse, and I had the distinct impression that all his furniture was glaring at me. After a few moments of convincing myself he hadn't embedded his personality into his furnishings, I peeked around.

I wandered over to the bookshelves. The titles were foreign like all the titles in their hidden library back at Yosemite. *Magic. Weaponry. The Art of Defense. Tenets of Tracking. Elementary Antidotes.* They were probably related to his studies. If I weren't so uncomfortable, I would've loved perusing his book collection and have Alex introduce them himself. I certainly could use the distraction. As it was, I hesitated to touch anything. I didn't feel like I'd earned the right to pour through his personal belongings.

There were a few odd shaped objects leaning against one corner: a couple fat, wooden sticks, a thin metal rod, and something else with a bronze handle. I stepped closer and pulled it just enough from its case to see the metal gleaming in the candlelight. A real sword. Alex and I always fought when we were little, but never with weapons. Had he learned how since then?

There's probably a lot you don't know about him. Maybe you could find out if you just talked to him.

Frustrated, I slid the sword back in its sheath, walked to his bed and sat on the thick wool blankets. Was this what it felt like to have an identity crisis? Except it wasn't my identity in crisis, it was everyone else's. The identities of every person of worth in my life had been overturned and replaced by something fantastic and bewildering.

I pulled my dad's letter out of my pocket and read his words again. Just seeing his handwriting comforted me. At least one thing in my life hadn't changed. Dad still loved me.

I wanted to keep my letter somewhere safe, so I opened the little drawer in Alex's nightstand. Just as I started to place the letter inside, I paused. There was a photo in the drawer. It seemed out of place in this world void of technology, at least from my experiences so far. Curious, I pulled it out.

It was a photo of Alex and me, taken years ago. I remembered the day perfectly. One summer, Dad had let me stay with the Del Contes—Andersons to me then—for a few weeks. Alex and I, the adventurers we were, had decided to build a treehouse. Well, I had decided I wanted us to have a treehouse and Alex had figured out how to build it. He had always been the industrious one, so good with his hands.

We'd spent every day, from dawn till dusk, sawing and nailing boards together. When I kept missing the nails and hitting my fingers, Alex had insisted I stick to painting. I hadn't listen and instead worked harder with purple nails and saw-dusted hair. It'd been completed in no time. On the day we finished, we had brought his camera. I even remembered arguing with him on how to use the timer function, but he'd wanted to take the photo himself. So, the photo ended up being a close up of us, our cheeks pressed together with blurred wooden slats in the background. Not much to show for our hard labor.

That was the Alex I remembered, dark hair in disarray over his forehead, tanned face with sun burnt cheeks, those green eyes bright and full of life, and a smile that always lifted my spirit. That was the Alex I cherished, the Alex who didn't care at all about me now. But if our friendship didn't mean anything, why would he keep this photo here?

A knock sounded on the door. I shoved the photo back in the drawer and placed the letter on top of it. Just as I closed the drawer, the door creaked open and Sonya peered in. "Are you too exhausted to talk for a moment?"

"Yes...I mean, no, I'm not too exhausted."

She stepped in the room, her black hair in a plait over her shoulder. In her hands was a burlap sack, the one Alex had brought from my home. I'd forgotten all about it. She sat beside me, setting the bag in her lap.

She looked over me as if checking for external damage. "How are you feeling?"

"A little overwhelmed."

"I'm sure you are, but you're holding yourself together exceptionally well. Your spirit is much stronger than mine." Her smile widened in response to the doubtful look on my face. "You weren't supposed to find out like this. Life never obeys our plans, I'm afraid. But, I don't want to keep you awake much longer so I'll get to my point. I brought you something for our journey."

She held the bag before me. I took it from her, set it on my lap and opened the flap. Varying shades of brown leather lay folded within. Sonya nodded for me to continue.

One by one, I pulled the items out: a thin, brown leather top and pants, a matching leather belt, and a pair of tall, earthy-brown leather boots. A pattern of swirls was etched into the belt with small loops attached around it, and, strangely enough, everything looked as if it was exactly my size.

"They belonged to your mother."

I stared at the pile of keepsakes in my lap. I'd never owned anything that'd belonged to my mother. I'd never even seen anything of hers.

"They were her traveling clothes. I know they may seem unusual to you, but they are normal here—for travel. Alaric planned to give them to you the day he brought you here. I know he'd want you to have them now. They should fit. You and Aurora have the same build."

My mother. A woman I never knew, who never knew me. I'd heard more of her in the past few days than my entire life, and with everything that was happening, I felt as if I needed her more than ever. I couldn't help but think, had she been alive, none of this would be happening. Dad wouldn't be gone, the Del Contes wouldn't have lied, and Alex...

"She would be so proud of you." Sonya's voice turned quiet. "I remember the day she told me she was pregnant with you. She was thrilled when she found out you'd be a little girl. She used to dream of you, you know. We talked about all the memories the two of you would share." Sonya's voice cracked. Her eyes turned glossy as she stared at nothing, as if the memory played in the spaces of the room for only her to see. She shut her eyes for a moment and took a deep breath. Her large dark eyes settled on me again, and great sorrow poured over me. "I loved your mother with all my heart, and I count myself blessed to have the liberty of knowing her daughter and watching her grow into such a beautiful and strong young woman."

My throat and chest constricted as I gazed down at the precious folds of leather in my lap. I wasn't strong. I tried to be, but I failed.

Sonya stood beside my bed, laying her hand over mine. "Get some rest, dear. I'll wake you in the morning."

She bent over, kissed my forehead, and crossed the room.

"Sonya."

She paused, turning her head to look at me.

"Thank you."

She smiled a weary smile, and left.

Sonya's words pricked my heartstrings. They shaped the vague idea of my mother into an actual person with feelings and desires. A woman who had loved me. A woman who had been excited to share memories with me—her only daughter. A woman who might have taught me to deal with everything I was feeling.

My fingers brushed over the supple leather. Leather my mother had worn.

I sat on Alex's bed, listening to the soft patter of constant rain. After everything I'd experienced, this last part had been the hardest to hear because my already strained mind had no more strength left. I had clothing from a mother I'd never known, a letter from a dad who'd left me in a strange world, and a photo from a friend who, at one time, meant the world to me. My eyes stung and my vision blurred.

I walked the clothing to Alex's dresser and carefully set them on it, stroking the fabric before returning to his bed. There was an ache deep inside of my chest as I tugged off my boots and lay down, and my strong wall crumbled around me.

Just as another wave of heavy rain shattered across the window, my tears burst free, streaming down my cheeks. For the second time in my life, my churning emotions surged beyond restraint and my body responded in the only way it knew how. With laments only my pillow could hear, I cried myself to sleep.

Chapter 9

Rook

The sound of sharp scraping pulled me out of my nightmares. I'd been running away from shadows, fighting against the invisible sea I trudged through, my legs sluggish and immovable. Alex had appeared, the Alex from my youth. His hand extended as he pleaded for me to hurry, that he wouldn't let anything happen to me. But when I grabbed on to his hand he faded into a fine, white mist that floated toward the sky and disappeared into the clouds above.

I woke with a start, drenched in sweat. My room was dark except for a line of light that shone beneath my door. I heard soft shuffling about the house. Everyone must be awake.

That scraping sounded again, followed by a very high-pitched whine.

Crawling out of my warm blankets, I made my way to the door, careful not to run into anything. My bedside candle was the only source of light in the room, but I needed matches for that. Why didn't these people use electricity here?

My lids felt heavy and swollen, and my eyes were tender as I creaked the door open.

Egan rammed right into my legs.

"Oh, good!" Sonya said. "You're awake. I was on my way to get you."

Sonya stood at the end of the hall wearing a very strange outfit, and as much as I tried, my murky vision couldn't make sense of it.

"Go ahead and change into Aurora's clothing and meet us below. We'll be leaving in a bit." She disappeared down the stairs.

Thick slobber now coated my hands, wrists, and most of my arm. If I wasn't awake before, Egan was fixing that now.

"Egan!" Thad exited a room off the hall. He smiled at me. "Morning, Rook. You look terrible. Awake yet?"

I rubbed my temples, and immediately dropped my hands. They were soaked. "Getting there."

"Better hurry up and change," he said, and started down the stairs, calling Egan after him.

Egan slumped his head, tail between his legs, and followed Thad.

I walked back to my room—Alex's room—and shut the door. It was too dark to do anything so I opened the brown curtains. The moon still hovered in the sky, lighting the room just enough to differentiate the shadows. And I changed into my mother's clothes.

After squeezing myself into the tight leather pants and top, I realized I wasn't just like my mother. She'd obviously had hips. The pants were loose where my hips should be, but the belt helped, and the top sagged a little at the bust. The boots pulled snug over my legs, but they'd be comfortable enough to walk in.

For a few moments I moved my arms and legs, getting used to the feel of the leather. If anything, this outfit made me confident in my decision to follow the Del Contes. It would've taken me awhile to find something to wear—especially something that would fit.

After combing my fingers through my long, wavy hair, I made Alex's bed the best I could in the dark, grabbed my dad's letter out of the drawer, and made my way down the stairs.

Of course Alex was right in my path, crouched beside the front door and fiddling with the ties on one of the packs.

The leather threads on his ivory tunic were left untied at his neck, showing off a lean, muscular chest. An array of daggers hung around the thick belt at his narrow waist, and his leather pants and boots boasted of the slender strength beneath them.

The boy from the photo was gone. Replaced by this...thing.

He stopped what he was doing and stood. A wave of amusement washed over me.

When I glanced up, he was looking at me with a raised brow and a grin. "You look...charming."

I narrowed my eyes. "Save it."

His grin disappeared but he continued to study my face. "Your eyes look swollen. Was my bed...uncomfortable for you?"

Before I was forced to come up with some excuse for my puffy eyes, Egan came bounding in, Cicero right behind him. He was dressed just like his son, carrying another pack full of gear that was smaller than the others.

"You're awake." Cicero smiled, standing before me. "You're the specter of your mother. Here." He set the pack at my feet. "This one's for you."

Egan examined it with his nose, and then his slobbery tongue.

"Have you mapped out our route?" Alex asked his dad.

"There's an alternate path through the woods that should get us there by nightfall."

Alex adjusted his belt. "Isn't that a little late?"

"We aren't in any particular hurry, and I want to avoid the main roads. Besides, Stefan isn't sending the horses to Rex Cross till tomorrow morning."

"I bet Otis is having trouble containing his enthusiasm."

Cicero frowned. "It's just one night."

"But one glance at us wreaks havoc on him for a few months," Alex countered. "You know members of the king's guard aren't considered good company by most of the realm these days."

"We have no choice. Plus, it'll place us near the Kirkwoods, which will cover our tracks until we reach the Arborenne."

More names. More places. All of them bouncing around in my head, and none of them sticking anywhere. What I needed was a map and a good month to study it.

Sonya appeared with everyone's cloaks. She wore leathers, just like mine. However, hers had sheets of deep green fabric attached at her waist, hanging down to her ankles with long slits for movement. It didn't matter what the woman wore. She always epitomized elegance.

She paused before me in appraisal. "You look just like her dressed like that." She handed me my cloak. "How does it feel?"

"I'm not sure yet. Ask me tonight."

She laughed, then lifted one of the packs and shrugged into it. Cicero and Alex did the same, so I followed. Its weight wasn't unbearable, but a week of this might be painful.

I noticed the gleaming silver handle of a long sheathed sword attached to Alex's pack. Well, this answered one question. He *had* learned how to fight with weapons, and apparently, so had the rest of the Del Contes. Between Cicero and Sonya, there were daggers, swords, and a bow and quiver. And I had nothing.

Thad's words drifted through my mind. *"Makes you wonder what else they're not telling you."*

When Alex and I fought, back when we actually got along, we were pretty evenly matched. I'd thought it was because of my skill, but the more I thought about it, the more I realized he probably let me win those times that I did.

Thad stood beside me, eyeing the small loops on my belt. "They aren't supposed to be empty."

"Would you like to make the first contribution?" I asked.

"What, give you a dagger?" He laughed. "No, thanks. I don't want your blood on my hands. The secret service would kill me. But I do have something for you—something even you can't hurt anyone with."

He held out his fist, palm side up. His hand opened, and sitting on his palm was a chess piece. The rook. "Remember me on your travels, Rook," he whispered. "When you get tired of Del Can't's charms, you can brainstorm your strategy."

I chuckled. He pushed his palm closer so I took the rook and shoved it in my pocket. It was a tight fit, but it would work.

"Are we ready?" Cicero fastened the last dagger to his belt. How many did the man need? I was surrounded by an arsenal...with legs.

"Thaddeus," Sonya said. "Thank you for your hospitality."

"Always a pleasure, Mrs. Del Conte." Thad bowed.

Sonya and Cicero were making last minute adjustments while Thad walked to Alex and smacked him hard on the back.

"Don't miss me too much. Oh!" Thad leaned over and whispered something in Alex's ear. Alex grinned, shaking his head. I had a strong feeling whatever he said had to do with me.

84

Thad turned his mischievous face to me. Seeing I was on to him, his smiled widened. "Have fun with the secret service, and remember what I told you...about the shadows."

He winked and disappeared down the hall.

Alex still had the grin on his face as he looked after Thad, then his gaze found mine. He lost the smile. It was good to see I elicited the same feelings in him as he did in me.

Cicero cleared his throat.

Alex and I both turned our attention to his dad, whose face was serious. "We must remain undetected, so no speaking, at least until I say. We'll rest once we're farther away. And Daria...it's imperative you stay close at all times. This world isn't a safe place for you. Follow our instructions, even if you don't agree. Trust us implicitly, even if you don't want to. We will get you to Alaric without harm, as long as you do what we say. Do you understand?"

I understood plenty. They expected me to hand over my freedom on a silver platter and trust them to keep it safe. Exactly what I didn't want to do. But I'd been down this thought trail. There weren't any other options for me, at least none that made any practical sense. I was forced to accept their offer and take my consequences later.

Maybe Thad had been on to something.

The morning air was crisp, the world quiet with anticipation as we walked away from the cottage. We headed in the opposite direction from which we'd come. Our path remained unmarked all morning, not that it would've mattered. I rarely noticed where I stepped because I was so enthralled by the scenery. It wasn't because this forest was so different than any forest back home. Sure, the trunks were thicker and grander, and the canopy above was the most vivid green I'd ever seen, but what kept me entranced was the life all around me. I could *feel* it.

With every light breeze, every swaying branch, every rocking treetop, there was life. Not just the chemical life all natural plants share. Here, in this place, it was as if they had a soul, as if they were connected to one another, speaking to one another in whispers. Just as I thought I could discern a word, the sound would flit away, drowning in the breeze.

Rays of sunlight streamed through the trees, dusting the earth below with halos of gold. As we walked through the patches of light, I lingered. It was as if my leather and skin were a porous covering, allowing the heat of the sun to travel to my body's core.

Light, cheerful melodies chimed in the forest. The sound mesmerized me—the ringing familiar, somehow, and there was an ethereal quality to it. Throughout our walk, I searched for the source of the beautiful sound, but I searched in vain. The little musicians were obstinate things, never showing themselves.

In this wooded chamber of serenity I thought the weaponry of the Del Contes seemed out of place. Violence couldn't exist with such beauty. Not to mention, I hadn't noted any sign of civilization. Not one. On occasion, Cicero would stop, his fingers trailing the soft earth, but then he would continue leading us forward, always silent, always vigilant.

It wasn't until midday when Cicero showed signs of stopping for more than a minute. He crouched beside a tree trunk three times his own width, sloughed off his pack, and began digging through it. Sonya and Alex stood apart from him, eyes scanning the perimeter. Considering our uneventful morning, their constant surveillance seemed unnecessary.

Cicero pulled out a small item that looked like a bronze coin. Something was engraved on the surface but I couldn't tell what. He set the coin in a dark knot on the bark. When he moved his hand away, the coin was still in place. And then the coin moved.

It sunk into the tree as if the bark was quicksand, inch by slow inch, sinking until the bark closed its wooden fingers around it. The bronze coin was gone.

"The tree...it just..." I stuttered.

Cicero held a finger to his lips.

A dark crack appeared in the bark. It was about as tall as Cicero was crouched, and the bark pulled back like a curtain, leaving darkness in its wake. When it stopped, it left a hole so large I thought Cicero might be able to climb inside. Cicero smiled at me then, and did crawl inside.

Sonya waved for me to follow.

"There's no way that's big enough for all of us."

Sonya's gaze was firm as she held a finger to her lips, still waving at me to move it.

I took a deep breath and followed, expecting to be crammed inside. But I wasn't.

The inside of the tree was huge, much larger inside than I thought possible. It was hollowed out into a single room, one so large I could easily stand. There were a few candles lit, hanging from the tree walls, and Cicero sat smiling at me from a wooden stool.

"You were saying?" He grinned.

"What is this place?" I looked up, the room unending as it stretched into the tree's utmost heights.

Cicero glanced around. "Technically, I suppose you would call it a tree."

Sonya and Alex joined us.

"No, I know that, but how is this possible? It didn't look this big outside."

"That's because it's a shroud. It was a tree once, but it's been infused with magic and changed into a hiding place. A safe place. They're difficult to create—only the greatest masters have been able to construct them. Your father and I stumbled across this particular one when we were much younger. Sometimes, if you're really paying attention, you can find others, but you have to know where to look."

"Come—" Sonya patted the ground beside her "—you need to eat something."

Gawking at the expansive innards of the tree, I sat next to her. She handed me a small loaf of moist bread, its aroma rich and sweet. Alex was already digging into his, seated near our entry, watching.

I took a bite and the flavors exploded in my mouth.

"What ith thith?" My mouth was full of food.

Sonya chuckled. "Brownbutter Loaf. Another Thad specialty."

I swallowed. "Wow, Alex, you have quite the little housewife. She fights and cooks for you. Does she clean too?"

Cicero and Sonya laughed, but Alex didn't respond. He kept staring outside.

Cicero smiled at his son. "Did Alex tell you he built that cottage?"

87

I studied Alex. I knew he was skilled with his hands, but I never would've expected that.

"Dad, I didn't build it," Alex muttered, not bothering to turn around.

"Might as well have. Come to think of it, building it from the ground up might have been less work than what you did. The first summer he was here—" Cicero glanced back at me "—Alex spent all summer on it. You should've seen the place before he moved in. It had been abandoned all these years because we were living in Yosemite. Right before his training started, I went to check on him. Was I in for a surprise. He'd added rooms—another floor, even—gutted the entire thing, rebuilt the cabinets and all the furniture. You must have worked on that thing all day and night your first summer in Gaia...so focused on that house." Cicero admired his son.

Bitterness powered through me in the same moment I caught a sideways glance from Alex.

Everyone was quiet, enjoying the meal compliments of Thad. He was quite the cook, if he had made the food I'd tasted in the past few days. Or maybe food just tasted better here. Everything else was more vivid. After my stomach was satisfied, my mind wanted its turn.

"Where, exactly, are we going?"

Cicero swallowed his bite. "Rex Cross. It's an inn near the junction of three main roads throughout the land. From there, we'll get horses and a few other necessary supplies before we continue through the forests and on to Lake Amadis."

Trying to map out a journey in a landscape I'd never seen was impossible. I had no points of reference, no ground to start from.

A tightly wound scroll landed at my feet.

"Open it," Alex said. "It's a map." He turned his attention back to the outside.

Untying the thread, I unrolled the thick papyrus. It was a map, and on it was a single continent surrounded by ocean on all sides, save the northern boundary.

"Gaia?" I asked.

Sonya nodded. "Most of it."

There was a dotted line with the word *Icelands* scrolled upon it, foreign mountain ranges, rivers and lakes, forests with strange names. The landmass was separated by natural topography into four major territories: Orindor, Alioth, Campagna, and Valdon—the one Rex Cross was nestled into. And from each major territory trailed a single road, all of which led to Valdon. At the point where three of the roads intersected was written the word *Rex Cross.*

Sonya moved to my side. "Here." She pointed her finger at the lower right-hand corner, near a star with King Darius Regius written beside it. "King Darius of Gaia resides here, in Valdon."

Valdon was surrounded by mountains, and the largest peaks were near King Darius' star.

"We're somewhere here." Her finger hovered over a small, unnamed patch of trees. On the other side was a main road that led from King Darius to Rex Cross.

I saw Alex's dilemma. "I know you want to keep us hidden, but seeing as this Rex Cross is right at a major intersection, doesn't that defeat the purpose?"

I didn't miss the sound of Alex clearing his throat. Cicero didn't either. His face was stern as he looked at his son and then me.

"Its popularity is what I'm counting on. It'll be easier to hide. We know the owner personally, and Alaric trusts him. It's the only safe place for us to make an exchange before heading into the forests. Plus, we may learn some information that could be of use to us. Otis sees and hears a lot of things."

"I still don't like it," Alex said.

The candles inside the tree flickered. Dried pine needles and loose dirt swirled into our temporary shelter. The air twirled before me, wrapping me in its fingers, lifting strands of my hair, and then it stopped, dissipating as quickly as it started. I peered into the faces of Cicero and Sonya, who were looking curiously at me. Even Alex looked back, his eyes narrowed on me.

"What was that?" I looked around.

Cicero collected his things. "I think it means we should get moving. Can't be too careful nowadays. Not even concealed in here."

Chapter 10

Rex Cross

Cicero and Sonya led us forward through the trees while Alex brought up the rear. It was strange, but every so often I would get this sense of frustration, and what bothered me about it was that it wasn't my frustration. It was his. Without warning, the frustration pulsed through me and I would look back to find Alex's brow furrowed as he hacked through a branch in his path. I could feel all of their emotions at one point or another: Cicero's determinedness, Sonya's caution. But Alex's frustration was always strongest. In fact, it was difficult separating his feelings from mine, and it made it difficult keeping him from my thoughts, like I tried so hard to do.

The shadows thickened as the sun set, and my entourage remained silent. My mind was left to itself, driving me mad with the same questions. Where was Dad in this strange land? What did he have to tell me? Why had he made the Del Contes swear not to say a word? Who was after me, and why? And why hadn't he told me any of this sooner?

The colors of the forest transformed from greens and browns to varying shades of black. Although I couldn't see the sun through the green barrier above, I knew it was nestling into the horizon for the day. I hadn't heard anyone mention anything about stopping, and I was starting to worry about how much farther they intended to go. My legs were tired, my feet were swollen, and I had the eerie feeling that we were being followed. I silently cursed Thad for his story of the Black Bard. I'd have to remember to yell at him when we returned. If I returned. Before I could finish the thought, something rammed into me.

But there was nothing there.

The air became so thick I was smothered in it. I tried pushing the ubiquitous force away, but it wouldn't budge. Its

90

grip only tightened. It was noxious, reaching its tendrils into my mind, searching. My skin turned to ice, as if all the light and warmth in the world was being pulled into itself, and my lungs burned as I tried stealing a breath, but the shear force made it almost impossible. Just when I thought my lungs would never taste air again, it ceased.

The others huddled around me, an aura of fear surrounding them.

"What's wrong?" Sonya gripped my shoulders.

I closed my eyes, trying to recover my senses, my breathing still ragged.

"What happened?" Cicero demanded.

"I...I don't know." I looked at Sonya. A shadow of realization darkened her features.

Without a word, Alex unsheathed his sword and disappeared into the forest.

"Where's he going?" I stared after him, fear writhing up my spine.

Sonya ignored my question. "What did you feel?"

"I'm not sure." I continued watching the trees for Alex. "There was this strange pressure. I couldn't breathe and my vision turned dark and...what's Alex doing out there?"

Sonya looked at her husband. "They're following us."

"Who, the pykans?" I asked. When they didn't answer, I said, "And you let Alex go out there by himself?"

Cicero frowned at the woods. "Alexander is fine."

Cicero seemed to think everyone was fine, except those who were actually present, like me.

I searched the opening in the trees where he'd gone, looking for any sign of movement. Sonya and Cicero seemed confident in their son's abilities, but I felt sick. I was considering marching in after him when he emerged from the shadows, and the relief I felt surprised me. The blade was in his hand, his expression fierce. His eyes settled on me. His concern wrapped around me tight, but it let go as fast as it had come.

"He's gone."

"You're sure?"

"Yes." Alex squinted through the trees. "I found tracks. There was only one rider. Heading in the opposite direction."

Maybe it wasn't the pykans then.

Thad's words flitted through my mind again. What else weren't they telling me? Or worse, what if Thad's story was true? I studied the shadows with renewed vigor.

"We've got to hurry." Cicero's worried eyes briefly met mine before he spun around and marched forward.

Alex placed himself at the back of our procession, his blade ready at his side. It was strange seeing Alex carry such a powerful weapon with so much ease and confidence. What bothered me more was how worried I'd been when he'd left. I wasn't supposed to care about him anymore.

The forest ended as night crept up on us. Flatlands spread beyond, lit by the eerie glow of a full moon. The enormous round orb floated above the horizon, shading the land in silver hues, sharpening the contrast of shapes and shadows. About a few hundred yards away, tiny dark shadows sliced through the long grass, hurrying toward what looked like a large barn.

Riders. Three of them.

Alex stood still beside me, his disdain evident even without my ability to sense his emotion.

"Daria, pull on your hood. Keep it low." Cicero's voice was quiet.

"As if that's going to help," mumbled Alex.

Cicero ignored him, leading us forward from beneath the tree cover.

As ominous and secretive as the forest seemed, crossing open land was far worse. I felt so vulnerable, so exposed, even though the riders showed no signs of seeing us. We were near a major crossroads. There was no need to assume every traveler was after us.

The riders disappeared into the barn. The same one we were headed for.

So, this must be where we're staying tonight.

The building looked solitary, sitting unaccompanied in the middle of nowhere. I wondered what it saw—what it witnessed each day. Since this was the major junction joining the territories, I imagined many people had sojourned here over the years, all with various purposes. Some good, some bad. Some in hiding, like us.

The building was much farther away than it looked from the forest, which was shrinking in size with every step. The forest had turned into a dark wall, veiling its inhabitants in shadow. I was suddenly thankful we were no longer there.

The barn began to look less like a barn and more like an inn—a very rustic inn. It had the same overall shape to it, but it also had little square windows evenly spaced about what I guessed was a second floor. The windows along the first floor glowed a soft orange, but they lacked transparency due to the thick residue on them. A pillar of smoke rose from a chimney, the silver threads curling and fraying endlessly into the black night. I took in a deep breath of chilled air, tasting the wood smoke that filled it.

Our boots crunched across the dried dirt road as we approached the entrance. Torches burned bright on either side of the heavy wooden door, illuminating a sign above that creaked as it swayed back and forth in the soft breeze. The words "Rex Cross" were etched in the wood and painted in red that had since faded with time and wear.

Cicero motioned for us to stop while he walked up the few wooden steps to the door. He rapped three quick times and then waited, his stance perched and ready. A slat in the door slid open and two beady black eyes filled the gap, peering out at us. They examined our group and vanished as the wood slammed back into place. The door creaked open and light sliced through the darkness, blinding me for a few seconds. Cicero motioned for us to follow then stepped into the glow.

The air inside was thick with smoke, sweat, and ale. We were met with a small waiting room of some sort with a few rotted chairs and an uneven table. A counter ran along one side, vacant and covered in dust as if it'd been built a long time ago and never used since. Even so, I heard the sounds of people snoring.

That's strange. There's no one here besides us.

On the wall next to the counter was a series of thick wooden shelves with an assortment of skeleton keys dangling from them. Long and short, rusted and gleaming, and they didn't appear to be attached to anything.

Curious, I walked toward them, and the snores grew louder and louder. Some swelled with each snore and others shivered as if they were cold.

I must be more exhausted than I realize.

Just as I reached out my hand to touch one of the keys, they all dropped from their perch on the shelves, darted past me in a whirl then swirled and twirled in a golden cloud overhead. The snoring I'd heard was gone, and in its place was angry clanging and ringing.

A door swung open and a burst of irritation clouded my senses. A stout man, about as tall as he was wide, rushed past me. His tattered brown cloak hugged his round belly, and his face was so swollen and hairy, it looked as if it'd stolen the grizzled grey hair from his head and moved it to his beard, leaving nothing but wisps on his crown. Grumbling, his plump arms reached behind the counter and pulled out a small treasure chest. He dropped the chest on the counter with an angry thud and threw open the lid. Inside was a large, rusty metal lock. The moment the keys laid eyes on the lock, the horde of them forgot me and raced into the chest, and the little man shut and locked the lid after them.

A few moments passed before the chest ceased skidding and thudding along the countertop.

All eyes were on me, including the beady black eyes of the fat man.

"Sorry," I said, embarrassed. "I didn't know...I was just...curious."

His eyes were almost lost in the folds of his crinkled forehead. "How would ye like it if someone 'ere were pokin' you when ye were sleepin'?" The man shoved the chest full of keys beneath the counter.

"I didn't..."

"Follow me." He cut me off, glaring. "An' don't be curious!"

I didn't miss the looks of irritation from Cicero and Alex as we followed the little man out of the room and down a short hall. The sound of muffled chatter and clanking dishes grew louder, and at the end of the hall was a set of double doors. The little man pushed them open and the noise exploded in my ears.

It was a large banquet room, littered with all kinds of people. Tables were filled with men in armor and some in garb like our own. The women all wore tattered dresses or worn leathers, much like mine, and they all looked as if they

94

could kill me with their pinky toe. Whatever their temperament, Alex's appearance was the one attribute that unified them. They all gawked at him as we passed, and then they whispered and giggled and glared at me.

A rustic round iron chandelier of candles floated overhead. It just hovered there, suspended between the ceiling and the heads of the people beneath it. Hanging from the walls were heads of creatures I'd never seen before, mounted to large wooden plaques. One reminded me of a deer, but its prominent fangs, catlike green eyes, and the fact that it was presently yawning, reminded me that it wasn't.

Seven varying shaded banners hung by invisible threads from the ceiling. All of them were tattered and old, and across each was stamped a word: Alioth in oranges, Orindor in reds, Campagna in blues, Valdon in greens, Gesh in browns, Arborenne in silvers. The seventh banner hung in a dark corner and was more difficult to distinguish than the rest, being that it was frayed and soiled. The light flickered, catching the faded golden lettering so that I could just make out one word: Pendel. Sonya was right. The map Alex had given me hadn't shown all of Gaia. If anything, it'd shown a very small portion of it.

Most of the people sat around laughing, sloshing the contents of their mugs. Some held cards marked with strange symbols and drawings, with a mound of gold coins as a gamble. Daggers were thrown, oddly shaped dice were rolled, money was traded, and everyone seemed to be enjoying themselves. Music echoed throughout the hall from a trio of stringed wooden instruments, huddled and player-less in one corner. The strings plucked themselves, bows weaved un-manned, and no one paid them any attention.

We followed our guide through the throngs of people and tables. A few glanced up, inquisitive. The women were more than curious, batting hungry eyes at Alex. He at least pretended not to notice.

My observations of the people in this world didn't fit the image I'd formed in my mind. In a world of kings and lords, I expected at least some sense of refinery. These men and women were filthy, salted with sweat residue. The faces of the men hadn't seen a razor in weeks, and their armor was battered and rusty.

The man motioned for us to sit at a round wooden table, shoved in a dark corner away from the commotion. Alex and Sonya each took my side. Alex kept one hand fisted on the table, but I noticed the other was rigid at his waist.

A lady appeared wearing a low cut dress. In her hands was a tray filled with mugs that she proceeded to pass around the table. As she handed Alex his, she winked and sauntered away. I peered at Alex, wondering how long he'd keep up his act, but it only earned me a glare, and I averted my eyes.

The stench wafting from the mug before me smelled rancid and sour, but Alex didn't hesitate before throwing back a gulp. I gaped at him, horrified, and he knew it. Although he didn't turn to look at me, I didn't miss his grin.

"Does anyone else know ye left?" The little man grumbled just loud enough for us to hear.

"We told no one." Cicero scanned the room. "But we think we were followed through the forest."

"Well, no tellin' what crazy folks be wanderin' 'round these days." The man chuckled, and I caught a strong whiff of spirits and rot. Someone needed to show this Gaian a toothbrush.

The lady reappeared, passing around bowls of some putrid smelling soup. This time she offered Alex a generous view as she reached across him to hand me my soup. He, however, still acted as if he didn't notice and stared up at the ceiling.

Everyone dug in. I pushed the ladle through my bowl of broth. Blue tinged spheres floated to the top, wrapped with long translucent grey-green veins, and my stomach turned.

"Otis, meet Daria." Cicero gestured toward me.

The little man called Otis scrutinized me. "That's her?" He frowned. "You said she'd be a young woman. How old is she...eleven?"

Alex laughed, then coughed and washed it down with a drink.

Well. I sat up a little straighter. "Eighteen."

A smile of blackened, rotted teeth greeted me. "Course ye are, darlin'."

"How has business been here?" Sonya nodded toward the room.

Otis looked at Sonya. "Busier. People in the territories aren't happy. Says King Darius is to blame for the droughts, and that he's keepin' all the goods for 'imself. So they all come here and drink down their concerns, bloody barbarians." He narrowed his eyes at two men who were trying to strangle each other but kept stumbling over their own feet. "Only I'm worried that their concerns aren't goin' down like they use to."

Cicero rubbed his chin. "There's a surprising amount of soldiers here, considering there's no war."

Otis leaned forward over the table. "Rumor is we're about t' be."

"What do you mean?"

A pitcher of that foul liquid floated through the air toward our table. It tilted itself over each cup, a stream of its contents falling with precision into a mug below, refilling it, then moving to the next. Everyone acted as if a floating pitcher full of liquid was a common thing. I held my hand over my untouched mug and it passed.

The woman must have given up then.

"Some o' the men are talkin'. Says there's someone mighty powerful—someone that sold 'is soul to," his voice dropped lower, "Mortis 'imself. Rumor is those that 'ave joined burned a strange mark on their necks. I've never seen it meself. Not sure I want to either. They're s'ppose to 'ave been given some dark powers." Otis forced so much of his breath to a whisper I feared my nose might be stained with the scent of rot and ale forever. "I'm afraid it's more serious than we think."

"Any idea who this man is?" Sonya asked.

Otis shook his head. "No, but he be recruitin' some o' the men with his 'elpers. It's an easy feat when the people are so unhappy. I 'ear the plan is to overthrow the king. Says the Regius dynasty well needs to come to an end."

"That's ludicrous," Cicero said. "If it weren't for King Darius and his armies, this world would be flooded with creatures of shadow."

"I'm not so sure anymore," Otis said, staring off into the room.

"You aren't suggesting he's failing?" Cicero's reprimand was immediate.

"Now, I'm not speakin' no treason." Otis wiped his forehead. "I see a lot of people from all over, and some of the outlying villagers—they've got some stories that'll make yer toes curl. Of evils returning." Otis leaned forward. "Gargons, even."

Alex went still beside me.

"Impossible," Cicero hissed.

Otis held up a fat, square hand. "Whatever it is, the things they speak of 'er gruesome things. I don't much like it when they give me th' details."

"Have they informed the king?" Cicero asked.

"They says they sent word, but can't get through. King's too busy. Probably planning his banquets, they says."

Cicero and Sonya exchanged a glance.

"Do you think this person—if they exist—could also be the one who sent Pykans after her?" Cicero nodded to me.

"Pykans, eh?" Otis took a swig of the foul liquid. "That's not good. But I can't think o' too many others who would have the nerve to go after that one." Otis glanced at me.

I was about to ask Otis what he meant by this when the chatter in the room abruptly died. Even the instruments stopped playing.

Three men wearing full armor stood in the hall. Their silver was dented and tarnished, their chain mail kinked and dirtied, as if they'd just escaped years of imprisonment. They scanned the room as they took seats at the bar, their faces dark and brooding.

The room began to return to its normal volume, but the music didn't resume. I felt a wave of anxiety from the Del Contes, who glanced askance at the new guests.

Beads of sweat formed on Otis' forehead, his black eyes shiny. "Time to show you to your rooms, I think."

The Del Contes stood from their seats. Alex grabbed my forearm, pulling me from mine. His grip was delicate, but I knew it would be difficult breaking free even if I tried. We all followed Otis along the outskirts of the room while keeping our heads low.

But my eyes kept returning to those men. Something about them was wrong. There was a blackness in them—an evil presence I could *feel*. One of them turned his head just enough, the hair falling away from the back of his neck, and the edge of a black symbol became visible. I strained to see the rest, but it was hidden beneath greasy black hair. The man beside him turned around and locked eyes with me.

A deadly chill moved through me.

"You there!"

I froze, and the room fell silent once again.

The man jumped from his stool and made his way toward us. Alex yanked me behind him, and Cicero and Sonya flanked us, hands at their waists.

The man halted, a terrible grin stretching across his face. His eyes were cold and hard, like looking at onyx.

The room watched, apprehensive.

"You aren't from around here, are you?"

"We're just passing—" Cicero started.

"Not you," the man hissed. No one missed the candlelight flicker when he spoke. "I was talking to the...young lady." He tilted his head, his dark eyes straining to see me behind Alex.

"Come, now," Otis grumbled. "I don't need no problems 'ere."

The man stared only at me, and I couldn't pull my gaze from his malignant, hostile face.

Alex pulled me closer behind him.

The man's grin widened, his companions having joined him. "Well, well, well," he laughed. "It seems I have competition. I'm not sure it's considered fair to duel with a noble, considering they train you boys in the art of handling women's undergarments rather than swordsmanship."

Light chuckles erupted about the room. Alex's blood ran so hot it heated my body.

"Where are you from, young lady?" the man continued, his dark, hostile eyes burning through me. "There is a uniqueness about you I've not seen since—"

"Leave," Alex growled in a voice that frightened me. There was a sharp scrape as he drew his sword half from its sheath.

The man's eyes widened in recognition. "Alexander Del Conte."

Air whispered through the mouths of many people in the room, and I glanced up at Alex. How did everyone know who he was?

"You've no business here," Alex said.

"I'm curious," the man continued, now noting Cicero and Sonya's presence with great interest. "What business could bring the entire Del Conte family to these parts. Aren't you supposed to be *comfortable*...on the other side?"

Cicero drew his weapon, the eyes of the onlookers wide in expectation. "Our business is none of yours," Cicero spat. "Remember who you serve, soldier."

Hatred simmered in those black eyes, and when he spoke, his voice threatened to wither all life. "I do not serve *your* king."

"Who do you serve, then, traitor?" Cicero challenged.

"Someone who will be very interested in knowing *you* are here." The man's eyes darted to me.

One of the men in the rear of their group—the man whose neck bore the marking—was drawing something from behind his back. I couldn't tell what it was, but I could feel his violence directed toward Alex, to get to me. And it didn't seem like any of the Del Contes noticed.

I had to do something.

A half-empty glass sat on the table next to me. In one swift movement I snatched the glass and chucked it between the two in front, right at the third man's face. A dagger fell from his hands and clattered on the ground as he hurried to catch the glass hurtling straight at his forehead. Cicero and Alex had their swords at the throats of the leader's companions, and Sonya held a dagger high, prepared to throw it at the instigator.

The leader stared hard at me. "Sharp senses for an outsider."

The room was so quiet I could hear my heart pounding.

The man raised his hands, nodding toward his companions with a wicked grin. All at once they left through the door, the hinges creaking after them. Then, silence.

Everyone ogled the four of us, their curiosity overwhelming.

"Git back to yer business, ye bloody barbarians!" Otis yelled.

The room filled with movement, the instruments took up their plucking, and the people conveniently forgot what had just transpired.

And Alex yanked me after him.

100

When the door to the room closed behind us, Alex spun me around. A fire burned in his eyes. "Are you *trying* to get yourself killed?"

I was taken aback. "No."

"You're already being hunted. There's no need to draw more attention to yourself."

His harsh tone angered me. "That man was about to kill you!"

"I knew what he was doing."

"Could've fooled me."

"That's the point, Daria. They aren't supposed to know what I'm thinking."

"What are you, a professional liar?"

"What's going on?" Cicero looked between us.

Alex seethed as he lowered his accusative finger from my face. "We never should've come here. It's not in her nature to follow directions."

Had Alex and I been on good terms, I might not have been hurt by his reaction. But this cut deep. He'd acted like I was a complete idiot, and that I was responsible for putting all of us in danger. Even if it was true, he didn't need to be so berating.

"It's not my fault," I said.

His eyes narrowed to fine slits, his face inches from mine. "If you would've done as you were told and kept your eyes in front of you, that wouldn't have happened."

Well, that explained it. He had caught me staring. "If you wouldn't have overreacted, they wouldn't have been suspicious."

"They were already suspicious—"

"Alexander," Sonya interrupted. "That's enough."

Alex stepped away from me, but his irritation spilled freely over me.

Otis, who had been quiet during this little conversational aside, watched me with a smirk on his face. "Quite the popular one, aren't ye?"

I scowled, trying to calm my rage.

Otis continued walking down the corridor and turned up a narrow flight of stairs, and we all followed. Cicero and Alex lingered behind speaking in whispers. It was obvious they were bothered by what happened. And what had happened? How was it those men knew anything about me?

We continued down a long, narrow hallway, passing door after door. People lingered about and candles in sconces sent shadows dancing across the walls. Even here the women made eyes at Alex, and then looked me up and down with disdain.

Otis stopped before a pair of doors spaced a few feet apart. He pulled out a large, rusted key ring, jingled one of the large keys into each door, and then faced us.

He lowered his head and spoke so that only we could hear. "I got two rooms set up for ye. In order to keep this one 'ere—" He nodded toward me "—safe, best have her stay with the young master."

Cicero gave Otis a solemn nod, and beside me Alex went still as a corpse.

"Master Durus will be 'ere right before sunrise, out back by the stables."

Cicero sighed. "Thank you again, Otis."

"Bah," Otis grumbled with a wave of his hand. He glanced at me as he tottered by, leaving us standing in the hallway full of doors and a few onlookers.

Cicero looked sternly at his son before turning a soft eye to me. "You'll need to stay with Alexander tonight. It will be more difficult for people to recognize our importance this way, and we don't want any questions. Not after what happened below."

My eyes widened in disbelief, and for a moment I stopped breathing. I couldn't stay in a room alone with Alex, and definitely not all night. Desperate, I looked at Sonya to intercede.

"Don't worry. You're safe with Alexander." Her eyes drifted to her son, and something passed between them. Placing her hand on Alex's arm, she leaned over to kiss me on the cheek. "Good night, dear. We'll wake you early in the morning."

And then Cicero and his wife vanished into their room.

I wasn't sure what was worse: standing in this dark and shadowed hallway full of strangers, or spending a night with Alex. On second thought, I did know which was worse. The latter.

Chapter 11

An Uncomfortable Night

Alex held our bedroom door open, his expression granite. "After you, princess."

"Don't call me that."

He raised a brow, but didn't respond.

This was a fabulous way to start the evening. Delaying the inevitable wouldn't make the morning come any faster. So, setting my jaw with determination, I strode past him and into our room. He followed after me, closing and bolting the door behind us.

It was just as I feared. One queen-sized bed.

Other than that, the room looked comfortable enough. A fire blazed in a stone hearth, and a large colorful woven rug hid the rotten floorboards. A few lanterns clung to the walls, lighting the corners. An antique wooden armoire stood off to one side and a square table sat in the middle of the room. On the table was a pitcher of clear liquid with a few empty glasses. I hoped it was water. After inhaling all the smoke below, I was dying for something to drink.

A loud thud sounded. Alex had dropped his pack and sword at the foot of the bed and was winding out of his cloak. He hung it on a small hook beside the door, and walked to the table, pouring himself a glass of the mystery liquid. Instead of taking a drink, he glanced up at me.

"I know you're thirsty. You didn't drink anything earlier."

My parched throat was turning drier by the second, but I couldn't reply. I still couldn't believe I was going to spend the night with Alex. Alone.

"Here, the glass is on the table if you want it." He set it down, poured another for himself then took a seat.

The fire crackled and spit. Alex studied the glass in his hands, turning it in his fingers, and his eyes moved back to me.

I couldn't take it. "Remind me again why it's safer for me to stay with you?"

A grin twitched at his lips. "Unfortunately, those in the king's immediate company, including the Aegises, don't have a very—" he looked to the ceiling for his word "—*honorable* reputation when it comes to women. No one will suspect your value this way."

"So your method of safety is ruining *my* honorable reputation?"

He folded his fingers together and rested them on the table. "Daria. Anyone that actually knows you knows they'd be better off going after a porcupine."

He wasn't smiling. There wasn't even the hint of one. I glared back at the fire, wishing the night would hurry up and end.

"Sit with me."

I looked back at him. The muscles in his face were tight but there was a disarming warmth in his eyes.

Oh, come on. Quit being so melodramatic. It won't kill you to sit next to him.

It might. Or I might kill him.

As I hung up my cloak, that little voice kicked it in high gear and I thought only of my parched tongue. I felt Alex's gaze on my back, waiting to see what I'd do. What I wanted to do was walk right back out the door and take my chances with the strangers. But my dry mouth was screaming so loud I gave in and made my way over to the table. Alex was on his feet at once, pulling out my chair.

"Really, this isn't necessary."

"I know."

He stood there, waiting for me to sit. Taking a deep breath, I sat as he pushed in my chair.

"See, that wasn't so bad." He seated himself across from me.

"No. There are only a couple of things I can think of that might be worse."

He looked straight at me. "Do me the favor of keeping those to yourself."

"Done." I picked up my glass and sniffed.

The liquid was odorless, so I took a cautious sip. It was water, and the most refreshing water I'd tasted in my entire

104

life. In no time, the glass was emptied and I returned the mug to the table. Right next to a fresh roll.

I peered up at Alex.

"I thought you might want this since you didn't eat earlier."

I wish he'd stop acting like a gentleman because it only made it harder to stay angry. But I was so hungry I shoved the roll into my mouth. As I ate, he turned sideways in his chair and stared at the fire. The angles in his face were sharp in concentration, his eyes distant with thought. There was a quiet strength to him, as if there was nothing in this world he feared. It was that confidence that made him even more threatening. Which reminded me...

"Um, Alex, I was wondering..."

He seemed apprehensive, but his gaze slowly moved back to mine.

"How is it that everyone knows who you are?"

He drummed his fingers on the table and looked back at the fire. "I'm an Aegis. The Aegises are usually known throughout the realm."

His answer sounded recited. "People don't react the same way to your parents."

Alex took a sip of his water and then thumbed his glass on the table. I started wondering if the answer to that question had something to do with this apparent reputation of people around the king. And, in Alex's case, he was...better looking than the average male. Every other woman in this world seemed to think so, too, because they all gawked at him as if they'd never seen a man before.

Maybe I didn't want to know what he was famous for.

"For some reason," he started, his choice in words careful, "I have—"

"That's all right." I didn't want to hear it. "I don't need to hear about your female conquests."

He choked on his laughter and looked at me with a gleam in his eyes. "You think *that* is why I'm famous?"

I eyed him, unsmiling.

"Please, I know you like to forget we grew up with each other," he said, "but I hope you know me better than that." His eyes bore into mine, the firelight reflecting in his, and I suddenly felt self-conscious.

105

"I don't know what I think about you anymore." I glanced down at my glass. "Everything I knew about you wasn't true."

"You're right." His humor was gone. "Everything you knew about my circumstances wasn't true. But I'm still the same person, and I still find that behavior detestable, like I always have."

Even though I wanted to argue with his claim about being the same person, I knew he wasn't lying. Not this time. I could feel his sincerity, but I wanted to believe he was lying. It was easier staying angry when I found fault with him.

"I...have a reputation with my blade. Sword fighting is natural for me. I don't realize the impact it's had until I'm recognized by strangers. I thought my skill was average."

From what I knew of Alex, he was anything but average.

"Oh."

Silence.

"So did you just let me win all those years?" I asked.

He grinned. "Not always."

Silence again.

"Nice throw by the way," Alex said.

Well, I felt ridiculous. As if Alex needed me throwing a mug at some person's head to "help" him. "By the way, I wasn't trying to give us away."

"Daria, I'm sorry." He sighed. "I was angry but I shouldn't have spoken to you like that. It's just...since we are Aegises, people naturally assume the person with us is valuable—especially if we're away from the castle—and no one can know you're here."

His last statement made me think of the conversation we had with Otis before three madmen arrived.

"What was that man Otis talking about...some secret army?"

Alex took a deep, thoughtful breath as he gazed past me. "There's been growing unrest in Gaia for years, most of it caused by drought and famine. Many blame the king and his lords, accusing them of hoarding all the profits."

"Profits?"

Alex looked back at me. "Gaians are artisans. Each region is known for different trades. Take Alioth, for example. It's primarily agricultural because they have the most cultivable land. Lord Commodus' territory, Orindor, is known for mining..."

"Goods are redistributed throughout the realm?"

Alex nodded. "And lately, with all the famine and drought, people are blaming the king, saying he isn't fairly distributing produce. The people also believe their financial compensation is well below what it should be, and that the king is abusing his power."

"Is it true?" I asked.

Alex raked a hand through his hair. "Yes and no. There isn't as much produce the past few years so the distribution is less. Still, I don't believe the king is to blame for it, but he's not exactly helping. The people are hungry, and angry because he does nothing. We, meaning at least my family and your dad, believe something greater is happening to this world—something greater than we even realize. And after listening to Otis, it sounds like there is someone recruiting people—like those men—for an army. Who it is and where they are, we've no way of knowing. We'll have to inform Alaric, and hope he's heard of something from Lord Commodus."

"What about these things happening to some of the outlying villages? Otis mentioned gargons?"

Alex didn't answer immediately. "That is news to all of us, and it's unsettling if it's true. The king needs to be warned, if he hasn't been already."

"You'll have to tell him then, Mr. Protector."

Alex glanced up at me, a funny grin on his face. "Sure thing, princess."

I grinned back.

See, talking to him didn't kill you.

Maybe it wasn't *so* bad being around him, at least not when there were things to talk about. But that was the problem. Talking with him reminded me of how we used to talk about everything, because I'd trusted him. That was before time proved his character, as only time can, and hjs character proved to be a false one.

Alex stood then, and walked to the armoire in the room, pulling out a few blankets. He moved to the fire and spread them out on the floor beside it.

"What are you doing?" I asked.

"I," he said without looking at me, "am tired and going to bed."

"On the floor?"

He paused to look up at me. "Well, I'm not sharing the bed with you, and there isn't the smallest possibility I'd let you sleep on the floor. So, yes, I am."

Once he finished arranging his blankets, he lay down. He tucked his arms behind his head and stared up at the ceiling, deep in thought. For some reason, I couldn't pull my eyes away from him. I wanted to, but I couldn't. I searched for the boy I knew, the boy hidden in the body of this man. But there was something about this man version I liked, the strength in his face, his arms...

"Why are you staring at me?" Alex was looking at me.

Shoot. "I just...you don't look...how you used to."

If he felt anything, his face didn't show it. He just stared right back with stoicism, and it made me even more uncomfortable. "I'm sure I probably don't look the same either."

Just stop talking.

A grin brightened his face. "Three years hasn't changed you all that much. And I could never mistake anyone else for you."

His words were surprisingly delicate and sensitive. Personal. For a long silent moment we were still, studying one another. A hardness returned to his features and he looked away and rolled over. "Good night."

I watched his chest rise and fall with each breath.

Why was I watching him sleep?

This was a disaster. I'd fallen right back into talking with him how we used to. I'd let down my guard, but it wouldn't happen again. I couldn't let him hurt me again.

I glanced toward the mattress and stuffed pillows. My muscles ached to rest on the bed and get lost in the pile of warm blankets. I glanced back at Alex, lying on the hard floor. No, I couldn't.

I grabbed my cloak, yanked the quilt off the bed, and arranged it on the ground, using my cloak for a pillow. The floor was unforgiving, but I was exhausted. Besides, Alex had been enough of a gentleman. If I let him do any more, it would be impossible to keep finding fault with him.

Warmth on my cheek woke me. Once I pushed my lids open, my eyes rested on a pair of deep green ones hovering close.

"Time to leave." Alex's breath tickled my nose.

He held my gaze a long moment before walking toward the fireplace and folding the blankets. Blankets we had slept on. Except, I wasn't wrapped in those blankets. I was on the bed, beneath the covers.

I sat up. "How did I get here?"

Alex didn't turn around. "I moved you."

He stacked the blankets into a pile. "It's our last night of relative comfort for a while. Trust me, you'll hate yourself later knowing you wasted a good bed." He walked over to the armoire and piled the blankets inside.

"But what about you?"

"I'll be fine."

"I can't believe I didn't wake up," I muttered.

"I can." Alex faced me. "You were talking a lot, even for you."

Fire licked at my neck and I felt horrified. When Alex and I were younger, we used to fall asleep in their library all the time. He'd always teased me for talking in my sleep, but now I was nervous about what my subconscious might have said. I already knew it wasn't on my side. "What did I say?"

Alex's gaze dropped and he raked a hand through his hair.

Oh, no.

"It was gibberish," he said.

"Was it that bad?" I almost didn't want to know.

His gaze lifted as he fought to suppress a grin. "Your subconscious has a...better opinion of me than you."

I knew it. My cheeks burned and I glanced away, embarrassed.

When I didn't say anything, Alex made his way to my bed and sat on the edge, careful not to sit too close. His mouth opened, but his hesitation surged and he closed his lips. "I think I'll keep it to myself."

I stared at him, mortified. "You wouldn't."

109

"I know. It's not fair." He pinched his lips together. "But you don't need to worry. I know none of it's true."

He looked back at me then.

I had been about to say, "Well, now you know how it feels," but I couldn't. Whether it was the way he was looking at me or something else, I didn't know. But this morning, the fight in me was gone.

A firm rapping sounded on the door.

Alex stood and walked to the door as I crawled out of bed.

Cicero peered in. "We don't have much time."

Alex handed me my cloak and pack, and helped me— despite my resistance— sling it over my shoulders. Sonya waited for us in the dark, empty hall, her smile widening the moment she saw me.

The inn was asleep, the corridors and rooms devoid of life. We exited through the front entrance and stepped into the sharp, cold morning. Thick banks of fog obscured the landscape, casting an opaque haze over everything in our path. Remnants of wood smoke lingered and the damp morning air chilled my bones. I pulled the cloak tighter, trying to retain my body heat as we walked around the corner.

Once we reached the stable, Sonya halted before a dark mass. It was a man about the size of a mountain, and from what I could tell, he had the strength of one. He loomed above me, solid as a rock, dark skin pulled taut over bulging muscles. An endless well of power emanated from him— power so great, it would've scared the life out of me under any other circumstances. A single leather vest covered his upper body, hanging open and exposing his defined torso. Leather cuffs were strapped around his bulging arms that were folded over his chest, and an enormous sheathed sword hung from his hip. The sword was quite possibly as long as I was tall. His black eyes bore down on me so intently, it was as if he was trying to burn a hole in my skull.

"A child? I was expecting someone older and more dignified." His voice was the lowest bass I'd ever heard, and it was difficult distinguishing his words because they all sort of rumbled together.

110

I straightened my posture, trying to appear more confident than I felt.

"Hmm." The man examined me without expression. "A young woman. Impetuous. Inflexible. Insecure."

I wasn't sure why every stranger we'd met had some grand expectation of who I was supposed to be, but I was tired of it. Particularly this morning.

"Excuse me." I stared right back into the eyes of the giant. "But who do you think you are, going around insulting people you don't even know?"

My companions stiffened, but the man continued staring, unaffected.

"Master Durus." He placed a hand over his flat stomach, giving me a slight bow. "If you find the truth about your character insulting, I suggest you change your character, my lady."

I opened my mouth to respond, but all that came out was an indignant puff of air.

"The horses?" Cicero said before I could embarrass them further.

"Follow me." Master Durus spun around and disappeared into one of the stalls.

Sonya and Cicero briefly glanced in my direction then followed Master Durus, but Alex stayed put. In fact, he was fighting back a grin.

"What are you smirking about?" I asked.

His grin widened, and he motioned for me to walk ahead.

I stepped past Alex and marched after the others, feeling Alex's amusement flourish behind me. The others whispered around a group of four horses but ceased the moment I entered.

"Please give Stefan our thanks," Cicero said.

"Certainly," Master Durus replied. "You have the book?"

"Yes, thank you." Cicero patted his cloak.

"The roads are clear." Master Durus nodded at Cicero. "Sonya, Alexander." Then his eyes settled on me.

I stared at him, waiting for him to say something. Instead, he bowed and vanished into the cold morning air.

"There's one for each of us." Cicero grabbed the reins of the black horse he called Nova.

My heart lifted at the prospect of riding horseback. Something familiar, something I could grasp onto—a remnant from my life on Earth. It lessened my feeling of displacement in this new world.

Cicero led his horse out of the stable, followed by his wife. Sonya had grabbed the reins of an elegant white one she called Orion. Alex handed me reins belonging to a beautiful chocolate brown horse with a rich ivory mane and a single patch of white fur along the breadth of his nose.

"Daria, meet Calyx."

Calyx flicked his tail and fixed his glossy black eyes on me. There was an intelligence in his gaze, much more intelligent than any average horse. It was as if he was appraising me to see what kind of person I was. Maybe this was what Thad had been referring to and why my dad only rode Gaian horses. But so help me, if Calyx started talking, I would walk.

"Hello, there." I rubbed my hand along the breadth of his nose, his fur velvety beneath my fingertips. He whinnied, rubbing his wet nose into my neck and I chuckled. Good, he didn't talk. I had the distinct impression that we were going to get along just fine.

Alex fastened his pack to the saddle of a black stallion he called Parsec. Relieved, I slipped out of my heavy pack and strapped it to Calyx. "Thanks for that," I whispered in his ear.

His ear flickered and his tail whipped again. It really did seem as if he understood me. Once my bag was secured, I hooked my foot through the stirrup and leapt into the saddle.

Alex was watching me. "Still riding, I see." He smiled. I couldn't remember seeing him smile like that. Not even when we were younger.

"Of course." I stroked Calyx's mane, trying to push Alex's smile out of my mind. "I suppose your life of luxury and self-importance doesn't give you much time for this sort of leisure."

"Lucky for me, this supposed life of luxury I lead requires I ride." Even his eyes teased. "I might even be better than you now."

I grinned. "This I have to see."

112

I'd always been a better rider than Alex. Although if I thought about it, "better" might be the wrong word. Reckless was more accurate.

Just as he lifted his foot to the stirrup, Parsec sidestepped. Alex's foot plummeted to the ground, landing with a squish into something green and slimy. Manure.

"Better?" I laughed. "Well, at least I know your reputation has nothing to do with riding."

Alex sighed and shut his eyes in resignation, but he was smiling. I laughed even harder. Shaking his head, he scraped his boot clean and fluidly hopped into the saddle as if he'd done it a thousand times.

The two of us exited the barn to where Cicero and Sonya sat, mounted and scrutinizing the land ahead. Beyond the blanket of fog, I could just make out a wall of shadow. It looked like a forest. A dense, tall forest. That must be the Kirkwoods.

"You two ready?" Cicero asked us over his shoulder.

Alex responded with an affirmative while I focused on keeping a straight face. I kept thinking about the manure.

"Run hard, straight for the woods. We can't be followed. The fog should hide us till we reach the trees, and we'll reconvene once we're under the cover of the forest. Daria?"

I clenched my teeth to keep from smiling. "Yes?"

"Remember what you agreed to."

I nodded. What he meant was that he expected me not to run off. I would keep that promise, as long as they kept theirs.

Chapter 12
Magical Missives

Once we reached the forest, Cicero didn't waste time. We stopped just long enough for Cicero to say it was all right to talk, but don't yell, and we were safe, but keep our weapons ready. And never, under any circumstances, was I allowed to go off on my own. Not even when I went to the bathroom.

The fog followed us into the forest, filling the empty spaces with haze. The trees looked like dark veins in the mist, stretching and bending, angling up from the ground like claws into a grey abyss.

I had no idea where we were or what direction we were headed. Everything looked the same: grey, dark, cloudy. Every so often, I'd hear a crow caw. It was always off in the distance, echoing endlessly in the mist, but it was the only sign of life aside of ourselves. For the most part nature was quiet, letting us pass through her uninhibited.

Calyx proved to be an incredible mammal with a remarkable temperament. He didn't startle, and he didn't require much—if any—guidance. Before I'd even reach to pull him in a certain direction, he'd walk that way. I wondered where Master Durus had found the horses and how they'd been trained. Out of all the horses I'd been exposed to, none were so controlled and intuitive. If this was what my dad was used to, no wonder he couldn't stand riding Cadence.

My thoughts drifted back to Thad and his words repeated again. *"Makes you wonder what else they're not telling you."*

Shoving my fingers into my pocket, I pulled out the little rook Thad had given me.

A tower with impenetrable walls. For all its strength in battle, what was it hiding inside? What was it fighting to protect? To Thad it was the most important piece. To me, it just sacrificed itself for the king like all the other pieces. But

Thad had employed this little rook again and again, using it to dismantle every strategy I didn't have.

The wind stirred, and shadows moved in the mist. Wasn't that what Thad had warned? That the Black Bard would come as a shadow? Was it possible he was real and following us right now?

"What are you worried about?" Alex gazed sidelong at me. He and Parsec walked beside me, and I hadn't even heard them approach. "Nothing."

He raised an eyebrow. "Parsec, I don't believe her." He patted his stallion's mane. "See how she's playing with her hair? She always does that when she's nervous."

Parsec and Calyx both whinnied and I dropped my fingers from my hair.

I glared at the perfidious pair. "Just something Thad said before we left. About a Black Bard."

"Ah." Alex swayed with his horse. "I might advise you *not* to listen to our dear Thaddeus. He's a professional jokester and gets some sort of sick pleasure from distressing others."

He had a point there. "Well? Is it true?"

Alex gazed ahead, his face fixed in concentration. "It depends on who you ask. I would say no. People have a habit of blaming any unusual or unexplainable event on the Black Bard, but no one has ever seen him. I think he's more myth than anything. Don't waste your time worrying."

A dark shadow sliced through the mist, right over my head, and it cawed so loudly I jumped in the saddle.

"Daria, seriously." Alex smiled at me. There was that smile again. "There's nothing to worry about. If he really exists and tries to attack, we'll hand you right over and be done with it."

I rolled my eyes. "Yeah, you'd like that, wouldn't you."

He chuckled. I hadn't heard his laughter in years, but the sound of it had changed. It was deeper and richer, and it resonated inside of me.

"What's that in your hand?" He nodded at my rook.

I'd forgotten I was holding it. "Thad gave it to me before we left. Thought I might practice my strategy so I don't have to talk to you."

Alex stared at the rook in my hand, his expression growing distant. Without another word, he slowed Parsec and walked behind me, and I suddenly wished I'd kept my mouth shut.

Darkness began to consume our clouded, narrow trail, and Cicero halted. He jumped down from Nova and led her toward the overhang of a tree branch fat enough to sleep on. "This looks good."

I hopped down from Calyx, grateful Alex had moved me to the bed last night. Well, a little grateful, because with that gratitude came guilt.

"I'll help you." Alex stood at my side.

"I don't need your—" he took my pack off the saddle "—help," I finished quietly.

"I didn't ask if you needed it."

"Daria," Sonya called over to me. "Grab Parsec, will you? There's a stream nearby and I'd like to get them some water while we fill our canteens."

Alex held the reins out for me, his face hard as stone. "There's no need to punish Parsec because you're mad at me."

"Mad? I'd have to care about you to be mad..."

Alex dropped the reins and walked away before I could finish my sentence, thus leaving me with both Calyx and Parsec. I couldn't be sure, but it looked as if the horses were glaring at me.

I led Calyx and Parsec after Sonya, Orion, and Nova, and I hadn't gone very far before I heard the sound of bubbling water. A few paces more and we reached a narrow stream trickling through the trees. It was shallow enough to walk through, but wide enough to ensure one got wet if they tried. The water was crystal clear, glittering through beams of sunlight as it bounded over and around small rocks. The horses were already sucking it up.

Sonya knelt along the bank a little downstream from me, filling hers and Cicero's canteens. I grabbed mine and Alex's.

Alex. He brought out the worst in me. Mad? I wasn't mad at him. He was the bane of my existence. There was a difference.

But I couldn't let him go without water.

I dipped my hands in the stream, the water icy cold against my skin. I filled his canteen first to make sure I didn't conveniently forget, and then I filled mine. After some of the water poured in, I lifted the canteen to my lips. The water was so refreshing I gulped down the rest before dipping it back in the river to fill for our journey.

A gust of wind whispered past my ears. With it came voices, layers of hushed voices, all whispering at once. I glanced around, but all I could see were trees. Thinking I imagined it, I went back to my canteen. The whispers sounded again. I looked back toward Sonya. She was focused on the stream, filling the canteens, but feeling my gaze, she glanced up at me and smiled, then returned to her task.

I must've been hearing things. I hurried to fill the canteens and secured the caps.

Just as I stood, a bright red leaf caught my attention. It fell from the sky, floating back and forth through the air. It looked out of place amidst the green of the trees. Nothing was red here, except for this leaf.

It continued to fall, sliding gracefully back and forth through the air until it landed in front of me, right on the water. But rather than glide downstream with the current, it just stayed there, floating. I watched the leaf as it spun in place, its deep red edges curled upwards as if reaching for me. Then it moved. Upstream.

It glided across the surface of the water, away from me, away from Sonya. Sonya was still fixed on her task, now tending to the horses, and the leaf kept moving away. Farther and farther it went.

Careful and quiet, I set down my canteen and followed after it.

The leaf grazed the surface, threads of water streaming behind. It glided with purpose, as if being pulled forward by an invisible string. Sonya was soon out of view and the leaf stopped moving.

It floated in place as before, fighting against the current with little effort. I crouched and picked it up, and something glittered in the water right beneath it.

I bent forward to get a closer look. Nestled in the stream, amidst the bed of rocks, was a strip of silver. A dagger. I dipped my hand into the cold water, folded my fingers around the hilt and retrieved it.

The dagger was remarkably light, the metal old and dulled, and engraved along the flat of the blade were what looked like runes. The same kinds of runes I'd seen on the amulet the Del Contes had used to travel to my home back in Fresno. The hilt was wrapped in a coil of copper wire with a sort of round medallion at the end, split into four engraved quadrants. Power pulsed from within the dagger, and even though I'd pulled it from the cool stream, the metal warmed my hands.

It was then I realized I wasn't alone.

The wind rustled again, with more strength this time.

I peered over my shoulder and saw a shadow a few yards away. The ground beneath it swirled as the shadow thickened into a dark mist, and then it floated toward me.

"Daria?" Sonya called from up ahead.

A sharp gust of wind snatched the leaf from my hands, lifting it to the canopy and hiding it in the green sea above. When I looked behind me, the mist and shadow had vanished, and the ground beneath it was still.

Whatever it was had gone.

"Coming!" I shoved the dagger beneath my cloak and through one of my empty belt loops.

Taking one last glance at the place the shadow had been, I jogged back to Sonya and our horses. I didn't mention what I'd seen, or what I'd found. I was still trying to make sense of it myself, and there remained a part of me that didn't trust her completely. Not yet.

The sun had hidden itself by the time we reached our camp: the tree branch.

The sounds of metal clashing upon metal greeted us. Cicero and Alex were fighting with swords. My eyes had a difficult time following their movements as they darted around each other, feinting this way and moving that. Metal jarred, arms were almost dislocated, and I'd never seen such smiles.

"Nice to see you haven't wasted your time either." Sonya left Orion and Nova beneath another large branch.

I left Calyx and Parsec beside them.

"Your son is pretty good." Cicero laughed as he spun around just in time to block Alex's thrust. Cicero always referred to Alex as Sonya's son, unless Alex did something exceptional.

118

"But, Daria—" Cicero rolled away, repositioning himself "—if you really—" *clank* "—want to learn, watch me."

I smiled as Alex darted across the space between him and his dad. My whole life I'd thought I'd known this family. It didn't matter that I'd seen them carrying the weapons, because it was astounding watching them use them. Round and round they went, swords piercing the air. Always controlled, always with power and strength.

Mesmerized, I stepped closer. Alex was smiling, but his focus was laser sharp. I could feel his raw power, determination, and skill. Where had he learned that? He moved with accuracy and grace, each movement fluid and precise. And then we locked eyes.

It was all Cicero needed. In the split second I had Alex's attention, Cicero kicked out his leg, uprooting Alex's stance. Alex fell on his back with a thud, his sword falling victim to the underbrush behind him, and Cicero's laughter boomed.

"I am the victor!" Cicero held his sword at Alex's throat with a smile. "And your son is my prisoner."

I laughed and Sonya shook her head. Cicero re-sheathed his weapon as Alex hopped to his feet with a grin and dusted himself off. His cheeks were tinged pink.

"You got lucky." Alex re-sheathed his sword.

"Pure skill, my boy." Cicero patted Alex on the back.

"So you admit to me being your son then?" Alex laughed.

Cicero beamed. "No, absolutely not. Not until—"

"Cicero? Alex?" Sonya called over her shoulder. "Where's the firewood?"

Cicero and Alex froze, eyes wide. "Still in the forest," Cicero said.

Sonya gave her men *that look.*

"Be right back," Alex said, bolting into the forest with Cicero on his heels.

I joined Sonya beneath the tree branch. "I've never seen Cicero so excited before."

She sighed, staring after them. "Duty and responsibility have done that to him, but I know his light heart is in there. It just doesn't always show itself."

I sat on a blanket beside her. She reached into her pack and pulled out a tattered leather book.

"Was he like that when you met him?" I asked.

"More so." She opened the book and began reading.

I wanted to ask her more about the transformation to duty-ridden Cicero, but she had focused her attentions on the page in her hands.

"What are you reading?"

It took her a moment to hear my question. "A documentary."

A documentary? Out here?

Whatever her reasons, it was obvious she was consumed by her reading, so I turned my attention to the storm barreling its way into the forest. I hoped the men wouldn't be gone long. Any moment the clouds would unleash their terrible fury on all the poor souls caught beneath it. Namely us.

Just as the soft patter of rain descended upon the treetops, Alex and Cicero returned, each carrying a few chunks of wood.

Alex arranged the logs for a fire.

"Any word?" Cicero asked his wife as he lay down his pillage.

Alex's hand stilled on the wood, his shoulders tense. Sonya exchanged a look with Cicero, and I immediately felt Cicero's irritation at himself.

"What do you mean?" I glanced between the guilty trio. "What word?"

Sonya took a slow breath, exhaling her irritation. "Your father has made it to Orindor safely and should reach Lord Pontefract by tomorrow evening."

"Love..." Cicero's tone held warning.

"How do you know that?" I asked.

"This." She waved the journal in her hands.

"Sonya!" Cicero was incredulous.

"*Dear,*" she said. "You already gave us away. Daria is dealing with many things right now. We aren't breaking any promises. I just read it myself."

He held his wife's gaze a moment before sighing and sitting down. Alex turned his attention back to the small fire he'd created. He was staying out of this one.

"This—" Sonya said to me "—is a bindingbook."

"You said it was a documentary."

"It is." She nodded. "But it's a documentary of our travels. It's a way to communicate with another person across long distances."

I wanted to remind her that obscuring the truth was still lying, but since she was the only one willing to share information, I kept my mouth shut.

"This book," she continued, "has a mate in Stefan's possession. He writes in his, and we see it in ours, and when we respond in ours, he can see it in his."

"How is that even possible?" I asked.

"Magic. Both are created from one, each being a representation of the whole. What happens to one happens to the other."

"Stefan...does he share a book with my dad?"

"Yes. Stefan is representing your father at court in his absence. With this book, Alaric can instruct Stefan what to do. Stefan is also relating our travels to your father and vice versa. According to Stefan, Alaric is right on track, about a day's journey from Lord Commodus Pontefract. From him, we hope to learn information about the Pykans, or at least Alaric can raise a warning before meeting us at Amadis."

"And you're just now telling me this?" I stared hard at the three of them.

Sonya glanced at Cicero, who gave her a very pointed look that said "I told you so."

"It hadn't come up," Sonya answered simply.

My anger flared. "Ever since you showed up at my house I've been asking you about my dad. You could've let me read this—actually, you could've let me write Stefan myself and ask him how my dad's doing."

"I'll let you read, but you aren't allowed to write in it." Sonya's gaze did not falter, despite her open-mouthed, disbelieving husband sitting beside her.

"Sonya." Disbelief had transformed to pure horror.

"Cicero," she continued, unfazed. "Let her at least see that her father is fine."

"Deal," I said before she changed her mind. "No writing."

Cicero frowned as Sonya handed the journal to me.

Sure enough, on the first page was a letter addressed to the Del Contes and signed by Stefan. Next page. A response written by Sonya to Stefan. Another from Stefan. The rest of

121

the book was filled with blank pages. How had I missed this? When had she been writing?

Most of its contents were about things I didn't understand, but there were certain items of interest I collected to my memory. Dad was fine, his travels were uneventful, he was anxious to see us—see me—and relieved to know we were safely on course.

After looking through the book, I couldn't understand why the Del Contes—namely Cicero—didn't want me reading it. But Sonya had put herself out there to let me see it, so I didn't ask any more questions. I handed the book back to Sonya, thanked her, and warmed myself by the fire Alex had made.

Cicero and Sonya spoke in hushed whispers as far away from us as possible. Considering we were all huddled beneath a tree branch, it ended up being around the distance of a few yards. Whatever dissension I had created was soon settled, and the pair joined us as strong in their unity as ever. How they did that was always a mystery to me. Having one parent didn't give me the opportunity to witness couples working through differences, and the differences between Sonya and Cicero only seemed to make them stronger.

The rain picked up, its patter drowning out the world as if nature was applauding its own beauty. I felt a sort of peace listening to the falling rain and crackling fire, and I was thankful for the flames because with the storm had come the cold.

Cicero passed around dried meats and stale bread.

"Aren't you glad you remembered the firewood?" Sonya grinned at her husband.

He smiled. "I'm not sure what you're talking about. I remembered, but your son insisted..."

I didn't hear the rest of what Sonya's son insisted, because they were huddled in chatter, their smiles satisfied with each other's company. They were quite the pair—Cicero and Sonya, justice and mercy. They'd always balanced each other well. When I was younger, I often thought that if the day ever came where I considered marrying someone, I would want a relationship like theirs. They were equals. They were each other's favorite companion. They had utmost respect for each other, which was also probably why they were able to work through any disagreement, like what had just happened.

My eyes found Alex's.

There was something in his gaze I couldn't place, some emotion brimming at the surface, but before I could find out what it was, he severed the moment and looked back at the fire. A wave of his frustration crashed against me, as if I'd offended him somehow.

No, I wasn't mad at him. I was furious. Furious at him, at myself, because *I* still cared.

Chapter 13

Flame

The next few days blurred together.

Since Sonya had let the bindingbook out of the bag, I wasn't as anxious about dad's safety. According to the venerable Stefan, Dad was visiting with Lord Commodus. And this Lord Commodus, whoever he was, knew nothing of the Pykans, was disturbed by the news, and planned to travel with my dad to nearby ports in order to ensure the safety of Orindor's citizens. This extended my dad's stay by about two days. Not that I was keeping track.

The forest remained saturated. The clouds nestled themselves on the ground, and droplets of water clung to the trees, making them shimmer when the sun's rays touched them.

I'd grown accustomed to my leathers. They felt like a second skin, doing a fantastic job moderating my body temperature. They always moved just the way I wanted, stretched just the way I wanted. A wardrobe of these might not be such a bad investment. They were practical and durable and pliable; these Gaians might be on to something.

I'd wondered how Cicero had been navigating through the homogeneous grey veil until I'd noticed a device in his hands. A compass.

The little bronze object didn't have the usual directional markers of north, south, east, and west. Other shapes and symbols dotted the circumference. Every time I'd looked, the arrow hovered over a symbol resembling the letter "R", and sometimes when I'd looked, that "R" glowed a faint gold.

"It shows the direction of one's needs and desires, if you know how to use it," Cicero had said. He'd even let me hold it, but the arrow would only spin round and round.

When the fog lifted and the sun began its descent, we stopped.

We'd reached the far boundary of the Kirkwoods. A narrow valley spread before us, and on the other side was another forest. From here, the trees looked much too packed with green to give us room for traveling.

"The Arborenne." Cicero looked at the dense forest ahead. "Follow me and keep your eyes open as we cross. I don't want to be seen entering the forest."

The four of us tore across the strip of open land, our horses panting. The cool air ripped through my hair, and Calyx's mane splayed in a thousand directions. His legs powered across the ground as he kicked up clumps of soft earth. It was a momentary freedom for us both—open sky above, open land all around. As we ran, something cold grazed my senses.

I looked over my shoulder. Two dark figures stood in the distance. Their cloaks beat in the wind, but they were still, standing like two black pillars, watching us. I looked back at the Del Contes. They hadn't noticed, being so intent on the approaching green wall, but when I turned back to the onlookers, they had vanished.

Cicero stopped before a net of vines. Everything was so thick, so overgrown, I couldn't see an entrance anywhere. Air ripped through the valley with so much force my eyes stung. Then the vines started moving. They pulled back like a curtain, revealing a trail that led deeper into the forest.

I didn't like the looks of this.

One by one we walked through. Hot, sticky air engulfed me, chasing away the chill from outside. My leathers turned soft and damp, sticking to my skin like glue, and my hair clung to the back of my neck. Once we were all inside, the vines wound together again, clearing all trace of our entry and hiding the valley beyond.

This exotic jungle felt alive. Everywhere—in everything— all I felt was power, deep and ancient, radiating from the trees, the grasses, the earth. The air was thick with the fragrance of flowers and heavy with humidity. Jolts of pinks and oranges and blues burst from deep within the green. Leaves as big as my body swept the ground, belonging to trees the size of small houses. Thick vines draped from branches like tinsel, snaking around trees trunks covered in thick, lime-green moss. The sides of the trail were flanked with grasses, the shortest reaching my waist, making it impossible to wander off. Chimes rang through the air, their melodies reminiscent of those I'd heard our first day through the forests. Except here, they had an ethereal quality, giving the breeze a beautiful voice. This place felt...magical.

"Stay close. We'll stop before nightfall." Cicero led us forward, deeper into the verdant jungle.

Our trail was a single black thread, barely wide enough for us to walk single file.

Sonya paused before a tree.

It reminded me of a willow, but its tendrils of green hair were much thicker and longer, and each strand was lined with exotic orange flowers, some of which draped over our trail. The tree looked as if it was covered in tiny bursts of flame. The flowers belled open into the shape of a star with blinding yellow centers, and their scent infused the air with something passionate and intoxicating and...familiar.

"Cicero, look!" Sonya pointed at the tree.

"How can I forget?" He smiled at his wife, plucking one of the flowers and smelling it before handing it to her. I didn't know why he bothered smelling it. I could smell the flowers from here. Any closer and my nose would probably never recover.

The moment Sonya's fingers touched the petal, the flower flared blood red at its edges. Sonya and Cicero continued on, lost in their memories with each other.

"Ardor's Flame," said a deep voice in my ear.

Alex was right behind me, gazing at the tree.

"Why did that flower just change color?" I asked.

He gazed after his parents. "The tree is enchanted. It sees the heart. Legend says that if you pick a flower and give it to someone you love, it holds its bloom as long as that love lives."

"So the color change depends on...love?"

"Yes. The flower feeds off the love two people share. Common thought is the greater the love, the greater the color change. But you never know what to expect—just how they'll change. My parents still have the flower my dad gave my mom when he confessed his love."

126

The flower. The one floating in the water bowl at their home on Earth. It was from this world. All these years, it had been the same flower.

"The water bowl," I said.

He nodded.

I reached out my hand to touch one of the bright stars, but just as my fingertips touched the soft velvet, the flower retracted into itself. In its place was a tiny green bud sticking out from the strand of the tree. As if that wasn't enough, it began recruiting all the other flowers so that in a few second's time, there were no flowers left on the tree. Nothing but clusters of green buds.

I pulled my hand back. "Why did they do that?"

Alex looked amused. "The flowers are afraid of you."

"Do you enjoy watching me struggle to figure things out on my own?"

He frowned. "No, actually, it's the most frustrating thing about you."

He gave Parsec a soft kick, squeezed past me and walked on after his parents.

"I'll tell you who's frustrating," I mumbled.

Calyx whinnied as we walked on. But when I looked back at that tree—that selfish, haughty tree—the flowers were out again in full bloom, and all of them were facing me.

We had been walking parallel with a solid, rock wall when Cicero finally stopped. Except, I couldn't really be sure the wall was still there. The sun had faded and the mist became so dark and so thick it was as if we were walking through a cumulonimbus.

"Ah, there it is." Cicero said.

I had no idea what "it" was. All I could see was cloud. Before I could ask, Cicero veered Nova off to the right and Alex and Sonya continued after him. Calyx hurried to follow so we didn't lose them.

They stopped before a cave, its opening just visible through the fog. Cicero dismounted, and led Nova after him through the narrow crack.

Calyx's irritation surged through me as I leapt from the saddle. I tugged his reigns forward but he shook his head and tugged back.

"Oh, come on. You're not afraid of a little cave are you?"

He whinnied and pulled harder.

"Fine, then. Want me to leave you out here?"

He stopped pulling, stood tall, and snorted. I couldn't help but chuckle at his obstinacy. When I grabbed Calyx's reins again, he still wouldn't budge. "Well, are you coming or not?"

Calyx whinnied but clopped forward and followed me through the narrow opening. Rough rock wall hugged us on both sides, but it ended after a few yards, much to Calyx's relief, and opened into a single, large domed room. Fuzzy balls of light floated near the arched stone ceiling, gilding the walls of the rock chamber.

"There, that should do it." Cicero dusted his hands and looked back at me with a smile.

"You made those?" I asked.

He smiled then shuffled through his pack. I gazed at the lights above, hovering weightless in the air. How he had managed them was beyond me, as were most things in this world.

"How did you know this was here?" I asked.

"I didn't." Cicero pulled a few reddish, round objects the size of softballs from his bag. "But I knew it existed. Alaric told me about it once. Said he used to come out here as a boy when he didn't want anyone to find him, like me." Cicero grinned.

"Not that it helped." Sonya winked at me and turned her attention back to Orion.

"Yes, your poor father. Appointed me as his Aegis because I wouldn't leave him alone. Figured he might as well pay me for it."

Everyone knew more about my dad than I did, even strangers like Thad. Funny the most reliable creature in my life should be a horse I met a few days ago. No, it wasn't funny, it was depressing. Extremely depressing.

Calyx nuzzled my palm and I sighed.

Wallowing in your woes isn't going to get you anywhere.

Thanks for understanding, Conscience.

I started un-strapping my pack, but Alex placed his hand over mine. His touch startled me.

"I'll do it. Sit down."

I jerked my hand away. "I don't need your help, thanks." I yanked down on a strap, tightening it rather than loosening it. Calyx shifted.

"Daria."

I was not in the mood for this—for him. "You're a protector, not a gentleman."

"Is it impossible to be both?"

"For you?" Snap. "Yes." I had now broken one of the leather straps, and Calyx was so furious his nose flared and he was showing me his big, white teeth.

"Daria? Would you come here please?" It was Sonya. "Oh, don't worry about your pack. Alex can handle it."

I expected Alex to give some indication that he was angry with me, but he'd already turned away and busied himself with my things.

Why didn't he ever fight back?

Frustrated, I joined Sonya, who had piled a few logs in the middle of the room.

"Where did you find those?" I asked.

"Over there." She pointed to an orderly stacked pile. "Your father was always prepared."

She was right about that one.

"You asked how Cicero made the light appear," she said.

So they weren't totally ignoring me. "Yes?"

"I'll show you," she continued. "I wanted to show you sooner, but it wasn't safe. And now, considering where we are, I think it's safe."

My curiosity soared. "Safe?"

Rather than answer, she closed her eyes. I felt a surge of her power, and a tiny flame appeared, right in the center of her woodpile. It was small at first, licking and grasping at the air, but it grew larger and hotter until it was blazing so hot I had to back away so my skin wouldn't melt off. "How did you do that?"

She smiled. "Magic. It's a force of its own here. Gaia is filled with it. Some of us can use it by drawing on its power, but not without exchanging our own energy."

"You exchanged your energy to make the fire?"

"Yes, but that's not what Cicero did. Conjuring light like that takes a bit more practice, but it's the same general concept."

129

"You mentioned *some*, so not everyone can do magic?"

"Yes. Good," she said, pleased that I'd been paying attention. "Most everyone can tap into its source a little, but not everyone's connection is strong, and no two persons interact with it the same way. Those with the strongest connections usually serve the king, but the most gifted are members of the Guild."

"If this...Guild is as powerful as you're implying, why can't they hunt down whoever's after me?"

Cicero scratched his chin. "Alaric doesn't trust everyone in the Guild."

"That's a high position of power for people you can't trust."

Alex's irritation brushed against me.

"We know," she said.

No wonder Dad wanted the Del Contes to hide me in a place protected by ancient magic. If someone at the castle—someone with great magical ability—was at all involved with my attempted assault, they might as well just hand me over.

The magical fire snapped and crackled, and a thought struck me. If I expected to make it in this world on my own, I needed to learn how to use magic, and fast. "I want to try," I said.

"No."

The response had come from Alex, who'd moved behind us. His arms were folded over his chest, and he stared at his mother as if my request was a personal affront.

Of course he would pick this moment to fight me. "Why not?" I asked.

He ignored me. "It's a bad idea. They could still be following us."

"Alex, I understand your concern," she said, "but Daria needs to be able to recognize it, for her own safety. Besides, it's too small an amount to attract anyone."

"I don't think you *do* understand. I know her, and she could—"

"Alexander." Somehow Sonya had turned his name into a reprimand.

"Help me with dinner?" Cicero asked his son.

Alex stared at his mother, not wanting to relent, but at last his eyes flashed to me and he joined his father, who was already cutting the red softballs into pieces.

Sonya watched after her son and I felt her anxiety pulse. She drew her attention back to me and smiled, but it failed to touch her eyes. "Magic is a skill you must learn, particularly your own limitations. Many great sorcerers have died over-extending their energy, so as long as you to do exactly as I say, you shouldn't have any problems."

"Fair enough," I said. "So how did you just do that?"

Loud scraping filled the rock chamber. Alex sat on the floor sharpening his sword. His eyes were hard and focused on his task, and his features were sharper than the sword's edge.

Cicero, however, joined us and handed out fruit. "Don't be disappointed if you don't take to it immediately. Magic takes a lot of practice. Some can't do anything for years, although I don't think that will be the case with you. Are you ready?"

I nodded, impatient for instructions.

"All right," Sonya said. "Close your eyes."

I closed my eyes before she finished. The scraping stopped, and I was overwhelmed by Alex's intrigue.

"This is the challenging part. Reach out with your mind, and connect with the wood."

I knew what she meant by "connect" because I'd felt "connected" to this world ever since I stepped foot in it. I tried thinking of the wood, picturing it in my mind.

"Wrap your mind around it. Focus on nothing else."

With my mind I focused on the wood, the grain, its shape. I felt Alex's complete attention. His curiosity and intrigue were so powerful it was dizzying.

"Keep your focus. Once you think you've connected, imagine heat with your mind. Feel it grow hotter and hotter. See it consume the wood."

Something pricked my mind. The sensation surged, melding with my thoughts—my being. It was much more powerful than I expected. It seeped through my veins, into my soul. My mind wouldn't pull away—couldn't pull away. My focus was trapped, and my spirit felt...complete.

131

I thought of heat, tried feeling it with my mind and body, when warmth burned deep inside of me. I was startled at first and had to fight to keep my concentration on the wood. The heat simmered deep in my gut and spread quickly through my veins, down my limbs, and surged beyond, flowing outside of me.

The moment was interrupted by yelling.

"Daria...stop!" It was Alex. And he was on fire.

I jumped to my feet. Cicero dumped the contents of his canteen over his flaming son. The water licked up the last of the flames, leaving Alex's shirt steaming and scorched, and his sleeves were charred like a marshmallow.

"Alex! I'm sorry!" I stuttered, pressing my palms to my temples. "I can't believe...I didn't...are you okay?"

He gaped at me, water dripping from his face and singed shirt. I tried and tried but I couldn't detect any pain from him, only irritation. Acute irritation.

Alex slowly turned to his father. "Do you have a spare shirt?" His tone was low and too even.

Cicero, however, gawked at me with his jaw hanging open. "Incredible."

"Dad."

"Check my bag." Cicero continued staring at me.

Alex brushed past me, his irritation so strong I couldn't even think about what I'd done. I just felt...mad, with his anger.

If I hadn't focused on the logs, I'd been focused on...

"Alex, I'm so sorry. I don't know how that happened! I focused on the logs, just like you said." I looked at a bewildered Sonya. "And...anyway, I thought you said it was supposed to be difficult to use magic the first time?"

The sound of Alex rummaging through Cicero's things was particularly loud.

Sonya grinned to herself, as if she found something amusing that had nothing to do with my failed attempt at magic. "I think that's enough for one evening. Next time, we'll have you practice things that aren't so...destructive."

"There shouldn't *be* a next time. She'll be destructive with anything at this point," Alex mumbled as he pulled on a fresh white tunic.

132

I didn't argue. He'd earned himself some verbal slack since I'd just set his shirt on fire.

After Alex threw the remnants of his charred shirt in the fire and the surprise from my mishap subsided, Sonya and Cicero passed around more of the fruit and some salted meats. The fruit's bright blue flesh tasted bitter despite the hundreds of sweet black seeds inside.

Alex didn't join us and instead returned to his daggers. From the way he acted, one would've thought I'd planned all that. When chatter finished and drowsiness set in, we crawled into our beds. Sonya kissed me goodnight and crawled into her blankets, which were close to mine.

I wasn't sure how long I lay there, watching the golden remnants of our firelight flicker on the ceiling. When I stole a peek at Alex's profile, I noticed his eyes were wide open, too.

"Alex," I whispered.

He didn't flinch, but I knew he heard me.

"I'm sorry about your shirt."

Still, he said nothing, even though his anger burned like an invisible halo around him.

"Look, I don't know why you're so upset when it was just an accident."

He turned to face me, frowning. "Are you apologizing, or telling me why I shouldn't be angry?"

I bit the insides of my cheek and glanced down. "Just...I'm sorry."

"Don't try that again until we meet your father," he said. "You have no idea how to control your power and you'll end up killing yourself. We can't protect you from you."

His anger hurt.

"You're just an overbearing egotist." I hadn't meant to say that out loud.

Too late. He'd heard. His aggravation surged. I watched him fight against words he wanted to say but his self-control wouldn't allow it.

"Daria," he said in a very tight, controlled tone. "My parents don't know you like I do, and you didn't catch them on fire."

This again? "What do you want from me, Alex? I told you I was sorry. It wasn't like I was trying to hurt you."

"I know. You never *intend* to hurt anyone."

I was taken aback. "What is that supposed to mean?"

His eyes refused to let mine go, and then he turned to face the ceiling and closed his eyes. "Never mind."

Frustrated, I flopped on my back and glared at the ceiling. Maybe he should reconsider our circumstances. Last time I checked, I wasn't the one lying to everyone about how I felt and who I was.

A few more days. That's all I had to wait until I would see my dad. But what would happen once we met up with him? Would all of my issues just dissolve? What if he expected me to return to our home on Earth?

No, I couldn't go back there. Not after knowing this.

I stared at the ceiling with my conflicting thoughts, but each thought ended with the anticipation of reuniting with my dad. Everything would be made right once he explained.

It had to be.

Chapter 14
Off the Beaten Path

"It's up ahead," Cicero called over his shoulder.

The sound of rushing water poured through the forest as we neared a river—the one Cicero said we had to cross. But when we reached the gorge, all that remained of a bridge were two fat wooden posts. Wrapped around them were remnants of rope with frayed ends, and there, hanging from the opposite cliff, was our bridge.

We all stood in solemn silence, gazing at the white frothed rapids below.

"Well, this looks promising," Alex offered.

Cicero frowned.

"What now?" Sonya asked.

"Looks like we'll have to cross further upstream," Cicero said.

"Will it put us far behind?" I asked.

Cicero shook his head. "Not more than a day."

I wasn't sure I could handle an additional day. The current wait was already long enough.

Alex leapt from Parsec and walked over to examine the rope, rubbing the frayed ends between his fingers. "This was cut."

Alex continued searching the ground, pushing aside grasses and fallen leaves, and Cicero joined him.

"Here." Alex had pushed aside a few leaves.

Beneath was a small indent in the soft earth. Even if I'd seen it, I doubt I would have stopped and called it evidence. But since Alex had pointed it out, I couldn't deny it was a footprint. Whoever had made it had been very careful to cover the rest of their tracks.

Alex looked across the gorge, his features hard. "Do we have any other options?"

135

Cicero took out his compass, and the little arrow floated over that ostentatious "R".

"No." Cicero stood, his brow furrowed. "Not unless we turn around."

"Then let's," Alex said.

"You know that's not possible."

"It *is* possible." Alex's voice grew louder. "Notify Stefan. Let him know we're being followed. He can tell Alaric. I'm sure Alaric will understand, and have us meet him somewhere else."

"Where, Alexander?" Cicero's voice was hard.

"I don't know! Somewhere with less variables than this bloody forest!"

As if to emphasize its own mystery, a large gust of wind blew through the trees, stirring the leaves off the ground.

Sonya dropped from her horse and walked to her son. Her features were tender, like they always were when she was about tell me something I didn't want to hear. And by the look on Alex's face, he knew what was coming.

"Dear," Sonya's voice was low, soft.

"Don't—"

"Alexander Del Conte."

Her tone silenced him.

"You know those variables you mistrust are the same variables that are concealing us from all of Gaia. Alaric knew that. If someone's on our trail, we are more than capable of handling them. Otherwise, they would've shown themselves by now."

Alex's gaze didn't falter, but the muscles in his neck tensed.

"Remember." Sonya placed her hand on her son's forearm. "You are not the only one here who cares."

Alex's anger ebbed and, thus overruled, he walked away from Sonya. Our eyes met just before he mounted his horse, and then he walked Parsec in the direction Cicero had suggested.

"You'd better be right about this," he called over his shoulder.

We stayed parallel with the river, sometimes with it in view, sometimes with only the sound of it for company. The gorge, however, showed no sign of ending. I wondered if it was going to take us more than one extra day. We'd been walking for hours and always away from the bridge. Cicero and Sonya had taken the lead, guiding us through the thick, green maze while our path narrowed.

Alex walked behind me for the most part, but moved to my side when the path was wide enough. He never spoke. Neither of us did.

It was during those silent, awkward moments I realized something about Alex. He had changed, and for the worse. There was no semblance of the boy who grew so fast his muscles couldn't keep up. This one filled out his clothing, wore it with strength and pride, but his features were too sharp, too chiseled and broody.

"What is it?" he asked, not bothering to turn and look at me.

"Nothing."

"You've been staring at me for the past five minutes." He fastened those deep green eyes on me then. I decided those eyes saw too much and I should probably avoid looking into them.

"I was just wondering what happened to you," I said, looking ahead. "Why you look like that."

He paused. "I'm not sure how to take that."

"Don't take it as a compliment."

He glanced sideways at me. "You're saying I look different and you don't like it?"

I shook my head. "Tall, dark, and handsome isn't a good look for you. It makes you look...stern and broody."

"So you think I'm handsome, do you?"

There was a smile to his voice, and I felt a rush of his amusement. I couldn't believe I'd just said that. Heat rose to my cheeks. Calyx didn't need to be kicked in order to understand his time with Parsec was over.

Night fell, and there was still no way to cross. With each step my heart grew heavier. We were walking farther and farther away from our intended meeting place. Cicero directed us uphill on a path so overgrown I had to hold an arm across my face to fend off attacking branches and vines.

137

Between two giant trees, I saw the dark outline of a small building. It was a dilapidated structure, square in shape and spanning two stories, with walls constructed of crumbling stone. Narrow windows lined the sides—most of which were missing. A small stable stood beside it, equipped with rotted thatched roofing. It was probably an attractive and sturdy building at one point but weather and time had stripped away its strength, leaving bare bones behind.

Apprehension swelled from the Del Contes. Cicero leapt off his horse and landed with crunch.

"What is this place?" I stared at the ruins.

Alex walked Parsec past me, his unease palpable.

"It looks like an old outpost," Sonya said.

"An outpost? In the middle of nowhere?" I asked.

A strong gust of wind barreled through the trees again.

"This region didn't used to be the middle of nowhere," Cicero said. "Time has segregated the magical and non-magical creatures. Many of the magical live here now, and because of the divide, humans have stopped frequenting this forest."

"Look at this." Alex held something black and curved and very sharp.

Cicero rubbed his chin then gazed back at the vacated building. "Well, it's more dangerous if we travel in this part of the forest at night."

Alex threw the lone talon hard at the overgrowth and led Parsec to the stable.

Calyx whinnied, his steps nervous. "Sh," I whispered, patting his mane. "It's all right."

Calyx believed me as much as I did.

Cicero and Sonya were already walking their anxious horses toward what was left of the stable. I slid off Calyx and glanced around. The air whispered as it rustled through the treetops, its cold fingers reaching beneath my cloak, chilling my damp leather. Calyx jittered nervously again, pressing his nose against my side.

"I know. That cave doesn't seem so bad now, does it?"

There was something powerful here. Something...evil. I could feel it in the air, in the trees, in the silence. I couldn't imagine I'd get any sleep tonight.

138

Alex was fiddling with his pack when I approached with Calyx. His movements were quick and angry. I didn't need my ability to sense his emotions to know he was furious.

He didn't glance up, but as he walked past me, out of the stable, he paused. "Don't go off on your own."

"When has that even been an option since your family dragged me out here?"

He looked straight in my eyes. "I'm serious."

Before I could say a word he was off into the forest, slashing through the overgrowth with his sword.

"Planning on sleeping in the stable?"

The voice was so close I jumped. Cicero was standing behind me.

"Where's Alex going?" I asked.

"To check our perimeter."

"Shouldn't someone go with him?"

"He'll be fine. Ready to come inside?"

I didn't know if they placed too much faith in their son, or if I placed too little.

"Sure." I patted Calyx, who was very unhappy about my leaving him. "Don't worry, I'll just be on the other side of that wall," I whispered for only him to hear. Taking one last glance at Calyx, I followed Cicero through an old shabby curtain of a door.

The space inside smelled of dried, rotted grass. There was no furniture, only dirt flooring. No glass filled the windows on ground level, just holes covered with shabby burlap cloth. There was no floor where the second story should have been, except for a small wooden ledge clinging to a portion of wall. I could even see parts of the sky through the thatched roof.

I sure hoped it wouldn't rain tonight.

Sonya had brought in our blankets and was already spreading hers along one wall. Cicero inspected the building, moving methodically around the perimeter. He trailed his hand along the walls, pausing at increments, and every time he paused, I felt a surge of energy, as if a current ran through my body.

"Will it work?" Sonya asked.

Cicero frowned. "I hope."

I was about to ask what they were talking about when Alex returned with some edible looking fruits in his hands.

139

My heart swelled knowing he was all right, but then I was frustrated at myself for being so concerned about him.

He handed the food to his mother. "All clear."

Sonya took the little purple fruits from Alex. "Oh, I love these! Thanks."

Alex nodded. "What, no fire?" he asked his dad. "Don't tell me it could attract attention."

A firm look from Cicero kept Alex from commenting further.

Cicero transferred his stern gaze to me. "Try to rest now. It could be a long night."

I'd been lying there for hours, staring at the same hole in the roof. So much time had passed that I saw some of the stars move in their orbits. I'd counted them. At least ten times. I tried sleeping, but my mind wouldn't stop thinking. Dad, this world, the secrets, Alex. All of them screamed in my head, holding me hostage from slumber.

Frustrated, I sat up.

The Del Contes were scattered around me, and they were all sleeping. I assumed Alex was asleep, even though I couldn't see his face. He had his back to me, but he wasn't moving.

Wrapping my cloak around myself, I crept over to the door and sat down, leaning against the doorframe. Thousands of stars glittered the night sky. I searched and searched but I couldn't find any familiar constellations. No Big Dipper. No Orion's Belt. These were all foreign, like everything else in this place. I swore everything in this world conspired against me, just to remind me I was a stranger.

A breeze rustled and I wrapped my hands around my knees, the little rook in my pocket wedging itself further into my hip. The tower with impenetrable fortifications. What I would give to have that now, for my physical and emotional safety.

So many questions haunted my thoughts. What else were the Del Contes not telling me? What would happen if we got to Amadis and Dad wasn't there? Would I be able to get away from them? Even if I did, where would I go? I'd have to take Cicero's map with me.

140

That was, if Alex didn't catch me first.

A faint pressure on my shoulder startled me. Fate was not on my side this evening.

"Mind if I join you?" Alex whispered.

I looked away. I couldn't deal with him. Not now.

He removed his hand from my shoulder, but instead of going back to bed like I'd hoped, he sat down. Right beside me. Now both of us were crammed in the doorway.

Silence.

The night seemed quieter, as if it was waiting to see what would happen. It was probably expecting some sort of explosion. I was, and I hoped Cicero and Sonya were heavy sleepers.

It was Alex who eventually interrupted the silence. "I know you don't want me here, but I need to know something."

I waited, distracting myself by picking the dried mud off my boot.

"What did I do to make you hate me?"

I looked over at him then, into his hurt and troubled face. He was such a good actor.

"How can you even ask that?" I asked.

"I wouldn't be asking if I knew the answer."

"But how can you *not* know?" I couldn't believe it. "Unless you really *do* think that highly of yourself and your ideas on what friends..."

He clamped his hand over my mouth, nodding toward his sleeping parents. "That's not the only reason," he whispered. "Please, think hard about what you're about to say and see if it's worth it, because chances are, it'll take awhile for both of us to get over it."

There was pain in his eyes, one so poignant it made me forget what I was about to say. He slowly removed his hand. And I was silent.

"I just...all I want is to know what I've done."

His humility breeched my defensive wall.

"Alex." I had a difficult time keeping my volume manageable. "I trusted you with everything. Everything! If I'd been in your shoes, I would've told you. You've lied to me my *entire* life, and you expect to just show up...after three years, and I'm supposed to be fine with that?"

His features strained. "No...I don't expect...look. I *am* sorry. It was the hardest thing I've ever done."

"Then why did you?"

"I didn't have a choice."

"You *always* have a choice."

"Not with your father."

"What does my dad have to do with any of this?" I struggled to keep my voice low.

His face moved close to mine, his features sharp in the low light. "He made me swear...swear that I would never say a word to you about it. When I told him I couldn't, he said I wouldn't be allowed to see you again. What would you have done?"

"But I never saw you again anyway!"

"And that would have happened sooner if I'd told you."

"Then you should've," I said. "It would've saved you the misery of my company all those years."

He leaned his head back an inch to look at me, his eyes searching mine. "What...are you talking about?"

This wasn't at all a topic I wanted to discuss. Not now, and especially not with him sitting so close.

I glanced away. "Nothing. Never mind," I said a little too quickly.

Alex placed his hand on my cheek, turning it so that I was forced to look at him. There was something in his eyes that made my heart ache, and I couldn't take it.

"Don't touch me!" I ripped his hand down, staggering to my feet.

He stood beside me. "Daria, *please*. Just talk to me."

His tone paralyzed me. It was vulnerable and honest, just like he used to be.

"I know," he continued with a slight tremor to his voice, "you refuse to remember I understand you better than you do. Just tell me what I've done, and...I swear I won't ever ask you again."

The look in his eyes, on his face. It was too hurt, too pained. Too believable.

Step by slow step I walked back to him, peering up into his face. "Why do you keep pretending you care?"

His expression changed from hurt to perplexed. "You think I don't?"

"I *know* you don't. It was hard enough when you just up and left, but then to find out I meant *nothing* to you? All those years you'd been trying to find a way to tell me you couldn't stand me. You had to be my friend, because of our parents. Because you were sworn to protect me, just like you are now. Just...stop pretending."

His parents stirred. He grabbed my arm and yanked me out the door. "How did you get that ridiculous notion into your head?"

I yanked my arm back. "I heard you say it yourself!"

"When?"

"The last day I saw you."

He frowned. "You went home sick."

He remembered.

"Of course I went home sick! I wasn't going to stay anywhere near you after hearing how you really felt. I just don't understand how I was so oblivious—"

"Hold on. Hear what? What are you talking about?"

I was so frustrated by his willful ignorance I could've punched him. He was going to make me spell it out for him—replay the memory, detail by painful detail.

"I was standing in your doorway, Alex." I said each word slowly and deliberately. "I heard the whole thing. You were talking to someone on the phone about me. Your exact words, in case you forgot, were that you were going insane and your parents made you be my friend my whole life." My throat constricted. "There. Are you happy now? You can end the charade. I may have been stupid then, but I'm not now."

Alex's lips parted as I fought back my tears. I couldn't believe I'd admitted all that. I knew it needed to be said, but I wasn't expecting to say it all now. Not when it was still so unbearable for me to deal with.

His eyes moved over my face, and so many emotions crossed over his before his features settled into comprehension.

"For three years," his voice was so low I barely heard it. "All this time, you believed that? That *none* of it was real? That I never...cared?"

My strength crumbled like the walls around me. "What else was I supposed to think? It's not like you were around to prove anything different."

"No." He grabbed my hands in his. "I wasn't."

I tried to break free, but he only squeezed tighter.

"Daria," he sighed. "I remember that day. I was anxious to see you because I thought it would be the last. They were going to send me here. My parents. When you arrived, I was on the phone with...someone from this world, and I was talking about you."

My palms sweated in his, and I was trembling.

"But it wasn't what you think." He stared into my eyes.

"Stop—"

"No," he cut me off, squeezing my hands. "Listen to me. I *was* going insane. Because I couldn't tell you the truth about this world, and also because I knew I'd have to leave you soon. My parents—the only thing they ever *made* me do was keep this world from you. What I couldn't stand was knowing I was leaving without telling you why. I was afraid...well, I was afraid you'd treat me like this."

I went utterly still, unable to say a word.

Was everything he said true? It couldn't be. It wasn't possible that all of that had been a simple misunderstanding. Except when I filled the gaps in my puzzle with the pieces he laid out before me—without bias—they fit. Every single one of them. The way he'd been acting, his silence, his distance. It all made sense. For once in my life I could step back and see the entire picture the way it really was, not the way I'd drawn it.

"When I saw you standing outside my door," he continued, "I was so worried you'd overheard me talking about this world, and that I'd broken my promise to your father. I won't lie, part of me hoped you'd overheard. Maybe your father could forgive me if it was an accident. But when I saw your reaction, I knew you hadn't heard anything. There was no...life in you. I believed you were sick."

With every word he said, I felt more and more ridiculous. And furious, with myself. "The note," I whispered. "The one you left in the *Count of Monte Cristo*."

"It was what I'd decided—how I would tell you while not completely dishonoring myself in the eyes of Alaric. I was so certain you'd find it that day since you'd been turning to it every time you came over. I wanted you to find it. I wanted you to find it with me there, and when you left, I'd hoped you'd find it on another trip to our house."

"I didn't find it till a few days ago."

"I realize that now. I thought you found it and were still furious. I guess I didn't consider you'd be so angry with me you'd never set foot in our house again." His gaze was so penetrating I had to force myself not to look away. "But why were you so quick to draw those conclusions about how I felt about you? After everything we've been through, why didn't you just ask?"

See! I told you that you should've asked him. This is your own fault.

I swallowed and glanced down at my hands that were hidden in his. "I'd been noticing a difference in you for a while. You were withdrawn and more private. It wasn't like you, and I...took it personally, I guess. It makes sense now, with everything you were dealing with."

He didn't speak, but his frustration pulsed through me. The past three years had affected him just as much as they had affected me. I could feel it surging inside of him, and that frustration slowly chipped away at the stones of my emotional barricade.

"If what you say is true," which I knew it was, "then why didn't you say something sooner?"

"It's been hard for me, knowing what to say to you after everything that's happened," he said. "Especially after seeing how angry you were. And I know you. Once that fire burns, only time can put it out. I wanted to talk to you about it— alone." He squeezed my hands gently this time. "At first I thought I'd be patient—give you time to adjust before apologizing with even the smallest hope you'd forgive me. But you seemed more resolute than ever with your anger and even I have a threshold."

I couldn't stop my smile. "You? A threshold?"

He returned my smile, and then leaned against the wall, tilting his head back toward the night sky. "I hate that I've become a liar to you, but I couldn't leave this world. I couldn't contact you without being caught. The only reason I was able to see you a few days ago was because I finished my training, and your father was planning to tell you the truth."

145

My breath stuck in my throat. "He was...going to tell me about this world?"

His eyes found mine as he nodded.

That close. Dad had been about to tell me everything that night at the Del Contes. "What stopped him?"

"He received word there was movement by the portal. Of course he decided it wasn't safe yet, and took you home, away from any possible danger."

"But the danger was waiting at our home," I whispered.

Alex stared into my eyes. "I'm so sorry." He placed his palm on my cheek, the warmth melting the rest of my anger. I couldn't move. I didn't want to. Three years of hurting from a ridiculous misunderstanding.

"I give you my word—if there is any part of you left that can trust it—I will never lie to you again. Will you ever forgive me?"

I was lost, staring into his eyes. Eyes I'd trusted, eyes that made me feel...whole, again. I was overwhelmed with so many emotions, his hope and my joy, his relief and my regret at how I'd acted toward him. It was so much I almost didn't hear the horses.

And they were whinnying. Frantically.

Alex snapped his gaze to the forest, intent on the blackness ahead. He dropped his hand from my face and yanked me behind him.

The horses were in a frenzy. I'd never heard them make such noise. But what startled me even more than that was the shear amount of terror I felt from Calyx.

"What is it?" I asked.

"Shh." He focused on the trees, my hand clutched in his. "Wake my parents. Now."

Then, just between the shadows, emerged a pair of glowing blood red eyes. My entire body went numb as relentless hunger and death filled my senses from the creature hidden in the shadows.

Chapter 15

The Shadow's Creatures

The deep crimson glow smoldered in the shadows. I felt the creature's pure hatred, its lust for death and thirst for blood—our blood. It took one step into the moonlight, and I forgot its hatred because I was consumed by my own fear.

It was a dog from hell. Four long, sinewy legs supported a thick muscular frame. Striated muscles flexed as it prowled, the breeze lifting a few strands of wiry hair from its taut, black leather skin. Gnarled bat-like ears stood erect from its fury-wrinkled forehead, its nostrils flared at the end of a long lipless snout, boasting a wall of razor sharp fangs. A whip for a tail lashed at the air as it took another step forward, sharp black claws raking at the earth. It was the creature from the book, the one I'd seen in the Del Contes' hidden room. The barghest.

"My parents," Alex hissed as he pushed me back through the doorway.

I was paralyzed with fear. The horses were going berserk, drowning in terror, and then they bolted into the forest and disappeared in the shadows. But the barghest didn't go after them. Its eyes were intent upon me.

Alex sprinted toward it with his blade overhead.

What was he thinking? I tried screaming at him, but no sound came. The barghest took a single powerful swipe, but Alex deftly rolled away and jumped to his feet, sweeping his blade around himself. His sword jarred against the barghest's chest with a *thud*, grazing its tough, leathered skin. Alex leapt away, and the barghest's massive fangs snapped at the space he'd stood just seconds before.

Those same jaws snapped me back to my senses. I reached for my dagger and started toward Alex. I didn't know what I was doing, but I wasn't leaving him alone. Not with this monster.

"Get back!" he yelled.

"I'm not leaving you alone!"

Before I was able to go anywhere, a flash of white light shot out from the end of Alex's sword. It hit the barghest, enveloped it in light and seeped into its skin. The barghest tensed, eyes squeezed tight while its entire body contracted and curled into itself. It flexed in a surge of rage, eyes burning, and the white light rebounded in all directions. Alex dodged a beam and I dropped to the ground as one flew inches over my head, blasting the rock wall behind me.

Dust and debris fell everywhere, and I wrapped my arms protectively over my head. When I glanced up, the monster lifted its nose in the air and opened its jaws, filling the night with a bloodcurdling scream. Layers of dissonance blared, deafening and alien, compressed into one terrifying sound. My soul iced over as I covered my ears, trying to block out the horror now filling them.

"You can't kill a barghest with magic!" Cicero bounded over me with his sword in his hands. "What are you thinking? You'll get us all killed! Sonya, get Daria out of here."

Sonya gripped my arm and pulled me back into the shelter as Alex and Cicero sprinted forward, swords ready.

"We have to help them!" I yelled.

"You're not doing anything."

The barghest tried rushing past Alex to get to me, but Alex jabbed at its leg. It leapt in the air, over his head, and landed behind him. Alex whirled around with his sword, but the barghest's hind deflected it.

"How am I supposed to kill this thing?" Alex shouted, barely missing the barghest's jaws as they ground into the earth where his feet had been.

"With the skill you're *supposed* to have." Cicero brandished his sword.

I felt a surge of Alex's irritation as he rolled across the ground, thrusting his sword at the barghest's underbelly. It leapt and Alex missed, and the barghest landed closer to where I stood inside the doorway.

"Well, are you going to help me or not?" Alex heaved.

"I'm still thinking about it," Cicero smirked. "That beam almost blew my head off."

148

"Stay where you are." Sonya released my arm and readied an arrow on her bow, her eyes locked on the barghest.

"Sonya?" Cicero glanced back at his wife.

Her strength surged as steel flashed in my periphery. Cicero ran straight at the barghest. His movements were so quick and fluid my eyes could barely keep pace. Pure enjoyment moved through me. There was a loud clang, and one of the barghest's bloodied claws sailed through the air, landing at my feet with tufts of wiry hair and bloodied skin still attached.

"Nice of you to help," shouted Alex. "I was beginning to think you'd lost your nerve."

"My nerves aren't nearly as fickle as your focus when—" Cicero dodged a claw "—a certain person is around."

The barghest was furious, thrashing its head in the air, trying to get at the Cicero, but Cicero was too fast. He charged at the monster with a yell, and at the last second, he dropped to his feet, sliding beneath it with his sword and emerging on the other side, unscathed. The tip of Cicero's blade dripped with fresh black blood.

The barghest's agony shot through me as it let out another bloodcurdling scream.

"I was focused! How was I supposed to know not to use magic?" Alex yelled at his father as he charged the wounded monster. Only this time, it sideswiped him and Alex went flying through the air.

"I think," Cicero shouted at his son, dodging the large fangs he had jumped in front of, "that I need to take more interest—" Cicero brought his sword down, sending another claw sailing through the air "—in your education. Or were you just showing off?"

I couldn't believe they were arguing right now. The barghest was injured. Why didn't they just finish it off?

"No, I was—" Alex started.

"Now!" Sonya yelled.

Together, Alex and Cicero jumped clear of the beast and the roof above me burst into flame. The beast charged, and Sonya shoved me from behind through a back window.

Air and light exploded and a wave of heat engulfed me. I flew through the air and hit the ground, hard. Pain exploded

149

up my spine, and for a moment I couldn't breathe. The fire roared in my ears, its heat burning my skin, but I couldn't move. It took a moment for my lungs to start working again, but when they did, they kept choking and coughing on smoke. It was like inhaling an ashtray. When I glanced up, a fire blazed where the building had stood.

Where were the Del Contes?

Coughing, I scrambled to my feet, searching for the others, when another burst of fire shot from the flames. It knocked me over again, shoving me to the ground, except this time, I didn't stop falling.

Round and round I went, sliding down a steep decline. My hands grabbed at the ground, trying to find purchase, but every small branch and vine gave way and slid down with me.

I stopped sliding and was thrown on moist, flat ground. This time when I breathed in, I swallowed mud and soggy leaves. Choking, I spit the mud from my mouth. My entire body ached, and I hoped I hadn't broken any bones. With a groan, I opened my eyes and staggered to my feet.

My world was pitch black. The trees here were so thick, I was surprised I hadn't run into one. And there was no trace of Alex, Sonya, or Cicero anywhere.

I was alone.

I couldn't have rolled very far. All I needed was to climb back up the hill. I could feel my way back. The Del Contes would wait for me.

A chill slithered down my spine, and I ripped my dagger from my belt and scanned the shadows.

Something was here with me, hiding.

My eyes darted between the shadows, searching for the source of rage, but I couldn't see anything. I took a step back, the pounding in my ears faster as adrenaline surged through me. My back grazed against something and I jumped.

It was just a tree. Relieved, I slid around with my back to it, my eyes glued to the shadows, my dagger shaking in my sweaty palm. I slid around a little faster, and I was about to start up the hill when I caught a whiff of rotted flesh.

My blood turned to ice.

I stared at a wall of fangs, blood dripping from each sharp point. Its red eyes burned with violence as a guttural growl rattled the earth.

"Daria, get down!" screamed a voice behind me.

I dropped as something whirred over my head, and an enraged howl filled the night. There was a flash of silver, and then a shadow leapt over me. One by one, more barghests emerged from the shadows, fangs barred and eyes glowing. Alex was my only barricade between life and death, but if he was afraid, he didn't show it.

I was too horrified to move.

Alex's movements were swift and he used his surroundings to propel him. He rolled along the ground, jumping to his feet just in time to ram the hilt of his sword into the jaw of another hungry mouth.

Cicero darted past me from somewhere, joining the fray. Father and son moved fast, plunging into the pit of death with a ferocity that was both astonishing and frightening, and they didn't slow.

Arrows flew past me from the shadows. I couldn't see Sonya anywhere, but her arrows never stopped coming. They didn't kill, but they disabled enough barghests to give Alex and Cicero an advantage.

"Can you start another fire?" I yelled.

"There's nothing to burn," replied Sonya's voice from somewhere, sending more arrows into the horde.

Alex's sword was still reverberating from impact when another barghest lifted its head behind him, preparing to strike. And Alex hadn't noticed. I screamed at him but no one heard over the din of the battle.

My anxiety spiked, and my heart hammered against my ribs. If anything happened to him...

Time slowed to a halt.

The others were frozen in movement, each vibration of Alex's sword was sluggish, its oscillations traceable with my naked eye. The barghest behind him had leapt and was suspended in air, gaining ground inch by inch as its slow-moving jaws hinged opened.

The burning in my palm startled me from paralysis. My dagger.

With a flick of my wrist, I hurled it across the clearing at the barghest with open jaws. End over end it flew, splitting through the air and the horde, until it sunk into the barghest's skull with a loud *crack*. With a shock of immense pain, time returned to normal.

The pain faded as fast as it had come, and the barghest fell to the ground with a thud, dead.

Alex's sword was still reverberating in his hands as he looked back at me. I could feel his shock as easily as I could see it on his face, but he quickly returned his focus to the next attacking dog.

Red points of light flickered off in the distance. There were more. We'd never get out of here alive. There were too many of them.

Sonya started pulling my arms behind me, away from Alex.

"What are you doing?" I tried shaking free.

Another dull thud sounded. Alex had downed another beast, pulling his sword from its abdomen, its entrails spilling on the ground. Another one landed with a thud as Cicero split open its throat, black blood spraying the earth.

Suddenly, sharp pain seared through me—so sharp it buckled my legs beneath me. Sonya's grip was the only thing keeping me on my feet. At first I thought I'd been attacked, but when I glanced down, I couldn't find any wounds. When I looked back, Alex was clutching his left arm to his chest, his white sleeve slowly changing to black.

"Alex!" I yanked and pulled against Sonya. "Sonya, let go! Alex is hurt!"

I could feel him struggling to suppress the pain.

Sonya fought against me. "We have to get you out of here!"

"I'm not leaving him!"

The air around us convulsed. The wind ripped up dust and dried foliage from the ground, whipping my hair in my face, but there was no sound. Not even as the wind gained momentum and force, forming a vortex right in the middle of the massacre.

Everyone stopped fighting—even the barghests, that were snarling and gnashing their teeth as they backed away from the silent vortex.

Without warning, the vortex contracted and exploded. A deep sonorous boom blasted forth, ramming into my frame as it barreled through the forest, flattening the barghests and pinning them to the ground. But we were all still standing. Whatever had pinned the barghests did nothing to us.

"What in Gaia's name...?" Cicero's gaze darted everywhere. "Alex! Get back!"

Alex's blade was still in the air as he and Cicero ran toward us. Once they were a few feet from me, a soft white glow appeared in the space where the vortex had been. The glow was moving. The air itself took on a soft sheen as the glow spread and diffused, flattening out across an invisible barrier, arching around our predators that had begun to stir.

We looked to each other. No one knew what was happening.

"Run!" Alex yelled.

He grabbed my hand, holding his sword with his wounded one, and yanked me after him. We sprinted up the hill with his parents on our heels.

"Are you all right?" I heaved, my lungs burning trying to keep pace with him.

"Fine."

I knew he was lying.

"What is that—" I huffed "—thing back there?"

"Some sort of shield." His breath was ragged.

I didn't have enough air to ask more questions, and I was certain he didn't have enough energy to respond. His pain was acute, and his energy was fading quickly despite his powerful steps.

We sprinted hard. My legs ached and my lungs heaved so hard I thought they'd collapse. We ducked beneath low branches, leapt over thick roots and vines. I had no idea how Alex was running so fast. Sonya and Cicero passed us and ran ahead, their panic filtering through me. We ran past the burning building, the smell of rot and death still thick in the air.

I glanced over my shoulder.

The red eyes below blazed with fury, locked behind the wall of light that was beginning to fade. Whatever it was gave us just enough time to get away, but I knew once that wall fell, those beasts would catch up to us, and fast.

We sprinted through the forest. Alex still gripped my hand in his, pulling me after him as his parents led the way. Twigs bit my face and arms, and pulled out my hair. A chorus of that horrible screaming filled the night again, renewing my will to run faster. The barrier must have dropped.

And then Cicero and Sonya stopped.

We were standing at the edge of a low cliff. The river glittered far below, the silken thread carving into the black forest. The sound of the hounds behind us grew louder and louder. I could almost hear the tearing of the trees as they stampeded through the woods. We were trapped. We'd never get away in time.

Alex yanked me around and stared hard at me. "Hold your breath."

Before I could respond, I was jerked forward and falling through the air. Ice-cold water engulfed me, choking off my scream as I swallowed it. A thousand tiny pricks stung the open wounds in my skin. I fought for air as I struggled to swim upward, weighed down by my heavy cloak.

With a gasp I resurfaced, water slapping against my face. I spit it out, choking on air and water, but my boots pulled me back under. Something grabbed my arm and I swung at it in an attempt defend myself.

"Stop...it's me!"

Alex grabbed my wrist, stopping my hand inches from his face. "Are you all right to swim?"

I nodded, the blaring screams echoing from everywhere. He guided me as we swam against the current. The heads of Cicero and Sonya bobbed in the water ahead, and they glanced back to make sure we were following. I swam hard, always watching Alex, making sure his arms were carrying him forward. His face showed none of the agony I knew he felt, only determination. We were halfway across the river when my hope sank. Red eyes dotted the opposite bank, pacing with anticipation.

When I looked back to Sonya and Cicero, I couldn't find them. My heart pounded as I scanned the river, the banks. Where had they gone? Alex couldn't swim forever.

I noticed two dark shapes hanging from a large shadow, fixed in the middle of the river. It was a rock, and Cicero and

Sonya were crawling up its side. As Alex and I approached, they waited with ready hands. Alex pushed me up so that my hand could reach Sonya's. She pulled me onto the rock and Cicero helped Alex up after me.

Crimson eyes lined both banks and their yips and screams rang in my ears. The eyes paced back and forth, hungry and seething.

"There are so many of them," I said.

Cicero looked back at me. "They can't cross the water."

"Are you sure?" I asked, but even as I watched, I noticed none of them dared to go near the river's edge.

Alex's wound burned through me and I scooted to his side. Sonya hovered over him, eyes closed in deep concentration as she held his arm. His entire shirtsleeve had changed to black, and the black was spreading fast. The flesh in his forearm had been ripped away, revealing mangled muscle oozing with thick blood. My stomach turned over.

"We have to stop the bleeding," I said.

Sonya crouched with her eyes closed, Alex's energy fading with every drop of blood that seeped from his open wound. Frantic, I pulled up the corner of my cloak and tried ripping off a piece.

Alex winced. "Daria, please."

Sonya's eyes snapped open and fixed on me, her expression blank. I glanced back at Alex's arm. Not only had it stopped bleeding, but it was coagulating along his forearm at an alarming rate.

Sonya sighed and sank down on the rock, her husband at her side wiping the hair back from her face. Whatever she had done put great strain on her.

I knelt beside Alex, examining him for any sign of further harm and wiped his arm clean with my cloak. The wound had stopped bleeding and was protected by a solid clot. How had Sonya done that?

"Sonya's a healer." Cicero said in answer to my unasked question.

"Wounds never heal that fast."

"You've also never seen a wound healed with magic. It greatly weakens the healer—especially for a wound like his. Barghest saliva carries poisonous toxins."

155

"It isn't healed..." Sonya struggled for air. "Not all the way. It was...all I could do..." She fought against invading fatigue.

"Shh." Cicero pulled back her hair, holding her hand. "You need to rest, love. You've done more for him than anyone else could. He'll be fine."

Sonya hunched forward, her breathing shallow. She'd depleted so much strength tending to Alex I could hardly detect traces of her life. That might have been because Cicero's anxiety was so strong it drowned out everyone else's emotions.

Alex's pain was acute, but it was noticeably fading. Relieved, I sat beside him and wrapped my arms around my knees to keep myself from shaking. With all my worry about Alex's health, I hadn't noticed the cold. The water had soaked through my cloak and skin, and now my bones were frozen.

"We should've turned around." Alex winced. "Alaric will be—"

"There's no point in arguing about it now," Cicero interrupted.

"...Should never have let her try magic," Alex mumbled.

Cicero glanced sideways at his son, his brow furrowed as his gaze returned to the blood rimmed banks. The eyes glowed from all directions, floating back and forth in the shadows, watching and waiting.

"Are th-th-those things usually prowling this f-f-forest?" I asked, unable to keep my teeth from chattering.

"No. Hellhounds existed in this world ages ago. They were created from the shadows by dark wizards. They couldn't live peaceably with humans, or any creature of light for that matter. It took decades to send them all back to the shadow world."

As if to emphasize the point, the horrible alien screaming blared all around us, the points of crimson shining with madness. I knew this was going to give me nightmares for a very, very long time. Probably the rest of my life. "Then wh-what are they doing h-h-here?"

Cicero rubbed Sonya's hand, as if trying to rub warmth into it. "Someone has brought them back."

"The same someone that's b-building an army?"

Cicero was quiet and contemplative as he gazed ahead.

156

Someone let the Pykans through the portal. Someone was building an army to overthrow King Darius. This same someone was sending hellhounds after me.

What had I marched my eager, ignorant self into?

I was suddenly glad I'd decided to follow the Del Contes. "How do w-we get rid of them?"

"We don't." Cicero's attentions were split between the prowling red eyes and his weakened wife. "But they can't stand water, and sunlight is toxic to their skin. Until then, we'll wait here."

My wet hair clung to my back, each droplet sending shivers down my spine. Alex lifted his good arm and wrapped it around me, holding me against him. I wanted to protest—he was the one wounded—but my ravenous body drank in the warmth of his, and my shivering died down.

There was just one more thing.

"Cicero, what was that light back there?"

Cicero scratched his chin. "Something that contained the essence of sunlight, or enough of it to keep the barghests at bay."

"How did you make it?"

"I didn't make it."

"Who did then?"

"No *human* possesses that power." He looked at me with curiosity in his eyes. "It appears that Gaia wants to keep you alive."

Chapter 16
Awkward Beginnings

I was alive.

Nature was in full glory this morning, celebrating our victory over death. The sun was hot, baking my leathers and shading the backs of my eyelids a burnt orange. Water bubbled by, birds chimed through the air, and a bed of rock had never been more comfortable. Everything was perfect, except for the acute pain stabbing the back of my skull.

I heard a sharp scraping and forced my lids open.

The world was white—blinding white—and the scraping made the ache in my skull pulse. After a few moments, my eyes adjusted and different colors came into view.

Alex was sitting beside me. His elbows rested on his kneecaps and he fidgeted with something in his hands. His dark hair curled around his ears and neck, hanging in his face, shielding his eyes. And his shirt was off.

For a moment all I could do was stare. It wasn't like I'd never seen Alex without a shirt. We'd known each other since we were crawling on all fours. I just didn't remember him looking like...that. His golden skin was smooth and perfect, his arms and torso were hard with lean muscle. There was no lying to myself now. He was gorgeous. So gorgeous it made me a little self-conscious.

And I had been wrong about him. It didn't take away the fact he never told me about this world, but I'd been wrong about one very important thing: our friendship *had* meant something to him. All those years of thinking my memories were false, that I had to destroy and hide them and pretend they never happened because he never cared. He *had* cared, and I could hold on to that truth with confidence.

So now what?

I pushed myself up, my head throbbing as if someone was beating it with a sledgehammer.

"Hey." Alex angled his face to look at me. His expression was still guarded, but there was new warmth to his eyes this morning.

"Hey."

"Sleep all right?"

"I...think so." I rubbed my temples and gazed around. There was no sign of the horrors from last night—the barghests. There was also no sign of Cicero and Sonya. "Where are your parents?"

Alex raked a stone across whatever was in his hands.

"Trying to find the horses."

Calyx. Poor thing had been so scared. "You think they made it?"

Scrape—scrape. The sound wasn't helping my headache. "Those horses are fine. What we're not so sure about is if they'll come back."

"I wouldn't blame them. We're risky transport."

There was a gleam in Alex's eyes as he looked at me. I wish he didn't look like that with his shirt off. It was distracting.

"Those barghests are gone for good?" I asked.

Alex narrowed his eyes at the ledge we'd leapt from. "For now, but they'll come back tonight. As soon as my parents return, we'll be on our way away from this place." He looked back at me and studied my face. "How are you feeling this morning?"

"Fine, besides a massive headache. What about you? How's that gash in your arm?" I bent toward him to get a look, but he hid his arm behind his back.

"It's fine."

"Let me see it." I grabbed his arm and his pain surged through me. The gash was much longer and deeper than I'd thought. The clot had crusted over with a shade of red so dark it looked black, and the skin around it was tinged pink, filled with a web of blackened veins. "Alex, that looks terrible."

He grinned, pulling his arm away. "That makes twice now you've insulted my appearance."

I rolled my eyes. If he only knew. "Can your mom do anything else for it?"

159

He flexed his arm, turning it over as he examined it, and I tried hard not to ogle. "She used almost all her energy restricting the poison to the wound. No, it needs other magic for the rest. Magic that's beyond her ability."

"There has to be something. We can't just let it fester like that."

"We don't have a choice. There's supposed to be a small village not too far from here. They'll have a witch doctor."

He'd better not be serious. "If your mom couldn't heal that, I doubt some witch doctor can."

"Witch doctors can be incredible healers. Besides, they'll have elixirs that would take my mother weeks to prepare."

He was serious. "I thought we were trying to avoid civilization."

"Lucky for us, this part of civilization doesn't stay up to date with news of the realm."

"I don't like it."

We both stared at the black mass on his arm, and then our eyes met. There was something in his gaze, something warm and comforting and...tender. Even more than I remembered, before my life had turned complicated and thrown me from its good graces.

We broke the silence at the same time.

"Last night—"

"About last night—"

We grinned at each other and I felt the heat rise to my face.

Alex held my gaze, and I fought to hold his. "I won't ask you to trust me. That's something I have to earn. I know that. But is it too bold to ask forgiveness? For leaving and never telling you about this place—this life?"

Could I? Was it even possible for me to forgive him for that? I still wasn't sure I could trust him, but he wasn't asking for my trust. Just forgiveness. Trust could—might—come later.

He didn't show the hopefulness I knew he felt, but his words were sincere and filled with regret. I couldn't deny him a second chance, not when I sat there, missing him so much. "No, it is not too bold," I said.

His eyes moved over my face. "You forgive me then?"

"Yes. And...I'm sorry I've been so difficult."

160

An imperceptible grin touched his lips. "It's a good thing I like challenges."

I laughed, shaking my head. "Challenge" was the nice way of putting it, and by the look on his face, he'd chosen that word with deliberate care. "And what I said to you, in your library. About hating you..." I looked away, growing increasingly embarrassed by my childish behavior.

But even before I finished what I was going to say, he extended his hand. "Friends?"

I grinned, placing my hand in his. "Friends."

His fingers closed around mine. "Thank you." It was as if his spirit had spoken to mine.

How strange that one moment could wash over the years, cleansing them from filth and grime. This was our chance at a new beginning, and he was still holding my hand. I wasn't sure how I felt about that, or why I felt anything about it at all. We'd always held hands as kids, but now it felt...different.

"Just so you know." I pulled my hand free. "You may be off the hook for leaving me out of, well, everything, but I still don't trust you."

His eyes held me entranced. "Fair. I know I deserve it. But you will someday. I'll make sure of it."

"You really are that confident," I teased.

He laughed then, and the sound of it massaged my heart. "Here." In his hand was a dagger. My dagger. "I tried sharpening it for you."

I took the blade from his hands. It was still dull. "You said you *tried*?"

"Yes, and apparently it's as stubborn as you are. Where'd you get that anyway?"

The little strip of metal flickered in broad daylight.

"In a stream, when Sonya and I went to fill the canteens. Any idea what these markings mean?"

His forehead creased in concentration. "None. I was trying to make sense of them, but they're of a kind I've never seen before. By the way—" he glanced up at me "—how in the world did you kill that barghest?"

I'd almost forgotten what I'd done last night with this dagger. It had sailed, end over end, straight at the barghest's skull and landed with the skill and precision of an expert. And I was no expert, at least not with knives.

161

"I have no idea. I was just as surprised as you were when it hit."

Alex thought this over. "Well, I guess I'm glad we didn't meet those hellhounds any sooner, or you might have let it kill me."

I laughed. "Oh, come on. I was mad at you. I didn't want you to die."

He raised a doubtful brow and I laughed harder. When my laughter faded, nature's voice was the only one left speaking.

Three years. How do you pick right up from where you left after that amount of time passed? Especially when time had taken that someone to another world, trained him as a fighter, and shown him how to use magic. Not to mention, turned him into the most beautiful man I'd ever seen. Time hadn't been so generous with me.

I felt his eyes on me then, hesitant yet curious. He was apprehensive just as I was. Old habits. The way we communicated and the closeness we had shared. They'd worked with such ease before, but time had rusted the joints, making them creak as we tried to operate them again. We had to start over, build new habits and new communication, and we had to assemble the parts from scratch. I wasn't sure I knew how to do that.

"Strange, isn't it?" Alex said.

"Mm?"

"Starting over after how well we knew each other."

Alex. Always perceptive, always accurate, and it was always irritating.

"You can obviously still read me just as well." I grinned.

He grinned back. "Maybe we can start with you filling me in on your past three years."

Well, this conversation could be devastating to my reputation. "Ah, well...there isn't much to fill you in on. The most exciting thing that's happened to me has all happened in the past week, but you've been around for that. I say we start with you."

He pulled his gaze from mine and looked toward the bubbling river. "All right." He took a deep breath.

I waited, suddenly impatient to hear anything and everything about him.

162

"My past three years have been...challenging. When I came to this world, it was to attend the Academia." Alex was quiet a moment. "My life has been consumed by that ever since. Training to fight and use magic, learning all about this world and the powers within it as well as the creatures that live here. I just finished my training a couple weeks ago."

His life sounded incredible, and I felt a twinge of jealousy. "So what will you do now?"

He glanced sideways at me. "Now I'm here with you. After that...I'm not sure. As an Aegis, I'm expected to serve someone of power, much like my dad's always watched over you and Alaric."

Birds sang and darted overheard in jolts of bright pink and orange and blue.

"Do you have anyone in mind? Not that I'd know who they are."

Alex raked a hand through his hair as he stared at the river. "My father wants me to accept the role as Aegis for Lord Tosca. He's been requesting me since I started training."

"Who's he?"

"He presides over Alioth, the territory farthest from Valdon."

I didn't know exactly how far "farthest" meant, but I did know I didn't like it. Not after finally getting my friend back. "I can't imagine your mom being okay with you moving to the place farthest from her." From me.

"She's not, but it's a highly coveted position. The people of Alioth face many enemies. They're attacked from their northern border—the Icelands—and since they generate most of our produce, they tend to see the bulk of raiders. The king takes great interest in Alioth, and it would place me in direct communication with him, making it possible to gain position, which my father sees as a unique opportunity for me. My mother understands that as well. It would be an incredible chance to make a name for myself."

I studied the set of his strong jaw, the disquiet in his eyes. "But you don't care about making a name for yourself."

He rubbed his thumbs together as he watched the river. "Enough about this." He looked back at me. "Tell me about you."

The way he was looking into my eyes—the way he seemed to sift through my soul—made me suddenly nervous and uncomfortable. I didn't want to share my uneventful life with him. He'd trained to fight, had probably made all sorts of interesting friends, and was being sought after by powerful people in this magical world.

Who was I?

The farm girl who didn't even live on a farm.

"Really, I don't want to bore you with that."

"Don't be ridiculous. Nothing about you has ever been boring." He grinned, showing his perfectly straight, white teeth.

Stop looking like that!

"Right." I smiled, my cheeks feeling flush. "I might have believed that *before* you went off to another world like the hero in some fantasy."

"Oh, come on. I'm no hero."

"I saw you fight. People write stories about men like you, not about me. You tell me which is more interesting."

"If you saw what I see, you'd never say that." The warmth in his eyes held me captive.

"Well, good morning!" It was Sonya.

She and Cicero stood side by side along the opposite bank. Sonya was smiling, but Cicero was frowning. And there weren't any horses.

"No luck?" Alex hollered.

"None. I couldn't even find tracks," Cicero said. "They're probably halfway home now, with our things."

Alex stood. "You're sure you know where you're going?"

"I've got the compass and the village can't be far. Either way, we're not going back."

"Of course we aren't," Alex mumbled.

"And," Cicero continued, "since we're so close it would be ludicrous not to visit them and see if they've heard or seen anything out of the ordinary."

"Because a barghest attack is completely ordinary," Alex mumbled again, his frustration surging again. He still wanted to turn around and go back the way we'd come. Anywhere but farther into this forest.

"Well, are you two coming or are you going to wait for the barghests to return?" Cicero asked.

The sun had warmed my leathers so effectively that the cool water felt refreshing during our short swim to the other bank. The water stung Alex's wound and pricked through me as we swam. I kept my eyes on him, making sure his wounded arm kept him afloat, But by all appearances he showed no weakness, only strength.

No one said another word about the barghest attack. I knew Alex was still upset about it, and I could tell Cicero and Sonya were unsettled, but they wouldn't say it. As if speaking about it might bring the barghests back.

We walked on, around the trees, picking through vines. There were no signs of the horses. I hoped Alex was right. I'd hate my last memory of Calyx to be him running for his life away from those monsters. On occasion I glanced at Cicero to see if I could sense any doubt or hesitation, but he showed nothing but the determination of a leader. Until he stopped and held a finger to his lips.

Alex walked to his dad's side, gazing in the same direction, and that's when I detected the sharp scent of wood smoke. Someone was burning a fire nearby.

Cicero motioned for us to follow him. He led us forward, his movements quiet, calculating. Soon we were standing at the edge of a small cliff and peering into a narrow green valley. Wooden buildings were scattered throughout: small homes, large buildings, and a few barns. Some had fences, some didn't. Smoke streamed from stone chimneys, dispersing into the thin blanket of fog nestled into the valley. A wide stream cut through the middle of the village and a single stone bridge joined both halves. Beyond all of that was more forest and mountains.

People were visible, tending to fields and various other chores, and by the looks of the few I saw, they appeared to be a rough bunch.

"Any idea where he'd be?" Sonya whispered.

Cicero shook his head, eyes darting between the wooden buildings below as his unease simmered. "We'll find someone who knows," he said. "Wait here. Give us one hour."

Sonya nodded, glancing back at me.

"Alex?" Cicero looked back at his son.

Alex nodded as he adjusted his sword, and I suddenly realized their plan. "Why aren't we all going?" I asked.

"You're staying here with me," Sonya said.

Now I felt uneasy. "No. If that village isn't safe enough for all of us, then—"

"Wait."

It was Alex. His eyes narrowed as he stared at the valley below, and I immediately saw what'd caught his attention. Guards. There were three of them exiting one of the larger buildings.

"Lord Vega's?" Sonya asked.

"Not sure." Alex's jaw tensed.

"Who's Lord Vega?" I asked.

"His territory is near here," Sonya whispered.

"Let's get out of here." Alex started backing away.

"Get down!" Cicero hissed, and shoved me to the ground. Sonya dropped down beside me. Alex went still as a statue.

The three men stood in a pack, all facing different directions, surveying the landscape. One of the men had stepped ahead of his companions, his movements like a warrior on the prowl, all the while staring in our direction. Even from here I could see the dark shadows beneath his eyes and the scruff on his neck and face.

I knew who those men were.

"The men from the inn," Alex snapped. "I told you we should've turned around."

Cicero glanced back at Alex, then his wife.

Alex began scooting back, tugging on me to follow him. "We need to get out of here before they see us."

The man below motioned for his companions to join him, all of them now staring at the spot where we lay hidden. In unison, they drew their swords and began walking toward our cliff.

"Looks like they already have," Cicero mumbled, gripping the sword handle at his waist. He and Alex exchanged a weighted glance, and then both looked at me.

I knew what was coming. They were going to tell me to run and hide myself, and there was no way I'd agree to that.

Alex noticed. "Daria." He placed a hand on my arm. "Please, you need to stay out of sight."

Something rustled in the trees behind us. Right as I peered over my shoulder, a black bird shot out of the leaves and flew straight for the valley below. It reminded me of a crow, but it was the size of a vulture. It soared to where it finally landed on a solitary wooden post just a few yards from where the men stood. The bird cawed, an eerie, lonely sound in the fog.

For a moment the guards stood there, glancing at the bird, then back at the spot where we lay. After what seemed like an eternity, the leader re-sheathed his sword and motioned for the men to follow him, and they disappeared back into the house. The black bird cawed again, extended its giant, black wings, and disappeared into the forest.

A gust of wind barreled through the forest and the fog below grew thicker, the world unusually quiet.

Cicero glanced at Alex. "Looks like you got your wish. Best pray that wound doesn't spread before we get help."

Chapter 17
The Fiori

We didn't see the guards again. Still, the Del Contes walked with one hand on a weapon, and their eyes never stopped searching the forest. And that feeling, the one that makes you think someone's watching you? It nagged at me like a dripping faucet, but every time I looked, I saw nothing but shadows.

The trees were also starting to get on my nerves. Maybe I was going crazy but it seemed like they were alive. Not in the way normal trees are "alive," but in the get-out-of-my-forest sort of way. I could've sworn a few branches conveniently swung into my path as I passed. I'd be walking, minding my own business, then all of a sudden—*whack*.

After a few hours of getting sideswiped by the trees—well, me getting sideswiped—our horses returned. The moment started out with a fright, but when we realized the strange rustling and crunching sounds were the result of moving horse hooves, relief presided over all else.

Poor Calyx. He was still so shaken and upset. It took me about two hours to calm him, and after that, all I felt was his regret. "It's all right," I'd told him. "I'm glad you ran away. They would have killed you."

That seemed to make him feel better, at least for a little while.

The trees didn't attack me again after that. I didn't know if it was because of the horses or because of something—or someone—else. Every time the trail allowed it, Alex rode beside me.

We spent the entire afternoon reminiscing and laughing. Alex reminded me of one particular day—I'd been five and he'd been seven—when he'd decided to give me a haircut. Dad had never able to bring himself to cut my long hair. That day, my hair had been in one long braid, so Alex's job had been quite simple. One snip of the scissors, and my braid detached. Alex had been so pleased with his handiwork, but my dad hadn't shared his enthusiasm. He had promptly accused Alex of turning his only daughter into a boy. I laughed so hard at the memory I earned myself a funny look from Cicero. Actually, he looked a little irritated, though I didn't know why.

Alex and I revisited all of my favorite memories: hours in their library, forts we'd built, fights we'd had, food we'd cooked that not even the squirrels would eat. Neither of us had been adept at following directions. Well, as Alex liked to remind me, I was the one who was terrible at following directions, and I also happened to be bossy.

The sting in Alex's arm had lessened, at least from what I could tell. He was pretty good at keeping that arm hidden from view. Every so often I would feel a shock of his pain, but it would always fade away.

Evening cast its predictable shadow over the forest, and we stopped for the night beneath another behemoth of a tree.

Sonya walked to my side. "Cicero wants you and Alex to fight."

I knew it. Cicero was angry with me for some reason. "Did I do something wrong?"

"Oh, spirits, no," Sonya said. "He just thinks you should practice, you know, keep your skills sharp."

"Oh," I said. "You mean actual fighting."

"What in the seven territories did you think I meant?" She laughed.

"Um, I don't know." I swallowed down my embarrassment. "But, do you really think he's in any condition to, you know..." I pointed at my own arm.

"I heard that!" Alex called from beside Parsec, hooking a few daggers to his belt. "And, to answer your question, I'm perfectly fine."

"Sure, fine shape for losing," I added.

He flashed me a challenging smile.

"Alex is going to show you how to fight with daggers," Sonya said.

"Really?" I'd never fought with weapons before, and the thought of it filled me with excitement. It also meant I

169

probably wasn't winning any fighting matches today, even against an injured opponent.

Alex approached us, his eyes fastened on me. My heart beat a little faster and my stomach filled with a swarm of butterflies. What was wrong with me?

Sonya placed a hand on my shoulder. "Are you feeling all right, dear?"

I swallowed forced a smile at her. "Uh, yeah. Fine."

She searched my face. "Don't worry. Alex is a natural with blades. He won't hurt you."

I held my smile and said nothing. It wasn't the blade I was afraid of. The thought of taking my training to the next step—weaponry—was thrilling. It was the fighting with Alex part. We hadn't done that in years, and he certainly hadn't been built like...that.

"Ready?" Alex stopped before me.

His smile made me catch my breath.

Calm down, take a deep breath. You've fought him a thousand times.

"Are you trying to intimidate me into surrendering?" I nodded toward his arsenal.

"As if that was possible." He grinned. "Anyway, these aren't for you. They're in case we encounter any real danger."

I blinked at his daggers, confused. "So what, exactly, are you teaching me then?"

"She's all yours." Sonya turned to me. "Don't be easy on him, not that you ever were." She grinned at her son, patted me on the back, and joined Cicero beneath the tree.

Alex stood there with a funny look on his face. I couldn't decide if he was amused or a little nervous, like I was. I tried getting a sense of his emotions, but for some reason I couldn't feel a thing, and that bothered me.

His eyes shone with something I hadn't seen in a very long time. "Don't worry, I might not have inherited many of my mother's good qualities, but I did inherit her patience."

Why was my heart beating so fast? "I'm not worried." I smirked, trying to shake off my nervousness. "But you also inherited her sense of caution. I want to be functional in a knife fight, not be the damsel in distress."

Alex leaned close to me and my skin suddenly tingled all over. His eyes were bright and unusually penetrating. "I don't

170

think you have anything to worry about there. You're the damsel who distresses everyone else."

With that, he strode into the forest. My face felt hot as I trudged after him. I didn't know why my body was acting so strange. Maybe this was all part of getting used to him again. I mean, it had been years since we'd done anything like this.

We wove through the thick trees, which, to my relief, kept their branches to themselves. I gave myself a silent pep talk the whole way, trying to convince myself nothing had changed and there was no reason to be nervous around him. Alex didn't stop until he reached a patch where the trees were spaced apart a little farther, the sun peeking what remained of its bright yellow head through the canopy, illuminating the forest floor.

The little clearing was beautiful. Splashes of color were everywhere from large flowers that lined the thick vines dragging along the forest floor, to the sound of falling water whispering faintly through the trees. Something buzzed past my ear, but when I looked, all I saw was a leaf about as long as I was tall with something slinking on top of it. It looked like a caterpillar the size of my hand. Short, stiff bristles of silver hair stood out all over its body, making it look like a fuzzy slinky. It inched along the leaf, leaving a shimmery, moist trail in its wake.

I reached out to touch it.

"I wouldn't touch that if I were you." Alex was looking up at me from where he was crouched on the ground, a few yards away.

I glanced back at the caterpillar but all traces of it were gone, except for the shimmery trail. Even as I watched, the shimmer darkened until it turned black as tar, and the leaf dissolved with the faintest sizzling hiss. All that remained was the stalk with an end that looked as if someone burned it, and there was no sign of the caterpillar.

"What was that?"

Alex studied me a moment. "This forest doesn't have its reputation for nothing. It's home to many dangerous critters. In fact—" a grin teased his lips "—I think you fit in nicely here."

I narrowed my eyes but he went back to searching the ground, using his foot to move tall grasses and fallen leaves.

171

"What are you looking for?" I left the deadly slinky and approached Alex.

"These." He picked up a couple small sticks. He tossed one to me. "What you're going to learn with."

"A stick." I stared at him. "You're going to teach me how to fight with a stick."

He made a face that said he didn't understand the problem.

Figured. "I'm having flashbacks to my kindergarten days."

"Do you want to learn or not?"

I made a face of my own but he pretended not to see it.

"Knives are a lot more dangerous than wrestling. You *will* get cut. That hurts a great deal more than getting the wind knocked out of you."

"Mr. Protector, you're already inhibiting my first lesson." I waved my stick.

He raised a brow. "Daria, you're dangerous with anything in your hands."

For some reason, I didn't like how he said that.

"First rule," he continued. "Point the stick away from you."

"Yeah, wouldn't want to get stabbed with a stick now, would we?"

"Good, you're paying attention."

I rolled my eyes as he continued. "Defend against the blade, not me. *Always* keep your eyes fixed on the blade. It's the greater threat."

"Considering your weapon of choice, I think you're the greater threat."

He crouched, his features sharpened with focus as he held the stick before him. Starting the match without warning, as usual.

"How's your arm?"

"Never felt better."

I mirrored his movements, crouching on the balls of my feet as we circled each other. "Are you going to explain what you're doing?"

"Once I see you understand what I just said."

"Okay, I'm going to get a small sting and we need to keep these pathetic excuses for weapons between us. Next?"

The answer I received was a physical one. He feinted with his stick, his body twisted around it, and I was nowhere near ready.

He was much faster than when we used to fight, and the wound wasn't slowing him. Not at all. It took all my focus to watch him, anticipate his moves, but I couldn't predict them like I used to. His style had changed. He was faster, smoother, and better. Much, much better.

He thrust the stick toward my stomach fast and I bent back, but he used my momentum against me. He grabbed the wrist of my stick wielding hand and reached around with his other hand, pinning me against him. My spine arched backwards at an uncomfortable angle and my limbs were immobile. Alex's smirk was inches from my face, his breath even and calm despite my own panting.

"You've certainly improved," I grunted.

"And you certainly haven't."

I scowled and he chuckled, and the sound of his laughter resonated through me. He let me go.

"I wasn't ready." I rubbed my shoulder.

"Obviously." He grinned.

"Why are you smiling?"

He shook his head with a gleam in his eyes. "Again."

His features hardened with focus and he came at me again. His movements blurred and the next thing I knew my hand was kicked and my stick flew through the air, landing about ten yards away from me.

"Well, you're supposed to hold on to it," Alex said.

"And you're supposed to teach me how. You haven't taught me anything, actually."

"I am teaching you something. Reminding you why you need to follow my instructions instead of depending on your usual method, Miss I-Can-Figure-it-out-Myself."

"And you said I was distressing. Your dad was right. You just like showing off."

He laughed as he ran over and retrieved my stick. I liked hearing him laugh.

"Here." He placed the stick in my hand. My hand looked so small next to his, and fragile. "Form a tight fist around the end." He manipulated my fingers and I was suddenly aware of how warm his hand felt on mine. "But keep your wrist

173

flexible. It helps maximize power and penetration." He stepped away and the stick flopped between my fingers.

"This is ridiculous. It's too small to get a good grip, but a knife handle—"

"—*will* be simple once you learn how to fight with this." He finished for me. "Now—" he positioned himself a few feet away "—always keep the weapon between us. Your free hand should protect vital areas, like your heart or throat, or you can use it to distract or grapple."

I sighed with irritation and rolled my eyes.

"Now, come at me."

Crouching low, I moved opposite him, making sure to keep my stick pointed at him. His joy flowed through me despite the seriousness of his expression, and I was glad to sense his emotions again. Even though it'd only been a recent development, I'd grown use to feeling them.

I feinted with one hand and slashed the stick across his torso, trying to trap him, but he was too fast. Before I could react, he spun around and knocked my legs out from under me. My next view of him was from the ground. That was it. I yanked out my dagger, and with it came that same surge of supernatural strength.

"No." His eyes narrowed.

I crouched low, taunting him with my dagger.

"Daria, I'm serious. You'll kill yourself."

"Quit being such a baby and fight me. I'm not a little girl anymore, so stop treating me like one."

He raised both eyebrows at that.

The strange power burned through my arm, and my hand gripped the hilt with ease. It felt natural, comfortable, as if I'd trained with one my entire life. My muscles knew what to do, just like the night before when I'd thrown it at the barghest.

I charged. He looked like he was going to stand there, but just before contact he pulled his dagger. With a loud *clang* our blades slammed into each other.

Our eyes locked, just inches apart, and I had never felt more alive.

He tried to trap my dagger, but this time, I moved faster. Spinning away, I kicked out my leg, trying to unbalance him. He leapt away at the last second but I didn't miss his

174

surprise. Or was it my own surprise? It was too difficult to distinguish. He tried again, spinning around, bringing the flat side of his blade down on my back. I just managed to avoid him, rolling away and jumping back to my feet.

The surprise was his. "Did you forget to tell me Alaric's been letting you play with knives for the past three years?"

I grinned, emboldened by this strange secret knowledge of mine. We danced around each other, searching each other for vulnerabilities while trying to remain unscathed.

"Don't be easy on me." I came at him again.

He trapped my arm, but I writhed free, slashing my dagger across his front, cutting at the air as he jumped back. His eyes narrowed as he stared at the dagger in my hands.

"Let me see that." He reached for my blade.

I jumped away from him. "Come and get it." I baited.

A smile spread across his face. I knew he couldn't resist. He never could.

Our eyes locked again as our feet moved in a circle, anticipating the other's movements. As long as I could hold his gaze, I could sense his direction. But just as I sensed it, he would sense mine. He slinked around me, his steps strong yet graceful, his movements lithe as a cat.

This time, he came at me so fast it was all I could do to keep my limbs intact. He grabbed on to my free hand, spun me around, trapping me against him, and strain pulled through my shoulder. His heart pounded against my back and his ragged breath was loud in my ear. I wrapped my leg behind his, bringing us both to the ground. My dagger flew out of my hand and slid fast across the dirt. We scrambled over each other on the ground, each of us fighting to reach my lost weapon. I thought I had it, too, when I twisted his arm behind his back, but he used his legs to trap and roll me beneath him. And then he secured my arms overhead, my wrists clamped in his grip, as we gasped for air.

"Not fair." I panted, while trying not to laugh. "You're too strong."

He grinned, his chest heaving with each quick breath. "You never let my superior strength excuse you before."

I tried ignoring how close he was. "You were never that superior in strength before."

175

He leaned so close his breath warmed my lips. "Then you need to find another advantage and use it."

The green in his eyes so intense it swallowed me whole. Our faces were so close I could feel the rush of every breath he took. My blood ran hot and I suddenly felt...confused.

I didn't remember feeling like this when we fought. We'd been close before, but I didn't remember being so aware of his proximity. My mind raced against my pounding heartbeat. My eyes were trapped in his. I wanted to pull them away but I couldn't. The way his beautiful dark hair fell around his face, the strong lines of his jaw and cheekbone, the perfect shape of his full lips. I wanted to reach out and trace my fingers over them, touch his skin with...

My hands. The ones currently trapped in his grip because we were suppose to be fighting. And I was lying on the ground admiring him like a fangirl.

I had to move. I had to get away from him.

Think, Daria!

His grip on my wrists had weakened, emboldening me. It wasn't over, not yet.

I ripped one hand free, pulled a dagger from his belt and held the flat side against his throat. "How's that for an advantage?"

He blinked. Something akin to amusement flashed through his eyes then his focus returned. He shook his head, leapt off me, and pulled me to my feet. He held my hand longer than necessary before letting go.

"Not bad for your first try." He didn't meet my gaze.

I handed him back his dagger. "Not bad? Admit it. You lost to an amateur."

"Amateur?" He re-sheathed both blades. "Please. You knew what you were doing."

"What? Getting your pretty white shirt dirty? Yes, I'm a real expert." I poked his now brown tunic.

He looked back at me, his grin tight. "That's enough for one day, I think."

Without giving me the opportunity to protest, he strode off and started picking through the underbrush.

"What are you doing?" I asked.

He didn't look up. "Searching for your dagger."

Oh, yeah. That.

I didn't know what had just happened, or why in the midst of a fight, I had decided I wanted to touch his face. He was my friend, right? It was okay to acknowledge he was...decent looking. Okay, maybe he was the most gorgeous guy I'd ever seen, but that shouldn't matter. He was practically family, but as I thought over it, my stomach filled with butterflies again. He wasn't saying anything either, which didn't help matters any, and try as I might, I couldn't sense any of his feelings.

My face flushed as I went to work, pushing aside leaves, kicking aside twigs and underbrush while searching the ground. Odd, it hadn't seemed like my dagger landed that far away.

A light breeze whispered through the trees, lifting the hair off my neck and cooling the sweat on my skin. It had been invigorating, the two of us fighting. Much like it had always been. Except Alex had been a lot skinnier then and he had never made me feel so aware of myself.

And still, no dagger. I glanced over at Alex, who was picking through some of the bushes, when I heard my name.

"Daria."

It was only a whisper. I glanced back at Alex. I hadn't seen his lips move, and he certainly didn't look as if he was trying to get my attention. Thinking I'd imagined it, I went back to searching for my dagger when I heard it again.

"Daria."

"Did you hear that?" I asked.

Alex glanced over at me. "Hear what?"

"I heard someone whisper my name."

He held my gaze. "I didn't say anything."

I gazed up at the trees swaying overhead. "I know. I didn't think you had."

"Daria."

"There it is again, did you hear it?" It sounded as if it was coming from somewhere off to my left.

Alex stilled and surveyed our surroundings, looking wary.

I had to find out where the sound was coming from. Step by slow step, I began walking toward the source.

"Where are you going?"

"I have to..."

"Daria."

I walked faster.

"Daria, wait!"

And faster. I stalked forward, intent on the direction of the sound. I felt Alex's eyes on my back as he started after me, his anxiety growing. But I didn't share his anxiety. All I felt was intrigue. The voice had a hold on me and kept pulling me forward.

I rounded a large boulder and stopped. A beautiful field of flowers spread out before me, flooded with brilliant oranges and yellows and reds in the most vivid pigments I'd ever seen. Their aroma was noxious and hypnotizing, binding me like a spell. Surrounding the field was a rim of large trees, a natural barrier to the alpine garden. I'd never seen anything so beautiful or enchanting in my entire life.

"This way."

I stepped out of the forest into the sea of color, my feet disappearing beneath layers of flower petals. I walked forward, intoxicated by the life in this field. There was a power here—an ancient power—that filled every petal, every leaf, and every bit of earth.

I took another step forward. A field filled with so many lush colors should be thrumming with movement: bees, butterflies, and birds. Maybe not those creatures in this world, but something. Nothing flew in the air. Nothing disrupted the ground.

I stopped, bent over, and touched the soft petals of a red flower. It resembled a rose, except the middle was filled with a glittering gold dust that sparkled in the bright sunlight. I plucked the flower from its stem and held it before my eyes. The petals dissolved into a fine red powder and the breeze carried them out of my hand, into the air, scattering them from sight.

"Daria, don't move."

Alex stood at the ledge, his face rigid. His fear pulsed strong but I didn't understand it. This place was too magnificent to fear.

Something blurred past my vision. I stayed perfectly still searching the empty field of flowers, but I couldn't find any signs of life.

178

Then I felt it—a faint pressure on my shoulder. I turned my head slowly and froze. It was a tiny person—a girl—about the length of my index finger. She sat upon my shoulder, her legs crossed, with a shimmer covering her tiny, delicate frame. Her hair looked like long strands of silver thread and large exotic pale blue eyes gazed up at me as her translucent wings fluttered behind her. The wind rustled her silver strands so that they floated weightless in the air around her beautiful face.

I couldn't breathe. I just stared, and she stared back. Despite her size, there was an endless well of power in her. She tilted her head to one side, studying me.Then my vision went black.

Before I had time to react, my sight returned. But I wasn't looking at the beautiful garden. I was gazing out at an endless desert. The landscape was dead, the air black with smoke, and I was overcome with excruciating pain. Cries of lament wailed in my ears, ripping apart my soul, and I fought to keep from screaming. The world's pain was my pain, and it was too much to bear.

And then the scene changed.

It was Alex. He was lying on the ground, his body still and blood soaked the ground beneath him. Someone covered in armor ran to his side, their blade drenched in black blood. The person ripped off their mask, and it was me. I kneeled over Alex, frantically feeling around on his body as tears streamed down my face, and I screamed at him to wake. He didn't move, and I knew he was dead. Sorrow tore through my soul. The armored version of myself sobbed uncontrollably, choking on her breath in absolute misery as she tried to shake life into him. I wanted to die, unable to bear the sight in front of me, but I couldn't close my eyes because they weren't open.

I heard a soft whisper that seemed to come from everywhere at once. *"There shall be much violence in your future, young daughter of Alaric and Aurora. See that you are prepared, for if you are not, the world around you shall dissolve into nothing, and everything you cherish will die at your hand."*

I drew in a sharp breath. There was no pressure on my shoulder, no desolation around me, but my body was

179

moving. Someone was carrying me away from the nightmare. It was Alex.

He carried me out of the garden, beneath the shade of the trees and laid me gently on the ground as he brushed the hair back from my face. "Whatever you saw, it's not real."

I clung to his voice with everything I had. His voice was real. He was alive. Everything I'd seen and felt—the agony, his death—it was all just a dream. He was here, real, and crouched beside me. Slowly I lifted my hand to touch his cheek. His skin felt hot beneath my fingertips.

He covered my hand with his and my stomach retched.

I rolled over and the contents of my stomach spilled on the forest floor. Alex held my hair back, his other resting lightly on my back. Now I could feel his anxiety without even trying, and it was overpowering.

Once my stomach had nothing left to give, I rolled on my back, my body still shaking, and my mouth burned with the taste of acid. I was a wreck.

He searched my face, his own features strained. "Please, tell me how you're feeling."

"I'm...I feel okay. I think."

His eyes filled with doubt and his concern surged. I must've looked even worse than I felt. "Really, I'll be fine. I swear I don't feel as bad as I look."

He looked a little relieved as he tucked a strand of my hair behind my ear. "We'll stay here as long as you need."

The agony I'd felt still ached within me. I'd woken up from nightmares before. It always took a few moments for the horror to fade before I believed it wasn't real, but the memories of these visions—and the feelings—they wouldn't leave. A tear slid down my cheek.

He wiped the stray tear from my face, and glanced back in the direction from which we came. "I should've known better."

"What do you mean?"

He looked back at me with eyes full of worry. "The pixie—that creature back there. They live in the Arborenne, particularly in the Fioris."

"Fiori?"

"That garden. A few exist in this forest. They are like a sanctuary for Gaia's rare and dangerous creatures—like the pixies and that other creature on the leaf. Fioris aren't considered very safe for human travelers. When you said you heard a voice whispering your name…" His voice trailed as he shook his head. "I was foolish to put it out of my mind, but I didn't think one would be so interested in you. Not yet anyway."

"But you said you didn't hear anything."

"I didn't. You can only hear a pixie if they want you to hear them. It's the same with their visions." He leaned closer, his gaze tender. "She showed you something, didn't she?"

I shut my eyes. "It was more…a feeling." I couldn't elaborate further. Even though they were images, they were too powerful. I watched Alex die again, all over in my mind.

"They see the past, present, and future. Whatever she showed you, if it hasn't happened or isn't happening, then it will happen."

No, I refused to believe that. It wasn't possible for that much pain to exist. The world had been bleeding to death—me with it. And Alex…

"Do you want to talk about what you saw?" He placed a palm on my cheek, and his warmth brought feeling back to my limbs.

But the image of him lifeless beside me was persistent, stabbing at my insides. My throat clamped down as my eyes filled with water again. I shook my head. "Not now. I will tell you. Just…later."

He stroked my hair and waited.

We remained still and silent together, my hands in his as I lay on the ground. The pain flowing through me began to subside. It almost seemed as though Alex knew how I was feeling, as if he could feel it himself. By the expression on his face, one might've thought he'd seen it, too. Once my pain became bearable, without me saying a word of it, he let go of my hands.

My hands felt cold.

"We need to get you something to drink. Are you okay to go back?"

"Yes, and I think I'd be just fine if I never met another one of Gaia's rare and dangerous creatures again."

Alex looked past me. "Don't worry about that. I'm beginning to think you're the most rare and dangerous creature of them all."

Chapter 18

The Festival of Lights

When Alex and I returned to our temporary abode—the tree—Sonya took one look at us and leapt to her feet.

"Alexander." Sonya's hands rested on her hips. Never a good sign. "You promised me you would behave yourself."

Alex looked affronted. "Behave myself? What are you talking about?"

"Look at her!" Sonya pointed at me. "She looks like a refugee!"

"Uh, Mother, I hate to break it to you." He scratched his neck. "But that's kind of what we are."

Sonya appraised me with a frown. "I can't trust that child."

Okay, so I didn't look bad. I looked terrible. Alex handed me his canteen while gifting me with his quit-acting-so-innocent look. He used to give me that look so often I'd thought his face was stuck that way.

"Thanks," I whispered, taking the canteen from his hands. I could sort of see my reflection on the metal. There were splotches of peach, which was my skin, but it was barely visible through all the dark brown. Apparently my hair had taken over. I reached up to pat it down when I felt something thin and crunchy. A leaf, with the twig still attached.

I glared at Alex. "You could've said something!"

"Here." He grinned and he moved behind me. Right behind me. He started untangling the twig from my hair, his hands surprisingly gentle.

"Alexander." Sonya's hands hadn't abandoned their position on her hips. "I think you've done enough. I'll take it from here."

"This is ridiculous!" Alex dropped his hands and the twig fell from my head. "I didn't..."

Sonya held up a hand, looking only at me. And I took a drink of water.

"A little help here," Alex whispered in my ear with a smile in his voice.

I smiled wryly and he rolled his eyes. After almost eighteen years of knowing him, he should know better. He nudged me lightly in the ribs and I choked on my water as I laughed.

"What happened to her?" Cicero joined us, gesturing at me with a stick of charred meat in his hands.

"Your son," Sonya accused.

And now, Alex was Cicero's son.

Cicero raised a brow, taking a bite of the meat. "Alexander, what did you do?"

"Me? Might I point out that *my* clothes have taken the greater beating?" He tugged at his brown tunic.

"Your point?" Cicero asked.

Alex fought back his laughter. "Why do you always take her side?"

I took another swig from the canteen to hide my smile. It had always been like this, his parents taking my side, my dad taking his, and neither of us missed the opportunity to let the other suffer. Ever.

"When you stop being the culprit, we'll take your side." Sonya folded her arms.

Alex shook his head. He leaned close to me then, his lips brushing my ear. "I *will* get you back for this. And that's a promise."

There was a smile in his eyes that made my heart skip a beat. He walked over to the tree trunk and sat, sharpening one of his daggers.

When I looked back, Sonya and Cicero were studying me. After Alex's last comment, I didn't feel the need to hurry to clear his reputation, so I took another sip from my canteen. It still tasted bad, but eventually started tasting less like puke and more like water.

My "nice" side soon found its voice and decided to liberate my resurrected friend. Well, in my own way. "Don't worry." I cleared my throat. "Alex did exactly what you asked him to do, but the problem is—" I grinned at him over my shoulder "—I'm still better than he is."

184

His gaze lifted to mine. Challenge flashed through his eyes as a smile spread across his face and he went back to sharpening his knives.

When I turned back to Sonya, she looked skeptical. Her gaze halted at my shoulder and her brows knit together. She hurried toward me and touched my shoulder. When she pulled her hand away, something glittered on her fingertips. "What's this?"

Glitter? Where had that come from? Oh, maybe..."I wonder if that's from the pixie."

Cicero stopped chewing. Sonya went perfectly still, her eyes burning holes through her son. Alex leaned back on his arms, and glared up at the tree.

Apparently, I wasn't supposed to share that information.

"You saw a pixie," Sonya whispered.

Alex moved his glare to me and I swallowed.

What? I mouthed.

He answered with a tidal wave of irritation.

"You were in a Fiori?" Cicero's anger sawed through me.

Alex moved his gaze to his father. "Yes."

"And you let her near one?" Cicero was so mad his ears turned red and a thick blue vein bulged at the side of his neck.

"It wasn't—"

"Do you have any idea what could have happened?"

Alex's gaze was steady as he held his father's. "Yes, I'm very well aware—"

"To let her wander into such a place—really, Alexander, I'm surprised..."

Sonya placed a hand on her husband's arm. "Dear."

But Cicero wasn't finished. "Of all the—"

"Cicero."

This time Cicero heard her. Slowly, he removed his death glare from his son and looked at his wife.

Sonya held his gaze. "They're obviously unharmed, and you know he would *never* let anything happen to her."

Her eyes flickered to Alex, and I thought I saw something pass between them.

"I don't care." Cicero was still mad, but the fury was fading. "The fact remains that he—"

"It was my fault," I interrupted.

185

I looked back at Alex. His expression filled with warning, but I ignored it. I couldn't let him get in so much trouble for something I'd done, and besides, I'd never seen Cicero this angry before. It was beyond fun and games now. Alex and I had just become friends again and I wasn't about to let Cicero ruin it.

"Alex tried to stop me but I—"

"Nothing happened." Alex's tone silenced me.

I caught his gaze and held it before he turned back to his dad. "We saw a pixie flutter by and I pulled her out of the garden before anything happened. Some of the dust must have landed on her, that's all. I won't let it happen again."

Cicero and Sonya's confusion was strong as they looked to me for confirmation. I wasn't sure why Alex lied, but his gaze was so intense and his apprehension so strong, I slowly nodded.

Cicero's fury disintegrated. Alex's masked his feelings from me once again and he went back to sharpening his daggers. Cicero sighed, and the color of his ears returned to normal. "Sonya, I'm glad we never had a daughter. It's hard enough worrying about Daria. Alaric had better take over soon because I'm about to leave her to the fates." Cicero grinned at me.

For some reason, his grin made me mad. As if a smile would erase everything they were hiding, like their smiles always had. Like they were still doing. Sonya must have noticed because she felt the need to remind me Cicero was only teasing.

Good to know. I mean, for a second there I thought Cicero was going to march me right back to those barghests with a bow on my head.

I dug into my meat, trying to forget my anger. The flavor was smoky and sweet on my tongue, its juice dripping liberally into my mouth. I'd forgotten all about my hunger in my evening with Alex, Nightmare, and Lies, and now I was ravenous.

"I suppose that's the first magical creature you've seen, isn't it?" Sonya said, picking up a stick of seared meat for herself.

I swallowed my bite. "The pixie?" I wasn't about to mention our dear friend Deadly Slinky after how they'd

186

reacted to the pixie. Alex was already in enough trouble, and I wasn't sure I could handle the amount of retribution I was accruing.

"Yes." Cicero wiped a drop of oil from his chin.

"I guess so," I said. "Are they all so psychotic?"

Cicero chuckled. "They're all slightly bizarre. Magical creatures have a unique bond to the power within Gaia, which lends them access to knowledge and abilities we don't have. They also aren't limited by our laws of nature, so some may live hundreds of years. Mind you—" he took another bite "—most magic folk think our limited lifespan a waste of natural resources, so they care little for us. Most of them avoid us by living inside this forest." He looked up at the treetops as if he expected them to be hiding something.

"The barghests…they're magical?"

"Yes, but barghests are created from shadow," Cicero replied. "The forces they draw upon are dark—Gaia's antithesis—and she has no control over them. But the pixies belong to Gaia."

How comforting.

The barghests had never struck me as the kind of creature you'd put on a leash and walk through the park anyway. But pixies? If they belonged to Gaia, and Gaia had control over them, I didn't think I liked Gaia very much.

"Pixies are remarkable creatures," Sonya said. "They can see the past, present, and future and they share some of those visions with humans, though it's rare. Their visions have always proven true and it's considered a great honor to receive one."

I almost choked on my bite. Honor? I wondered if she'd feel the same way if they showed her that "honorable vision" of her dying son. Even as I thought about it, the horror and agony began to resurface. The image of Alex flashed through my mind and my heart ached. I turned back to my dinner, feeling the weight of Alex's gaze.

Cicero continued. "I haven't heard of an account for years. Even so, the only time most people ever see a pixie is at the Festival, and pixies rarely attend that."

I swallowed my bite. "What Festival?"

Sonya exchanged a quick glance with her husband. "Every seven years," she answered, "Valdon hosts the Festival

187

of Lights. It is a commemoration for a war fought centuries ago. The Festival is the one time the magical creatures join us. Like Cicero already said, these days they don't bother with human affairs, but on that day, many of them celebrate with us."

"Which war are you talking about? One of Earth's wars?"

"Spirits, no," Cicero answered. "Earth would have crumbled beneath such raw power. When Gaia took her powers from Earth, she brought another with her, a malevolent one."

"Wait a minute. If she left Earth to create her version of a perfect world, why would she do that?"

"She didn't have a choice. This evil is also a magical being, and when Gaia took all that was magical, it all came: the good, the terrible, and everything in between. In order to keep her world safe, she banished him to a spirit realm so he was unable to physically harm a living soul."

"He?"

"Mortis."

A stiff breeze blew by and the light of our low fire flickered.

Cicero took a deep breath and continued. "He's not a physical being, but his powers can reach through the barrier into this world. Creatures like the barghest belong to him. Some people try to tap in to his power, but serving the dark always ends in death because the dark is never satisfied. It always tries to gather more souls, which is what happened during the battle over whose victory we now celebrate."

Here Cicero paused, but I didn't question him. I was too curious to hear more.

"Many years ago, Mortis found one such soul to possess—one who would do his work for him on the surface. Mortis abhors his prison and has tried escaping ever since Gaia sent him there. This man was given Mortis' power and strength to control armies in an attempt to destroy Gaia and break down the barrier.

"But Gaia also found a man to trust, someone called Galahad. She entrusted a great shield to him, one that harnessed the power of the elementals."

"Elementals?"

188

"Yes, just as you would think. Air, water, fire, earth. All can take physical shape in this world. They are the most ancient and strongest of the powers and once that shield was created, man was able to channel their power. Hence, Galahad was given the power of Gaia."

"Well, that seems like an unfair advantage."

"Galahad didn't win the war."

"But with that much power, how—"

"I was getting to that." He smiled. "Always impatient. When Galahad took up the shield and channeled its power, it defiled him. Sometimes great power brings out the worst in us and, unfortunately, it isn't until people are given it that we see the true shades of their character.

"What ended the war was the death of Mortis' chosen agent. Gaia was lucky Mortis' agent was weak. He was killed while the world was deciding how to hide from Galahad. At that point Gaia destroyed the shield by tearing it into pieces. The very action killed Galahad. Stories say his screams of agony were heard in all the lands, even on Earth."

That sounded...painful. "So the destruction of the shield freed Gaia of evil?"

"The shield wasn't destroyed."

"But you said—"

"It was torn to pieces. Seven, to be exact. There is an order in this world called the Keepers of Light and their members are called Dalorens. The Dalorens have access to magic no others can use, and it is the Dalorens who used magic to protect the seven pieces. Gaia couldn't destroy the shield without destroying her world, since they represented a physical embodiment of her powers and the elementals. The Dalorens placed magic on the pieces, each piece holding power that belonged to the whole and can only be activated by a rightful lord. Once all the lords unite, they could select one to rule sovereign amidst them. It was a way to share the power without one man having too much."

So. Much. Information. I sat for a moment rubbing my temples, mulling over everything Cicero had said. A war, magic, elements, pieces of some shield being protected by some special group of magicians until some rightful lord came along. And I'd thought Earth was a crazy place. "There are seven lords?"

189

"Six," Sonya answered this time.

Arg. "You specifically said—"

"The seventh has been a mystery for over a century. Pendel's territory."

The image of the tattered banner in the shadows at Rex Cross flitted through my mind. "Pendel has no lord then?"

"A steward governs Pendel in lieu of its rightful lord. Rumor has it only the Dalorens know the location of that missing bloodline."

"This shield isn't currently active?"

"Correct," Cicero answered.

"Then how does Gaia have a king without all seven lords present?"

"How indeed," Alex murmured.

I realized I hadn't heard the sound of Alex's scraping for a while. When I looked back at him, his expression was all hard lines.

"Alexander." Cicero warned.

Alex shoved his dagger into its sheath and joined the horses.

"The people—" Sonya's eyes followed her son "—needed a ruler. Too many years passed without one and society crumbled. So they elected King Darius. He was the strongest, most able of the lords, so the decision was simple."

"Simple?" Alex said with his back to us while scratching Parsec's nose. "He all but forced the position."

Cicero's intake of air was sharp but Alex didn't show any signs of acknowledgement.

"Why didn't someone just ask these Dalorens who the seventh heir was so they could choose a rightful leader?" I asked.

"The Dalorens are dangerous." Cicero answered. "Their access to knowledge has granted them access to rare powers. They also happen to pride themselves in exclusivity and none who have gone seeking them out have ever returned."

"Not to mention—" Alex turned around and looked pointedly at his father "—*someone* has convinced the world we don't need that knowledge."

"What Alexander fails to acknowledge is King Darius protects the people from evil. It is his power that protects our physical and metaphysical boundaries. You can't have a world without order, and King Darius is a fair and just ruler."

"If it helps him to be." Alex smarted.

Cicero frowned his son. What was Alex's problem?

"Not everyone is pleased with King Darius these days," Sonya interjected. "There's been severe drought in Lord Tosca's territory. The people there are farmers and provide most of our food."

Lord Tosca, Lord Tosca...where had I heard that name? I glanced back at Alex and met his gaze briefly before he looked away. Wait. Lord Tosca was the guy Cicero wanted Alex to work for. The one who lived farthest away. My stomach flopped. Alex glanced back at me, inquiring, and I looked away.

"The people need someone to blame, like people usually do," Sonya continued. "And leaders are the easiest targets."

"That's because leaders are usually the ones with enough influence to do anything," Alex said.

"That doesn't make it his fault, Alexander."

"And what of all the rumors about gargon raids?" Alex stepped forward. "For all his protection and power, the king has done nothing to investigate."

"Alexander, mind your tongue," Cicero's tone was low.

"Gargons?" I asked.

Alex stopped pacing and held my gaze. "Dragons."

My jaw dropped. "Dragons? They're real?"

"It isn't possible," Cicero said through clenched teeth. "If gargons had been unleashed, we would've seen them by now."

Dragons.

They existed. No way. This I had to see.

"Brilliant." Alex glared at his father. "So we'll just wait for an attack like you waited for the barghests."

"Not another word, Alexander." Cicero's gaze did not falter as he stared down his son.

Alex's fury burned hotter than our crackling fire. I'd never seen him argue with his father like this. Actually, never—not in all my years of knowing him—had I seen him this angry. And if I knew anything about Alex, his anger was never unwarranted.

I wanted to talk to him without Cicero and Sonya around to get a more holistic picture of this almighty king. But at this rate, Alex was going to earn himself nothing short of dismemberment. I thought I'd better step in and change the subject.

"So when is this grand Festival?" I asked.

The blanket of tension slowly lifted. Cicero looked at me, and the creases in his face faded along with Alex's rage. Good, it was working.

"Actually, it's happening this very year, on November sixth."

"But that's..." My birthday.

Sonya smiled. "Yes, we know."

"It technically starts on your birthday," Cicero continued, "but the games don't begin until the seventh and then continue for seven days. People travel from all over Gaia to celebrate. It's the one time we all get along." He grinned. "Even your father isn't as argumentative."

My heart sank. "I guess my dad's been?" It was a silly question to ask—I already knew the answer. But it was just one more thing I'd been left out of, something else they'd done while I'd been twiddling my thumbs alone in Middle of Nowhere, California.

Sonya smiled at me in an attempt to be encouraging. "You'll be going this year."

Great, well, that fixed everything.

"Convenient timing if you ask me," Cicero added. "The best way for you to meet the people in this world—including the Great Lords."

Even better.

I didn't want to meet any all-powerful lord of anything. What I wanted was to find my dad so that I could get some answers and move on with my life.

"Oh, yes, the Festival is exciting," Cicero continued. "The décor, the competitions, the dancing." Cicero flicked his hand in the air, and then looked at his son with a mischievous grin. He must have forgotten his anger. "Alexander is looking forward to the dancing aspect in particular, I think."

That got my attention. I turned around and caught Alex's gaze. "You...know how to dance?" I teased.

Alex's eyes held warning, and then he sat beside me and watched the fire. He was so close I could smell the forest on his clothing.

Alex dancing? I wondered if he was any good, which made me picture Alex in a tux twirling in circles to the sound of violins. The mental picture made me snort out loud.

He turned to look at me, the challenge returning to his eyes. "Don't even think about it."

I grinned. "Already did."

"Oh?" A grin twitched at his lips. "And how did I look?"

"Humiliating."

He smiled and I suddenly couldn't breathe.

Snap out of it!

His brow had risen while I'd been stuck staring at him like an idiot. I looked away before I made a bigger fool of myself, but I could feel his eyes on me still.

"Dear." Sonya grinned at her husband. "You used to step on my feet all the time."

Cicero chuckled. "True, and Vera did tell me the other day that Alex's improvements are remarkable, well, for him. She's been able to keep her toenails during practice, not that she cares for them."

Every other word faded as my ears zeroed in on one: Vera.

"Vera," Sonya laughed. "Did you write her back? Before we left?" She was looking at Alex expectantly.

And Alex poked at the fire with one of his daggers. "Didn't have time."

He looked...uncomfortable.

"What's the punishment for that, then?" Cicero grinned. "Twenty lashes? You must be the only man in Gaia who isn't afraid to make her mad."

"Alex is also the only man in Gaia who *can* make her mad." Sonya grinned.

I suddenly felt sick.

Chapter 19

Competition is Ugly

I peeked back at Alex to find him studying me. His face was unreadable and my heart beat faster, so I looked back at the ground. A pit began forming inside of me, attempting to punch itself through my stomach lining. What was wrong with me? I didn't even know her and I didn't like her. Who was she? What did she look like? Were they good friends? It hadn't occurred to me that Alex might be...dating. The thought never even crossed my mind, and now it was there, forcing every other thought out of it.

"I'm done," I said. "Does anyone want the rest of this?"

"You've barely touched it. Come on." Cicero waved at me. "Eat a little more."

"No, really, I'm full. I'll toss it in the fire if no one wants it."

Cicero looked skeptical, but when he realized I really was done, he reached out and took the meat from my hands.

I didn't speak much the rest of the evening. I doubted Cicero and Sonya thought much of it, distracted with their memories of past festivals. Alex stayed seated beside me, but he didn't say much. Sometimes, he would chuckle or comment at something his parents said. Other times, his curiosity would poke at me, but I never turned to look directly at him. I was too afraid he would see right through me—see how I was feeling. And I knew how I was feeling was ridiculous.

Alex could do whatever he wanted, talk to whomever he wanted, even date whomever he wanted.

But why wouldn't he say anything to me about it?

Why do you think you have a right to know?

Round and round went my thoughts. Until someone mentioned Stefan.

194

"Hey, has Stefan mentioned anything about Dad?" I asked. I wasn't sure, but everyone looked a little uncomfortable.

"No," Sonya answered.

No. That was it. Just no.

One full day, a barghest attack, Alex gets poisoned, and nothing. I didn't believe her. Not one bit. "What do you mean, no? Shouldn't he be on his way by now?"

"We're still waiting for him at Amadis as planned," Cicero answered, his words guarded. Too guarded. "And with our small detour, he may even beat us."

They were hiding something and after the little Vera incident, I was so not in the mood for this. "How can you be sure if he hasn't said anything? Maybe you missed something. Can I see the book?" I held out my hand.

Cicero and Sonya exchanged a glance. Alex was quiet beside me.

"Maybe later," Sonya said.

I dropped my hand. "What happened?"

"Nothing has happened," Sonya answered a little too quickly.

"How do you know? You haven't heard from him, so you can't know that."

"If—" her eyes bore into mine "—Stefan thought Alaric was in the smallest threat of danger, he would send guards. I promise you that. Please be patient. It's only a few more days until your father can explain."

As much as I didn't want to hear it, it was the same thing I'd known all along. I was supposed to bide my time until Dad could explain the rest. No matter how much I wanted answers now, the Del Contes were under oath. These were the consequences I'd accepted without thinking through my decision. This was my punishment.

As I sat, wallowing in self-pity, Cicero declared it was time for bed and Sonya kissed my forehead goodnight. She worried for me—I could feel it writhing inside of her.

"May I speak with you a moment?" Cicero's eyes locked on his son.

A storm of apprehension and frustration passed over me as Alex stood and joined his dad. The two of them walked past our ring of light and into the forest. They didn't go far. I

195

could still hear their voices, but most of their words were too soft to distinguish.

Alex's frustration surged so strong that even from this distance it was hard to separate his frustration from mine.

"—I'm concerned," I heard Cicero say.

"You think I don't know that?" Alex spat. "Not once have you stopped reminding me."

"Remember your place," Cicero answered, and I heard nothing more.

When they returned, Cicero was distracted with thought, and Alex's features steeled. As Cicero walked passed me, he gave me a weak smile, then joined his wife in their bed of blankets. Alex, however, sat beside me at the fire, but he sat a little farther away this time. He kept his face from me, his gaze intent on the flames.

"Are you okay?" I whispered.

At first, I thought he hadn't heard, but then he glanced sideways at me. "Fine." His expression was distant, just like it'd been years ago before he vanished from my life, and it hurt.

"Don't lie to me, Alex."

He held my gaze. There was pain in his, a deep-rooted pain I didn't understand, and he turned his attention back to the fire. "I'll *be* fine."

I glanced at Cicero, whose breathing was already even beneath his blankets.

"What was that about?" I asked. "Not this afternoon, I hope?"

A low sigh escaped his lips. "Partially. But, it's nothing you need to worry about. I can handle it."

He was building a wall again. "I didn't ask if you could handle it." I forced my voice to stay low. "We're friends. I'd like to understand, unless you changed your mind."

"Daria." He met my gaze. "I'm not..." He took a deep breath and closed his eyes for a moment. When they opened, there was something sad in them. "He was just reminding me to...adjust my attitude. He thinks I need to be a better influence." One corner of his lips turned upward.

"As if that ever mattered."

196

"You don't have to remind me." He tossed another log on the fire. Sparks flew as flames licked around the fresh offering.

"Sorry about earlier." I said. "I didn't realize Cicero would get so mad."

"It's just as much my fault. I forgot to warn you, but I don't think it would matter. If my parents had had the choice, they would've given me away long ago and adopted you."

I smiled. "My dad's the same way with me—always taking your side."

"Seems Alaric is the only one with any brains."

I was about to ask him why he didn't want his parents knowing about the pixie when Alex turned to look at me. The way the light warmed his skin, the way it reflected in his eyes. My heart sputtered in my chest and I had to look back at the fire to calm myself.

But calm had been completely overthrown. Nervousness had turned tyrannical, massacring all of my other emotions and simultaneously throwing all of my words out of my brain leaving them in broken bits somewhere inside of me.

What is wrong with you?

"What's wrong?" he whispered.

I had no idea, but I had a sneaking suspicion that once I found out the answer, I wouldn't be so eager to share it with him. "Nothing."

I felt his eyes on me as I fought to master my nerves. A few silent moments passed before I gathered myself and was able speak. I also tried keeping the times my eyes found his to a minimum. "Why did you lie to your parents about the pixie?"

He stared at the fire. "I saw how it affected you and I didn't think you would want to talk about it."

That was it? That was...thoughtful. "Thanks. I didn't." I paused. "But, I'll tell you now...if you still want to know."

He didn't look at me. "Only if you want."

I recounted both visions to him in detail, fighting against the emotions that threatened to return, but I left out the extent of my agonizing over his death. That, I felt, was a little too personal. His face didn't change as he listened.

197

When I was done, he grabbed my hand in between both of his, and though his lips were grinning, his eyes were not. "That's terrible."

"I know, so why are you smiling about it?"

He brushed a strand of hair from my face, his fingers lingering for a moment. "No wonder you don't care to meet another magical creature."

"But, what does it mean?" I tried ignoring the feel of his fingers on my skin.

He peered off into the forest. "I've no idea. But..." He looked back at me. "I don't think you need to worry about killing me. Unless you grow two feet and gain some serious muscle mass."

I chuckled, shaking my head.

He let go of my hand and leaned back on his arms, watching the fire. Despite his attempt at making light of my vision, I could feel that it bothered him. "Maybe next time they'll show me a vision of you dancing. I can only imagine how catastrophic that would look."

He tilted his head and looked back at my face, his suspicion strong. "Are you...jealous?"

"Don't be ridiculous." I answered a little too quickly.

He smirked. "I think you are."

"I am not." My body felt warm all over. "Why would I be jealous of your bad dancing?"

There was a gleam in his eyes that didn't come from the fire. "You know that's not what I'm talking about."

Of course I knew, but if he thought I was going to talk to him about it he had another thing coming. He was my friend. I had no right to care about his love life. But I did. I couldn't stand not knowing, and there was no way I was going to ask.

I glared at the fire as Alex's amusement poured through me.

That was it.

"I'm going to bed." I got to my feet.

His gaze followed me, but he said nothing. He knew what was wrong with me. He knew what was wrong and wasn't saying a word to deny it. It felt as if someone was squeezing my stomach into a pulp.

"See you in the morning." I spun around and walked to my blankets, feeling his eyes on my back.

198

"Daria..."

I kept walking. "Alex, it's fine. You don't have to explain..."

"Daria..."

This time I paused but didn't turn. The night listened as I waited. I heard him sigh.

"Good night," he said.

Without answering, I lay down, pulled the blankets overhead, and closed him from view.

I woke shaking, startled from my dream of Alex lying dead on the ground, me sobbing hysterically over him.

I sat up. All that was left of our fire were glowing embers. The night around me was thick with shadows. The Del Contes were all in a deep sleep, and Cicero's heavy breathing sounded particularly loud in the silence.

A glow off in the distance caught my eye. It was a faint white halo, floating in the shadows a few yards from where I sat.

"Follow me," a sharp whisper sounded in my ear.

I started and looked around me. Nothing but shadows, and the Del Contes all had their eyes closed.

My breathing quickened.

"There is something I must show you."

The voice was in my head.

"Daria, you cannot trust them," the whisper continued, the light pulsing with each word. *"Your entire life they have lied to you. They keep things from you still, and now they refuse to tell you about your father."*

I jumped to my feet as the halo floated away from me, deeper into the dark woods.

"Yes, I know where he is and what has happened to him. Your companions don't want to tell you. There are many secrets they continue to keep—many dangerous secrets. Listen to your heart. You already know you cannot trust them, and I cannot tell you with them near."

The light was moving away fast. Fear and curiosity battled within me, each fighting for dominion, but curiosity won. I had to know. And whoever—or whatever—was trying to get my attention knew about my past. Which also meant it

199

was feasible they knew about my present. My alternative had presented itself earlier than expected.

I glanced back, making sure the Del Contes were still asleep, and tiptoed after the light into utter darkness.

Chapter 20

Misleadings

The light moved fast. I stumbled over roots, grabbing low hanging vines for support as it pressed on.

"Who are you?" I asked, now well out of range of the Del Contes.

It was silent, a white orb swimming through black, and then it stopped. Something cold touched upon my senses and the light disintegrated, leaving me in total darkness.

Alone.

I gripped the handle of my dagger and pulled it free. My breath was the only sound in the night. A puff of stale air, cold as death, tickled my neck. I jerked my blade around. "Who's there?"

Something chuckled a few yards away. The sound was deep and gurgling.

"That was almost too simple," hissed a bone-chilling voice.

"What do you want?"

The voiced paused. "It is incredible how much trust you've put into those who continue lying to you."

"What are you talking about?"

"Your...*friends*." The word was filled with loathing. "They've led you here," the hiss continued, now on my other side. "In a direction opposite your father. All your life they've lied to you and are lying to you still, yet you do not question them."

"Who are you?" I wanted to believe he was lying. I needed to believe.

"Haven't you questioned them and this power they worship? It isn't as good and pure as they would have you believe. How could it be when its followers are forced to lie to those they hold dear? How can a power so good and pure enable such corruption and tyranny? The one I serve is greater. He can give you the answers you seek. He can give you power so that no one—not even your companions—will dare lie to you again. Take your future into your own hands. Do not trust it with them."

Each word cut through me like a blade because each word was true. "What do you want?" My dagger trembled.

A light breeze rustled the trees above.

A distorted human face appeared. His skin looked as if it was made of dirt, cracked and dry like the ground when it hasn't seen water. His eyes were orange and cat-like, and he had no nose, just two fine slits. His lipless mouth smiled, revealing a row of spaced, pointed dagger-like teeth, and its tall, cloaked form hovered over me with breath that smelled of decaying flesh.

I opened my mouth to scream but no sound came. My dagger burned in my hands, bringing me back to life. I lashed out, slashing across his torso, but he vanished and appeared on my other side faster than I could blink. Horrified, I tightened my grip on the handle when a bolt of blue light shot past me.

Fury filled his orange cat-like eyes and a low growl rumbled from his chest. He leapt straight into the air, cloak whipping after him, out of sight. A ball of green light exploded from the trees, arcing into the darkness beyond. Another bolt of blue light twisted above from somewhere close, stretching its blue fingers high into the tree, illuminating the silhouette of my attacker.

My feet were stuck in place as I tried making sense of what was happening. Bright lines of light streaked through the darkness—green, blue—each vying for dominance. Whatever had led me here was producing the green. So who—or what—was making the blue?

Before I could find out, something clamped around my wrists.

I tried to break free but it was like trying to pull off my own arm. Someone was dragging me away from the battle of blue and green lightning, farther into the shadows. Another streak of blue light flashed and I saw my captor's orange cat-like eyes glaring at me.

There were two of them.

I flexed and twisted to free my wrists but his grip was like iron. "Let go!"

He just pulled me after him.

With all the force I could muster, I kicked out my leg and struck him hard in the back. My leg jarred as it made contact, sharp pain shooting up my shin. I might as well have kicked a rock. My joints burned and my leg throbbed, and the pain I felt was all mine. None of it belonged to the creature. I couldn't even detect the slightest discomfort. He just pulled and pulled and pulled, leading me farther away from the battle. What was this thing?

My dagger singed my palm again. Heat spread through my blood, bringing life back to my aching limbs, and this time when I twisted my wrist, I broke free.

Everything slowed and my senses sharpened.

The light overhead froze mid-arc and my captor's face was stuck in ugly surprise. Gripping my dagger, I slashed across his arm, freeing my other wrist. Surprise and pain jolted through me as he let go.

Light shot from his hands, but the light came slowly, creeping forward as my blade rose to meet it. The burst of energy hit the metal with a spark and deflected into the trees in a hundred directions. Another bolt of light came and I rolled toward the creature. The light singed the place I'd stood only a moment ago. I leapt to my feet and thrust the blade up into the creature and a burst of pain shot through my ankles.

My legs were yanked out from under me and I slammed to the ground, hard. I choked on my breath as I fought to move, but my legs were stuck together. A thick root had snaked around my ankles and pulled tight. I hacked at it, chopping away as hard as I could, but my dagger didn't even make a scratch. The creature grabbed my feet and started pulling again, the rest of me dragging after him.

I slashed at the air, screaming at the monster. Light flashed above and I saw another shadow move from the trees.

My heart sunk. Another one? I'd never escape.

There was a burst of white light so bright I was blinded. The grip around my ankles vanished and the light dimmed to black. Flames exploded, filling the night with smoke and fumes, engulfing my captor. His agony and fury powered through my body as I struggled to get away.

Sweat dripped into my eyes from the heat as I pulled myself from the flames, dragging my legs behind me. The fire suddenly disappeared, as if someone snuffed it out, and everything returned to darkness.

"Daria!"

It was Alex. I couldn't see him, but within seconds his hands found my shoulders and he was trying to get me to stand.

"I can't. My ankles are tied."

He was quiet, his mind racing, then I felt his resolve. "Don't move an inch."

"Okay."

The sword in his hands started glowing white.

"Daria..." He leaned closer to me, his eyes shining from the glow of his sword. "I'm serious. You can't move."

I held his gaze. "I won't. Promise."

Satisfied, he took a deep breath and stepped away, focusing on my ankles. He raised his sword and looked back at me with a warning so strong I might've been scared if I wasn't in such pain from the thing binding my legs.

The sword flashed and he brought it down in a white blur. The root snapped and fizzled, and the shards wriggled and writhed back into the earth. He dropped his weapon to the ground and crouched at my side. "Did they hurt you?"

I wiggled my ankles and flinched. "Not too bad. I'll live."

The glow from his sword faded. "Come on, I'll help you up."

"I don't need help." I tried pushing myself to stand, but the pain in my ankles was too much.

"Let me guess." He ignored me and wrapped his arm tightly around my waist. "You have everything under control?"

His breath tickled my ear and I swallowed. "Yes."

He helped me to my feet, and I was thankful for the dark because I could feel my cheeks burning.

Pain ripped through my ankles and legs and I stumbled. Alex held me tighter so I didn't fall, and I bit my lip, fighting back tears. My ankles were sprained, badly. Come to think of it, breaking them might have been less painful.

Alex slowly sat me back down. "Looks like I'll have to carry you."

No way. "I'm fine."

"Yeah, you look fine."

"Just...give me a minute, okay?"

He sat himself beside me, our sides touching.

I felt his curiosity. He wanted to know what I was doing out here. He wanted to know why I'd left, but for some reason, he didn't ask. His hesitation pulsed as strongly as the burning sensation in my ankles, but before he said a word, something snapped a few yards away.

My heart sunk. Not another one.

Alex leapt to his feet, sword in hand. "Don't move," he whispered.

As if that was an option.

A tiny light appeared, hovering in midair. Standing just a few feet away from it was an old man. His hair hung long and straight and white at his sides, and his wrinkly forehead wrinkled further in curiosity as his clear blue eyes stared at the pair of us.

This man had saved me. He had been the one who had produced the blue light. I didn't know how I knew that, but I knew it with certainty.

Alex stood over me, blade ready, as the man approached. The man halted one small step before the tip of Alex's sword.

"Who are you?" Alex growled.

"Great mages, young man, do you always introduce yourself like this?" The man's voice was raspy, but not threatening, as if he spoke too much and his vocal chords were wearing out. "I warn you, it will never encourage friendliness."

Alex pushed the blade toward the man's throat, creating a dimple. "Answer me before I kill you."

I started. Alex? Kill someone? "Alex." I touched his leg. "I think this man helped me before you came."

His blade didn't lower. "Then explain what you're doing here."

The old man smiled. It was a smile that made you feel like you could tell this man anything in the world, and he would protect you. "Our aims aren't so different, Alexander Del Conte. Like you, I want only her safety."

Alex's eyes narrowed. "How do you know my name?"

"I know many things about you, dear boy, but I must admit that I don't particularly enjoy friendly discourse when one has a sword at my throat."

Alex lowered his sword, but not his scrutiny.

The man rubbed his neck and turned to me. "Now, that wasn't so hard, was it?"

"Tell me your name before I change my mind," Alex said.

The old man gave a slight bow and his long, white hair hung in a curtain around his face. "Tran Chiton, or more commonly known as the Black Bard."

I couldn't believe it. Thad hadn't been telling stories.

"That's not possible," Alex whispered.

"I assure you, it is."

"You're real, then?" I asked.

The man laughed, a light melodic laugh. "I certainly hope so."

"Thank the elements she's safe!" Cicero arrived out of breath with Sonya sprinting through the forest right behind him.

They both stopped in their tracks and Sonya looked as if she'd just seen a ghost. "Master Tran?"

Alex's attention snapped to his mom. "You know this man?"

Sonya walked to Tran with a light in her eyes. She stopped a few feet before him and threw her arms around him.

"Careful, dear Sonya." The man chuckled. "My bones aren't what they once were. My spine upsets easily these days."

Sonya backed away with the smile of a little girl spread across her face. Alex looked between his mom and the old man. Cicero stood back just as baffled.

"I can't believe it's you!" she said. "You're really—"

"Now, now, there's time for this later. We must see to the girl." The man stared at my ankles as if he was deciding what ankles were used for.

Sonya looked down at my legs. "What's wrong?"

"I think her ankles are broken," Alex answered for me.

Sonya crouched at my side and placed a hand gently on my ankles. She took a deep breath and looked back at me with a frown.

"There was some kind of root wrapped around them," I said. "I don't think they're broken, just sprained."

"We'll see about that." She pressed gently on my ankles and I cried out in pain.

"And what, exactly, were you doing out here?" Cicero asked.

Everyone was looking at me for my answer, and I looked down. "I don't know what happened." I couldn't tell them what that creature said. I was still sorting it out myself. "I went...for a walk, and— "

"It seems Daria was lured away," the old man answered.

I studied his wrinkled face. "How do you...know my name?"

He smiled, waving a withered hand. "I've followed you for quite some time, and those pariahs have been following your trail ever since you entered the Arborenne. They may be cursed but they're not fools, being outnumbered by such a talented escort. They tried luring her away from your protection to take her to Gaia knows where. I've been waiting for them to do it. Would have had them too if they weren't so skilled at that 'vanishing back into the earth' act." He sounded personally offended by this.

Tran stepped past our group and knelt beside a pile of ashes—all that remained of the creature. His brow furrowed as his hands sifted through the debris and he stopped. Inch by inch he drew out a golden chain until it ended in a round metal object. It was a medallion.

Runes were engraved on the surface, and it looked just like the medallion the Del Contes had used to transport themselves to my home in Fresno. Was that only a few days ago? It seemed like ages.

"A magical device?" I asked.

"Yes, and your intended transport, I believe." The man gazed at the object, deep in thought. "Here, Aegis Cicero, I believe I will leave this in your possession. Perhaps it will aid you in your investigations."

"Shouldn't you keep it?" Cicero asked. "With your power, you could destroy the problem now."

207

Tran rubbed his chin, head tilted as he studied the object. "No, I doubt this will lead us straight to our man. Better to keep it safe for now. Once we know more, you can use it. Until then, it isn't safe and your lives are too valuable to put at such risk—especially hers."

Everyone seemed to agree with his answer.

"Thank you, Master Tran." Cicero took the medallion and tucked it in his pocket. "I'll wait and see what Alaric thinks we should do with it."

Tran nodded in agreement.

"There were two of them. Where's the other?" Alex studied the shadows.

"I'm afraid he got away." The old man stood to his feet. "Which means whoever—or whatever—they serve will soon be aware of my existence, which is rather unfortunate. I do enjoy having most of the realm thinking I'm dead." He grinned, glancing into the night. "But come. Currently, my home isn't far from here, and I insist you stay with me tonight. After so many years, I know there is much to discuss."

"I'm sure there is." Cicero glanced at his wife.

Sonya smiled. Whatever doubts Cicero had about this man's true identity, Sonya's complete confidence swayed them. But they didn't sway Alex's. His grip was still tight on my shoulder, so tight, in fact, it was starting to hurt. "She still can't walk."

"Right, right," Tran said, frowning at my leg. "Skinny things, I'm surprised they get you anywhere really. We'll have to fix your ankles at the house. Terribly young to have such health problems. Alexander? How about carrying our invalid?"

Not this again. "I don't need anyone to—"

"To do what, child?" Tran asked. "Carry you? Did that root wrap around your brain? You can't walk! No, no, let Alexander be a gentlemen. I'm sure he doesn't get much of an opportunity with a spirit like yours."

Well, if he was trying to gain Alex's trust, it worked. Alex's amusement was already filtering through me, but at least his grip on my shoulder ceased.

Thunder clashed overhead and the breeze stirred.

208

Calyx. He would be furious if I left him alone in this. "What about the horses?" I asked.

"Grool will fetch them for you," Tran answered.

My hearing must've been affected during their fight with colored laser beams because I thought he said "drool." "Who?" I asked.

"You'll meet him soon enough. Come, come, the rain will be here any moment. You can't come down with a cold on top of broken bones. Then our dear Alexander would have to spoon-feed you, and I know how much you would *love* that."

Alex raked a hand through his hair and Tran's smile spread from ear to ear. I suddenly wasn't sure if I liked this old man.

Alex crouched beside me and slid one arm around my back and his other beneath my legs. "Ready?"

"Do I have a choice?" I mumbled.

He smiled. "Seems fate is bound to make a damsel out of you."

I scowled. "You're not helping."

He lifted me off the ground, as if I weighed no more than a feather, and held me tightly against his solid frame. I was acutely aware of him, the scent of pine and musk and woodsmoke on his skin, the feel of his arms around me. I felt safe and protected, like any *friend* would feel, right? Except I liked being in his arms more than I thought I should.

"Shall we?" Tran asked.

We followed Tran Chiton, Master Tran, the Black Bard—whoever he was. The very man I had been set on not finding. The very man I'd thought Thad lied about. As it turned out, Thad was the only one telling the truth. Mostly.

Chapter 21

The Black Bard

I couldn't see anything beyond the golden halo of Tran's lantern. Not the trees, not the ground—not even Cicero and Sonya, even though I knew they were near, because I could hear them talking. I couldn't hear what they were saying, but I knew it wasn't bad because I could feel their surprise and disbelief, unlike Alex, who was unusually tense—even for him.

And it wasn't that he had a problem carrying me. In fact, he almost seemed to be enjoying himself. He just didn't like having his sword-hand occupied.

What did he think Tran was going to do? Wag a finger and make me grow a fifth limb? Alex's parents didn't seem too worried, and if there were anyone besides my dad who'd overreact, it would be Cicero. Besides, Sonya somehow already knew the man. He was like Gandalf's hippy brother, the one full of all goodness and magic and wisdom, but probably spent a little too much time behind the pipe—and no telling what he put in it.

But none of that seemed to matter to Alex. His grip around me was tight and protective, and his eyes remained fastened on Gandalf's forgotten, slightly deranged twin.

"Tran Chiton is dead." Alex's deep voice reverberated through his chest and in my ear.

His statement was so simple, so confident, I was surprised to see Tran grin in response.

"I am sorry to disappoint you, dear boy, but life hasn't chosen to end my time yet. I suppose Gaia still has need of me. However, I'm sure once I've fulfilled my purpose, you shall most definitely have your wish."

Rain began whispering on the treetops and cold drops splattered on my skin. Alex pressed me tighter against him and I was grateful for his warmth.

210

"I don't wish that," Alex continued. "It's just that everyone says you died. Years ago."

Tran wagged a bony finger, and to no one's great surprise, I still had only four limbs. "And it is that which has kept my life intact. Ironic how it works out, don't you agree?"

"But people say you were...are evil," I said. He didn't need to know by "people" I meant Thad.

"Do they?" The old man chuckled. "Oh, my. I suppose it depends upon whom you ask. If I'd destroyed your life, you would think me evil. But if I'd destroyed the life of your enemy, I would be quite the hero by your standards."

Suddenly, Tran stopped, and we were drenched with rainwater.

Alex adjusted me in his arms, and I could tell he was poised to reach for his sword.

Tran moved the lamp forward and an old wooden door appeared, right in front of us. Windows popped into view, the golden light behind fuzzy and distorted from the thick film that covered them. I couldn't see the rest of the home because trees and overgrowth concealed it. Even though the house seemingly appeared out of nowhere, it also looked as if it had always been there, as if it'd erupted from the ground and nearby foliage gathered around to form walls and a shaggy roof.

There was a soft creaking, and we were guided through the door.

The interior was not what I expected. It was carefully constructed, with wooden beams and perfectly laid stone—no traces of forest. A fire blazed in one corner and the air smelled sweet and yeasty, like freshly baked bread. There were thick rugs covering the wooden floorboards, a comfortable looking sofa and a couple well-kept chairs. Sort of what I expected a Bed and Breakfast to look like, minus the location and Gandalf's twin.

Along the far wall was an enormous bookshelf. Half of it was lined with shimmering glass vases and the other half was stuffed to the brim with thick, worn books. Beside that was a wall of macabre-looking metal objects, like hooks, pickaxes, and warped rings with barbs sticking out all over.

Okay, so maybe Bed and Breakfast meets Frankenstein's lab.

Who—or what—is this man?

"Please," Tran said. "Make yourself at home." He turned away from us and paused. "Great mages, I almost forgot!"

He placed his hands on Alex and me. The water in our clothing began gathering into little beads. Larger and larger they grew until they looked like glass marbles and fell to the floor in a single shower. The beads rolled along the wood, soaking into the grain until they disappeared completely.

I gasped. "How did you do that?"

Tran smiled, patting my arm. "No spoon-feeding for you this evening. Alexander, would you lay our invalid down on the sofa? I'll return shortly. I've got to ask Grool for the medicine."

That name. So my ears hadn't been malfunctioning. He hadn't said "drool," he'd said "grool." Who in their right mind would call themselves something that sounded like rotten food?

Assuming that person was in their "right" mind...

Tran went over to Cicero and Sonya, dried out their clothing, then disappeared down a narrow corridor.

Alex carried me to the couch, very carefully set me down, and placed a hand on my leg. I winced.

He searched my face. "You okay?"

I took a deep breath, pushing back the pain. "How's your arm?"

A creature suddenly appeared, about half the size of any normal person. His skin was tinged a light brown and scraggy tufts of hair piled between two prominent pointed ears. His eyes looked like two black marbles, and he glared at our group as if we just ruined his life. A potato sack covered his scrawny frame with holes cut out for his head and gaunt, knobby arms, and he had two brown stilts for legs supporting it all. A dark leather belt hung at his waist filled with sharp, maniacal looking tools, similar to the ones on the wall.

Little Frankenstein scuffled right over to me, pushing through Sonya and Alex until he was at my side. A glass jar was in his hand, filled with something black that looked like tar and smelled like ammonia, only worse. And I thought growing up on a farm was bad.

The creature dug his gnarled hand into his over-sized potato sack pocket and pulled out a small vial filled with

212

clear liquid. With his fingernail, he scooped out some of the black paste and dipped it into the flask. But the liquid didn't turn black. It bubbled viciously for a few seconds and turned a puke-green. The smell was nauseating.

He thrust the flask inches from my face and spoke in a grinding voice, "You drink!"

There was no way I was going to drink that.

Alex bent his head so that his lips were at my ear. "It's for your ankles. It's not going to kill you."

"The smell might."

Alex chuckled and backed away, and the creature held the flask before my nose.

Even though the vial smelled like death, I knew one fact for certain. If there was one thing Alex didn't lie about, it was my safety.

Hesitating, I took the mystery flask from Little Frankenstein's hand. His round, black eyes followed my every move, scowling as if he was completely insulted I was taking so long. As I lifted the flask to my lips, the little creature grunted loudly for emphasis—just in case I missed his visual demonstration.

Very slowly, I tilted it until the liquid touched my tongue, and then I gagged. Right over Little Frankenstein's scrunched face. He clenched his fists at his sides as a frothy mixture of green liquid and spit dripped from his nose.

"That's disgusting!" I wiped the residue from my lips.

"Well, your highness, it's not hot chocolate," Alex said.

"All right, Mr. Protector," I said. "Why don't you give it a try then?"

"Grool," Alex turned to the fuming creature. "Do you have a cure for obstinacy? She's desperately in need of one."

I opened my mouth to argue, but before I could say a word, Little Frankenstein had pinched my nose and shoved the flask to my lips.

The liquid burned. I felt as if my throat was dissolving, then my stomach, and the burning continued down, through my limbs, into my legs, through my ankles, all the way down to my toes.

My ankles. There was no more pain. I wiggled them to be sure, but they felt fine.

The creature ripped the flask from my lips and shoved it back in his belt. And just as I thought he was going to leave, he paused before Alex. He stared at Alex's arm with wide eyes, and scrunched his face in disgust. Pinching the large flaps of his aquiline nose, he fixed an icy glare on Alex and scurried away.

"Your ankles are healed, I see." Alex lifted his hand from my leg.

Now that we were safe and sound in the confines of Frankenstein's Bed and Breakfast, his hesitation was gone. All I felt was his anger toward me for leaving them.

Maybe I should've pretended my ankles were still broken.

"What happened?" Sonya sat beside me.

All three of them waited for my answer, but Sonya's gaze was the only one tender enough to give me confidence to answer.

"I just...needed some air, so I went for a walk—"

"Was the air so different a hundred yards away?" Cicero's face was bright red, and that vein started bulging in his neck again.

I set my features. I didn't need to feel guilty. Not after all they'd lied about. "Yes."

"You're lucky you weren't killed!" Cicero continued. "You have no idea what's in this forest. Don't *ever* walk away like that again, do I make myself clear?"

I glared at the fire. Any clearer, I'd be looking right through him. It wasn't my fault I was ignorant about the dangers in this world. It was theirs. They'd never bothered telling me.

Tran lingered in the doorway with a large cloth covered basket in his hands. There was a sad smile on his face, but it warmed his features and erased any hesitation I'd had with the man. I'd never known a grandfather, but if I had the choice, I think I would've picked someone like him.

He left the shelter of the narrow doorway and approached us with the basket. The smell of sweet bread was so strong my mouth watered. Also, I was anxious to rid myself of the taste of Grool's rancid liquid.

"Oh, wonderful." He smiled. "I see your bones are healed."

214

Tran pulled back a cloth, tempting me with a steaming treasure of enormous fluffy rolls. I dove into the pillage. They were warm and doughy, falling apart in my hands as I shoved a bite in my mouth. It was almost better than Thad's brownbutter loaf. Almost.

"Grool informs me you've received a rather nasty injury." Tran looked at Alex.

Alex waved it off. "It's fine."

I was just about to tell Tran that Alex was lying when I caught myself. If I said that, then they'd ask how I knew and I'd have to explain how I'd been sensing their feelings. I didn't want them knowing that yet.

"I restricted the poison to the wound," Sonya said. "His health has been strong ever since."

Tran smiled, leaning toward Alex. He reached out a withered palm. "May I?"

Alex was wary but didn't argue. Tran's movements were slow and deliberate as he rolled back Alex's shirtsleeve.

I had to keep myself from gagging. The scab oozed, threads of his shirtsleeve were stuck to it, and the skin around it was bright red. I felt a surge of immense pain from Alex, but when I met his gaze the feeling disappeared. He'd been suppressing more pain than I realized. "You carried me with...that?"

His expression was blank.

Tran ran bony fingers over the scab, brows fixed in concentration. "Sonya." He glanced up. "I'm surprised you had any strength left after this."

Cicero clutched his wife's hand between both of his.

"I did everything I could," she said.

Tran's smile was proud. "And you did a marvelous job. This should have killed him."

"Killed him?" I choked on my roll. "Alex, what were you thinking?"

"He was thinking he wanted you safe," Tran said. "Barghest poison is one of the deadliest. It's almost impossible to cure, but I believe—" he examined the wound "—after your mother's excellent care, I should be able to rid you of it for good. It is fortunate you have such a talented mother."

Alex met his mother's loving gaze.

215

Tran shut his eyes. He trailed his fingers along the wound, his lips barely moving. At first nothing happened, but as I watched, the scab started changing. It fell away and disappeared into thin air, piece by small piece, and in its place was a patch of new skin. The last piece fell away and a black wisp of smoke curled into the air. A horrible barghest cry pierced through the room so loudly I covered my ears. The smoke began to disappear, like a black thread being pulled into a vacuum, and suddenly vanished, taking that alien shrieking with it.

The room was silent.

When I looked back at Alex, his arm was as good as new, aside from a faint pink scar.

"There." Tran rested his hand on Alex's arm. "I think that should do the trick."

"Thank you." Alex looked respectfully at Tran.

Tran smiled. "I'm afraid that scar will remain a permanent addition to your physique. Hope that's not a problem?"

For some reason, Tran was looking at me.

"By the way, child, you fought well against that Pykan."

"That was a Pykan?" I didn't know what I expected them to look like, but the picture in my head was definitely something more...human.

"Yes, and he might have had you, too. His friend was pretty good at keeping me distracted. We were fortunate Alexander arrived because once that Pykan wrapped his blasted snakeroot around your ankles, I was certain you were lost."

"Snakeroot?"

"A Pykan trademark. Their powers lie with the more...sadistic vegetation in this world. Snakeroot is one of their tools, and can only be removed by magic."

"You said they've been following us?" Cicero asked.

"Yes, and you've also had a trio of guards on your trail, though I think we got them off your scent." Tran scratched his chin, thoughtful.

That village—the one where we'd tried finding a witchdoctor for Alex. Three guards had been there, waiting for us, and at the last moment an enormous, black bird had flown out of the trees. Had it been...Tran's? Had he helped us then?

"But," Tran continued, "Pykans aren't quite as easy to divert. Grool has been keeping an eye on them. Grool was also the one who noticed our dear Daria walking away."

Oh, no, not back to this.

"And *why* were you walking away?" Sonya asked.

I looked away from her, right into Alex's penetrating gaze.

"I believe—" Tran's warm eyes settled on me "—Pykans can be quite hypnotizing when they want to be. Poor Daria found herself entrapped."

Little Frankenstein returned, this time carrying a tray of steaming ceramic mugs.

"Ah, yes. Have you formally met our guests?" Tran eyed Grool, and Grool glared directly at me. Come to think of it, glaring might have been more polite. Grool looked as if he wanted me to drop dead on the couch.

"Cicero, Alex, Daria, meet Grool. Sonya, I don't believe introductions are necessary?"

She grinned and shook her head.

"Grool has remained a faithful and trustworthy companion for me all these years." Tran waved Grool over to his side and whispered something in his ear. Grool slammed the tray down with a loud *clank* and stalked out of the room with his fists clenched, mumbling and grumbling all the way.

"Forgive him," Tran whispered. "Brownies are quite territorial and don't understand the concept of manners."

So Little Frankenstein was a brownie? My list of "things that shouldn't exist, but really do" was growing so long I was going to have to start organizing it into subcategories. I could see it now, "Brownie" written right above "Deadly Slinky," "Pixie," and "Barghest" under a heading entitled "Things That Want Me Dead." Actually, I didn't think there were any other categories.

I heard a quick patter and Grool reappeared. He marched straight to his tray, yanked it from the floor, and practically threw all the mugs in our faces. Well, except mine. He dropped that one at my feet, letting the contents spill all over the floor, and he stormed back out of the room. Tran frowned after the little fiend.

"Tran," Cicero said. "Do you hear much of the realm in these parts?"

"Not the kind you seek. I hear the usual: pixies fighting for flowers' rights, the conscia trees boycotting fruit production. You know—" Tran held his hand to his mouth as though he were telling me a secret "—conscia fruit are Lord Commodus' absolute favorite. They're vengeful creatures, those conscia trees, and their memory is quite astounding. Still angry at Lord Commodus' great-great-great grandfather for cutting one down centuries ago. Bah." He waved his hand at the air like he was slapping it. "They're all histrionics. If magical creatures weren't plagued with narcissism, this world might be a peaceful place. But I digress." He sighed and his ashy brow furrowed. "I know what you're asking, Aegis Cicero," his tone turned serious. "And I have heard rumors. Ones that are very disturbing indeed."

"About the villages outside of Orindor?" Cicero asked.

"Yes." Tran's mouth formed a line as he watched the fire. "Gargons."

"That's what Otis said." Alex looked at his father, every ounce of I-told-you-so written across his face.

"But that's impossible," Cicero said, ignoring him. "No one I know has seen anything."

"Recently, I traveled to a few villages beyond the interest of King Darius," Tran said. "There are a good number of them, you know. Upon such a visit, I saw one myself. Wouldn't have believed it otherwise. Burnt down half the village before I frightened it away."

"A gargon is a dragon...right?" I asked, trying to remember what Alex had said.

Tran walked over to a low bookshelf and pulled a thick volume with a tattered leather cover and began flipping through the pages. He halted on one and gazed over it with a frown. Thus satisfied with his findings, he handed the book to me.

"A concordance of monsters. Watch out, though." He winked. "They tend to forget they're on paper."

Yes, he was definitely Gandalf's crazy twin.

I took the book from his hands. The word *"Gargon"* was scrolled across the top of the page. Drawn beneath was a creature that matched my idea of a dragon: narrow, dark,

218

and muscular reptilian body with enormous bat-like wings. But the wings were...moving, flapping on the page without actually going anywhere. A tail whipped behind it, one with sharp points jutting out from the end. Fiery red eyes glowed on the paper with fury, white fangs curved over a narrow black lip. Two long slits existed where its nose should have been with steam billowing out of them, even out of the page. Its powerful jaws opened, revealing more layers of razor sharp teeth, which, unfortunately, also decided to come out of the page. I slammed the book shut before the drawing could bite me.

Note to self: Add "Drawings" to list of "Things That Want Me Dead."

Tran grinned. "Don't say I didn't warn you."

"That's what attacked that village?" I handed the book back to him, not wanting to peruse it further. I intended to keep my fingers.

"Without a doubt," Tran said.

"It doesn't make any sense," Cicero said.

Tran clasped his hands. "There are many things lately that lack sense."

"How long have you known about the Pykans?" Sonya asked.

"Not until recently, and I believe the council isn't aware of them either, or at least they aren't saying."

"The council is in session?" Cicero frowned.

Tran nodded.

"But Alaric's gone."

"Apparently, the king is being blamed for the attacks and the drought—which you were already aware. They accuse him of practicing dark magic and want him to step down from the throne until his reputation is cleared."

"Bloody traitors!" Cicero gasped. "How dare they make such a ridiculous accusation!"

"Calm yourself. Even you can't deny the manner of Alaric's absence looks suspect—what, with no one knowing his whereabouts. And the lords, as you know, are easily influenced."

My dad must be higher up on the food chain than I thought.

"But that's ridiculous," Alex said. "Stefan is there."

"Precisely," Tran's voice was low.

Alex opened his mouth to argue, but stopped. "Someone on the council knows we're here. The Pykans were sent after Daria as a distraction."

Tran was silent.

"That's absurd," Cicero said. "Lord Commodus can verify where Alaric has been."

"Ah, but Lord Commodus isn't there, now is he?" Tran said. "His son Danton is acting in his place."

"Of course." Alex paced the room. "No one trusts Danton and Stefan is too weak to fight them on it."

"Don't worry too much quite yet," Tran continued. "The lords haven't acted, which means they aren't entirely convinced."

"Whoever the traitor is behind this," Cicero continued, "he's powerful enough to summon the barghests."

"About that," Tran said, with a long, bony finger poking his chin. "Would you mind filling me in on the details of your attack?"

Sonya recounted those horrific details, all the while Tran's pale face grew paler and paler.

"It has to be a Guild member." Alex stopped pacing beside the fireplace and looked back at his dad. "They're the only ones with that kind of power."

"Not necessarily, dear boy." Tran's brow furrowed. "There are others—like myself—who have remained hidden all these years. But we can be certain of this: whoever is behind these attacks is giving intelligence to someone inside the castle. I'm afraid, as you were already suspicious, there are enemies within the council."

The more I learned about this world, the more I feared it. Was there anything in this world that didn't want me dead?

"The soldiers you mentioned," Cicero continued. "We ran into them the first time at Rex Cross. They wore the armor of Valdon, but their necks were branded."

Cicero had seen it too.

"I know." Tran scratched his beard. "I do not know who or what they serve, but it worries me."

"What is the king doing about the accusations?" Alex asked.

220

"King Darius is responding much as he always does. Predictably unpredictable. Silent and manipulating, which doesn't help the case against him, I'm afraid. You know how he is. His own advice has always been his most valued asset. It is well Daria is with you, away from the people of this world, at least until you join Alaric. Then maybe some sense can be made from all of this, hopefully before they decide on a course of action."

I didn't understand much about what they were saying, except for one important fact. My dad's absence was causing problems, and this was bound to put him in more danger.

"Maybe that's why you haven't heard from Dad." I interrupted the silence. "Maybe he's in trouble."

No one would meet my gaze. In fact, they all looked a little guilty. My fear expanded as I became certain it was true. "You know how strong those Pykans are. It took Tran *and* Alex to get rid of them, and now my dad is out there alone—"

"Your father is just fine." Sonya still wouldn't meet my gaze.

"How do you know that?" I got to my feet. "Stefan hasn't said a word about him, unless you're lying to me..." I stopped before Sonya. "*Again.*"

"Daria." It was Tran. His blue eyes were thoughtful as they studied my face. "I know you really have no idea who I am, nor any particular reason to trust me, but I am certain Alaric is able to handle himself, if any in this world can make such a claim. Have faith in him, my dear. You will see him soon, or I am no sorcerer."

I didn't know how he did it, but each word he said was like throwing a bucket of water on a raging fire. He was the first person I'd spoken to in over a week who I knew was being completely honest with me. I believed him, and took a deep breath. "You are a sorcerer?"

He smiled. "Well, 'was.' I am more of an entrepreneur at present."

"Don't let him fool you," Sonya said. "Tran Chiton is well known for being one of the most powerful mages who ever existed."

Tran's gaze drifted absently to the flames. "History does a fine job remembering and disregarding what it wants."

"Why aren't you still serving the king?" I asked.

221

"That, my dear, is rather complicated. Certain events transpired and I felt it my time to withdraw from society. My work these days is more easily done when people think I do not exist. Plus, Grool's inventions keep me well entertained. I must say, in all my travels, his antidotes and sprite traps are exemplary."

"So that's what you have on the wall?" Cicero nodded toward the collection of metal death traps.

Tran smiled. "That is only some of them. Grool is quite the expert at catching pesky creatures. The only disagreement we have is that he likes to keep them." Tran gestured toward the bookshelf containing all the vases. "Please be careful with them. If one breaks and releases one of those creatures, they are quite cumbersome to control."

Grool suddenly reentered the room. His potato sack covering was soaked through, and he was carrying a mug half his size. The contents sloshed upon the floor with his jerky movements, and something sour filled the air. Grool hobbled to Tran and grumbled something into his ear.

"Thank you, Grool," Tran said.

Grool wobbled straight to the bookshelf and meticulously inspected each vial. He sat down, glaring at each of us in turn as he took a swig.

"What's that smell?" I asked.

Tran stood to his feet. "Grool's mead. It's made of rat droppings."

"Rat droppings?"

Grool scowled at me as he took a large sip.

"There is a seed here rats eat. Once their stomachs digest its coat, they excrete it whole in their droppings. That partially digested seed is what they make into ale. I find the drink horrid myself, but it is a delicacy to brownies—like Grool."

"You've actually tried it?" Cicero asked.

"Of course." Tran grinned. "How else can I claim distaste? But it is late, and you have more traveling ahead. I offer you my hospitality for the remainder of the night. Grool has already taken care of the horses. They are close by and hidden, and here, I've got just the thing…"

He waved his hand over the sofa. The cushions began growing. They grew longer and longer, until each were about the length of a bed. "There, that should do it."

I didn't think Sonya and Cicero looked nearly as startled as they should have.

Tran looked at me, then Alex. He walked over to the wall, tapping one spot about eye level and one nearer the floor. A few wooden planks in the wall buckled, and two horizontal slats of wood moved out parallel to the floor. Bunk beds. Tran shuffled to a small cupboard, pulled out a stack of blankets and passed them around.

He glanced between Alex and me. "My apologies if your bed is a little firm, but you haven't earned the right to share something more comfortable." He smiled. "Not yet, anyway. Goodnight."

My cheeks burned hot as Tran disappeared, Grool mumbling something after him.

Cicero interrupted the silence. "Wait till we tell Alaric this one."

"How do you know Tran?" I asked Sonya.

Sonya stared off at nothing. It seemed as though her mind was sifting through memories, all of which caused her pain. "I knew him a very long time ago, when I was a child. He recognized my ability then—to heal. And when I came to Valdon with your mother, he served King Darius."

Wait a minute. "He knew my mom?"

Sonya's smile was nostalgic and sad. "Gaia was not the same when Tran left."

I could tell she was deciding whether or not to tell me more, and I desperately wanted to hear more, but her hesitation won. She kissed me goodnight, made her way to Alex, kissed his cheek too, and then crawled into bed with Cicero. When I turned around, Alex was sitting on the lower bunk, arms resting on his knees, his expression inscrutable.

He glanced up at me and I knew. He knew what the Pykan had said. He'd known why I walked away. He'd known all along and didn't say a word. It was this strange connection we seemed to share where nothing I kept deep down was hidden from him. I wondered what else he already knew and realized this couldn't be good. Did he know what a mess I was? Did he know how his touch made me feel? Did he know just how angry I was and that I would leave if they didn't follow through with their promise?

I searched Alex's eyes but couldn't find answers there. I couldn't sense them, either. He just sat studying me as I studied him with an invisible brick wall between us. I hated that wall, and it was back with a vengeance.

Alex abruptly stood to his feet, raked a hand through his hair and climbed into his bunk. He didn't look at me again.

The room was quiet. The Pykan's words echoed in my head. It had known too much about my circumstances and feelings.

"Makes you wonder what else they're not telling you," Thad had said. And now Alex was withdrawing again, just like he had years ago. Was following the Del Contes the worst decision I could have made?

Sighing, I crawled on my hard wooden slat and shut my eyes. If Dad wasn't at Amadis, I would leave this family—leave Alex—and find him. No matter what happened, after tomorrow, I would only trust myself.

Chapter 22

Amadis

I woke with a start, freezing. My blanket had been ripped from my body. Grool was scurrying about, tidying up the place, eager for us to leave, and I realized my blanket was draped over his scrawny arm. He fixed his black marble eyes on me, saw I was awake, and then my bed started melting back into the wall. I all but fell out of it.

Guess he still hadn't forgiven me for spitting on him.

The Del Contes were already awake, and the sun peeked through the curtains. I made my way toward the bookshelf propped against the wall. The vases were all different: fat, narrow, tall, short. Some were filled with liquids of varying shades and viscosities, some with shimmering vapors. Little white tags were tied to each with strange scribble written on them. One vial in particular was glowing a bright orange, swirling and dispersing inside its transparent trap. Just as my finger brushed the glass surface, something flew out of nowhere, slapping me on the hand.

"Ow!" I waved my hand, my fingers stinging.

I'd been hit with a long, narrow bone. It apparently belonged to Grool, who was also pointing a long black fingernail so close to my face I went cross-eyed.

"What was that for?" I shook my burning fingers.

"No touch!" Grool waved his bone.

"But I wasn't going to..."

My words were cut short as Grool pushed me away from his prized bookcase and used a dirty rag to wipe the vials clean. If Tran thought Gaia would be a better world without narcissistic magical creatures, he should probably start by getting rid of Grool.

Tran appeared at my side.

"Here, you may want this." He held out my dagger.

I checked my belt. The sheath was empty.

"Grool has the unfortunate habit of collecting artifacts. It doesn't seem to matter where he finds them or who he finds them belonging to." Tran smiled.

"Thanks." I slid the dagger back in its sheath.

"Interesting item. If I may, how did it come into your possession?"

"I found it. In a creek."

Tran stared at the object, but his mind was somewhere else.

"Do you know what it says?" I asked.

He looked back at me. "I believe you must discover that for yourself."

Grool walked by and his eyes flashed to my dagger, grumbling and scowling all the way.

Everyone said their goodbyes, and the Del Contes thanked Tran repeatedly for his hospitality.

"Oh, and, Cicero," Tran said. "Follow the rounded symbol of your compass. That should be the most direct." He winked.

Cicero nodded. "Thank you, Master Tran."

Grool led them out the door, but Tran stopped me before I could follow. When I turned around, his expression was earnest.

"Do not fear your future, child. The fire in you burns strong, but is too volatile. I know you desire answers, but it isn't time for them yet. Be patient with the Del Contes. They are doing everything they can to help you. Trust them."

I sighed. "I'm not sure I can."

Tran placed his hand on my shoulder. "You should not cast judgments on what you do not understand. There is a responsibility that comes with knowledge, and, in your case, it is not a responsibility that I would be anxious for. There are great evils in this world—greater than you can begin to imagine—that would do anything to attain that knowledge. So we must do everything in our power to protect it, even if it means not telling you. But when the time comes, which is not far, I've no doubt you will be more than able to manage it.
"

And with that, he and his entire house disappeared.

Tran was right. Cicero followed the rounded symbol on his compass, and it took us all of one day to reach our destination. Much faster than we'd anticipated. But that last day was never ending.

What would I say to Dad? Where would I even start? It felt like ages since we'd sat in our Subaru, arguing about my future—the future he wouldn't disclose to me then. I'd been adamant about moving forward. Would I have been as desperate for change if I'd known this was going to happen?

Tran's words had imprinted themselves on my brain. *There is a responsibility that comes with knowledge.* What was this supposed responsibility? As much as I wanted to trust this family I'd known all my life, time only proved that I couldn't rely on them.

Alex rode in silence, bringing up the rear of our procession. His withdrawing continued. Not even my ability to sense his emotions could penetrate the barrier he was building. It was like the time before he left, when he'd pulled back into himself, and it felt as if someone were ripping my wounds open all over again.

I couldn't ask him about it. I tried convincing myself that my fear of confrontation had nothing to do with this Vera girl who managed to weave her way into every fleeting thought and feeling I had. But my mind kept returning to her, along with the realization that he hadn't denied anything. As far as I knew, he could be dating her. And, although I didn't quite understand why, it was the deciding factor that made it difficult for me to say anything to him.

The sunlight became softer, the shadows became longer, and Cicero stopped.

The trees here were grand—the grandest I'd seen—verdant and buzzing with life, covered in thick layers of bright green moss. The earth was dark with moisture, soft and pliable as I stood upon it. Soft chirps and melodies rang high in the trees, vines swaying in the light breeze. The air here was rich and aromatic, and just through the trees I caught a glimmer. Water. We'd reached Lake Amadis.

And for all its grandeur—for all its magic—a difficult truth began to set in.

I was off Calyx before anyone said a word. "He's not here." My voice fell flat.

227

Cicero exchanged a look with his wife.

"No. Not yet." Cicero's voice was too calm for my liking.

The others dismounted. The air was cool, and the breeze rustled through the trees, announcing its arrival even before it brushed over my skin. Cicero and Alex went to hunt for our dinner, and Sonya sat, mending arrows beside the fire she had made.

"Can I check to see if Stefan's written?" I asked.

Sonya didn't look up. "He hasn't."

"How do you know? Have you checked?"

"I will. Once Cicero returns."

I watched her as she attached silver and green feathers to the end of an arrow, and my frustration surged. Her pack was right beside her, the pack that contained the book.

Later, once they fell asleep, I would read it myself and plan my course of action.

Be patient with them. You know they are just trying to keep you safe.

No. I was done being patient.

Sonya and I sat in silence. She was preoccupied with arrows, while I simmered with frustration. He was supposed to be here. We were running behind, and he should've been waiting.

I could take Cicero's maps or his compass, but which direction should I go first? I'd feel guilty if I left them without the means to return. It was best if I left Cicero's compass to him—after all, I couldn't even read it. After about an hour of silent planning, I decided I needed to move and clear my head. "Mind if I walk along the lake for a bit?"

She looked up, and though she was looking at me, she didn't see me at all. "Not at all."

I started walking away when she spoke again. "Oh, and take your time. We'll have dinner ready when you return."

"So you can discuss things without me," I mumbled and kept walking.

I meandered through the dense foliage and brilliant blue glistened ahead. The breeze whispered through the trees, and the melodic chiming sounded again. This time it was right overheard. Craning my neck to focus, I peered up into the green. Thick vines festooned above, but there was something mixed in with them. Smaller vines shaded a silvery blue.

228

Clusters of them hung amidst the green like tinsel in the forest, and as the breeze blew through them, they clanged against one another, filling the air with harmonious melodies. Natural chimes.

I took a step forward when something squeaked at my feet.

I glanced down at a cluster of white mushrooms with large black spots. The biggest one stood directly at my feet, its umbrella tilted back as if it had eyes and was looking up at me.

Just as I was thinking I'd imagined the squeaky sound, it moved.

It scrambled off into the bushes with a trail of smaller mushrooms following right behind, all of them squeaking angrily along the way.

I sighed. Once I found my dad, I would ask him to take me far away from here, preferably somewhere without plants.

When I emerged from the tree cover, my breath caught. A crystal clear blue lake filled the crevice between mountains still covered in winter's snow. Bright orange and yellow flowers rimmed the perimeter, filling spaces where trees weren't, their vivid shades just as rich on the water's reflective surface. The lake rippled gently in the soft breeze beneath a sky streaked in lurid shades of bright orange and blazing pink. The moss covered ground dipped its fingers into the water, disappearing just beneath the surface.

I took off my boots, pushed up my leathers and stepped in the water. It was cold to the touch, but refreshing. It had been days since I'd had a bath. I braved a glimpse of myself in my reflection. My eyes were sunken, my long hair a tangled mess and there were dark streaks of dirt on my cheeks. I really did look like a refugee. No wonder I'd frightened the mushrooms away.

I scooped up handfuls of water, wiping them over my face. The thought crossed my mind to just get it over with and take a bath, but the cool breeze deterred me. I didn't want to air dry in this cold evening air. Plus, seeing how the water here was so clear and pure, it didn't seem right tainting it with my filth.

The perimeter curved until I stood at a small inlet with a single large boulder standing in the center of it. I stopped walking and gazed at the pristine lake. The water rolled gently, lapping at the base of the boulder. The breeze lifted strands of my hair into my face, and for a moment I closed my eyes, allowing my senses to drink in the nature around them. The sound of the water licking at the shore, the cool air tickling my skin, its fresh scent filling my lungs. My mind shut down. All my frustration, all my anxiety, all my planning, all of my doubts—they were lost in the tranquility of my surroundings. I'd almost forgotten what it was like to be alone.

Over the course of the past week, I'd been forced to deal with everything under constant surveillance. Soon I would have Cicero's map in my hands, and Calyx, my devoted traveling companion. After tonight, I'd be alone, like I was right now. But when I opened my eyes, I realized I wasn't alone.

Something shimmered on the lake's surface, off to my left. At first I thought it was a reflection, but when I noticed the glimmer was localized, I wasn't so sure.

The shimmer moved.

Swirls of water twisted and bubbled, flowing swiftly across the surface of the water, straight for the boulder. It paused, swirling and bubbling in place, and then continued forward—a small, localized current of water—moving straight for the rock.

Curious, I took a step forward and the movement ceased.

For a few minutes, the water was still, the evening quiet.

The bubbling returned, but more violently this time. The water churned and swirled, and then it rushed toward me.

I took a quick step backwards and froze. A narrow column of water rose from the lake's surface. Water fell away, leaving behind a girl. Her skin was ivory, her hair long and golden as it floated around her face as though she was still underwater. Her slender, elegant frame was covered in a shimmering gown seemingly made of water. Two exotic blue eyes stared at me as she raised one of her delicate fingers to her full red lips. Then she pointed beyond me.

My eyes followed the direction of her finger. There, spread out on a rock, was a familiar shirt, pants, pair of leather boots, and a sheathed sword. Alex's clothes. When I turned back around, her large red lips pulled up into a smile, and she disappeared back into the water.

I couldn't believe it. This woman, magical creature—whatever she was—was spying on Alex, and she expected me to stand by and let her.

I wasn't sure what to do. Should I let him know? My pride said leave him be. He obviously wasn't dressed and I didn't need him thinking I was the one spying on him. Except, if I was bathing, and someone had been spying on me, I would want to be told—immediately.

I made up my mind.

I took one step back in the water. "Alex."

The bubbling surged and the girl appeared before me. This time, her face was livid. She glided forward, arms extended as if to embrace me, but just as I braced for contact, her shape disappeared, transforming into water—water that washed over my entire body.

The surface of the lake stilled, and I was left drenched, freezing, and drowning in Alex's amusement.

Heat licked up my neck and face as I glanced up. Alex's head poked out from the side of the boulder, his dark hair matted to his head, part of his bare chest exposed. And I felt ridiculous.

He had a smirk on his face. "I never knew you for a spy."

Don't think of him naked....don't think of him naked....

My cheeks burned. "I thought you were hunting."

"I was."

His amusement continued crashing over me in waves.

This was what I got for being nice.

"Do you normally bathe with your clothes on?" he asked.

My blood ran hot as he eyed me up and down. I scowled. "Do you normally bathe with an audience?"

He looked satisfied. "So you were spying on me."

"No...I....she..." I stammered, pointing at the water as his smirk slowly stretched into a huge smile. "You're impossible."

He stared at me with that stupid smile plastered on his face, and I glared back at him, starting to freeze. I wrapped my arms around myself, trying to hold in my body heat and my composure—any ounce of pride I had left.

"Aren't you cold?" I asked.

"Yes."

"Well, then why are you just standing there with that look on your face?"

He raised a brow. "You *do* realize my clothes are behind you."

My entire body felt as if it was burning from the inside out.

"Well, are you going to turn around or not?" Alex asked.

Flustered, I spun around and shut my eyes tight. Alex chuckled as he moved through the water. Why in the world was I so embarrassed? I wasn't the one naked.

I felt him walk behind me and listened for his soft steps as he moved to his clothes.

"I wasn't spying on you."

He didn't respond. It sounded like he was pulling on his boots.

"Really," I continued. "There was this girl, only she came out of the water and she wasn't like any girl I've ever seen..."

"That was Amadis."

"That *thing* has a name?"

"*She—*" I heard him tug on his other boot "—protects this lake."

I was appalled. "Wait, you *knew* she was watching you take a bath?"

"Daria, honestly, I didn't see her. Besides, I don't exactly have any other options, now do I? Unlike you, I like going to bed dry."

I couldn't see, my fingers and toes were going numb, and I was now standing in a puddle of my own precipitation. It seemed to be taking Alex a bit longer than necessary. I wouldn't put it past him, in our current situation, to make getting dressed a drawn out affair.

My irritation surged. "What are you doing? Ironing your shirt?"

Nothing.

"Have I ever mentioned how adorable you are when you're angry?"

I opened my eyes. He was standing right before me, fully clothed, his dark hair dripping around his face. His green eyes were exceptionally bright, and that arrogant smirk was still on his face.

I'd had it.

232

I yanked up my boots and marched past him, back toward camp.

He chuckled, bounding after me.

"I don't see what's so funny," I said over my shoulder.

"You wouldn't."

He caught up and walked beside me. I could feel him watching me, but he said nothing else.

When we returned to camp, Cicero and Sonya were seated beside the blazing fire with a kettle right beside it. They eyed us as we approached, eyes darting from Alex to me.

"Should I even ask?" Cicero looked at Alex.

Alex plopped down on a log. "Daria made a new friend today." He beamed at me.

I rolled my eyes and sat beside the fire, trying to warm my fingers and toes.

Cicero grinned. "Ah, you met Amadis."

"Yes, I met Amadis." I motioned to my drenched clothing.

Sonya got to her feet and walked over to me. "I'm sorry, I forgot to warn you. Amadis doesn't like other females—definitely not attractive ones—and especially not when men are present. She's...insecure."

Alex snickered and began eating his dinner. I had the sudden urge to walk over and hit him.

"Here." Sonya handed me a bowl of steaming broth before I could act. "This should help."

"Thanks." I took the bowl from her hands, letting the contents warm my insides.

I didn't speak the remainder of dinner. Everyone must have sensed my mood, because no one tried to make me talk. Once I was done eating, I crawled under my blankets and shut my eyes. This night I would wait until they were all sleeping. Then I would take matters into my own hands.

****

The darkness was impenetrable.

The air was stale, cold. Everywhere I turned, I could see nothing but pure, thick black.

233

A wall of light cut through the night. My eyes fought to make sense of it. To adjust to the white, or adjust to the dark. Either made it impossible to adjust completely.

A large shadow filled the bright column. It was the silhouette of a man, veiled by a thick cloak. He took a single step forward and something creaked shut behind him.

The darkness returned but for a single candle spilling its glow into the empty square room. There was a man, hunched in one corner. Shackles bound his hands and feet and his head was covered with a black sack.

"You are a fool," hissed the cloaked man, his voice seething with hatred.

It was a voice that rang familiarity in my ears. It was the voice from the portal. The dark rider.

The cloaked figure took another step toward the man and that malevolent voice continued. "I warned you what happen if you failed to cooperate. I had hoped you would see reason."

The prisoner tensed. I could taste his fear, his agony.

"I'll ask once more," continued the sharp tone. "Where is it?"

Silence.

In one swift movement, the veiled man yanked the prisoner up by his collar, holding him inches above the ground. The prisoner struggled to keep his head lifted so that air could reach his lungs, legs and arms thrashing as he tried to relieve the pressure at his neck.

Beneath the hood of the cloaked man, white eyes burned. "Know this. I will find it, and when I do, I will give no pardon to its bearer. Remember, this is your doing."

With a flick of a wrist, the prisoner was slammed against the wall before sinking back to the ground.

"Curse you...Tiernan," the prisoner said in a barely discernable voice.

Tiernan reached deep into the folds of his cloak and pulled out a translucent cord. It wriggled and writhed in his hands, its hisses and shrieks revolting. Tiernan held it before his white eyes, watching the object struggle in his grip.

"It is you who shall be cursed. I have wasted much time hoping you would be sensible." His eyes fixed on the prisoner. "I am done."

He set the cord on the ground and took a single step back. At once, the cord knew its purpose. Its movements were snake-like, writhing along the ground straight for the prisoner. It slid up the prisoner's leg and right above the man's knee, wrapping around forming a tight, seamless band.

The prisoner jerked and spasmed in response, flexing his legs and arching his back in unnatural angles, his agonizing screams rebounding against the walls of the small room.

The band began throbbing and pulsing, glowing a pale white, and the man's cries lessened as he slumped in a heap on the ground.

The hooded man stood tall over the heap on the floor. Tiernan removed the cloth from the prisoner's head and yanked him up by his hair, craning his head back. The man's pain pulsed through me.

"I warned you," Tiernan hissed. "Now you will watch as your pathetic world is destroyed, and your loved ones die with it."

He threw the man back on the ground, his face falling in the candlelight.

It was my dad.

****

"Dad!"

Someone was shaking me as images of my dad stained the back of my eyelids.

"It was just a dream..." The voice was familiar.

I opened my eyes. Alex's face was inches from mine, his expression tight. His hands went to my cheeks, holding my face. But there was no dungeon. No pain, no sign of my dad.

I sat up. The embers from the campfire still burned beside us.

"Look at me." Alex's voice was strained.

My eyes moved back to Alex's as my body shook uncontrollably.

"What happened?"

My throat clamped down, making it difficult to speak. It had all seemed so real, as if I had been right there in that room with my dad. I could still feel the chill inside the stone tomb—smell its stale air and feel his agony.

Alex wiped the hair out of my face. "Was it the vision?" he whispered.

I shook my head.

Cicero and Sonya hovered over us. "What was it?"

I choked on air. "Dad."

Cicero and Sonya exchanged a glance.

Alex grabbed my hand. "What about Alaric?"

I saw my dad thrown onto the floor, his shape contorted in pain. The seed of fear began growing, wrapping and twisting around my veins. Very slowly, I recounted the details of my dream and once I finished, I glanced up. Each of their faces was tight with worry. It was all I needed to act. Right now.

"We have to find him!"

"Your father isn't in any real danger." Sonya placed her hand on mine.

I yanked it back. "How can you say that? You haven't heard from him in days, and my dream was so real...what if that's why you haven't heard? What if he's imprisoned and being tortured?"

The more I thought about it, the more certain I was. My dad was imprisoned somewhere, held captive by some person I didn't know. He was never going to meet us here. The Pykans had known that. The Del Contes knew that, and that was what they'd been hiding from me.

"How could they get to her here?" Cicero asked his wife.

"I've no idea." Sonya looked at me, deep in thought. "They can't penetrate physically, but it is feasible they could reach her mind. They've already done it once."

"We're wasting time." I started to my feet.

"Daria." Sonya's voice was firm. "I know you are worried about your father, but this dream—I think it's a trap. The Pykans know you're here, they know your weakness...."

"My *weakness* is that I've let you bring me here without demanding an explanation when I know full well that I can trust none of you."

Alex narrowed his eyes. "That's not fair."

"I'll tell you what's not fair. Since I walked through that portal and into this world, I've done nothing but do exactly as

236

you all have said. I've trusted you, I've believed you. Even though you've done nothing but hold back the truth from me—which, need I remind you, you've done my entire life. I'm telling you what I saw is real, so unless you help, I'm going after him myself."

There was a small voice in my head that warned of guilt, but I forced it silent. The sympathetic side of me had waited on them long enough. My whole life. My independent side was done waiting.

"You'll stay right where you are," Cicero said.

"I won't—"

"You will," Cicero interrupted, his tone final. "We'll discuss this in the morning. Alex? Keep first watch?"

Alex pulled his eyes from me, his jaw clenched. "Yes."

This was just great. Not only had I let my intentions slip, I had earned myself a personal guard. Alex. And he would anticipate me better than anyone.

Cicero and Sonya walked back to their beds. Sonya glanced back at me one last time, her expression remorseful.

"Feel better?" Alex wasn't looking at me.

"Don't talk to me."

My words hurt him, but I didn't care. He didn't understand. He'd grown up with the protection of two parents—two parents who had always been honest with him. Alex had never been lied to. Alex had never been alone.

There was one person in this world I could claim as a parent and he was the only family I had. Nothing they could say, nothing they could do could make me wait any longer.

I sat, my anger seething. Alex sat beside me but I'd never felt more distant. Neither of us spoke. He was my captor, I his prisoner. I couldn't believe this. He'd never let me out of his sight. He was controlling enough as a protector when he *did* trust me.

How would I get away now? I racked my brain, trying to think of an escape. How could I get away from them without them catching up to me?

Then I got an idea. I wasn't sure if it would work, but it was all I had.

I stared out into the forest and focused on the shadows. Craning my neck, I stared harder, intent on nothing, but Alex didn't need to know that.

237

It only took a few minutes for my vigilant captor to notice.

"What is it?"

"I think...I think there's something there."

He followed my gaze. "I don't see anything."

I shifted, still staring at the same empty spot. "Are you sure?"

He got to his feet and unsheathed his sword. "Daria, I swear, if you're lying..."

"And you would know all about that, wouldn't you?"

His lips tightened, and he walked in the direction I'd been looking. I only had a moment.

Once Alex disappeared from sight, I moved. As quiet as possible, I crept over to where Sonya and Cicero slept.

Where did Cicero put it? I searched his bag.

My fingers touched upon cool metal. I pulled the amulet from the bag, careful not to wake them, hung it around my neck, and crawled back into my blankets, just as Alex came into view again.

He stared hard at me and then glanced over at his parents.

"What did you do?"

I narrowed my eyes. "Don't tell me you don't trust me."

"Not when you put your mind to something." Alex sat on the other side of the fire this time, but kept me in his periphery.

So far, so good.

Now I needed to figure out what to do. Tran said it was a transport device and it looked almost exactly like the one the Del Contes used to get to my house. Was it something I had to think? Concentrate on?

My movements were slow as I touched the cool metal. I didn't know what I was doing, but physical touch couldn't hurt. If there was any possibility of finding my dad, this device should be my most direct route. Or at least it would get me out of reach of the Del Contes.

My fingers closed over the object and as I focused, Alex jerked his head around.

He leapt to his feet and scrambled to me. "Daria, no!"

I shut my eyes, concentrating on the object just like I had done with the fire, and right as Alex's hand touched mine, it

238

vanished. I heard a high-pitched hum and my body felt as if it was being squeezed through a small hole. Vomit rose in my throat and my ears popped.

And everything went quiet.

Chapter 23

Lord Tiernan

I was standing in a large stone room, lit by the glowing candles floating in the air overhead. Across from me sat a man in a sort of throne, crowning a small staircase of four steps, candelabras on either side. A hooded figure hunched beside him, whispering into his straight, jet-black hair. Two guards flanked his sides with swords at their waists.

The hunched figure froze and turned its face to look at me. It was a face of dried earth and orange cat-like eyes, and it emitted a low hiss as its eyes narrowed in fury. The man in the chair noticed me then, dark, powerful eyes taking me in. His lips lifted into a smile that, for all its intent, turned my insides cold.

"Daria." The man's voice sent chills down my spine.

It was the voice I'd heard when I'd first entered Gaia. The dark rider near the portal. The voice from my dream. And I began to feel very, very afraid. "Where's my dad?"

Without turning his eyes from my face, the man waved at the Pykan. "Leave us."

The Pykan moved past me, pausing at my side, its frame towering over me as its anger surged, and then it left. The door closed behind him.

The man steepled long fingers together. "I've been expecting you."

"Tell me where my dad is." I unsheathed my dagger.

At my movement, guards rushed to my sides. I tried positioning myself to fight but I couldn't move. I couldn't even wiggle my fingers. My body was frozen in place. In no time the guards had my arms locked behind my back and a sword was pointed at my neck.

The man stood, calculating each step he took. He stopped inches from me and took my dagger.

I struggled against the guards, but my limbs still wouldn't move.

He ran his fingers over the face of the blade, tracing the strange etchings. "Extraordinary," he whispered to himself. He shoved it in his belt and looked back at me. "You won't be needing this."

"Tell me where my dad is or—" The tip of the blade dug deeper in my throat, cutting off my words.

"Or what?" He stared down his long nose, hatred in his eyes. "Take her below."

My body went cold as my mind turned to darkness.

There was a sharp pain at my wrists and shoulders. It was the only thing my mind could grab onto, and it slowly pulled me back to consciousness. I tried thinking, but I couldn't sift through the haze. I tried moving, but my body would only sway.

I forced my lids open. A torch hung near a windowless door, keeping the room dim and filled with smoke. My wrists were chained above my head, hanging from a high stone ceiling and my feet dangled a few inches from the ground, rocking back and forth with every wriggle and writhe. I could just graze my toes along the ground, but each time I tried I'd sway and my shoulders and wrists burned. I tried calling out for help, but no sound came. My throat was parched. My whole body ached—it was hard just breathing—and my head pounded as the memories returned.

Where was I?

There was another question, one I was afraid to ask but my conscience asked it for me anyway.

What have you done?

I didn't know how long I'd been unconscious. Had I been left to die in this room? Then why lock me up at all? Was I that much of a threat? My shoulders burned from the strain, my wrists ached against the metal. I was certain the shackles would carve right through them.

The door creaked open and a tiny person walked through, concealed in an oversized cloak. The person walked toward me with a small cup in hand. It was a boy, and a young one from the looks of it. His features looked innocent

241

despite the dirt and grime caked on his skin. His face was pale and covered with countless little freckles and his eyes held a significant amount of sorrow and wisdom for one so young.

He held the cup to my lips.

"Who are you?" My voice scratched.

He pushed the cup to my lips, forcing the water into my mouth. The water revitalized me as I gulped it down. I finished it in two gulps, and the young boy stood before me, gawking.

"Help me...please."

He stood a moment more, and turned around and hurried out the door.

Hours passed in darkness and my shoulders burned so badly I thought they might fall off. My spirit was heavy with the same question: what had I done?

After what seemed like days, the door opened again. This time, a man walked through with a guard following after him. It was the man with jet-black hair. The guard stayed by the door, but the man approached me, halting inches from my face.

And I spat in his face.

Rage contorted his features, and he gripped my hair, yanking my head back at an uncomfortable angle. I fought to not cry out in pain. "I advise you cooperate if you value your father's life."

Seeing that I wasn't going to argue, he released my hair. My scalp throbbed.

"If that happens again, I will kill you."

"What have you done...to my dad?"

The man walked toward a stone basin filled with what looked like water, standing in one corner of the room. He kept his broad back to me. "I have done nothing to your father."

"Liar," I hissed. "I saw you—"

"You saw what I wanted you to see." He turned around then, his features severe. "Your father is not here, nor has he ever been. That vision was fabricated to lure you away from your friends and bring you here."

My heart dropped through my feet and fell to the ground. "You're lying."

The man smiled a wicked smile. "It is one of the few times I am not, I'm afraid."

The Del Contes had been right. It was a trap. A trap I'd walked into alone. I had no idea where I was, and chances were no one else would know either. Any relief I might have had about my dad's safety was being quickly replaced by horror. "What do you want with me?"

The man drew my dagger as he approached. My heart pounded against my ribs, and I momentarily forgot the pain in my arms.

"You have something I need."

"You've already taken the only thing I own."

"No, it is in here." He tapped the tip of the dagger on my temple. "A location."

"A location? Of what?"

He frowned. "The box."

"What box?"

His eyes narrowed. "The one that belonged to your mother."

I glared back. "I never knew my mother."

"Do not take me for a fool," he snapped.

"I swear I don't know what you're talking about."

He dug the edge of the blade against my neck, the cold metal digging into my skin. "I will not play games with you. Tell me where it is."

I struggled against the sharp pressure on my neck. "I don't know."

He took a step back and crouched to the ground. He extended his arm, letting it hover over the cold floor and his sleeve began moving. It wriggled back and forth as if something was trying to climb out of it.

Two brown threads appeared first—like antennas. A long, thin body followed, suspended between sleeve and ground, until a handful of its tiny legs touched the floor. It slithered from his robe, streaked in bright red and yellow, slithering toward me on jointed legs like a centipede. A centipede the size of my arm.

It writhed fast across the stone floor, straight toward me, the torchlight reflecting off its glossy, chitinous body. Once it reached my feet, its front end lifted from the ground until those spindly legs caught hold of my boot. I tried kicking it

243

off, but it was no use. Each and every leg was secured. Inch by inch, it pulled the rest of its body upward, crawling up my shoe, and then it began moving up my leg.

I squirmed, swinging on the chains as sweat dripped down my face, stinging my eyes.

The man watched with cold detachment as his centipede tickled up my leg and slithered up my torso, and once it reached my neck I squeezed my eyes shut. The feeling of each leg, tickling the skin around my collarbone—I couldn't stand it anymore. Its body was cold and wet, lingering there as if waiting for the command to strike. When it didn't, I opened my eyes again.

The man frowned. "Let's try this again, shall we? Where is it?"

Cold, slimy pricks tickled my ear. "I don't know!"

Those black eyes narrowed inches from mine, his fury palpable. "The slithe will kill you. All I have to do is give the command. Its poison will slowly dissolve your organs, saving your brain for last. You will be conscious through the entire process, begging for death."

His eyes bore into mine, and I felt him then, like tendrils sifting through my thoughts and feelings. His power was stronger than any I'd felt since coming to this world, save Tran Chiton. Closing my eyes, I waited for the pain to come, trying to ignore the feel of the slimy slithering creature on my neck. I was going to die here, without anyone knowing what happened to me. I was going to die because of my own foolishness.

The mental probing abruptly ceased. "You really have no idea, do you?"

I opened my eyes and was surprised to see amusement in his.

"I told you, I don't know what you're talking about." The pointed legs slid around my neck like a collar. "I came here for my dad."

"And did you in all honesty think that a man with the power of Alaric Regius needs the help of his daughter?"

I gaped at him, forgetting the slithe completely. "Alaric...who?"

244

His smile made my insides recoil. "I see your father picked a masterful guard in the Del Contes. Aegis Cicero never would break an oath."

"What...are you talking about?" The antennas poked my cheeks and its entire body tightened around my neck.

Tiernan frowned. "Your father is the son and heir of Darius Regius, ruler of Gaia."

It felt as if a rock lodged in my throat. "No. That's impossible. My dad is just a businessman...I mean, Ambassador. You're after the wrong man."

"Oh, no, no, no. The likeness to your mother Aurora is uncanny." He ran the backs of his icy fingers along my cheek. "And the power that runs through your blood." He trailed the tip of the dagger along my arms. "It seems you are as the prophecies have foretold—a blend of the unique powers from your mother and father, making you a dangerous weapon. Gaia has...surprised me."

Was this what the Del Contes had been forbidden to tell me—what Dad had planned on telling me? This was too much. This was insane. "I don't have any powers. I'm telling you, you've got the wrong person."

"I'm sure your father thought he was protecting you," Tiernan continued, "thinking I wouldn't harm you if you didn't realize your power, because power, once discovered, takes time to fully develop. Luckily, I have ways of extracting that information which doesn't require your knowledge. You may thank your father for this, because it's his fidelity to Gaia that makes his own understanding of magic very, very limited."

Tiernan picked up the creature from my neck, and it writhed and jerked in his grip, struggling to break free. He carelessly let it fall to the ground and with a blast of light, all that remained of the slithe was a black spot on the stone. The man turned back to me, and then he dug the dagger into my forearm.

Cold metal carved into my skin and I gasped in pain. Blood trickled down my arm as he pulled the dagger away, its edge coated in my blood. He walked over to the stone basin and rinsed the dagger clean in the water. The water shone shades of blue so bright it illuminated the room. He cupped

245

his hands together, scooped out some of the bloodied water, and drank.

My insides twisted.

He stood erect, his features in ecstasy at the power now trickling through him. My power.

"You are more powerful than I thought," he said, walking back toward me. "My Lord will be very pleased with you. Yes, Gaia will mourn when her precious daughter turns against her."

"I will never help you," I spat.

Tiernan gripped my chin and forced me to look into his eyes. "Those devoted friends of yours are on their way here now, in an attempt to rescue you, and when they arrive, I will kill them."

Horror gripped my soul. "No...please..."

"You have two choices." He shoved my chin aside. "Surrender your will and powers to my lord, *the* Lord, and your friends will be left unharmed—that is my word. Or, you will die in this room and I will take your strength and kill them. Either way, I will have your powers."

"You'll never get away with this! They'll kill you if you do anything to me. Let me go!"

He set something on the ledge next to the basin. It was an hourglass, one filled with blood red sand already streaming into the empty half.

"You have exactly one hour to make a decision, at which point the last grain will fall, and your life will end. I hope you make the right choice, for I should be sorely disappointed to waste such beauty."

With that, he left.

The guard lingered a bit, watching after his master, then fixed his black eyes on me. A sickening shadow passed over his face as he took soft, careful steps toward me. His breath reeked of rot and ale as he gave me a decayed smile that spread across his swollen face, glistening with perspiration. He lifted a fat, square hand and dragged his rough palm across my cheek.

"So vulnerable and such..." He licked his fat lips. "Delicious purity."

I conjured all the saliva I could and spit it on his face. He, however, held that black smile as he wiped off the spit, inching his face closer.

His chuckle was low, sending ice through my blood. "I'll enjoy you, *princess.*"

He patted my cheek, walked through the door and closed it behind him.

I screamed after him—at myself.

No one listened, and no one answered, just as no one came.

I was alone.

I fated myself to this. Dad, the Del Contes—Tiernan was going to kill them. All because of me. All because I wouldn't listen.

But Tiernan had given me a choice. A choice that would spare their lives. All I had to do was serve him. The Del Contes and my dad didn't deserve to die because of me. They'd done nothing but risk their lives to protect me—their entire lives, just as they were forced to do now. I felt as though a knife were being run through my gut. I didn't deserve any of them.

The red sands formed a threatening pile in the glass. My time would be running out soon. I could yell those words, serve this evil, and live the rest of my life as a lie. It wasn't so different, if I thought about it. I was used to living a lie, only now I was choosing to live one in order to protect those I loved.

Isn't that what you've been chastising everyone else about? That they'd all lied to protect you?

I hadn't understood their reasons, and I'd judged them for it. What I'd done—the way I'd acted—was humiliating. Now I might never get the chance to apologize for my behavior, and Alex...

My chest throbbed as I remembered how I'd treated him. All along he'd been trying to protect me from this evil. Dad had been right. My stubborn resentment was going to be the death of me, either physically or emotionally—probably both.

I didn't have much time left. Maybe they wouldn't blame me for this choice. Out of anyone, they should understand what I was about to do. I opened my mouth, prepared to yell

247

the words that would forever alter my person and take away my freedom, but I couldn't.

Even if I lived that lie to protect them now, what would happen later? When this unknown Lord's power had grown because I had given it to him and then I'd be forced to hurt them?

There must be another way. There has *to be.*

I searched the room for anything I could use to escape but there was nothing aside from that stone basin. Besides, what could I do chained to the ceiling?

The chains.

Maybe, just maybe, I could break free. After all, with my mind I'd been able to start a fire and I'd been able to use the amulet. Was it so far from the realm of possibilities that I might be able to use that same power to unlock the chains? Tiernan had said I was powerful. It was a power strong enough that he'd been hunting me for it. Just how powerful was I? Now was as good a chance as any to find out.

I shut my eyes tight, concentrating on the shackles. It was difficult, knowing the sands of time were running low on my life. I fought to focus on my wrists. The shackles had some sort of internal opposing force and rebounded my mental prodding. I focused harder, my face pinched in concentration, my teeth clenched as I fought against the pressure of the brace. My skull ached from straining and my teeth ground so hard I thought they might shatter. And then I broke through.

I pushed through the opening, searching for a latch until my senses found it. In a second I had one undone, followed quickly by the other. With a click, I crashed hard to the ground, and the wind was knocked from me. For a moment I lay, gasping for air. My wrists burned and my head pounded as I choked on my breath.

I looked up and realized I only had a couple more minutes. I crawled to my life timer and lay it on its side with only a few grains left. Sighing my relief, I made my way to the door and shoved.

Nothing.

The shackles had left me so exhausted I didn't have any strength left to force my exit. Slumping to the ground, I tried to calm my breathing so I could think. There was no way I had broken free of my chains only to be trapped by a rotted wooden door.

Footsteps sounded outside. Maybe the guard had returned. Regardless, whoever lurked there wasn't powerful. I couldn't find any of the evil presence I'd sensed in Tiernan. Struggling to my feet, I pressed myself against the wall. Whoever opened that door would be my means out. I would make sure of it.

I held my breath and gathered all my remaining strength. The door creaked open and a figure walked in. And I struck.

Within seconds, I had the intruder in a chokehold, preparing to smash my fist into his face when innocent eyes gazed up at me. The cup in his hands clattered to the floor and its contents spilled on the ground. Clamping my hand over his mouth, our eyes locked. He looked past me at my broken chains and his eyes widened with shock. But he didn't struggle—not once—as I pulled him away from the door.

I gave him a look, trying to convey in silence that I would be lifting my hand from his mouth and he had better think twice before yelling. When I lifted my hand, he didn't say a word. He only gaped, unblinking.

Well, he obviously wasn't going to get me in trouble, so maybe he would help me.

"Do you know a way out?" I whispered.

He nodded, his eyes never leaving mine.

"Will you help me?"

The boy smiled then, bringing a childlike glee to his features. He leaned closer. "Are you really Lady Daria Regius?"

His eagerness made me smile. "I'm not sure who I am anymore, but my name is Daria."

"You broke the chains?" His small forehead wrinkled.

"Yes."

"You are Lady Daria Regius, then." His tone was so confident for someone so young.

"Well, if you help me get out of here, then maybe we can both find out."

The challenge delighted him. Whoever he was or whatever had happened to him, the spirit inside him was strong and brave.

"Are there any guards out front?"

The boy held up a single tiny finger.

One guard. I could get past one guard. The training Dad had insisted on might prove useful after all. However, it was one thing to fight for practice. It was another to fight for your life. But I had to try. This might just be the deadliest test I'd ever taken, and it was very possible I would fail it.

I took a deep breath. The boy had taken off his cloak and was holding it out for me. His clothing was dirty and torn, and his arms and legs were starved for proper nourishment and looked out of proportion with his knobby elbows and knees. If we succeeded in escaping, I would see to it myself that he would be taken care of. Starting with a huge meal. And a bath.

"I can't fight. I'm too small," he whispered. "Wear this. He'll think it's me."

I nodded in understanding, and I wound the cloak around me. It was tight, but the low lighting would help, at least at first glance.

As I started again for the door, I turned around, grabbing the boy's arm. He flinched at my touch.

"What is your name?" I let go of his arm.

"I don't know. So if we get out of here, maybe we can find out mine too."

I smiled. "I promise I'll help you."

He seemed to like that answer. "The guards call me Fleck."

Appropriate for one with that many freckles, but not a proper name. We would have to change that.

"Wish me luck, Fleck."

"If you can do that—" he pointed to the broken chains "—you won't need it."

His confidence in my ability enabled me, no matter how false it might have been. I grinned, my strength renewed at having someone's faith. I would give it my all, at least for this boy.

Grabbing the cup, I pulled the hood far over my head and opened the door. Just as Fleck had said, there was one guard standing beside my door, his sword still in its sheath. It was the same disgusting man I'd met earlier in my cell. I kept my head low as I approached him, the empty cup in hand.

250

"Is the princess still alive?" the guard grumbled, licking his lips.

I nodded. The man's desires filled me with disgust.

"Think it's time I go in there." The guard patted his fat belly. "A beauty like hers shouldn't be wasted. Keep watch for me, eh, Fleck? Let me know if Master Tiernen is coming." He flashed hungry eyes at the prison door. "I've never had a princess."

I turned to him then, my blood boiling. His eyes widened just as I slammed the stone cup into his face. The back of his bald head rammed into the wall and he slumped to the ground, unconscious.

"And you never will," I spat. "Fleck! Open the door!"

The door creaked open, and I used all my strength to drag the heavy guard into my prison. Fleck watched with bright eyes and a grin on his face. "See, I told you, lady."

"Here." I handed him back his cloak and started taking off the man's armor. On the back of his neck was that same symbol I'd seen at Rex Cross. The entire mark was black, the center resembling an eye framed by triangles on either side. I'd have to tell the others—if I ever saw them again.

The guard's armor was too large, but it would have to work, and it was ridiculously heavy. I ended up taking off a few pieces to lighten my load, but I kept the breastplate. It seemed essential, even though it threw off my balance a little. I was certain that if anyone so much as touched me, I'd fall over headfirst. I tore off his shirtsleeve and wrapped it around my face, concealing as much of it as possible.

"You look like a boy, lady," Fleck whispered.

"Why, thank you, Fleck." I moved my body, trying to get used to the feel of this metal. "All right, do you know a way out of here?"

His little brow puckered. "I think so," he said after considerable thought. "But you have to use that power again." He nodded toward the chains.

"Sure." My answer didn't reflect my feelings. I wasn't sure I could do that again, but I wouldn't crush either of our hopes now. Not when we'd made it this far.

"Good." He smiled, a light in his eyes. "Follow me, Lady."

Chapter 24

Escape

Fleck and I hugged the hallways, pausing at intervals to listen. It was quiet in this maze of damp, dark caverns lit only by intermittent torches, and there was a chill that touched my bones. It was as if the air around us was a living thing, and whatever it was felt evil.

Fleck's knowledge of this place was more thorough than I could've hoped. Not only did he know exactly where he was going, he kept us on passageways that weren't frequented. Without him, I never would've found my way out.

We tiptoed along and I began to get used to the feel of the metal on my chest. I still felt top heavy and it clinked a little when I moved, but after awhile, I was able to walk in relative silence. It still worried me, though, the thought of fighting while wearing this thing. Would I be able to move fast enough?

We rounded a corner when I saw movement in the shadows. I shoved Fleck against the wall behind me and drew the sword I'd stolen from the guard. It felt a lot different than holding a dagger, and I couldn't seem to get the balance right.

Hold it steady, Daria. You have to get out of here...at least for Fleck.

The shadow moved toward me. Torchlight flickered and I caught a glimpse of shiny metal. Whoever it was wore armor, like mine. How could they see through my disguise so easily?

There was a flash of steel as I barely managed to deflect the strike at my throat, and due to my breastplate, I miscalculated my movement and almost toppled forward. My attacker's sword came at my side and I barely managed to spin away before being skewered. But something about his movements seemed familiar.

His foot landed hard in my chest, throwing me back against the wall with a crash. He lifted his sword over my head. I would've rolled away, but I was wedged against the wall.

"Lady, watch out!" Fleck screamed.

The sword came down in a blur and I shut my eyes, waiting for the blow that would end my life.

But nothing came.

I opened my eyes and stared at the tip of sword.

I felt a surge of the guard's curiosity as he reached over and ripped the cloth from my face. His sword clattered to the ground.

"Daria!" He ripped off his helmet and wrapped his arms around me.

It was Alex. He had come. He had found me, and had risked his life for mine. Again. "You're alive." He held my head against his chest.

Guilt and remorse flooded through me as he pulled back, his hands moving all over my face. A torrent of emotions crossed over his face. There were so many things I wanted to say, so many regrets that I didn't know where to start. He sighed and rested his forehead on mine.

"Alex...I'm so...sorry." My voice trembled and my throat clamped shut.

He pulled away, his face inches from mine as he held a finger over my lips. Then he noticed Fleck and his eyes narrowed. "Who's he?"

Fleck's eyes were wide and his knobby knees knocked.

"Fleck," I whispered. "He's helping me escape."

Alex's brow furrowed and footsteps shuffled behind him.

"Dad!" I struggled to my feet with Alex's help.

"Shh!" My dad whispered, folding his thick arms around me, smothering me in his relief.

After all this time. I couldn't believe he was here, right now, and alive. "Dad, I—"

"There's no time." His voice was low. "We've got to get out of here. Alex?"

Alex nodded, glancing at me before throwing his helmet back on. Dad grabbed my arm.

"Wait, Fleck?" I peered back to where Fleck stood, mouth agape. "You're coming with us."

Dad's apprehension was acute. "We don't know who he is."

"He helped me get this far. I'm not leaving without him."

My dad hesitated, but motioned for a shocked Fleck to follow.

"Prince Alaric?" Fleck whispered.

Prince? I mean, of course it made sense, since he was the king's son, but it was still odd hearing it. My dad, a prince.

"How did you get inside, sire?" Fleck asked.

Sire? This was going to take some getting used to.

"We recruited a borderline insane wizard for help," Dad said. "Although, we can use any help getting out. You must know a way?"

"I was going to use the main entrance."

"How's that?" I was staring at Fleck now.

Fleck looked down, embarrassed. "I thought you could pretend you have orders to take me somewhere, but that won't work with this many people. And everyone recognizes you, sire."

Yells echoed throughout the corridor, followed by pounding footsteps. We all pressed ourselves to the wall, holding our breaths, but no one continued down our tunnel.

"We entered through a side entrance," my dad continued, "but now that they're aware you're missing, that will be impossible."

"We have to try—before they seal the exits," Alex said.

The four of us ran down the corridor until we reached a much wider vein—a main passageway. A handful of armed guards shuffled past, intent in the direction from which we had come. My cell.

I gripped Fleck's sweaty hand. "I won't leave you here," I whispered in his ear.

He nodded as the color drained from his face.

We marched in the opposite direction, me holding on to Fleck as if he was my prisoner. It was difficult not to run, but that would give us away. Guards ran by—pushed by—none taking a second glance at us.

This might be easier than I'd thought.

We continued until the corridor descended, lower and lower underground, ending in a narrow, domed room. Guards were peppered about, standing, chatting, and no one even glanced at us. Beyond them was a dark slit in the rock wall. An exit.

If we could thread through the guards unnoticed, we would be free. It would be that simple.

"There you are. I was wondering when you'd come."

Or maybe not.

Lord Tiernan appeared out of nowhere, and now we had the guards' attention. Shuffling sounded behind us and I spun around to find them now blocking that path, too. We were trapped.

"You didn't honestly believe I would let you simply walk out of here with my prisoner, did you?"

My dad stepped forward. "You." That one word held so much loathing and disgust it seemed as if the entire room recoiled.

Lord Tiernan's smile pulled his taught skin even tighter over the sharp bones of his face. "Who were you expecting, *my prince?*" His velvety voice was laden with condescension. "Unlike you, I serve the *true* Lord of Gaia."

"The *true* Lord of Gaia is my father, King Darius Regius," Dad growled in a commanding tone I'd never heard. "You forgot yourself, Tiernan. My father rewarded you beyond measure for your services, and this is how you thank him." Dad waved his hand at the men in armor now gathered all around. "Selling your soul to Mortis." The light in the room flickered and dimmed. "You forget who you bargain with. It will be the end of you."

The smile on Lord Tiernan's face fell. "You have always failed to see the world as it is. Your father is a coward, just like the one he serves, exploiting the talents of others and using them against his people. I curse the days I called myself his servant," Tiernan spat, eyes narrowed in pure hatred. "It is your ignorance that will kill you, old friend."

Tiernan drew two swords from beneath his cloak, one for each hand, and he radiated so much power it was disorienting.

Dad drew his own sword, and his eyes shined with a ferocity that frightened me. What was he thinking? He didn't know how to use a sword.

"You should've died years ago for your treason," my dad said. "Today, you will pay for it."

Everything happened so fast that before I could figure out what they were talking about, Dad charged Lord Tiernan.

"Dad!" I screamed. I lunged after him but was yanked back by a firm grip.

"Leave him," Alex said.

I fought against his hold as I watched my dad cross blades with Lord Tiernan. "Alex, you have to help him! He can't fight..." My words trailed as I watched.

I was wrong. My dad *could* fight, almost as well as Alex.

Everyone's attention was engaged in the duel as Tiernan's spinning blades attempted to scissor my dad in half. Dad always moved at the last second, delivering counter blows that were knocked to the side.

"Close the exits!" Tiernan brandished his swords.

A few cloaks drifted toward our exit and raised their arms. I soon realized they weren't men. They were Pykans. A rock began sliding through our intended exit, sealing the narrow crevice.

"Alex! Get her out of here," Dad yelled, rolling away from a scissor of metal.

Before he could finish his command, Alex was already pulling me away.

"We can't leave him!"

Some of the guards turned their attention toward us now, drawing their swords.

Two, three, four at a time charged. Alex threw me behind him and leapt into the melee. He danced around them, fast and fluid, his legs finding a face, a knee as his sword slashed through tendons and arteries. I couldn't move, watching the sphere of death he created around himself. So much blood. So much violence.

As I watched Alex, I was thrown to the ground, suddenly unable to move. One of the guards had me pinned and was forcing a dagger at my face. Mustering my strength, I freed one hand, grabbed another dagger from his belt, and shoved it into his abdomen. His pain tore through my body as the force behind his dagger weakened. He toppled sideways off of me.

"Daria!" Alex yelled.

I heard scraping as silver flashed on the ground toward me. Alex had thrown me another dagger. Swinging out my

256

arm, I caught the blade and shoved it into the chest of my next attacker. His dark eyes widened in surprise and pain as he rolled to his side, lifeless.

I scrambled to my feet, my blood roaring in my ears. My blade was dripping crimson....with blood. I had just killed two men. I had taken their lives. My stomach turned just as another attacked me.

On instinct, my muscles brought the dagger around, right into the blade of my attacker with a clash. Everything around me slowed and I suddenly felt light and weightless. His movements were sluggish and predictable. Before he could reposition his sword, I spun around. Using my momentum for force, I plunged the dagger into an opening in his armor, right into the side of his ribcage. His jaw dropped as he slumped to the ground.

Alex was staring at me in disbelief, as a sword was being lifted over his head. And he didn't see it. I threw the dagger, and it sliced end-over-end through the air, right into the forehead of the guard. His movement froze as he and his weapon toppled to the ground.

Alex looked behind himself in surprise and then rushed to my side, pushing and slashing at anyone between us. He jerked me away from a sword that came within inches of my abdomen. Another guard rushed toward us, but was weighed down by an anchor named Fleck. Fleck sat on the man's feet with his arms wrapped tightly around his legs. The man realized his inhibition and raised his sword. I leapt forward, slashed across the man's raised arm and kicked him down.

Fleck ducked, still wrapped around the man's legs.

"Fleck, you're fine. Get up." I grabbed his arm and yanked him up beside me.

When I looked up again, my heart dropped. There were more guards. This time, the Pykans had joined them and they'd sealed our only exit.

A handful of the orange-eyed men began encircling us, their rotted mouths fixed in satisfaction. Out of the corner of my eye I saw a blur of brown and grey, and one of the guards fell. The blur moved again, and another guard fell—this time followed by maniacal laughter.

"Great Mages! I can't believe you started the fight without us," said a voice I recognized.

257

Tran appeared, flashing Alex and me a look of disapproval.

The Pykans hissed like a brood of vipers and the blur stopped spinning. It was Grool. He still wore his brown paper sack, but now he was wearing a helmet that was much too large for his odd-shaped head. Infuriated, he stomped on the foot of a Pykan, jabbed a wickedly shaped piece of metal into the folds of its cloak, and spun off again in a blur of silver and brown. The Pykan's pain shot through me and its cat-like eyes narrowed as a burst of light shot from its fingertips.

Tran met him head on. Green light pushed against blue, and sparks flew through the air as the two sorcerers dueled with a power only they could wield. Alex pushed Fleck and me to the ground just as another bolt of light shot through the space our heads had been.

The magicians leapt into the air using the walls and heads of men to rebound. Light flashed all around as rock crumbled after it.

Alex pulled me after him and we crawled away with Fleck right beside me.

The remaining guards had huddled off to the side to avoid the magical avalanche. Also because they were transfixed by something: the fight between my dad and Tiernan.

I took off, aware that Alex was yelling after me. My heart raced as blood pumped through my veins. I climbed on top of a small boulder that had fallen and peered over the group.

"You're weak, *sire.*" Tiernan's swords crossed with my dad's and he spun away. "You should've listened. Now she will watch you die."

Dad ran at Tiernan, his swords flashing through the air. I could feel his rage and power as it surged through me.

The ground began to shake. More chunks of rock fell from the ceiling, some tumbling down on the heads of the guards. Tiernan stumbled through the debris to regain his balance. His eyes shut, his features strained, and the shaking stopped. When he opened his eyes, there was a spark of amusement in them. "Is that all?"

Tiernan showed his teeth as his eyes glowed white. His swords fell to the ground and he stretched his arms high. A blanket of white light formed in the space between his hands and then he flung it at my dad. With an agonizing yell, my father dropped his swords and swung his arms outward against the enveloping wall of light. An explosion sounded. The light shattered into a million tiny crystals, falling like rain around him.

Once the last crystal shard fell, my dad slumped forward. Tiernan saw the opportunity. He swept up his swords with a yell, and charged.

Dad just managed to block the attack, but his back was bending from the pressure. Tiernan smiled and pressed harder. My dad's knees buckled. One of his legs turned at an unnatural angle and his pain shot through my body.

"Dad!" I screamed, petrified.

Tiernan smiled a wicked smile, holding one sword overhead. "Goodbye, old friend."

I didn't remember leaping from the boulder. I didn't remember pushing past the guards, but somehow I was standing behind Tiernan, my hand gripping the dagger that was deep in his chest.

Tiernan froze as I retracted my weapon. His eyes widened in shock and the swords fell from his hands, their clanging rebounding inside the silent stone chamber. He opened his mouth and screamed—the yell so horrible it turned my blood cold. And then he crumbled to the ground. All that remained of Tiernan was his cloak and my stolen dagger.

The room was silent.

I picked up my dagger and hurried to my dad's side, still shaking. Alex pushed through the horde of shocked guards and helped me get my dad to his feet. Dad's strength was fading fast.

I searched in desperation for a way out, but both exits were blocked. The guards' shock began wearing off and they started closing in on us. The show was over, and they weren't letting us get away. We stepped back, and Alex held on to my dad. Tran and Grool had joined us. Grool was holding an ax in his hand, gurgling strange insults at the men poised around us.

"Keep walking." Tran's voice was low as he moved back to the wall.

"Walk where?" I asked. "We're trapped!"

The guards crept closer, confident of their prey.

I glanced back at my dad. His eyes were closed as he leaned against the rock wall. His features looked strained and tense and the veins around his temple were bulging. And then the ground began trembling. Violently.

I grabbed Fleck and pulled him to me as I huddled over my father. Huge pieces of rock fell from the top of the dome, crashing all around—many of the boulders falling between the guards and us.

The wall right behind us began splitting. I clutched Fleck's hand and we ducked while large chunks of the cave crashed down behind us. A few plummeted toward our heads, but right before impact, and with a wave of Tran's hand, they exploded into millions of tiny shards. At once the crashing ceased and the room returned to silence.

I lifted my head. The wall next to us had split so that it formed a tunnel, and at its end was a narrow thread of light. My dad slumped to the ground.

Alex was already hoisting Dad up on his feet.

"Hurry!" yelled Tran, pushing us through the new exit.

We sprinted. Grool ran after us, dropping things on the ground while laughing maniacally at himself.

Tran led us forward through the dark tunnel. The soft light grew brighter and brighter, and the scent of damp air grew stronger. Enraged voices shouted behind us. The Pykans were already blasting the blockage into oblivion. We didn't have much time. Once they destroyed the rock barrier, we'd never outrun them. Not with my dad in this condition.

It felt like forever before the narrow tunnel ended and we were dumped on the sandy beach of an alcove. Our tunnel was at the base of a steep, rocky cliff that curved in a semicircle into the ocean. Rain poured down upon us from the dark clouds above and large white-capped waves crashed along the shore, desperately trying to reach us.

I had no idea where we were, but I knew we were far from Lake Amadis.

Tran kept us running straight for a narrow crevice in the rock, and we were soon stumbling out of the alcove.

The army emerged from the crack in the side of the rocky cliff. They were livid, gripping their weapons as they ran. Bursts of light fired at us with renewed vigor, and we ran and ran.

"Grool, now!" I heard Tran yell from somewhere ahead.

The ground shook and the air filled with loud explosions. Flames consumed the cavern, pouring out of its crack, reaching bright orange fingers toward the sky. The explosions continued, and the fire and smoke stretched higher and higher while the cliff imploded upon itself.

When I looked back at Tran, I couldn't find him. Or Grool.

"Up here!" shouted Cicero.

At first I couldn't figure out where the sound came from, but then I looked up.

Cicero and Sonya were flying. They were sitting on the backs of velvety black creatures that looked like horses, but their necks were longer, arcing outward from their extraordinary muscular bodies, and they had wings. Enormous, black wings.

"Mom, here." Alex helped Fleck climb on with Sonya.

If I hadn't been so concerned about the armed guards chasing us, there was no way I'd trust my dad on that thing. Cicero helped pull my dad on with him, and Alex threw me on a third rider-less creature and climbed in front of me.

"Hold on!" he yelled over his shoulder and I just managed to wrap my arms around his waist as we took off into the air.

Rain and wind slapped my face as we soared upward, higher and higher. I tried not to look down. I tried not to look anywhere. My grip around Alex was so tight, I wasn't sure if I'd be able to ever break it loose.

Below, the men screamed after us. A few stray beams of light shot past, but our winged horses swerved easily out of the way. The guards grew smaller and smaller as we soared farther and farther away. Just as I felt that overwhelming relief of survival, a blood-curdling shriek pierced the air.

I glanced back. Three creatures rose from the flames and ruin, flying through the air toward us. Gargons. So the rumors were true. These were what had been wreaking havoc on villages. These beasts were spitting images of the drawing I'd seen in Tran's monsters manual. They had been frightening enough on paper, but they were terrifying in real life.

"Gargons!" I yelled at Alex.

"I see them!"

261

Their sleek reptilian bodies sliced through the sky like darts as their powerful wings beat against the wind. Those fiery red eyes burned with hunger as their soul-splitting wails ripped through the air.

"Take Daria ahead," Cicero yelled. "We'll distract them."

Sonya was already reaching for her bow. Before I could blink, the dark green and silver feathers shot through the air, sinking deep into the skull of one of the creatures. It shrieked and blew hot steam as it clawed at the air, unable to bat its wings. Gravity took it then, pulling it down like a stone falling through the air.

Another took a swipe at Sonya. Her horse dove, missing the gargon's claw by a thread. Cicero threw one of his daggers and missed, but provided enough of a distraction for Sonya to restring her bow and loose another powerful arrow. With a shriek the beast tried to dislodge the point from its chest, its wings unable to keep it airborne.

Two down. One left. But this one was faster.

Sonya shot arrow after arrow, each missing by a thread. Cicero flew near enough to slash with his blade, but the gargon raked at him, sending him, my dad, and their winged horse spinning through the air away from us.

Infuriated, the gargon shot forward, intent on Alex and me. Sonya and Cicero were far behind now, trying with everything they had to catch up. The beast was too quick. The distance between us was closing fast.

"We have to go faster!" I yelled.

"This is as fast as it gets!"

"Can't you do something?"

"You drive."

Before I could ask, Alex was climbing over me.

Air screamed past my ears. The beating of the gargon's wings grew louder, and now it was so close I could feel its hot breath. Alex held on to me with one arm, his other clutching his sword as I tried to give him the stability he needed to do whatever it was he had planned.

The gargon swiped, but its claws were deflected by Alex's blade. Its teeth came down on us and our horse dropped before those powerful jaws could trap us inside. The next time it clawed at Alex, it took his sword with it.

No.

This couldn't be happening.

We hadn't come this far to die, splattered on the ground. I had to make things right. I refused to let this happen.

My anger surged, and a gust of wind blew so strong it sent our creature and the gargon spiraling through the air. Both of us struggled to rebalance against the wind. I held on tight to the horse, clenching my legs around its body so that I wouldn't fall, and Alex did the same. It took a minute for us to regain our balance until we were jetting forward again. But the gargon had righted itself as well.

Fury wafted through my body again, and the wind blew hard in my face. But this time the wind had words. It filtered into my ears, the whistling gaining volume, transforming into what sounded like a soft voice. *"Use the dagger."*

There was a strange tingling sensation over my body and the dagger burned at my hip.

You have to try. There's no other choice.

"Hold on!" There must have been something in my voice because Alex didn't argue. He let go of me and held on to the horse.

I ripped the dagger from its place beneath my belt and turned my body so that I could get better aim, my legs clamped tight for balance.

"What are you doing?"

"Just hold on!"

I concentrated on those eyes—those furious eyes that thirsted for my death. For Alex's death. I would not let that monster have it.

Pulling back the dagger, I focused, empowered by the wind. With a flick, the dagger left my hands.

Silver streaked across the black sky. It split through droplets of water and landed right between the red eyes of death. Within seconds, the red eyes dimmed and the air filled with the terrible sounds of agony as the ground reclaimed it.

Chapter 25

Return to Amadis

Alex stared wide-eyed after the fallen gargon. Our own creature slowed to a more relaxing pace so I carefully turned back around in my seat. Alex snaked his arms around my waist, holding me so tight against him I could feel his heart pounding against my back.

"How did you do that?" he asked in my ear.

Cicero and Sonya joined us. Their surprise was strong, their faces showing love and pride. A love and pride I didn't deserve.

"Did I just witness Daria slaying that gargon?" Cicero hollered over the wind.

"Yes!" Alex shouted.

"I thought we were going to lose you," Sonya yelled.

Alex squeezed my waist. "So did I."

We had made it. It was a good thing, too, because if anything had happened to them, I never would have been able to forgive myself. My dad was unconscious in front of Cicero, but at least he was safe. Fleck's eyes were still shut tight as he held on to Sonya with all his might.

"Fleck, it's all right," I yelled. "We're alive."

Fleck didn't move, not at first. But then the lid on one eye lifted to make sure it was safe to open the other, and his posture relaxed a little.

"How is he?" I motioned toward my dad.

"Breathing," Cicero called back. "He'll be all right."

I glanced back at Sonya, who, despite all efforts to hide it, was still recovering from the scare of almost losing us. All because of me. I fixed my eyes up ahead and felt Alex's concern. He didn't say a word, but held on to me a little tighter. I was suddenly aware of how close we were, the feel of his chest against my back, and my heart beat faster. I was glad he couldn't see my face.

The land remained in shadow from the heavy clouds above, though the rain had stopped. This was definitely an improvement. Constant drops smacking your face hurt at the speeds we were flying. The terrain was far below us, rolling and dipping endlessly in either direction. The world looked empty from up here. There were no signs of life or habitation—just open plains. The kind I would love to ride on, in any other circumstance.

Flying was a unique sensation. At these altitudes and with nothing like a seatbelt holding me down, I should've been scared senseless, but I wasn't. With every gust of wind and every whisper of the breeze, energy and peace surged through me. Their combined effort permeated every part of my being. It was difficult to explain, but the open air was invigorating in ways nothing else had been. It was purifying and revitalizing, and I felt as if I could stay up here forever.

The sun sank behind the glorious mountains of Amadis, warning of the pervading night. Our transport landed like a bird on water, and we stopped.

When I hopped down from the creature my legs ached from clenching so tight. Up close, the horse was gigantic, the tip of its nose still a few feet from the top of my head. Alex dropped to my side.

"What is it called?" I reached my hand toward its nose.

Alex didn't look at me. "A vox. They're native to the Arborenne. We were fortunate to find them."

"Great Mages, that was marvelous, if I do say!" Tran appeared behind me.

"Where did you come from?"

His blue eyes shone with the excitement of battle. "I've been here, waiting for all of you. It has been difficult being patient because I've wanted to discuss our most recent events and, well, Grool..." He gestured toward the trees.

Off in the distance, just visible between the trees, was a little person wearing a helmet the size of his body, waving a twisted piece of metal in the air at invisible attackers while laughing maniacally.

I grinned. "Tran, thank you. You risked your life..."

"Ah, ah." He shook a withered finger in my face. "Your father has arrived."

He marched past me, toward the others. Sonya helped an eager Fleck to solid ground, while Alex helped Cicero lift my father.

Seeing my usually robust dad limp in someone's arms made my heart squeeze. There were deep cuts along his arms and bruises were forming on his face. I had done that to him, every cut, every bruise—they were all my fault.

I rushed to his side as Cicero and Alex carried him to Cicero's blanket, careful to lay him down without further injury.

I hated to ask it, but I needed my dad. "Can you help him?" I glanced at Sonya.

She didn't meet my gaze. "I'm going to try."

She knelt at his side and placed a slender hand on his forehead.

"Sonya, maybe you should let Tran..." Cicero started.

Sonya ignored her husband, shutting her eyes. The strain on her was immediate. It was as though my own energy was being stolen from me. The look on Cicero's face was one of pure torture as his eyes darted between his wife and Tran, in hopes that one or the other might stop what was transpiring. Sonya had already done so much.

"Sonya, it's all right," I whispered, crouching at her side. "You don't have to do this."

Her body slumped forward, and Cicero was there to catch her and prop her up. "That's enough, love." Cicero carried her to her blankets and laid her down. Her breathing was shallow and strained.

A gasp of air sounded beside me.

"Dad!"

His lungs took in another gasp as his lids fluttered open. When his eyes found me he struggled to reach out with his hands.

"You're alive," he sighed, closing his eyes.

"Yes. Everyone's alive." I glanced behind me at Tran and this family who had saved my life, and then I felt a sharp pain in my chest. "Tran and the Del Contes saved us..." My throat strangled the rest of my words and tears spilled over my cheeks. Each of them stood in silence. "I'm...so sorry. The way I've acted...I should've trusted you all. I should've listened..."

266

Cicero came to my side then, his eyes warm. "I can't pretend I don't understand why you did it, because I do." He laid a hand on my forearm. With a sigh, he looked to my dad. "Alaric, why couldn't you have had a more obedient child?"

Dad coughed as he laughed. "Trust me, old friend," he whispered. "I've asked myself that since the day she was born. I like to think Gaia is getting back at me by putting ornery people in my life. You included."

Cicero chuckled as he looked back at me. "Sonya and I love you like you're our own daughter. We would do anything to protect you—not because it's our duty, but because you are our family. I forgive you. Had you hurt yourself, I might not have." He wrapped his arm around me.

"I don't deserve any of you."

"We are given many things in this world we don't deserve, so best appreciate it while you can. Life is...so very fragile."

He released me, then walked over to join his wife who lay exhausted on the blankets. My dad moved to sit and I hugged an arm around his shoulders to support him.

"On the bright side," Dad continued, "we now know the gargon rumor was true and the villagers have their predators destroyed."

"Unfortunately, we also have our evidence destroyed." Cicero motioned toward the unsuspecting Grool, who still fought the invisible foe.

"The safety of Gaia's citizens is more important for now," Tran interjected.

"Yes," my dad continued. "Hopefully it will help unify the territories once we present to the council that the Del Contes have slain three gargons."

"Daria killed the last," Cicero said.

My dad's gaze widened on me. "Is this true?"

Everyone looked at me, and I looked down.

"She did," Alex answered for me. "With a dagger."

"Sonya and Cicero killed the first two," I said. "Really, I was lucky."

Dad studied me a long moment. "Luck doesn't slay a gargon."

"You should've seen her," Cicero continued. "I'd never seen a more determined face—and for Daria, that has to tell you something."

267

The others chuckled but I couldn't even smile. I still felt too guilty for what I'd done and how I'd treated them.

"You haven't introduced us to your friend." My dad nodded toward Fleck, who sat off in the distance with his arms wrapped around himself.

"Fleck," I said. He didn't move. "Fleck, come here please. I'd like to introduce you to my family."

Nothing.

I got to my feet and walked over to him. He had his head buried in his arms and legs. I placed my hand on his shoulder and he flinched. "Fleck, it's just me. You're safe now. What's wrong?"

Muffled murmuring sounded from the pile of folded arms and legs—all of which was indecipherable. I crouched low, my mouth at his ear. "I can't hear you. Tell me what's the matter?"

"They'll make me leave."

"Why would they do something like that?"

"Because I'm marked."

"Marked how?"

He lifted his head and I started. Flecks of silver flashed bright in his eyes, glittering in the remaining sunlight. I hadn't noticed them before, being in the depths of the caves. So he hadn't been named for his freckles. It was because of his eyes.

"A Daloren child," Tran gasped. Tran was at our side in a moment. "Yes...yes...it was too dark for any of us to notice your eyes before." He tilted his head to the side, and Fleck, who was now altogether distraught, buried his head back into the safety of his arms.

"See!" Fleck cried.

"Fleck is a Daloren?" I asked. I remembered Cicero saying the Dalorens were dangerous, but I couldn't believe that about Fleck. "What was he doing there? I thought Dalorens live somewhere else."

"Not always," Alex answered. "The Daloren trait can appear at random. You're born with it. Once the trait appears—namely the eyes—the child is sent to Indanna's Keep, where the rest of his kind reside."

"Fleck." I kept my hand on his arm. "What happened to your parents?"

268

At first I thought he didn't hear me. He just sat huddled inside himself, silent, motionless. Then he lifted his head and the light caught in his eyes. It was distracting, the silver in them. "Murdered. I watched them..." He buried his head back into his self-created shelter.

I wrapped my arms around him even though he flinched. "We have to help him."

Tran studied the boy, his face revealing none of his thoughts. "He needs to be taken to the Keep. Immediately."

Fleck started shaking.

"We can't just hand him over to strangers! Look at him. He needs care. Who knows how long he's been imprisoned back there. He can stay with us—at least for a little while."

It was evident that Cicero, Alex, and my dad were wary of this plan, each looking at the other to give me the answer I didn't want to hear.

"Please," I begged. "Let him come with us. It won't be permanent. He risked his life for me. The least I can do is get him a warm bath."

The others chuckled at that—except Tran.

"You may be right, child." Tran rubbed his chin. "It may benefit us to find out where the boy came from and what Lord Tiernan wanted with him."

"Who is Lord Tiernan?" I looked at my dad.

His lips pinched together and he shut his eyes. Memories attacked him, all of them streaking pain across his features, until his wearied blue eyes opened once again. "There was a time, well before you were born, when Lord Tiernan was both a friend and confidant of mine. I don't know how much the Del Contes told you, but Tiernan is the brother to Lord Commodus Pontefract of Orindor."

"Lord Commodus Pontefract, as in the man you visited?"

Dad nodded. "Yes. Lord Commodus is a very strong and brilliant leader—I'll discuss that meeting with you all soon. His brother Tiernan Pontefract was just as brilliant— particularly with military tactics. Many members of the Guild hated him, because he was both powerful and influential in ways the Guild prides themselves in being.

"I first heard of his disappearance from Commodus—he hadn't seen or heard from his brother in weeks. Commodus was anxious, searching the lands for him. There was tension in the world then, much like there is now. Relationships were strained. Always over power." These last words uttered by him were laden with bitterness. "No one had word of him, not until a few years passed when we saw Lord Tiernan, looking much like you saw him, fighting against his own brother. Commodus wasn't the same after that."

To have your family—your very own brother turn so far away that they wanted to kill you. How could someone turn so far that they'd destroy the very ones they loved?

"But it doesn't make any sense. If Lord Commodus was so upset over his brother, they must have had a decent relationship. What could change so that Tiernan would kill his own flesh and blood?"

Dad winced, taking a deep breath. "Evil never happens at once. It finds a weakness and plants its seed. That seed grows, branching through all other aspects of your thinking. You don't realize its hold until it's too late. For some reason the dark is more potent. Many who tamper with it are drawn to the possibilities. The more power that is naturally given to you, the greater the temptation. Many think Tiernan kept his real intentions hidden for years, until one day, chance favored his prepared mind and he left. What his purpose is, only he knows. I—and the Del Contes—believe there are those like Tiernan, who exist within the palace gates, monitoring what is happening, communicating with the dark."

"Is that why you kept me on Earth?"

Sorrow radiated so strongly from him, I felt guilty for bringing it up.

"Yes," his voice cracked. "There is…so much to tell you."

My insides fought it out. Half of me wanted to tell him to stop and rest, but the other half, the side with cannons and flares, needed him to continue. I wanted the truth. I needed the truth, so that I could be free from its haunting once and for all.

"Your mother was a very powerful woman, Daria. Her tie to this world was a unique one and her abilities were greater than most—even equal to members of the Guild. But even beyond that was something more precious. A secret her family kept for decades." He hesitated. "She was a Pandor. It is said that when Gaia separated from Earth, she entrusted

270

something to the Pandor family: a box that held the secrets to this world, secrets even the Dalorens do not know. The knowledge of that box was passed on through generations and told only to the successor. Your mother never even told me—and that woman prized her honesty, telling me everything."

"Pandor...as in Pandora's box?"

He grinned. "No, but the Greek myth was a coincidental distraction. Your mother's maiden name was Pandor, not Pandora."

Too coincidental if you asked me. More probable the myth was planted.

"When I was imprisoned," I started, thinking back. "Tiernan asked me where a box was. I didn't know what he was talking about...but it must be this box you're talking about."

Dad nodded. "A prophecy exists—one that has been around for centuries. It says one day a woman will rise from two powerful bloodlines, and she will lead the people of Gaia against Mortis' return—the Great Lord of Shadow. And my family has also been blessed—or cursed depending on how you look at it—as being one of the strongest humans in this world. We seem to have a unique tie to the elementals."

"Cicero told me about them," I glanced at Cicero. "About the Great War and how their powers were used."

"Ours is the only known lineage that claims ties to the elementals. I've been able to shape the earth since I was a boy."

"You...created our escape back there? You split open the rock?"

He nodded.

I couldn't believe it. I mean, I hadn't thought much about it and I guess I'd just assumed it was Tran, but to think it was my own dad...

Boy, did I have a lot to learn.

No wonder he had fallen unconscious. And if his lineage really had this power, it meant he thought I had it too. But how? I hadn't seen any sign of an element.

But you have.

With the whispers of the breeze, gusts of the wind, flying through the air.

271

Dad smiled encouragingly. "His name is Cian. The elemental of wind. He's hidden himself from this realm for many years, but I'm almost certain it's him. We'll have to keep watch—see if he's returned or just feeling things out. He's a fickle one, much like the wind."

A tie to this world from my mom, a bond to an element from my dad. I wasn't sure what it all meant, but it was certainly a lot to think about. "So you think I am the one the prophecy talks about? A merging of two bloodlines?"

"I'm not sure, but I won't risk your life for something that seems more than coincidental. When your mother and I found out she was pregnant with you, we were afraid. We told no one except the Del Contes and...your grandfather."

"The king?" I asked.

I felt the surprise of the Del Contes and my dad. His eyes moved back and forth between mine. "You know?"

"Tiernan told me," I whispered.

He shut his eyes, his grief strong. "I'm sorry you found out this way. I thought I was protecting you. I thought that knowing certain things would put you in greater danger. I didn't expect Tiernan to simply try and take your power."

He sighed. "Serves me right, I suppose. When your mother was—" he shut his eyes briefly "—dying, she made me swear I'd keep you hidden until I found the evil behind Lord Tiernan. She'd never trusted him, even back then, and vowed Gaia wouldn't be safe for you until he was gone. We knew that they'd come for you if they knew she was pregnant with a girl—they all kept watchful eyes on her the moment we married. People can be vicious in their devotion to their beliefs.

"After your mother passed, I tried relentlessly to find out what'd happened to Lord Tiernan so I could bring you here, but failed. The Del Contes were nice enough to come with me to protect you, under an oath of secrecy—the same oath that prohibited them from telling you anything. I hated doing that to you."

"But even when you were little you were too inquisitive for your own good. I knew if I, or the Del Contes, told you anything about this world—even if I told you why you weren't allowed to go to it and of the dangers waiting for you here—

272

you would try to find it, and nothing would be able to stop you."

He was right about that. That's just what I would have done, and that fact wasn't helping my guilt, either.

"All these years the Del Contes have monitored the entrance, until recently when those Pykans made it through. I couldn't have you marching back into the castle—not only because most of Gaia doesn't know you exist but also because I wasn't sure it was safe. Before I could take you there, I needed to figure out what was going on. This place—" he waved his hand at our surroundings "—was the safest, most concealed location I could think of, a place where I could meet up with you and tell you everything myself. Try and salvage what little respect for me you may still have."

"Dad." I knelt at his side. "I was angry that you didn't tell me...angry at the Del Contes."

"I know how you feel about lies." His grin was weak.

I caught Tran's gaze then, his face tender and loving. *"You should not cast judgments on what you don't understand,"* he had said. Tran grinned then, as if he heard the thought himself.

"But—" I turned back to my dad "—I understand why you did it now. Knowing such a powerful evil exists...if I knew it was after someone I cared about, I can't say I wouldn't do the same."

I caught Alex's gaze then and looked away. I was so ashamed of how I'd treated him.

"How *did* you figure out how to use that amulet though?" Dad studied my eyes.

"Oh, that." I was so embarrassed when I remembered what I'd done and how I'd spoken to the Del Contes. How I'd tricked Alex. How I'd stolen the amulet from Cicero's pack. The list of things I'd screwed up was almost as long as the list of things that wanted me dead. Probably longer.

"I'm not sure, really. I was so desperate to find you. I knew they were talking to someone named Stefan and he hadn't mentioned you in a while, and they wouldn't let me read the bindingbook. I told myself I'd follow the Del Contes here, and if you didn't show, I'd try to find you myself. And then I had a dream about you...it was so real. I had to see you—find you and make sure you were all right. I wasn't sure

273

what I was doing when I put it around my neck, but it worked."

"I should've known better." He sighed. "Stefan hadn't heard from me because I was riding hard to meet up with you. He was worried someone knew we were communicating and didn't want to give away my location. And," he paused, his eyes strained. "Sonya didn't let you read the bindingbook any more because Stefan forgot himself and...asked how his sister Daria was doing."

At first I hadn't heard the words. I was still sorting through all the stupid conclusions I'd drawn. My judgments had been formed with such haste it was mortifying. And then the rest of his words reached my ears. "Sister?"

"Stefan is your brother."

I looked at him with a blank stare, unable to move, my breath lodged somewhere inside of me.

"I didn't want you to know." He searched my face. "Not until I told you. It was wrong of me, I know, and completely selfish, and I am so sorry for keeping him from you all this time. But I couldn't tell you about him without also telling you about this world, and the longer I kept his existence from you, the harder it was to tell you. Still, I never wanted you to find out like this. The Del Contes were only upholding their oath to me by not letting you know your connection to him."

Time passed in silence while his words settled in my mind.

I had a brother. Another living creature existed in this world that shared my own flesh and blood. For eighteen years I had been an only child, but there had been another who called my dad "dad." There was another who called my mom "mom."

I opened my mouth to speak, but only air escaped. My heart beat a little faster and my breathing turned shallow. I could feel the truth in his words, but they would not sink in.

A brother.

I had a brother. That meant I was the sister to someone.

Dad sat silently, his pale face never turning from mine. I could feel his anxiety and pain, but what I felt more than anything was his regret. Of all the untold secrets, this was the hardest to hear.

"So he lives here?" My voice was fragile. "In this world?"

274

He nodded.

The ground began rising, swallowing me within it. I closed my eyes, struggling against the sabotage of my calm. With each slow breath I fought to hold onto a thread of stability. My emotions were running rampant with so many conflicting feelings. Pain, fear, joy, and bitterness. It was difficult holding myself together without having anywhere to hide and sort everything out. In fact, that was how it had been ever since I'd left home—an onslaught of life changing information with no private sanctuary for my thoughts. Was it possible for a human being to hear so many things about their life and stay sane?

I stared at the ground, trying to find solace in its emptiness, but I kept feeling the concern of my dad and Alex.

Minutes passed in thick silence before it hit me. I had a brother. A sibling. No matter how upset I might be that I'd never known, I had finally been told. There were no longer just two in our small family, there were three. Curiosity pricked at my mind. "What's...he like?"

"Well, since you asked, he's the one who inherited all of *my* qualities, so you should be thankful for him, really." He grinned. "By the time you were born, there was nothing left of me to give you."

I smiled back. "No, really. I want to know."

"I'm being perfectly serious. So, as long as you don't constantly prove how much smarter you are, you two will get along just fine. You see, I've had a lifetime of learning how to handle being humbled by a woman. He's only had twenty years and been around women a fraction of those. It takes a man a good deal longer than that."

I chuckled. "Does Stefan...know about me?"

"Yes, *very* well. You might not have anything new to tell him." He grinned. "Stefan has quite the spy."

I followed Dad's gaze to Alex, whose eyes dropped.

Alex's voice sounded a pitch lower, if it was possible. "Stefan—your brother—has been my closest friend since I can remember. He's highly inquisitive, especially when it comes to you. Everything I know, he knows—mostly because he wouldn't leave me alone until I told him." He paused, looking back into my eyes. "He'll love you."

Chapter 26
Clarity

Our dinner that evening was probably the most cheerful in all my life. Dad laughed with Cicero and Sonya about memories that were finally safe to discuss in front of me. It was strange, listening to him talk about this world and all its magic, but it also felt right, somehow.

My mind had been prepared for all of this. If I looked back at the events of my life, there were little pieces along the way—fragments—that struck me as peculiar at the time. Now, they all found their way back to my mind, completing the full picture and identity of the man who was my loving father. He was still exhausted, but his spirit was light and happy, more so than I'd seen it in years.

Cicero and Sonya, with some interjections by Tran, described our very eventful journey to Amadis. News of the barghest attack disturbed my dad. He told us that Lord Commodus hadn't heard anything of the Pykans but would alert his territory. Dad had raced to meet us at Amadis and arrived right after my abrupt departure. From there, an omniscient Tran had suspected my actions, bringing the Vox to the rescue, and somehow, with his infinite wisdom and Cicero's magical compass, they had traced the movement of the amulet until they found me. The rest, well, I was present for and humiliated by, so I was just fine moving past it.

Even though I'd made a terrible mistake in leaving, something good had come out of it all. We had defeated the threat to the outlying villages, at least for now.

Fleck seemed to warm up some, sitting at the fire next to Alex. Alex had taken complete responsibility for Fleck's comfort, showing him his knives and teaching him how to whittle sticks. Fleck was fascinated—as every young boy would be—and his worries disappeared. Grool even joined them, glaring at the pair perfecting their craft. To him, the battle wasn't over. He sat sharpening his twisted piece of metal, scowling every so often over his shoulder and stabbing at the night.

A few times I met Alex's gaze, and when I did, I was humbled by the depth and warmth in them. My friend. I may not have been fair to Cicero and Sonya, but I'd treated him the worst. There was still one thing I needed to make right, if he would let me. Later, when everyone went to sleep, I would talk to him...alone.

"Hey, lady!" Fleck jumped to his feet and ran over to me. "Look what I made!" He held out a stick that had the bark chipped off in a spiral.

"It's great, Fleck. What are you going to use it for?"

Fleck plopped down beside me. "I was thinking you could have it."

Looks like I'd be answering that question myself. "Thank you."

Fleck sat beside me, calm as could be. "Told you that you were a Lady." He grinned.

I smiled back. "And I will keep my promise. We will find out your real name. 'Fleck' will never do for someone as brave as you."

He liked that. His grin widened, showing all of his tiny spaced teeth. His face turned thoughtful then as he glanced past me.

"You love him, lady?"

Startled, I followed Fleck's gaze to Alex, who sat intent on another project in his hands. "Well, he's my friend..."

Fleck looked doubtful. "The way you look at him is different."

"We're really good friends. We've known each other since we were little—younger than you even."

"You love him," he said with finality.

"No, it's not like that..."

"Lady." Fleck sighed with that same seriousness of an adult that made me want to laugh. "For being so smart you really are thick sometimes."

My lips parted as he laughed and bounded from my side, back to his new favorite—Alex. He leaned close to Alex's ear and whispered something. Alex's eyes found mine and there was a smile in them. My cheeks burned as I turned away from the pair of conspirators.

This wasn't good. If how I felt about Alex was obvious to Fleck after only one afternoon, I was kidding myself if I didn't think Alex noticed. I had to get better at hiding it. I couldn't let him see how he made me feel. If he knew, it might ruin everything, and our friendship was unstable enough as it was.

Everyone fell asleep early from the day's trials. Even Grool slept on the ground snoring, still wearing his enormous helmet. Tran slept sitting upright against a tree, and Fleck had fallen asleep beside Alex with a knife in one hand and a stick in the other.

It is time.

I stood and walked toward Alex. His eyes met mine and my heart sped. I didn't know if I could do it, especially after what Fleck had said. What if he saw right through me? What if he saw how he made me feel?

You have to. He deserves your apology more than anyone.

I took a deep breath and sat beside him. "You're nice to him." I nodded toward Fleck. "Thanks."

"Don't act so surprised." He smiled as he glanced at Fleck. "He's been through a lot."

"I wonder how long they've kept him."

"Hard to say, but it's dangerous for him, having powers he doesn't know how to control. Daria...I know you want him to come with us, but it can't be for long. He has to get to the Keep." He grabbed my hand and I struggled not to focus on the feel of his skin. "I promise you he'll be safe there."

My heart ached. He always cared about my feelings. He was always a friend I never deserved. "Alex, I..."

The green in his eyes was filled with such tenderness and...love.

He's just looking at you like that because you're his friend. You don't remember because it's been so long.

Uncomfortable, I glanced down, aware of how close we were. Aware of myself next to him and my hand in his. I liked the feel of his skin on mine.

He squeezed my hand gently and my heart sputtered in my chest. I forced myself to focus on my apology.

278

"The way I've acted to you." I looked back into his eyes, trying not to be distracted by the way he was looking at me. "I'm so embarrassed. I was so quick to...to judge you and you...you've done nothing but risk your entire life for me." My throat constricted, choking my words. "You had no choice....all for my protection. You could've lived here all along, but because..."

He grabbed my other hand so that both of mine were now clutched tightly in his as he gazed earnestly into my eyes. "And I would do it all over again."

He wiped something wet from my cheek. I hadn't even realized I was crying.

"I am so sorry," I whispered.

He pulled me close, wrapping his strong arms around me, my face buried in his chest. I could smell the earth on his shirt, mixed with that smell that was just...him. In that moment I felt peace, greater peace than I'd felt in years. Being here with him, with all barriers stripped away. Now we were both vulnerable in our honesty and it was freeing. My friend had come back to me days ago, but the relationship returned that moment. My stronghold wrapped around me, my anchor fixed to the ground. I'd missed him more than I even realized.

He held me there, letting my emotions dampen his shirt, saying everything he needed to say in loving silence. Which, of course, only made me feel worse. But this time, there was no denying that being in his arms felt different. Different than when we were kids. Different than when he would hug me goodbye or try comforting me because I'd hurt myself. This time, there was something else—something I knew I wanted to hold on to forever, and it also scared the life out of me.

As if reading my mind, Alex leaned back just enough so that he could look into my eyes. "Walk with me." He stood to his feet and held out his hand. I slipped mine into his, the warmth of his touch flowing through my arm. Together we walked, hand in hand, through the trees. We didn't speak as we stepped through the shadows, sounds of the night chirping and singing in the distance. Points of light floated in the air like fireflies, only these were much larger. They twinkled in a cloud, like glitter in the shadows, swaying and drifting with the light breeze.

When we emerged from the tree cover, thousands of bright white stars littered the sky. Their reflection mirrored undisturbed across the lake's surface. The entire landscape was veiled in an ethereal white glow, the mountains' rock spires close to puncturing the sky that illuminated them. Trees basked in the starlight and though the flowers were muted, some caught the light, sparkling and glittering white like stars hanging from the trees. The lake was magical at night—more so than during the day. If I'd seen this lake, knowing nothing of magic, I would have known without a doubt that magic existed.

"It's beautiful." My words felt cheap as I spoke them.

Alex smiled. My heart sped as he led me along the water, my hand still in his. He paused beside a large boulder, helping me sit beside him. Minutes passed and we sat in silence, our sides pressed together.

Everything had changed. We'd grown up to be adults, or at least he could claim that victory. Mine was to be determined. We had left a child's playground and entered the world's arena where we fought for our lives—where peril and trials would prove our characters for what they were. I was afraid to analyze mine. I'd seen Alex kill men. I'd killed men. My stomach turned, remembering. One, two, three, four—the fourth didn't count. I had left him unconscious. Still, with my hands, I had ended someone's life. That power seemed too great to be entrusted to a human. Who was I to take the precious gift of life from another?

"What's bothering you?" Alex asked.

I could feel him studying me, but I didn't turn to look at him. I picked up a smooth pebble and sent it bounding across the lake's surface. Tiny ripples spread from each point of contact. "Do you ever get over the deaths?"

Alex rested his elbows on his knees.

"The first time, I was sent on an assignment, I killed a man. A part of me died that day. I was deluded in my self-righteous sense of justice, but when it happened—I still remember that moment like it just happened. I sacrificed a part of myself I knew I could never have back." He paused,

280

taking a deep breath. "I remember all of them...each and every face.

"I know you're sick with it and I wish I could tell you it gets easier, but it doesn't. But—" he turned to look at me and I met his gaze "—you have to remind yourself why. You've seen what the enemy is capable of. If it goes unchecked, many innocent lives—hundreds and thousands of them—may be lost. The barghests, for instance...power like that unleashed on the land. Can you imagine what would happen? And the gargons—think how many lives they've destroyed. That is how I justify my actions, remembering all the lives I'm saving by the ones I'm destroying. Those men—the ones who have done so much evil—they already made their choices. They've chosen a path that doesn't allow for mercy or tolerance of any other way of life aside from their own. With every choice, there are consequences."

I understood what he was saying, but it was still difficult to digest. It was necessary, even though it sounded contradictory. Kill to protect life. But I didn't like the idea of him putting his life at risk. "Why does it have to be you?" I asked.

"It's who I am. I wouldn't say I'm as legalistic about servitude and propriety as my father, but I can't sit back and watch injustices. Not when I know I can help."

"Maybe...you can find someone else to protect. Someone who doesn't put you in as much danger."

"Daria." He tucked a strand of my hair behind my ear. "When it comes to protecting you, I never have a second thought. Your life is so precious to me that I don't trust anyone else with it. If any of them harmed you—touched you—I can't explain it but giving them a quick death would've been a difficult favor to grant. It surprises me—scares me a little. I've never...felt that way before."

I took a deep breath, trying not to think about how close he was. "You're saying I make you want to...torture people?"

He grinned and looked down at his hands. "When you put it that way..." When he glanced back at me, something in his eyes held me still. "Is that disgusting to you?"

"How can it be when I'm just as guilty? And I can't think of any other alternative, considering we wanted to escape alive. It's just taking some time for me to deal with the reality

281

of it. You know I've fought almost my entire life, but I wasn't wagering life and death then."

He gazed out at the lake. "Actually, it's pretty amazing how fast you've learned to use a dagger. You're almost as good as I am." One corner of his lips pulled up into a grin.

"Give me a few days. I'll be better than you." I nudged him in the ribs.

He smiled then, the starlight sharpening his already strong features. His dark hair fell around his face and eyes in a beautiful mess. He looked so striking that my breath caught in my throat and I glanced away, afraid to look back at him, afraid he would see the effect he had on me.

Daria, knock it off. He's your friend. It's okay to think he's handsome but you should probably stop drooling over him.

"What made you decide to forgive me?" His deep voice tickled my ear.

Friends don't drool. Friends don't drool...

"Tiernan gave me a choice. He said if I surrendered my powers to serve him, then he wouldn't harm any of you. And if I didn't, he would kill me and take them anyway. Then he would kill the rest of you."

I felt Alex's gaze on me, but I stared out at the water as if it was the most interesting thing I'd ever seen.

"It was then I understood why you didn't tell me all those years. You knew me better than anyone—that I would march myself right into harm's way, thinking I was invincible. But to know that nothing would happen to you—to have the promise of your safety if I lived a lie—that's what I would be doing. I would've done it. I would've hated myself for it, but I would've done it to protect you."

"But you didn't."

"That's because I had another option."

He was still watching me, but I couldn't turn to look at him. Not this close. Somehow I knew I'd never be able to finish what I wanted to say.

"I don't know how I managed it, but I thought if I could somehow manipulate a fire to appear, there might be a small chance I could manipulate my chains to break." I tossed another pebble in the lake and it splashed with a hollow *plop*. "I don't know. Thinking back on it, my logic sounds ridiculous."

282

"And it worked?"

I nodded. "Ironic, you have Lord Tiernan to thank for that. He's the one who convinced me I had all this power in my blood. I figured if it was something he wanted so desperately, I should at least try it out before he took it away."

Alex grabbed onto my wrists and I flinched. His brow furrowed as he rolled back my sleeves. "Why didn't you say anything about this?"

Even in the low light, my wrists looked badly bruised, with dark lines of dried blood etched around them from the chains. He pushed one of my sleeves up further, revealing the line Tiernan had not so delicately carved into my arm. He frowned at me. "Daria."

"Really, I forgot about it. And it's not like I could tell your mom. I feel bad enough that she used all her strength on my dad."

He stood and walked to the water's edge.

"What are you doing?" I asked.

He waved at me to join him. "We need to at least wash it."

"Oh, no, no, no, no," I said. "I'm not getting anywhere near that water."

Alex grinned. "She won't get you now. I'm with you." There was a gleam in his eyes that made my insides knot together.

Friends don't drool...

I stood and joined him, crouching beside the water. Alex helped splash water onto my forearm. It stung at first, but then numbed the pains in my wrists and arms as it cleansed my blood of grime and memories.

"Better?" he whispered in my ear.

I nodded. My heart was beating fast, and, even though the evening was cool, I felt warm all over. He stood and walked back to where we were sitting. The moment he placed about three feet between us, I heard quick movement, an irritating familiar gurgle of laughter, and found myself drenched from head to toe. Again. "Alex!" I clenched my teeth.

He cracked up laughing.

"It's not funny!"

283

"I know...but...." He could barely get words out, he was laughing so hard.

That was it. I charged at him, throwing myself on top of him and pushing him to the ground, making sure his clothing soaked up as much water as possible.

But he wasn't fighting me.

Instead, his arms wrapped around me holding me against him. His laughter died down as his hands trailed up my back and slid into my hair, and then he rested his palm on my face, holding me there, inches from him.

There was an intensity in his gaze that melted every part of my body. My eyes were trapped. I couldn't move, I couldn't breathe. He held his palm against my cheek as his breath warmed my lips. He leaned closer, and he kissed me.

His lips were velvety soft as they pressed against mine. He hesitated at first, fighting back a desire, unsure of my feelings. And I finally understood why everything had been so difficult, why his leaving had hurt so much. It was this. It had always been this. He had always meant so much more than just a friend.

Passion burned through my veins, and I started kissing him back. His emotions were intense and dizzying as they blended with my own. All of them were tender, and all of them were filled with longing. I drank in the taste of him as he rolled me beneath him, his heart pounding against mine. His fingers threaded through my hair and mine through his, each of us pulling the other closer. Our legs tangled as our mouths pressed together more urgently. And then with a soft groan he stopped. Resolve replaced his passion and he rolled away from me.

My heart felt as if it was going to explode out of my chest. My mouth still burned from his lips and the taste of him lingered on my tongue.

"I'm...sorry." His voice was rough.

"You're...sorry?" I gasped. "Why would you say that?"

"I should never have..." He shut his eyes, struggling to calm himself. "I forgot...myself."

"Forgot yourself?"

He turned to face me then. There was so much pain in his eyes as he reached out and tucked a strand of hair behind my ear. "I forgot who you are."

284

I finally discover I've been in love with my best friend all my life, and the first thing he does is say he forgot who I am? You don't kiss your best friend and then say "sorry, wrong person."

"What are you saying?"

He trailed his fingers along my cheek. "Believe me, I've wanted nothing more than to have that freedom with you, but I've always known that once you came to this world, things could never be how they were, or—" he ran his finger along my bottom lip "—how I want them to be."

"I don't understand."

"Once you meet your grandfather, you will."

My disrupted passion was transforming quickly into anger. "You're telling me that you're going to let my grandfather—a man I've never even met, and has never had any interest in my life—control our future?"

"When your grandfather happens to be king of Gaia, yes."

I couldn't believe he was doing this, making it about my situation—being the granddaughter of a king. It was like I'd stumbled into another time period altogether, when position and class actually mattered. This was the twenty-first century, and although I was currently in another world, I was from the United States. Born and raised there. I had freedoms—including the freedom to love whomever I wanted.

"Daria." He rested his palm on my cheek, his gaze never leaving mine. "I have always loved you, much more than a friend should—especially one who would do nothing to dishonor you. *We* can't be. I've known this since the day I met you. Your grandfather is, or will be, very protective of your position. You of all people should understand. I've known this. I've always known this." He rubbed his thumb over my cheek. "We can't be close, not like we were. This is Gaia. We can't do as we please—especially not you. I can never have you when you belong to the state, and I doubt anyone is as angry about that fact as I am."

The absolute truth and sincerity in his words filled my heart with bitterness from a discovery that was only going to cause pain. His feelings were so strong and intoxicating, I wondered how he'd hidden them from me this long. I had loved Alex my entire life—loved him as my best friend—but it wasn't until recently that I'd been so confused. He had

285

understood the depth of that love. He was always the one who understood.

"There has to be a way." I touched his cheek, feeling the stubble beneath my fingertips. "My dad loves you. He can talk to my...this king..."

Alex kissed my fingertips and smiled. "I've always loved your determination. I won't lie, sometimes it drives me mad."

I smiled back at him, our fingers intertwined in the small space between us. I wanted to close that space. So badly.

"I didn't plan on complicating this...relationship of ours any more than it has been the past three years. I just wanted some time with you alone." He played with a piece of my hair. "Without all the hordes of people who will be surrounding you from now on. Everyone will be watching."

"You're acting like I'll never see you again."

He gazed up at the sky and his chest rose with a deep breath. He shut his eyes, silent for a moment. "The connection you have to this world—the connection your mom had. What's it like?"

His question caught me off guard. I also wasn't sure how much of it I wanted to tell him. He might be upset if he knew I could almost always sense his feelings. Though I wondered how accurate that sense was, considering I had never known he felt this way about me.

"Well," I started, inhaling a deep breath of fresh air. "It's as if my spirit is aware of everything around me. Things I can't see I can feel—as if I'm being pulled in a thousand directions. I can sense others when they're near, as if their soul has physical properties. I know their feelings at times—not why they're feeling that way, just *what* they're feeling."

He was quiet, thinking something over. "You sense mine?"

"Yes."

"And are my feelings stronger than the others?"

I thought about this before answering. "Yes."

He nodded, staring at the sky.

"Why?"

"I can sense yours," his voice was quiet. "Ever since you've been here. That ability—I've never experienced it. But you are the only person I can feel."

286

Part of me was horrified that so much of myself had been obvious to him.

He glanced back at me and grinned. "Trust me, there were many points during the past few weeks I cursed that newfound talent. I thought you hated me so much I was beyond all hope of forgiveness. It might have been nice to be ignorant of it."

I looked down at our intertwined hands. "Alex, I'm sorry."

He placed his hand on my cheek again, our eyes glued to each other. Moments passed and we lay still. I yearned to be closer to him and my lips ached to feel his again, and as the thought would pass—as my desire would pulse—he would smile that smile I adored.

The air grew cooler and the breeze chilled my damp skin, giving me goose bumps.

"We should get back," he said. "Someone might wonder what happened to us, and I don't want to be held responsible for making you get sick."

I nuzzled myself against him. "I don't care."

I felt him fighting his desire. "I do. We can't have the king of Gaia meeting his snot-nosed granddaughter."

I smiled at that, and he helped me to my feet and wrapped an arm around my waist, holding me to him. He stared into my eyes as he moved the hair from my face. My need for him was bursting inside of me. All of a sudden, little white specks started floating around us, like snow. They landed in our hair, on our clothes—delicate, white flower petals that smelled of rich tuberose.

Alex dusted off a petal that had fallen on my nose. "Show off." When he saw that I had no idea what he was talking about, he continued. "Like your dad said, you inherited a connection to this world from your mother. A connection to Gaia. I think these trees are in tune to your feelings and are...adding to the ambiance."

Before I could argue, he rested his lips gently on mine. He pulled away too fast and grabbed my hand. "We better leave or I won't be able to help myself. My self-control is waning fast."

"I suggest we stand here then. At least five more minutes." I stood planted to the ground and another shower of petals fell around us. I didn't know how I was doing it, but

287

I wished it would stop. There's no being discreet when the trees give you away.

Desire flashed through him but he forced it down the moment it came. Alex had incredible willpower. I'd always admired that about him, but right now, it was driving me insane.

He shook his head. "You are going to be the death of me." He pulled me after him through the trees. My pulse ran fast, but so did his as we marched toward reality and away from something we both wanted. Responsibility was something I prided myself in, but I hated it when it conflicted with my desires.

Everyone was just as we had left them. Grool's snores had been replaced by grumbling and mumbling as he clawed at the air. Alex picked up Fleck and laid him down on his blankets.

"What about you?" I whispered.

"I'm going to stay awake."

"Then I'll stay awake with you."

"No, you're going to bed." He walked over to my blankets and lay down, motioning for me to join him. I was there in a heartbeat, lying on my side right next to him. His chest rose and fell quickly as he laughed in my hair. He draped an arm over my waist, holding me against him as I breathed in the scent of him.

I turned back and spoke into his neck. "I don't see how this is going to help your case—with everyone able to see, and all."

His breath tickled my ear. "I'm only staying until you fall asleep."

"Then I won't."

He squeezed me gently and kissed my hair, and he said nothing else. I soon forgot the chill of night being wrapped in a cocoon of Alex's warmth. Sometimes he would trace invisible patterns over my arms, or run his fingers through my hair and brush it away from my face. I'd never been more comfortable and contented. My eyelids felt heavy as I struggled to keep them open.

The last thing I remembered was catching a glimmer of silver flecks above a mouth smiling at me from beneath Alex's blankets.

288

Chapter 27

Valdon

Soft voices filtered around me as my consciousness returned. I curled into myself, my blanket doing an insufficient job keeping me warm. Alex wasn't behind me. I had fallen asleep.

When I opened my eyes, I found my dad off to the side, discussing something with Cicero, Sonya, and Tran. Grool was across from me, building something that looked like a trap with rope and wood. He placed a small object beneath it, hopped away with that maniacal laughter of his, and hid behind a tree, glaring at his creation.

I couldn't see Alex anywhere. Or Fleck.

"You're awake!" Dad beamed, walking toward me.

My muscles ached and my joints creaked as I got to my feet. Dad wrapped his arms around me and then appraised my attire. "You look just like your mother, dressed like that. I'm sorry I wasn't the one to give it to you."

"That's okay. I've got it now, and, believe it or not, I like them. By the way, have you seen Alex?"

A suspicious look passed over his face. "He went with Fleck to the lake. We thought Fleck should look more...presentable for our arrival. And when your little friend found out by presentable we meant a bath, his shaking was so inconsolable that Alex decided to go with him."

I ginned, picturing the scene in my head. "I guess Alex didn't tell him about Amadis."

"Glad to see you two are getting along again."

His grin made the heat rush to my cheeks, and there was no way I was going to discuss this sort of thing with my dad. "How long till we get to King Darius's castle?"

He smiled then, knowing he'd caught me red-handed. "One day."

"One day? But it took us almost a week to get here."

"Tran's offered to return the horses so we can take the Vox. It'll be much safer, and will put us there by late afternoon."

"So fast?" Only a week ago I'd been impatient for my fate, but now I wasn't ready for it. Especially if it meant going to a castle to meet this grandfather king of mine.

Dad placed his hand on my shoulder. "I thought we could ride together. I'd like some time alone with my daughter before I'm forced to share her with the rest of this world." His tired blue eyes studied me a moment. "Of course, I understand if you'd like to ride with Alexander."

The heat rushed to my face again. "Dad, I—"

"Look at me!" shrieked a little voice. Fleck came bounding toward us, cheeks pink, freckles bright, and eyes wide in admiration of himself. "I thought those stains were permanent!"

Alex followed after him, hair dripping around his face. He looked particularly gorgeous this morning. Our eyes met and my heart skipped a beat.

"Well done, Alexander!" Dad chuckled. "Fleck has turned into a presentable human being."

"Lady, that Amadis is so nice. How come you didn't like her?" Fleck appeared very disturbed.

"Who says I didn't like her?"

"Alex. He said you—"

"—didn't *exactly* get along," Alex interrupted, stopping before me with a smile in his eyes.

I narrowed my eyes at him, unable to hide my grin. "*Hopefully* he told you why?"

"Because she's so beautiful?"

Alex laughed.

"Of course not," I said. "It's because—"

"Time to go, I'm afraid," Tran interrupted.

Dad reached out a strong hand. "Tran Chiton, how can I thank you for all you've done."

"For now, by keeping my existence quiet. There is more I must do before the world realizes I'm still in it." He shook my dad's hand.

Cicero and Sonya joined for goodbyes. I was grateful to see Sonya's energy had returned. Her features looked refreshed this morning.

And then Tran turned to me.

His eyes were kind, studying my face as if wanting to remember it just as it was. He placed his withered hand on my shoulder, his grip surprisingly strong.

"My dearest Daria, it has been a pleasure and honor, and I shall look forward to seeing you again."

"Thank you, Tran. For everything." I reached my arms around his slight frame.

He laughed and patted my back. "That's enough, child. You'll squeeze the rest of my life from me."

I stepped away from him as he moved to Alex.

"Alexander Del Conte. I'm glad Daria has such a devoted companion in you."

Alex caught my eye. "And I'm glad you have Grool."

Tran laughed and Grool glared through the slit in his helmet.

"Until we meet again!" Tran mounted Calyx.

Tran and the horses left with Grool walking behind, swinging at the air with his makeshift sword.

"Strange, those two." Cicero stared after them.

"Strange, but brilliant." Sonya smiled. "Tran was always eccentric. It was one of the reasons I trusted him. And now—" she turned to me "—are you ready?"

She was always so kind. I almost wished she were angry with me so I didn't have to feel so guilty for how I'd treated her. "Sonya," I began.

She waited, those tender eyes patient.

"I...didn't have a chance last night to say thank you, for..."

She held her hand to my lips, a smile in her eyes. "All's forgiven, my darling. It is time we took you home. To your real one."

It wasn't long before we were sailing through the air on our flying black stallions. Amadis fell behind, hiding itself beneath the trees. The majestic rock spires began to shrink as we gained altitude, and soon, that extraordinary and peculiar Arborenne looked like nothing more than a thick green blanket covering the earth. From these heights I was able to note the actual scale of the forest. It was enormous— spanning all the way to a mountain range whose silhouette I could just make out in the distance. We had walked through

291

a small fraction of that endless green. No telling what else had been right there with us.

Just beyond, far off toward our right, was a wall of enormous jagged mountains.

"Orindor." Dad pointed, calling over his shoulder.

"Lord Commodus?"

He nodded.

So that was where he'd been. One of the first requests I'd make would be to get a tour of this land my grandfather ruled. It was disorienting observing a landscape but not knowing any landmarks. Where was the ocean? Which way was north?

As we flew, I felt Dad's anticipation. It was one thing for him to tell me about my new life. It was something entirely different for me to experience it. The day to day, the people. I was anxious for it too.

I shut my eyes, feeling the wind as it flowed over me. Air whistled past my ears. The flapping of the vox's wings was hypnotizing as they beat out my thoughts, my worries. My fears.

A few times I turned back to look at Alex. Fleck rode behind him, holding on to him for dear life.

What would happen to us now? My grandfather couldn't be that controlling, could he? It was cruel realizing my feelings for my greatest friend in the world when it was too late to act on them. It had to be possible. Maybe Alex was wrong. He had to be wrong, because I was afraid to think what would happen if he wasn't.

By late afternoon our powerful vox had descended into a deep valley, shaded by grand mountains on either side. My stomach jumped as we dipped down farther and farther as the landscape ran to greet us. With strong wings spread, our vox glided gracefully to the ground, and we stopped.

I jumped from the horse, my legs stumbling to find balance on solid ground. We had landed in a narrow clearing. Thick, towering trees surrounded us on all sides except for a single path ahead that wove deeper into the forest. Everyone else landed right after, and when Fleck's eyes opened, he smiled his toothy grin.

"I'm alive!" he said as Alex helped him down.

"Of course you are." I chuckled.

The moment we all dismounted, the vox leapt into the air with beating wings and soared back in the direction we had come. I watched the black shapes grow smaller and smaller until they were nothing more than dark specks in the sky.

Dad smiled at me. "How are you feeling?"

"How should I be feeling?" I asked.

He placed a sturdy hand on my shoulder. "Scared out of your senses."

"Gee, thanks for the pep talk."

"Daria, don't listen to your father." Sonya smiled, grabbing my hand. "You'll do beautifully. Everyone will adore you."

Great, just what I wanted. Everyone's adoration. I gave Sonya a face that said as much and she laughed.

"I say listen to Alaric." Cicero grinned.

Sonya nudged him hard in the ribs, and he lost the grin.

"Is Stefan here?" Alex asked my dad.

"He should be." Dad looked ahead. "I wrote to him earlier this morning."

Alex glanced at me before turning to walk ahead. The rest of us trailed after him. Fleck lingered by my side in a pensive silence. I wondered what a boy of his age could be so pensive about, but then I remembered he had an incredible—and inconvenient—amount of insight for one so young.

There was a light tug on my sleeve. "Lady?"

I glanced down at him.

"Don't be scared."

"Why do you say that?"

"Once those people see what you can do, they'll be the scared ones."

I paused, crouched at his side, and smiled. "Just as long as I don't scare you."

"Oh, no, lady. But I think you scare him." He nodded toward Alex.

Just as he scares me, I thought.

I patted Fleck on the arm and held his hand as we continued. Both of us were going to a place neither of us had been. Both of us were strangers in our own land.

A wall came into view, stretching in either direction. It was built of stones and stood so tall there was no way of telling what existed beyond. There was a large wooden gate

293

embedded in the thick wall and as we neared, I felt smaller and smaller. The gate was wide enough for all of us to walk through side-by-side with plenty of room to spare, and its height reached at least fifty feet. How the gate ever moved was beyond me.

Out of the corner of my eye, I saw movement in the shadows of the forest. I felt it then—a presence, one that felt familiar to me somehow. The feeling grew stronger and stronger until a young man emerged from the trees. His bronze hair shone in the sunlight, bordering a pair of striking blue eyes I would recognize in any crowd. They were my dad's eyes.

He was of average height and his fitted black attire showed off a lean, muscular frame. He was an exact replica of my dad, albeit much younger. There was a rigid structure to his face, but it was no reflection of his spirit. That, I could feel, was pure and good and honest. Even if no one had told me, I would've known that the young man standing before me was my brother. And I couldn't have hand-picked someone better.

My legs walked to him of their own accord.

We stopped a few feet from each other. His blue eyes twinkled and he beamed at me. A few of his bottom teeth were turned in the wrong direction, but their imperfection was somehow more endearing. Then, without warning, he pulled me into a tight embrace. His love and joy wrapped around me then, even more powerful than his arms. When he stepped back, large, prominent dimples framed the smile that spread across his face.

"Daria." His rough voice sounded proud.

I took a deep breath. "Stefan."

I didn't think it was possible, but his semi-crooked smile widened and his dimples deepened.

"It's about time you arrived. I've been waiting my whole life to meet you."

I liked the sound of his voice. It was strong and confident and...kind.

"I wish I could say the same," I said. "I've only known you existed since yesterday."

He looked past me at Dad with a grin on his face. "Father."

Father. Strange hearing someone else calling my dad "father."

Stefan looked back at me with my father's eyes. "He's a bit overprotective."

"You think?" I grinned. "Don't tell me he has thermal sensors around this place, too."

Stefan looked astonished. "You're serious?"

It was decided, then. Life really wasn't fair.

"He left that bit out." Stefan glanced back at my dad—our dad. "I guess we know who the favorite is." He smiled back at me. "Well, I can hardly wait to get to know you myself, especially after everything Alexander has told me…"

"Um, I'm not so sure I'd trust everything Alex has to say. He's a little biased."

Stefan looked thoughtful. "He was right about one thing. You are beautiful, and that's something I know for a fact he's biased about."

He studied my now red face and his suspicion surged. Then he glanced back at Alex and a smirk appeared. Dad joined us, his face full of love and pride, and his joy was overflowing at having his children finally united.

Dad and Stefan embraced, and smacked each other firmly on the back. "Thank you, Stefan. I know it hasn't been easy."

Stefan smiled and the dimples returned. "I only did it for her."

"Already uniting against me?" Dad asked.

I grinned. "Dad, you can't postpone the inevitable."

Both men beamed. It was like looking at two versions of my dad at the exact same time. Would I ever get used to this?

"Grandfather's waiting for you in his chambers," Stefan continued. "He dismissed the council for the rest of the afternoon after I told him you were on your way, but beware. They're all lurking about, wondering what in the blazes caused the king to shorten yet another pointless meeting."

"Good, you haven't mentioned Daria then."

Stefan shook his head just as the Del Contes joined us, Fleck trailing behind.

Heartfelt greetings were exchanged all around, Stefan and Alex slapped each other hard on the back. Stefan whispered something to Alex, and Alex just shook his head.

295

"A Daloren child?" Stefan said, noting Fleck.

Fleck hid behind Alex's legs.

I took a step forward. "He was being held prisoner and he helped me escape."

There was fear in Stefan's eyes. "But he needs to be taken to the Keep," Stefan said.

Fleck began shaking again.

"But he doesn't know anyone—he doesn't even know his real name. I promised him I'd help him figure it out." I grabbed Stefan's sleeve. "Please."

Stefan held my gaze. His fear faded and he crouched low, speaking in a voice that was softer. "What is your name, lad?"

Alex tried to comfort Fleck, but Fleck wouldn't budge. He was resolute in his position behind Alex's legs.

"Whoever you are," Stefan continued, "seeing as you saved my sister, I think you deserve a grand reward. I'm thinking—" Stefan rubbed his chin and stared at the sky "—a table filled with roasted meats, sweet breads, and all the callaberries you could fill your mouth with."

I could've kissed him. Fleck's little flecked eyes peered around Alex's legs. And then his nose appeared, followed by a mouth that was wide-open and grinning.

"Really?" his little voice whispered.

"All in celebration of your bravery." Stefan smiled. "But I must have a name to give the cooks so I know where to deliver your food."

"Fleck." He all but shoved Alex over and bounded toward Stefan.

"Fleck." Stefan smiled, extending a hand. "It is a pleasure."

I mouthed the words "thank you" to Stefan, who nodded and stood.

"Let's proceed, shall we?"

We stood before the guardian to my fate—the gate—and as my curiosity surged, the gate slid sideways into the stone wall, just wide enough for us to pass through. A mountain of a man blocked our passage. It was Master Durus.

Why was it, out of all the people in this crazy world, my family had trusted this man? Maybe it was punishment.

"Thank you, Master Durus." Stefan nodded.

296

"Sire." Master Durus bowed.

Stefan walked through.

The others said their hellos, but when it was my turn to walk through, Master Durus held up a massive hand.

Of course he would do that.

His black eyes bore down upon me. "A caution, princess," sounded his familiar low rumble. "King Darius has no tolerance for differing opinions. I might advise you not to speak...unless absolutely necessary."

Well.

I strode past him after the others with Master Durus on my heels. The gate closed silently behind us. Power poured through my body as I walked through the thick stone wall and the sensation ceased the moment I was on the other side.

There must be other defenses in place. Magical ones.

On the other side of the wall was a bustling marketplace. Stone and wooden buildings lined the inner wall, separated from others by narrow walkways. People gathered in the streets, in the buildings, chatting, trading, and pushing through the crowd. Some wore armor, others wore cloaks, and some wore clothing like ours. It was like I was looking at a movie set for King Arthur's Camelot. Only this was real.

Green and black banners hung from every high window, green and black flags crowned the tops of buildings. Fruits and oddly shaped vegetables filled stands as their tattered owners argued over price with others dressed in velvets. Other stands boasted an assortment of weaponry, tools, strange looking books, maps, objects I'd never seen before hovering over their counter.

Master Durus led our small caravan down a narrow alley. The Del Contes positioned themselves around me and Fleck. Alex walked right at my side. This part of town was quiet and eerie. The walls were too tall for the narrow lane, leaving only a thread of blue sky visible up above. Eyes kept peeking through high windows but I could never glimpse their faces. A curtain would ruffle or a window would close and the person would vanish.

"Where is he taking us?" I whispered to Alex.

He tilted his head toward me. "To the castle. We're using back roads."

297

"Back roads?" I motioned to the dark alley we were walking through. "I keep feeling like a ghost's going to jump out and scare me. No, wait. Considering the circumstances, it'd probably be a gypsy. You don't have any gold, do you?" I smirked.

Alex stepped closer to me. "I think they'd be satisfied with you."

I pretended to look offended. "You wouldn't."

He grinned and stepped away.

A couple people rushed by us in the opposite direction. They recognized Master Durus and ducked their heads to hurry past. I didn't blame them. The man was supposedly on my side and I was afraid he'd strike at any moment—either with words or something worse. Much worse.

But when they passed me, I felt a surge of their curiosity. They paused to glance behind them—at me—and then walked away even faster.

My stomach churned as we walked on, my heart beating faster. What did it mean, being a princess? From all my studies, being the daughter of a prince was anything but enviable. It meant your person belonged to the state, and that your life would be dictated by its decrees and those more powerful. Maybe it would be different here. Maybe I would have freedom—freedom to train to use magic and the freedom to train to fight. And maybe—the freedom I desired most—I'd be allowed to be with the person I cared most about.

Thinking down that line encouraged me somewhat. I caught Alex's eye and he reached out and took my hand in his, giving it a light squeeze before letting go. It had to be possible. This king couldn't keep Alex from me.

We reached the end of our narrow walkway and stepped onto a manicured lawn of deep green. The land was cast in the shadows of thick clouds, but the sight before me was transcendent, and I knew. It was the painting from the Del Contes guest room. It was of a castle in Gaia—this very one.

A stone wall circumvented a single hill, enclosed from behind by a monumental mountain range. Seated right on top of the hill was that magnificent castle. The painting had failed to capture its grandeur—not even the mountains could compete. Turrets stood tall, spires brushing against the sky. Arched stone bridges connected other, smaller turrets to the main building that dwarfed the hill it sat upon. A single bridge connected it to the rest of the world, extending over rushing rapids—overflow from a nearby cascade plummeting over a cliff.

It was medieval in every sense of the word. Medieval...and magical. And it was going to be my home.

Chapter 28
King Darius

"Master Durus," Dad said. "Would you take Fleck to Master Antoni? I think it best we save this surprise for later."

Master Durus nodded without the slightest hesitation, face fixed in his trademark scowl. I wondered fleetingly if he had any other facial expressions. Fleck's eyes widened as they took in the sheer height of the man, and his knees started shaking.

Alex crouched at Fleck's side. "Master Durus is one of the meanest, toughest, strongest men I've ever known. And—" Alex glanced back at me with a smile "—he is one of the best. If there was anyone on this planet I would trust to keep you safe, it would be him."

My urge to punch Alex vanished at once.

Fleck glanced warily at me and Alex continued, "Fleck, I promise you'll be in good hands. He'll take you straight to Master Antoni, and Master Antoni isn't like Master Durus at all. In fact, Master Antoni is very kind, and gentle, and understanding. You'll like him. And here—" Alex pulled a tiny whittling knife from a pocket and held it before Fleck. "Hold on to it till I come visit. I expect to see proof you've used it."

Fleck took the knife from Alex's hand and beamed. If Master Durus was offended by Alex's comment, I couldn't tell. His expression was the same as always: mad.

"You'll come soon, won't you?" Fleck asked.

"I'll try," Alex said.

Fleck sighed. "I understand. You have to go with the lady."

Alex grinned, ruffling Fleck's auburn hair. "I promise I'll come as soon as I can, and so will she."

Alex's warm eyes turned to me then.

"Of course I will," I said to Fleck. "I just hope my living situation is as nice as yours."

Fleck looked past me at Alex, and a funny smirk appeared on his face. Fleck understood way too much about things. It must be the Daloren wisdom in him.

Without a word, Master Durus began walking down a different street and glanced back for Fleck to follow. Beaming, Fleck spun around and followed the mountain back toward the bustling marketplace.

"Will he be all right?" I asked Alex as we continued toward the castle.

Alex leaned close. "I wouldn't trust him with anyone else."

Armed men on horseback rode past us, always saluting my dad and Stefan and extending their salutations to the Del Contes—Alex in particular. All they did to me was stare.

We reached the base of the drawbridge. From here, the castle looked as though it propped up the sky. No one guarded the bridge, but again there was a surge of power as we crossed. Rapids churned far below, racing back into the mountains. This was the only way in and the only way out.

Maybe you should turn back. Do you really want this?

I paused and looked over my shoulder. To be like the people back there in the marketplace, doing whatever I wanted, whenever I wanted, accountable to no one. Adventure and freedom. What was I walking into?

But I couldn't stop now. I couldn't turn around and run. No, that wasn't an option, not after everything we'd fought for. Today, I would meet my grandfather the king. It was the least I could do after what I'd done. I walked on, and I didn't look back.

Armored guards eyed us as we passed, all bowing their heads to Dad and Stefan, and we stopped at a pair of colossal doors. Without knocking, the doors swung inward and we stepped inside.

It took a moment for my eyes to adjust to the dim lighting, and when they did, I stopped walking. I'd felt small looking at this castle from a distance, but standing in this room made me feel microscopic.

The atrium we stood in was built for giants. God-like giants. White columns rose like trees from a foundation of granite, their tops disappearing in a sea of arches that formed the highest ceiling I'd ever seen. Heavy velvet green draperies cascaded along the sides of tall and slender windows, landing in puddles of green upon the floor. Rays of light streamed through the windows, streaking across the ground like ribbons of gold. The only other light was from an elaborate chandelier that floated overhead, filled with rows and rows of fat and flickering candles, which, I assumed, were responsible for the smell of smoke lingering in the air. But for all the attempts to warm the room, the space felt cold and empty.

"This is where we leave you, I think." Cicero smiled at me. "I'm sure you'll want to experience this moment as a family."

Dad and Cicero hugged. "You know I consider you family. But—" Dad gripped Cicero's shoulders "—thank you. For understanding."

Sonya hugged Dad, and then me. "Daria." She kissed my forehead and smiled as she touched my cheek. "Welcome home, my dear."

Sonya and Cicero said goodbyes to Stefan, Sonya whispered something to her son, and she and Cicero walked out of the atrium, disappearing through a corridor.

"Well, A." Stefan grinned. "See you later this evening?"

Alex smiled at Stefan—my brother.

I had a brother.

I would never get used to this.

"Probably not," Alex said. "A few weeks with your sister and I'm beat."

Stefan chuckled and Alex turned toward me. The green in his eyes looked greener somehow, and I felt a rush of his affection.

What now?

Alex wrapped his arms around me, holding me tight as he whispered, "Don't be afraid of them." His lips brushed my ear. "Let them feel the weight of who you are—who I know you to be—because that woman was born a leader."

For a moment we stood in silence, me encased in his arms. I didn't want him to let go. Ever.

"Alex?" I asked.

He tilted his head.

"Find me later," I whispered. "I need to see you."

His gaze was soft as he brought my hand to his mouth. His lips warmed the back of my fingers and he let go.

Without another word, he turned on his heels and began walking after his parents.

"Alexander," my dad said.

Alex halted and looked back at my dad. Both men stood tall and something passed between them.

"Thank you," Dad said in a voice full of emotion. "Thank you for keeping her safe."

Alex bowed his head slightly. "It wasn't just me—"

"No, it wasn't," Dad paused. "But I know you. And I know she's here now, because of you."

Alex held my dad's gaze a long moment. His eyes flitted to me before bowing his head, and then he left.

I was about to start after him when a low voice penetrated the room.

"Prince Alaric!"

A man approached us, dressed in rich cloth and vibrant shades of blues, walking tall as if he owned the whole world. His leather boots echoed as they clicked against the stone floor and his deep blue cloak fluttered behind him. His black hair was straight and grazed his shoulders, making his pale face paler and his hard features harder. He held a semblance to someone I'd met recently—someone that elicited very bad memories.

"Lord Commodus Pontefract." My dad smiled. "How did you beat me home?"

Lord Commodus Pontefract. So that was why he looked familiar. His brother had held me prisoner, in chains, and attempted to kill me. More than once.

"I know, it is miraculous." He smiled. I didn't like his smile.

His eyes turned to me. They were cold, like his brother's, and they were studying me so intensely I looked away. It was hard separating him from his brother, and I couldn't look at Lord Commodus without seeing an evil man.

"Who is this...stunning young woman?" His voice dropped in a whisper. "She reminds me of someone." He paused. "She reminds me of..."

"Daria is my daughter." My dad stood taller, the humor now gone from his face.

303

Lord Commodus' lips parted before he could hide his shock. I felt his mind mulling things over, putting pieces together and trying to find where he fit in that puzzle. Or where to place himself.

Lord Commodus rubbed his chin. "Is King Darius aware..."

"We were on our way there now."

Lord Commodus appraised me thoughtfully. "It appears Gaia has been keeping secrets," he said, more to himself. The smile returned to his face. "I won't detain you any longer, for I'm sure you are anxious to see your father."

Dad didn't answer.

Lord Commodus started to turn but paused, holding up a finger, forehead creased in thought. "Perhaps, of course, if there's time, you all might join me for dinner. Danton is here, as you know, and I should be delighted for him to..."

"That," Dad interrupted, "won't be necessary."

Lord Commodus looked at me. "Of course, sire. All in due time. Tomorrow then." He bowed his head. His robes flared around him as he spun on his heels and left.

Dad stared after him, his emotions masked.

"That didn't take long." Stefan smirked, staring after Lord Commodus.

Dad's lips tightened. He met my gaze before motioning for us to follow him forward. His forehead was lined with deep creases.

He led us up the grand staircase and Stefan kept his hand on my elbow. I tried shaking free, but after about three times of having him replace his hand, I gave up.

The halls upstairs were just as expansive as below. We walked down tall corridor after tall corridor, upstairs and downstairs, past portraits—all with frowning faces (I used to wonder why portraits never smiled, but then I figured if I had to sit absolutely still for hours while someone painted me, I'd be grumpy, too).

We reached a covered bridge. A lawn stretched beneath us and the air smelled of flowers—lavender, mint, tuberose—and at the end of our bridge was a pair of double oak doors.

"Father." Stefan inclined his head toward me. "Don't you think she should change?"

304

I put my hands on my hips. "What's wrong with my clothes?"

"They're just not exactly...for every day."

"I've been wearing them *every day* for the past few weeks. So they have a few cuts and scratches? They're holding up just fine."

He looked to Dad for help, but Dad stood back, amused. Dad knew better.

Seeing he wasn't getting any help, Stefan continued. "That's not really what I meant."

"So what *did* you mean?"

"Well, as a princess, you are expected to dress—well, wear a dress. And you—" he sniffed my hair "—desperately need a bath."

Dad chuckled and I narrowed my eyes. "Just because you prefer petty refinery to dirtied working hands, don't assume I lack manners. I just prefer honesty to pretty buttons." I thumbed the golden buttons of his double-breasted black coat.

Stefan looked aghast at Dad. "Did you teach her anything?"

Dad shook his head. "Tried. She never listened."

Stefan. The golden child, crowned with golden hair. Fitting. I had no idea how Alex could be so close to such a goody two-shoes. We'd have to work on that.

Dad waved his hand, shaking his head as he led us through the doors.

I didn't feel as small in this room. The ceiling was still ridiculously high, but at least it wasn't God-high. Huge maps covered the walls and a large round table stood at the opposite end of the room, surrounded by high-backed oak chairs—all of which were unoccupied, save two.

A man sat in the tallest chair with his back toward us, and another cloaked in crimson hovered at his side. They were speaking in harsh whispers, but at the sound of our entry, they talking stopped. The man in crimson stood tall, turned to face us, and I shuddered.

His face was drawn and narrow, the angles in it sharp and formidable as if his soul had gone, leaving nothing but a hollow shell. His lips tightened as he gazed at us and a shadow passed over his eyes. I was suddenly glad the Del

305

Contes hadn't brought me here without my dad. I didn't trust either person I'd met so far.

The man sitting in the chair stood and spun around.

Odds didn't look good I'd trust him either.

Silver hair hung just past his shoulders, and the rest of him was covered in elaborate emeralds, blacks, and silvers. His skin showed age, particularly around his frowning mouth. His features were hollow and severe, as if he'd been strong in his youth, but age had stolen his strength, leaving only shadows. But what struck me most were his eyes. They were my dad's, and now Stefan's, yet they lacked the warmth I cherished. These eyes were cold and cautious and...calculating.

My grandfather.

"Alaric." The single baritone word held such command even the walls stood at attention.

"Father." My own father bowed his head.

I'd never heard my dad so submissive. This man—this distant, unfeeling man—was my grandfather? I'd always imagined someone loving and gentle and, well, like Tran. Not him. Not someone who wasn't even happy to see his only son safe and sound—king or not. This man acted put out.

With a slight turn of his head, the king glanced at the man in crimson. "Leave us, Headmaster Ambrose."

Ambrose's dark eyes studied our group before he crossed the room. His step faltered—right in front of me. It was brief, and I doubted anyone else noticed it. He didn't turn. He didn't stop. But I caught his eye before he proceeded out the door.

The room was quiet. The king stood still as a statue with his hands clasped before him, staring at us.

"I expect that you intend to explain your absence." The king frowned.

Each word felt like a physical blow.

My dad didn't flinch. "And I will, but first—"

"Who have you brought with you?" The king interrupted, pale curious eyes sliding over me.

Slowly, I began to understand Alex's words. Not even one minute in the king's presence, and I was already afraid of him. The intelligence in his gaze made me feel as though I were standing naked before him, as if he could see every desire of my heart, and he was the last man in either world I felt safe sharing them with.

Before anyone answered him, he lifted his fingers to his lips and his eyes widened. "It can't be," he whispered.

"It isn't," my dad replied. "Daria is our daughter."

"Alaric, I know she isn't Aurora. You seemed adamant that you weren't going to bring your daughter here, yet." The king took a step toward us, those omniscient eyes never leaving my face. He continued to approach, coming to a stop right before me. He smelled of spiced cigar and mint, and his withered yet still able fingertips reached out and touched my hair.

Did the man expect to have rights to everything?

I pulled my hair away and took a step back.

He raised a sharp brow. "My apologies, my dear, but you are so like your mother. How old are you, child?"

Child? "Eighteen."

"Has it really been so long?" he whispered more to himself.

Dad didn't answer.

"Daria." The king's tone transformed to one of tenderness, his eyes matching the warmth in his voice. I was disturbed by how immediate his character had drifted between patron and ruler.

This was my grandfather. The king. Both persons would be a very interesting encounter, but combined? What did you say to the grandfather you never met who was also the ruler of a world you only recently discovered existed? Maybe I *would* take Master Durus' advice and keep my lips closed and let him do all the talking. And maybe, just maybe, if I showed the proper respect, he wouldn't be as harsh on my unique relationship with Alex as Alex seemed to think he'd be.

"Welcome home, my dear." He smiled, appraising me. "Alaric, she's the ghost of Aurora—particularly the large grey eyes, and there is undoubtedly Aurora's...wild air to her." He waved at my filthy attire. "And yet." He tilted his head. "How is it possible that you should have such a beautiful daughter? Had she not looked like Aurora I would deny your claim on her."

307

All chuckled but me. My grandfather was smiling, the mood in the room lightening at once. The control he had over the atmosphere unsettled me. I could feel his pride and admiration, but there was that other part to him—the king part. That was what I was afraid of. It seemed to me it wouldn't take much for that merciless side to show its face.

"I suppose I should introduce myself," he continued. "I am Darius Regius, Sovereign of Gaia, and, of no less importance, your grandfather. You may address me as Grandfather as Stefan has always done."

A little voice nagged at me to say something, but I wasn't sure what. I still couldn't believe what he had said, even though I'd heard it with my own ears.

"Well?" He glanced irritably at my dad.

Dad looked at me, silently pleading. Right, I needed to be on my best behavior, which meant I should probably say something.

I stuck out my hand. "Daria Jones from Fresno. You may call me Daria."

Stefan's anxiety spiked, but the king smiled, accepting the gesture. "Natural command, I see. But from now on you will go by your given name, Daria Regius, and we will have to do something with these clothes of yours." His eyes frowned over the length of my frame.

My cheeks flushed, but I stood tall, aware of Stefan's acute disappointment.

"And now that we're on the subject of your dress, you should know it isn't fitting for you—a princess of Gaia—to be covered in filth. I recall your father saying you prefer to be out of doors. That is fine, however, for now you shall remain inside the castle, until you learn our ways and what's expected of you."

I started feeling claustrophobic. Within moments of meeting the man, he built walls around my freedoms and dictated my future. He expected me to be a mindless, glittering, puffy-dressed pawn at his disposal. This man, my grandfather, the king.

Don't say a word. Don't say a word if you have any hopes of keeping certain freedoms.

At my silence, he continued. "I understand these changes may be a lot to absorb, but given the proper time, I'm confident you will learn our customs and manners as should be fitting. The lifestyle here is entirely different than what you're used to, I'm afraid. I will take great care in ensuring you are educated with the best tutors as your brother has been. That should be rather simple, now that you are to live here, but before any of that, we shall present you to the realm. Tomorrow morning should do."

"Father." My dad's apprehension was strong. "Don't you think it's a little early to—"

The king held up a jeweled hand. "All but one of my lords is present, although his son is serving in his stead." The king turned to my father. "Perhaps Stefan mentioned Danton is here?"

"Yes," my dad said, his tone flat. "We saw Lord Commodus Pontefract on our way here."

"Wonderful. He has arrived then. Things have been trying since your absence, and now that you've returned, you can fill the council in so they may find an appropriate course of action. Regardless, everyone is gathered who must meet her, and they can relay the information to the territories well before the Festival in November.

"And then." King Darius fastened calculating eyes on me. "We can introduce the world to my granddaughter. Wait until they see her. News of her beauty will travel far. I've no doubt she'll have her choice of eligible suitors come November."

I suddenly found my voice and, unfortunately, lost my discretion. "Suitors?"

A twinge of nervousness hummed from my dad and Stefan.

"Of course. As my granddaughter, you are expected to marry well. The union must be to the son of one of my lords. Not to worry. They're all present currently, including Lord Commodus' son, Danton. He would be very suitable, once you've...changed." He waved his withered hand over my frame again.

Their nervousness had transformed into pure terror.

"Marriage?" I gaped at him. "What on earth are you talking about? I'm only eighteen and I'm not...getting married anytime soon, and when I do—assuming I do—I'll pick him myself."

The room fell silent. Seconds ticked by, holding on for dear life. The horror of Dad and Stefan was practically screaming in my ears, but even beyond that was the flash of rage from my grandfather, though his face betrayed nothing.

My grandfather patted my arm. "We shall discuss this topic at a later time."

"There's nothing to—"

"Daria."

It was Dad this time. His eyes held warning. I closed my mouth.

"Alaric, it is alright. She is tired from so much travel, so many life-altering circumstances. I am sure that her judgment has suffered for it."

I wanted to tell him my judgment was fine. It was his judgment that suffered, but I didn't want to get Dad—or myself—in further trouble. Remnants of that powerful rage still permeated the space around him.

"I think perhaps it is time to introduce Daria to her chambers." Without giving anyone the opportunity to argue, he snapped his fingers. The sound was sharp in the empty room.

Within seconds, a woman poked her face around a wall. She had a sweet demeanor, slight frame, soft features, and warm brown eyes. She seemed to be about Sonya's age, but her skin had lost more of its elasticity, and when she smiled, the skin crinkled near her eyes.

"Yes, your grace?" Her voice was soft.

He motioned for her to come to his side, and she wasted no time in obeying. He whispered something into her ear and she nodded as her eyes moved back to me.

"Daria, this is Rhea, one of my attending servants. I'm relinquishing her services to you, unless you find them unsatisfactory."

He was giving me a maid? What was I supposed to do with a maid?

"Really, sir…sire…Grandfather, that's not necessary."

"I tell you it is." His tone was final, and the cloud of apprehension hovering around my dad and Stefan told me I shouldn't argue.

My grandfather continued. "Rhea, show Daria to her quarters. I have matters to discuss with my son and Stefan."

310

So now he was leaving me out?

"That's it?" I couldn't stop the words. "You're making me leave—just...go to my room after everything that's happened?"

The king's face was rigid and his eyes were like ice. "*Goodnight*, my dear."

No, not after everything I'd been through. He couldn't do this. "I am just as much a part of the past events as they are. Probably even more so. I was there for everything, if you didn't know. So you should hear what I have to say."

I had done it. Pushed too far. Much too far.

An inferno blazed in the king—one so strong the candles in the room flickered. The draperies ruffled as a shadow danced upon the king's features.

Dad's face flared red and Stefan was paralyzed in shock. The king looked so livid I thought he might start breathing fire. Wouldn't that be nice, to make it through all that only to turn into a pile of ashes. I should've turned and run when I had the chance. I should've fled at the gate.

I never should've come here.

"Father," my dad interceded. "You may find her account beneficial."

"My granddaughter's thoughts on diplomatic matters are unnecessary." Each word dripped from his tongue like acid. "I will not hear another word on the subject."

My dad bowed his head in secession. "One moment then, while I speak with my daughter?"

He earned himself a rather overt glare from his father, but made his way toward me regardless. Dad's face communicated everything he could not say while in the presence of a king. Mostly silent apologies.

"Daria," he whispered. "I promise I'll come and see you the first moment I can. And I'm hopeful—" he glanced back at his own father "—that given time, he'll learn to value your opinion." He wrapped his arm around me. "All right?"

"As soon as you can," I reiterated.

Dad nodded.

On the king's orders, I was escorted from the one remaining person I trusted.

This man was taking everything away from me. This king, my grandfather.

311

Chapter 29

Glittering Captivity

Angry, I followed Rhea to my room, along with an escort of two guards.

The guards weren't so bad, really. Their armor was obnoxiously loud as we walked, and they didn't say a word, but at least they didn't stare. Not like everyone else.

The people in the king's castle were about as nice as the king. In fact, I wondered if he somehow made an announcement to his entire court, ordering them to make the new girl feel subhuman, because when I walked by, they would look me up and down and frown as if they pitied me. Some even covered their mouths and giggled. But the funny thing was I pitied them. They looked like peacocks in their so-called refinery, and it was beyond a giggling matter.

Rhea turned down another hall—I was doubtful I'd ever find my way around—and stopped before a tall door with a round, iron knocker. The guards positioned themselves on either side and stared at the opposite wall. I had the sudden urge to jump and scream in front of them while making a funny face, but Rhea clicked my door open and motioned for me to step through. Maybe later.

"Your room, my lady," she said.

I peered inside.

There was a small sitting area near the door, with two mahogany chairs and an ivory sofa. Everywhere I looked was deep green and black and silver, and lots of dark wood. Sconces clung to the walls, surrounded by golden halos of light, and the air smelled so thickly of spice it numbed my nostrils. I couldn't see a window anywhere but I noticed a wall of black velvet, hanging from an iron rod and pooling on the floor below like a puddle of ink. There was an enormous bed off to one side, covered in rich green satins and black velvet with a mountain of pillows on top. Of course, it was equipped with four posts and way too much gossamer. This room was larger than my entire home back in Fresno, and it was apparently mine.

If my grandfather the king was trying to make me feel out of place, it was working beautifully.

Rhea followed me inside and pulled the heavy draperies open, the muted evening light softening the shadows in my room. Beyond the glass was a view of the mountains. Waterfalls cascaded into verdant greens and birds soared high, disappearing into thick clouds overhead.

It was a picture of freedom.

Note to self: add "cruel" to the list of my grandfather's attributes.

Rhea padded off through a narrow corridor on one side, and the sound was soon accompanied by a few splashes of what sounded like water.

These people didn't waste time.

After a few minutes of arguing with Rhea—well, me arguing with her—she capitulated to letting me scrub my own skin and wash my own hair. As much as she tried convincing me of its commonality, I was not ready for someone else to give me a bath. There were some freedoms I was going to keep. Like who got to see me naked.

My grand tub sat upon four curled legs on a pristine marble floor enclosed by an oval-shaped marble wall. I even felt too dirty for the bathroom. Once I was done scrubbing two weeks of filth from my skin—which hurt—I walked right back into my room to find Rhea had already laid out clothing for me across the bed: a black satin gown, a rich black shawl, and slippers.

That was it, then. Rhea must've heard the king's announcement, too.

Rhea noticed my hesitation and took a step toward me. "My lady—"

And that wasn't helping. "Please don't call me that," I said.

She looked at me as if I'd offended her. "It is your title."

"Title?" I grumbled to myself. "This is getting ridiculous."

"Excuse me, my lady?" she asked.

"Nothing...never mind. I just...you don't need to call me that."

Rhea studied me but I couldn't tell what she was thinking. "All right," she said at last. "As long as it's just you and me."

I didn't hide my relief. "Thanks."

She nodded.

I made my way over to my bed and stared at the silk.

"Do you not like it?" Rhea asked.

What I really wanted was a t-shirt and shorts, but I doubted Camelot could provide anything like that. "No, it's...nice," I said, rubbing the soft fabric between my fingers. "It's just not what I'm used to."

I missed my room back in Fresno, the one with scuffs on the walls, a missing closet door, and stacks of papers and books on the floor because there wasn't enough room for them on my dinky desk. I even missed the stench of farm on my clothes.

"I understand." Rhea's tone was so gentle I looked back at her. By the look on her face, I knew she really did understand, somehow. She continued, "I'll help you in any way I can. There are...ways to keep yourself beneath all the glittering layers." She smiled a warm, genuine smile.

I grinned. I might like this woman after all.

No one visited my guarded room the remainder of the evening. Not even Dad. That surprised me, but Rhea assured me it was because of the situation. Until everyone knew I existed, no one—not even my dad—could visit. Maybe Dad hadn't realized that when he said he'd come see me, but I could sacrifice this one night. Especially after everything my family had done for me.

Rhea spent the remainder of her evening attending me, and attending me well. I hadn't expected it, but I appreciated her company. For one, she didn't call me "my lady" again, but even more than that, she was real with me. Tomorrow would be a momentous day in Gaia, she'd said. Everyone would be anxious to meet me.

"And remember." She'd grinned. "It is only for a little while. You can return to these chambers and be yourself again."

Rhea and I might get along just fine.

314

I thanked her many times throughout the remainder of the evening, and the next morning when she brought me my breakfast through my guarded door.

"They're still out front?" I whispered.

Rhea nodded, grinning. She set a tray of food beside my bed: breads, unusual fruits, a couple slices of meat, and a goblet of a deep burgundy shaded liquid.

"Upon the king's orders. Oh, and I hope you don't mind." She set down a pile of deep brown leather fabric on my dresser. "But I took the liberty of having your leathers cleaned and mended. It will be a while before you are allowed to own anything like this." She smiled.

"Thank you." I grinned. "I'll be sure to keep them hidden."

"And I found this in your pocket. I wasn't sure if it was important to you or not."

In her hands was the little rook Thad had given me. It had cracked. Part of the tower was missing but it was otherwise intact. I wished my own tower—the one I was locked within—would chip away. Thanking her, I took it from her hands.

She nodded and disappeared into my bathroom.

I set my little chipped tower on my nightstand and began digging into my food. The bread was doughy and warm and sweet. I picked up the goblet and took a sip of the liquid, but immediately spit it back in the cup. These people were bizarre when it came to their tastes in beverages.

Rhea poked her head in. "Do you not care for Pom Ale?"

I eyed the drink in my hands. "You all drink ale this early in the day?"

She chuckled as she stepped into the room. "It's considered a delicacy. It's made from pomegranate trees on Earth."

"I didn't think it was possible, but you have successfully ruined their flavor."

She smiled. "Is there something else you like to drink in the morning?"

Was there ever. "Coffee."

"Coffee." She mulled the word over in her head. "Is it...black and smells much better than it tastes?"

I grinned. "That is an adequate description."

"And you like it?"

I nodded.

She peered into my goblet, held her hand over it, and closed her eyes. When she removed her hand, the substance inside the goblet was dark and steaming and smelled like...coffee.

"How did you do that?" I gasped.

She grinned, holding up a single finger over her lips. "Do not tell a soul. There are things I'm not allowed either, but I think this occasion excuses it." She took a whiff of the coffee in my hands. "And why you prefer that to Pom Ale, I'll never understand."

I took a sip. It was the best coffee I'd ever tasted. Finally, something familiar, something from home. I might survive here after all.

She began walking back toward my bathroom when a soft rapping sounded on the door. "Will you be seeing anyone now?" Rhea asked.

"Yes. That's fine." I pulled my black robe around my frame. The silk still felt slippery and cold against my skin.

Rhea unbolted the door and it creaked as it opened. Soft mumbling ensued and a head of bronze hair appeared. Great, Golden Child.

"Good morning, mind if I come in for a moment?" His voice sounded a little nervous, but his smile was so warm I couldn't tell him to go away.

"Sure, I mean, is that okay?" I asked Rhea.

"Of course...my lady." She grinned, and I grinned back. "Would you like me to stay?"

I eyed Stefan. "No, I think I can handle him."

"So sure of yourself already?" Stefan grinned.

"I doubt Mr. Prim and Proper would do anything to offend the one and only princess of Gaia."

Rhea covered her smile as she stepped out the door.

It was odd seeing this younger version of my dad staring back at me. We didn't look related at all, but then, I was used to that. I never had looked much like my dad.

"Have the guards left?" I asked.

Stefan looked at me as if my question was ridiculous. "It'll be a long time before you're left unattended."

My morning was getting better by the second. "Then where's my...our dad?"

Stefan folded his fingers and swallowed. "He'll be here in a little while. He was on his way this morning, but I asked him if I could see you first."

I eyed Stefan. Why he thought I'd want his company over our dad's, I had no idea.

Silence.

Stefan grinned awkwardly and took a few more steps into my room. "How did you sleep?"

"Terribly."

He looked over me a minute and grinned. "Perhaps we should move your bed to the woods. A says you slept great out there."

That was the second time I'd heard him use that. I raised a brow. "A?"

"Alexander."

I nodded. "So...you talked to Alex?"

"Last night over dinner. I was dying to hear the details of your journey."

Left out again. A prisoner in my own room. Scowling, I walked toward my taunting freedom called the window.

Stefan meandered to my side.

Just go away.

Unfortunately for me, he didn't hear my silent plea. "Daria, I came here because...I wanted to ask you something."

I waited.

"What...is that horrible smell?"

I looked at him then, his face winced in disgust. "It's not me. I had a bath," I said.

"No." He looked down at the goblet in my hands. "It's that. What *is* that?"

I tried to keep from laughing but I couldn't, not completely. "Coffee."

"Coffee? I've never heard of it before."

And I thought I'd been sheltered. "Um, it's—" What should I say? "—something to help wake me up. We drink it back home."

He looked intrigued. "Where did you get it?"

317

Mr. Goody Two Shoes couldn't be trusted with that information. "Rhea...managed to find me some."

"Is it good?" he asked.

"It's better than that Pom Ale of yours."

Stefan looked a little offended. "You didn't like it?"

I eyed him a moment. "Did you send it for me?"

"Yes."

"Oh. Well, thanks. But, no, I didn't like it."

He eyed my coffee. "May I?"

I handed him the cup. "Careful, it's hot."

He was slow to lift it to his lips, and he almost immediately handed it back. "How can you drink that stuff?"

I took a huge gulp. "So you came here to ask me about my diet?"

"No," he started, clasping his hands. And then he began pacing. "What I...wanted to ask you was..." He stopped walking and looked up at me. "I need your patience."

"What do you mean?"

"Well." He folded his hands again. "You see...you're different."

I raised a brow. I wasn't sure I liked where this was going. "Different."

"Yes, different. You're outspoken and self-sufficient and opinionated and...why do you look so angry?"

I realized my face was burning. "Hm, I don't know, maybe because you came all the way up here just to throw insults?"

He looked curiously at me a moment. "Daria, I meant them as compliments."

I opened my mouth to respond but I couldn't think of anything to say. I had never thought of being outspoken and opinionated as a good thing—in fact they usually got me in trouble—but Stefan was serious. And now he was starting to look confused.

"Oh," I said. "I just thought...well, those things usually irritate most people."

"I didn't say they weren't irritating."

I folded my arms.

"I'm sorry, that's not at all what I meant." He scratched the back of his neck and looked down at the floor.

"Then you better explain before I grab a fistful of that golden hair and drag you out of here."

318

He looked startled. "I just...what I meant was, you speak your mind and there's nothing duplicitous about you. And you're independent and you're...not afraid." He took a step toward me and lowered his voice. "I'm not used to that and I find it refreshing."

I searched his face. He was being completely honest, if not a little frightened that I might actually follow through with my earlier threat. I grinned and he grinned back, and his posture relaxed a bit.

"But..." he started.

"I knew there had to be a *but* coming."

He grabbed my hand. "No, listen to me." His eyes were even bluer than my dad's. "As refreshing as you are, it'll take me some getting used to. People don't...refute Grandfather. Not even Father. My upbringing tells me it's wrong, but my heart knows you're right." He squeezed my hand. "Daria, what I mean to say is...I'm so glad you're here. I think we can learn a lot from each other—at least I have much to learn from you."

Of all the things I had expected him to say, these words weren't even on my radar. My brother might be a little goody-goody, but he was sincere and his heart was good. He let go of my hand.

I sighed. "Between the two of us, I've got the steepest learning curve."

"And I'll do anything I can to help you," Stefan said. "Actually, that's the other reason I came."

"Oh?"

"Well, it was actually Father's idea, but I wanted to help you pick your attire for your...announcement." He said the last word in an ominous whisper.

"Is it really that horrific?"

"No, just all the great lords, the entire council, the Guild...basically anyone of importance. They've been discussing a course of action all morning after what happened to you in the south, but since you destroyed all evidence, Father and the Del Contes are having a difficult time convincing everyone about what happened. But the one thing they can all agree on is wanting to meet the famously returned Lady Daria Regius. Immediately."

I was supposed to meet everyone? Right now? All at once? My limbs started feeling weak and I had a difficult time filling my lungs with air.

Stefan grabbed my arm. "It's not terribly bad." He looked worried. "Really. It's just a bunch of powerful lords and..."

"You're not helping." I took a deep breath.

He sighed. "Right."

He looked lost, as if he wanted to reassure me but didn't know what language I spoke. "You'll be fine," he finally said. "Grandfather is the most powerful human in our realm. Plus, Father will be there, and I'll be there..."

I laughed. "Great. I feel better already." I took my arm back. "So. You're here to help me pick out a dress?"

He started to respond, and his face turned red. "Father was worried you might show up in jeans and a t-shirt."

"Wait, are there any?"

Stefan looked curiously at me as he shook his head, and then he turned his attention to my wardrobe. I wondered if we'd ever really understand each other. He flung the doors open and I was afraid. It was filled to the brim with all sorts of colors and fabrics, and lots and lots of pink.

"Father thought I should pick out your dress because—" Stefan searched inside "—he thinks—" he strained, reaching deep into the pile of clothes "—you don't have any idea how to flatter yourself."

In his hands was a wad of shimmering emerald green, and there wasn't nearly enough fabric to make a shirt—let alone a dress.

I eyed him with suspicion. "Dad wants me to wear that?"

"The king wants you to look appealing, and you need to make a good first impression at court. Whatever you do after that is on your head. Here." He smiled, holding the dress before me, letting the bottom part fall to the ground, and I stared.

It looked like an emerald dressed in diamonds. There was a single piece of green silk, contoured to the shape of a woman with a neckline lower than I was comfortable with. A sheer overlay of silver hung from the waist down to the floor, covered in tiny sparkling jewels that trailed behind like a glittering river beneath the moonlight. "I'm going to wear that?"

He smiled. "The silver will bring out the grey in your eyes. You'll look stunning, trust me."

He held it out to me, but I was afraid to touch it.

"It won't bite. Here." He draped it over my arm. "I'll get Rhea to help you and I'll be back with Father. Rhea can pick out your shoes. This is as far as I'll ever go with women's fashion."

I glanced skeptically at him as he laughed and walked out the door. I might like my brother after all. There was an innocence to him that a life of luxury and propriety had somehow managed to leave unadulterated.

Rhea entered right after, smiling as she observed the gown. It didn't take long to put it on. She fiddled with my hair, held brushes and powders to my face, grabbed a pair of satin black slippers, and I was soon standing in front of the mirror.

At first I thought I was staring at another woman. A crown of glossy dark hair was gently pulled back, spilling about her slender neck and strong collarbone in large rich curls. Thick dark lashes framed her large grey eyes and splashes of pink warmed her lips and cheeks. The emerald gown hugged her slim frame in all the right places and the silver sparkled as she moved. She looked...ethereal.

And I realized it really was me. I tried to find myself in the reflection, but around every angle and every exposed piece of skin, all I could find was a woman. Someone confident, someone that belonged here, as if she'd lived here all her life, knew how to act, speak—even think. And I didn't have a clue.

Stefan peeked his head in, and I noticed just in time to see his jaw hanging open.

I smiled, feeling my cheeks burn. "I feel like an imposter in this dress."

He let himself in my room. "But you look dazzling."

My face burned hotter.

"Good, keep blushing. It gives you a sort of innocence and vulnerability that is very attractive. It'll do wonders to your merit, at least until you open your mouth."

I punched him in the shoulder and he laughed.

There was a quick knock and Dad stepped into the room.

My father looked like a prince. He was dressed in fitted black with a silver and black waistcoat, and a sword was strapped to his waist. A rich green cape slung over one shoulder, attached by a large silver clasp.

Despite the luxurious costume, his person was unmasked and his features glowed with pride and love.

"What do you think?" He beamed.

"I think you'd better never leave me locked up in this tower again," I said.

"Princess." He kissed my forehead. "I'm so sorry. Your grandfather kept me occupied well into the morning, which, I'm sure, was intentional. By then it was too late and there were many curious eyes watching me. I didn't dare risk your safety."

Of course he wouldn't. "Then after this morning, you'll have no more excuses," I said.

"And I don't intend to create them—not after a lifetime of making excuses from telling you the truth." He sighed, and then took a step back, appraising me. "You look absolutely stunning. On second thought, maybe I should keep you locked up here." He grinned.

"If you want me to behave myself today, don't even dream of it."

"Something tells me she'd find a way out anyway," Stefan said.

My dad chuckled. "I brought something for you." He reached into the breast of his jacket and pulled out a delicate silver chain. From it hung a beautiful clear crystal. It caught the light, splattering it in fragments upon the walls. There was an energy radiating from it, as if it held life inside.

"This belonged to your mother," he said. "It was a Pandor family heirloom. I thought now might be a good time for you to have it."

I touched the smooth crystal. From leathers to elegance.

My mom seemed just as confused about her identity as I am.

I smiled to myself.

"Here, I'll help you put it on." He clasped it around my neck. The crystal felt cool upon my skin. He smiled and extended his arm. "Shall we?"

He led us down the wide stairway, Stefan following behind. Our footsteps echoed along the empty halls as we passed portrait after portrait of grumpy men. We finally came to a stop before a pair of enormous doors, guarded on either side by men in elaborate black and silver uniform. They didn't move and they didn't speak, but this time they stared right at me.

I liked them better when they stared at the wall.

"You'll be just fine," my dad whispered in my ear.

My hand sweated as I gripped his arm, thankful he stood right beside me.

The doors opened.

A swell of anger and indignation wrapped around me and loud voices filled my ears.

The noise ceased. The silence hit so fast I wondered if I'd lost my hearing, but then someone coughed.

One by one they all turned to peer at the doors. There were so many faces, and all of them craned their necks to catch a glimpse of us.

I was slammed with their curiosity and wonder, some hostility. Taking in a deep breath, I pushed their emotions away so I didn't rip free of Dad's hand and run right out the door.

Dad led me into the room and the sea of faces slowly parted to the sides. All of them stared, many of them whispered, none of them I recognized. Candles hovered in the air overhead, casting a soft glow upon their faces.

There was one, lifting his head from a short bow. I hadn't recognized him at first, veiled in a heavy crimson cloak. That dark face and permanent scowl. Master Durus stood near a group of men dressed as he was, all of their faces stern, their eyes narrowed as we passed—including the man my grandfather had addressed earlier as Headmaster Ambrose. A surge of power pulsed through me and then it clicked. This was the Guild. Master Durus was a Guild member.

We walked past more men and women, all of them bowing, dressed in lavish velvets and leathers, some wide-eyed in wonder, others glaring, angry that I existed. These were people of influence and power and their minds were already working, devising avaricious plans for me—me, the spark that ignited them.

323

Out of the sea of curiosity, I was touched by two fine points of tenderness. I caught Sonya's gaze, and Cicero stood right beside her. Their faces were bright beacons in the night. Thad stood nearby, clad all in black and standing with a group of similarly dressed younger people. Students of the Academia.

And then one point of emotion stole everything. I saw his dark hair first, then his eyes as they trailed up the length of my frame. Alex looked striking, all dressed in black with his thick dark hair messed perfectly around his face. My heart beat fast as I felt a surge of his love and desire, and his eyes finally lifted to mine. His gaze was so piercing I momentarily forgot where I was.

My dad yanked on my arm, hastening me forward.

Fine. I would find Alex later, after all of this.

Thinking on that, I found it easier to ignore all the faces and stare only at the green river of velvet that marked our path forward. The last of the sea divided, and there, in an elaborate bronze chair, sat my grandfather.

He was dressed even more lavishly than he'd been during our first meeting, and now a crown of jewels sat on his head.

I couldn't believe this. His crown—that thing filled with enormous sparkling jewels—it belonged in a glass case at the Tower of London. Not on his head.

"Ah, there you are." He stood, smiling with pride. "We were just discussing your victory over the gargons." He embraced each of us in turn, but it was stiff and formal and completely forced. I followed Dad's lead, faced the crowd, and gripped his arm harder. There were so many of them, and all of them were staring at me.

"Lords and ladies of Gaia, citizens of the realm," Grandfather's voice bellowed. "It is time I introduce you to someone long absent from this world—someone who has been kept safe since her birth so that she may devote her life to serving this realm as a daughter of the crown."

Whispering sounded about the room.

"She has already proven that service, slaying one of the greatest threats Gaia has seen in centuries. It is with great pleasure I give you my granddaughter, the daughter of Alaric and Aurora, Princess Daria Regius."

Hands clapped and chatter exploded as surprise and indignation poured through me. I could feel their scrutiny and expectations—all of which was left wanting.

Much as I was left wanting.

In my ignorance I thought the one thing I needed—the one thing I wanted—was to know the truth. That the truth would set me free. But as I stared at the faces—so many devious, manipulative faces—the truth made itself perfectly clear. And it was sending me straight into captivity.

EPILOGUE

The rest of my day was a blur. So many names were spoken, so many hands were shaken, and everyone commented on me slaying a monster. They thanked me as if their extravagant lives actually depended on it. I never said much. I didn't trust these people.

At some point during the commotion, Thad made his way to shake my hand with a funny smile on his face. He had known all along, of course. I asked him why he hadn't given me a pawn instead of the rook, but he said I'd never looked that innocent.

I never made my way to Alex, although I tried relentlessly. At one point, I caught his penetrating gaze through the group of black suits surrounding him. There was one in particular I noted, standing beside him—an exotic young woman with long blond hair who frowned at me. After a while, when that frown didn't disappear, I deduced it was Vera.

When the commotion died and surprise faded, I eventually retired to my room for the night. Alone. My dad and Stefan told me I'd done a fabulous job, but I'd done a fabulous job pretending and it sickened me. Ironic how the choice Lord Tiernan had offered me wasn't so much different at its core.

But this way no one was dying. At least not on the outside.

I tugged off my gown and pulled on my robe just as I caught a glint of metal. There it was, lying across my nightstand. My dagger.

No one had been to this room, no one but Rhea and me.

I picked up the slender object, and the metal felt cool. Strange that it should keep returning to my hands. I tucked it into my drawer and crawled into bed.

A light chill on my cheek woke me. The candle flickered beside my bed, but the rest of my room was dark, except for something bright orange on the pillow beside me.

326

A flower.

Ardor's flame. It was a burst of fire on my pillow and its fragrance was strong—much stronger than I remembered. Beneath it was a piece of paper.

My heart beat fast as I looked around. My room was empty. The draperies fluttered in the light breeze. The window. I had closed it.

I picked up the flower and the petals folded in on themselves and into a compact bundle. Typical. I set the compressed flower down and picked up the paper.

My hands shook as I opened the folds.

My darling friend,

I know you'll be furious I was here and didn't wake you, but I couldn't. I'd never be able to do this.

After what happened, the king has requested volunteers to take assignment with Lord Tosca in Alioth. Now that my training has completed, it is the perfect opportunity for me to establish my own person as an Aegis. When I offered my services to the king for this assignment, he was more than happy to grant my wish. Never doubt the intuitiveness of your grandfather.

This is where I risk losing your friendship forever. You may hate me for it, as I hate myself, but there is a plan for your life and as much as I want it to, it is a plan that cannot ever include me. Staying near you would only complicate things and make it impossible for either of us to live our roles as expected. I tried not to love you so that I could remain your friend, but I've failed.

Remember who you are, Daria. The strong pillar I know you to be, the confident woman who can do anything—conquer anything. This realm needs you much more than you need it, and one day, when you choose the man who is to be your equal and partner in this life, I can only pray that he deserves you.

Please forgive me.
I will love you always,
Alexander

The paper trembled in my hands.

He wouldn't. It wasn't possible. He couldn't just...leave. Not after...

I rushed to the window and pushed it open, searching the night. He couldn't have gone far. I could stop him. He would not take this choice from me.

Raindrops splattered on my face. It was too dark to see anything. There was no one. Nothing...but emptiness.

The words I tried to ignore screamed at my soul, ripping it to shreds. I was too late.

He was gone.

Gone in a world I could not navigate, amidst a people I could not trust.

I sank down beside the wall, my face wet with rain and tears, the letter still shaking in my hands.

How could he do this? How could he take away my choice—the only choice I would fight to keep?

Always protecting me. Always trying to do what he thought was best. Making the decisions for both of us. This time he was wrong, very wrong. And I already hated him for it.

Rain slapped against the wall behind me, the breeze chilling my bones through my thin silken shield. When I looked up, I noticed something bright red. It lay atop my bed, its vividness making everything in my room seem dull.

The Ardor's Flame had opened, and it was bleeding.

Connect with Me Online:

My blog: http://scribblesnjots.blogspot.com
Facebook: http://www.facebook.com/GaiasSecret
Twitter: http://twitter.com/barbarakloss

Acknowledgements

Oh, the "Acknowledgements" page. I've been sitting here, trying to figure out just where to start, because there have been so many people that have made my debut novel, *Gaia's Secret,* possible! This has truly been a group effort, and I wouldn't be here today, stumbling over the beginnings of this page, if it weren't for all the time and energy you put in, helping me realize my dream.

I've got to thank my family first and foremost, for being the initial set of guinea pigs (poor things). Mom, Uncle As, Annie, Teri Lee (a.k.a. Mom #2), Madeline, Hannah, Aunt Cynthia, Lauren, Joanna, no matter how badly I butchered that initial story line and character development, you always encouraged me to keep going until I got it right. Thanks for believing in Daria and Alex. Without you, they might not have ever gotten together.

To my friends at the Med Center, for letting me constantly talk your ear off about my imaginary friends, and not ever complaining about it. John, Scott, Janice, Laura, Chris, Kris, and Teri (who, by the way, also fixed all my plural possessive issues. If you find any, it's not her fault!).

And, of course, all my awesome beta-friends who were honest and encouraging all the way, giving me more insightful and thoughtful feedback than I could've dreamed. April & Troy, Misty, Gina, Amy, Sarah, Kim, Ashley, Kate, Tia. I couldn't have asked for better readers. You all are brilliant!

My awesome critique partner, Christine, who is a genius at catching everything I couldn't see. Thanks for always believing in my characters! And Laura, for giving me a very thorough crash-course in grammar.

Of course there's the fabulous bloggers. You guys have been crucial to my sanity. Your own stories and paths and advice and comments have been essential to this endeavor.

Last, but absolutely not least, I want to thank my best friend, and husband, Ben. If it weren't for you, I never would've written those first few (and embarrassing) words on paper. You've always believed in me, even when I was so frustrated that I wanted to throw my story against the wall and be done with it. You've been a constant sounding board, have read every draft I've ever thrown at you, encouraged me, challenged me, helped me keep the imaginative spark alive. You've been as invested in this story as I've been, and it wouldn't exist without you. I love you. Thank you.

Made in the USA
San Bernardino, CA
25 May 2015